Caer Perris

The Portchester Chronicles, Volume 1

Dan Canwell

Published by Dan Canwell, 2024.

Caer Perris

Volume I of The Portchester Chronicles

Dan Canwell

Part I
Sisal

BC 339 – the southern coast

Mist hung in the autumn morning air enhancing the stillness of the day. A solitary man stood by the water's edge, his sword and shield marking him as a warrior, and he looked around and was satisfied with the little he could see. He had ridden his horse round the land to this point and liked what he had found. There was water on three sides of the firm ground on which he stood and the stillness of the sea spoke of the safety of the anchorage. There were a few trees and maybe, just maybe the land was fertile. Slowly, the warrior, Perris the son of Sisal turned and took in his location, or as much as he could see, and he was content.

The call of a bird, urgent, screeching and piercing, from out on the water cut through the silence and the warrior heard the sound of wings beating as a flock took to the air. Everything told a story his father had said, so listen to it and learn the tale of your land; and the birds told him that either the water was a safe place, or that it was plentiful with fish to feed on. If he was lucky, very lucky, then it was both.

Perris drew his sword and using it as a staff, he leaned on it to take his weight as he sat on the cold damp ground, the smell of the salt water mingling with the earthiness of the land. Perris waited in contented silence breathing deeply, sensing the place and knowing that he had finally found what he had been looking for.

'I can hear you, you know' said the warrior, his voice deep and strong. He turned as he rose, the swiftness and grace of his movement a testament to his physical fitness and strength. Ten paces away was another man, dressed similarly in rough woollen garments, a cloak draped over one shoulder and the sharpened sword still held within the wide leather belt around his waist. The newcomer had his arms spread wide and a welcoming grin upon his face.

'All hail to thee Perris, son of Sisil' he intoned grandly. Looking at him, the warrior was almost looking at a reflection of himself, the shaggy mop of unruly brown hair and the full beard and moustache which hung well below the chin. Both men were barrel-chested, strong and powerful, though the newcomer was clearly the more matured, and Perris smiled in return. 'Greetings to you too Ferrax, also son of my father Sisil.' He laughed 'you loud bastard.'

Ferrax, the older of the two young men shook his head. 'I don't know how you heard me but I suspect you were dropped on your head as a child and your copious backside picks up more sound than those tiny ears. Something must have moved!' He too laughed and the two men sat down next to each other.

'Is this it then?' asked Ferrax, a hopeful note in his voice. His brother nodded his head, the shaggy hair and the metal rings he wore in it ringing in affirmation.

'It is certainly the landing, but I also think it is my place, I really think so. I will wait for the mist to lift and then . . . and then I will know.'

'In that case I can only hope it is' replied Ferrax 'because my arse is sore from riding, my guts are churning from the lousy food and I miss the, er comforts of home.' He nudged his brother who smiled as he turned to him.

'I don't know what she sees in you' said Perris

'It's a lie I told her' replied Ferrax as he lay down and stretched out on the grass. 'I told her that she had the choice either to be my woman or yours and that you stink of goat piss, fart like a sow and have a cock the size of an acorn . . . and only then when it's hard. Can't think why she chose me.'

Perris roared with laughter and leaned over and cuffed his older brother round the head playfully. The two of them were comfortable with each other on some levels and were as alike as they were different; for Ferrax, being with his brother was like a release from the responsibilities that were attendant on being the eldest child of the renowned Chief, for Perris being with Ferrax was a chance to be the stronger and physically more able, a role he could not play at home.

'Why are we here anyway?' asked Perris.

'Father requires that we greet an important guest, some merchant from Gaul and get him safely to our village. There is business to be discussed and arrangements to be made' explained Ferrax. 'And our father wishes us to make a good impression' he added significantly and with emphasis.

'So, that means you do the clever talking and I just stand around looking like I want a fight' said Perris.

'Something like that' agreed his brother. 'But I sense that this place means something to you. It's the way you look around and take the land in. Have you been here before?'

'Never' replied Perris truthfully, although he left out that he had been looking for such a place for the past two years. Perris knew that as second son his life was destined to be one of subservience and support to his older brother, and whilst he loved Ferrax dearly, and would support him into the heat of the sun, subservience was not a character trait that found much space in the heart or mind of Perris.

The young warrior knew that there would come a time when he would have to break with his family and establish a place of his own where he could be Lord. A place where he could defend himself against enemies and live life to be an old man, wealthy and wise just like his own father. This place, this land by the sea was perfect.

Perris was shaken from his reverie by a shout from one of the three men who had travelled with them. The man, Buldan, was pointing out to sea and shouting that he could see a sail. Perris and his brother scrambled to their feet and joined Buldan by the water's edge. As they looked over the water, Perris took in more of the surroundings; ahead of him was a large expanse of calm water, protected from the sea by what looked like a large islands on both sides. In the far distance Perris could see more land that formed the backdrop to the colourful red sail that pulled the small wooden boat along. There was water everywhere, a river came in from the place where the sun set, the water moving swiftly and freely. Over to the place where the sun rose was another smaller river that created one of the islands. Perris turned round, away from the sea, for behind them was a steep chalk cliff, and he was impressed. The islands protected the harbour from the ravages of the sea, the cliff protected the land from the most inclement inland weather, from the coldest winds that blew with such ferocity in the winters bringing snow and ice and death.

'Come' said Perris to his brother and the others 'we have time before that boat can get here, let us prepare a fire and welcome our guests. Buldan? See if you can find us something to eat, if not we can use the supplies we brought with us. Ferrax my brother, how do you wish us to greet our visitors?'

Ferrax spent the next ten minutes explaining how he would like everyone to behave, and explaining a few of the words he knew in the visitors' dialect. His concentration seemed to amuse Perris who smiled indulgently as he tried to contort his mouth to make the unfamiliar words. Strange he mused how men are so similar yet so different, how a man can become so important that he has the two sons of Sisal to run to him. Perris felt something that was almost resentment at his apparent subservience to this stranger, but knew that to his brother and his father this visit was of great importance for it added prestige and profit and that, to Sisal, was a mark of civilisation.

Having understood his brothers' instructions, Perris wandered once again over to the shore to stare at the approaching ship. Distance had distorted her size, she was much larger than he had at first appreciated; the distance to the open sea clearly much farther than he had at first thought. Perris looked at the sun and its arc across the sky. The boat had already taken time to travel as far as it had and he calculated that by the time it arrived about a quarter of a day would have passed. If it took a quarter of a day to reach this harbour from the open sea then the place was much easier to defend, with adequate warning of an approaching enemy, allowing warriors time to group and prepare an appropriate welcome for any aggressor.

'My Lord?' Perris turned round to see a grinning Buldan holding the limp bodies of four rabbits. Perris' face split into a smile as well as he instructed his man to build a fire and prepare the meat. It was not the largest feast but it would provide an appropriate welcome to their visitors who would probably have had their fill of fish.

Eventually the ship came as close as her captain dared to the shore and three of the crew manhandled a heavy iron anchor, overboard with a huge splash. Ferrax waded out into the harbour until he was waist-deep and was able to shout a greeting to the visitor. A small boat, constructed like a coracle was let down into the water and two men carefully lowered themselves into the craft and paddled towards their host. Ferrax, with a smile on his face, held the small, shallow boat and dragged it towards the shoreline whereupon the two men got out.

'My Lord and father, Sisal sends greetings to you sir' said Ferrax 'and sends you his finest warrior for your escort' he added indicating Perris who had strolled down to greet the stranger. The Gaul looked between the two young men and laughed easily.

'I see your father has more than one son eh Ferrax? He is a lucky man that has such men to serve him.'

'It is not only our duty, but also our honour to serve our father' intoned Perris 'sir' he added, almost insolently. 'We are preparing a meal, perhaps you would join us?

'Gladly young man, most gladly' replied the visitor. 'May I introduce to you my guardian Forrun, he travels everywhere with me as my protector.' The second man from the boat was large and well built, but although bulky, not any of the weight was fat; the man was pure muscle. 'Forrun alas has no speech my friends, having once been captured by raiders as a small boy and his tongue cut out, but what he lacks in conversation he makes up with by his prowess on the field of battle.' Forrun smiled and Perris sensed a keen intelligence and awareness in the soldier and so he approached him and half drew his sword from the sheath tied to his belt. Forrun, recognising and appreciating the gesture did the same thing and the two warriors swapped weapons each able to assess the sword of the other. It was a signal of mutual trust and respect, whereby each fighter showed that he had nothing to hide and no aggressive motive to the other.

Forrun admired the intricate pattern hammered into the blade of Perris' sword, whilst Perris hefted the weight of iron, feeling the strength and power of Forrun's weapon. After a length of time set by tradition, the two warriors reclaimed their own swords and then instinctively clasped wrists, a bond created. Ferrax appeared both impressed and pleased with his brother's demeanour and formally bade their visitor, Corillun, welcome to the land of Sisal. He then led the four of them to the fire where Buldan had the rabbits skewered on sticks and cooking well. He handed meat to the guests first, as custom decreed.

'A fine welcome after dried meat and fish for four days' announced Corillun. 'We had wind and tide against us for what seemed like most of the journey' he added, to explain the length of time at sea.

'How do you feel about our harbour?' enquired Perris. 'The journey from the sea is quite long.'

'Indeed so, young Perris' agreed the visitor. 'Your father is indeed lucky that the gods smile on him with all they provide, including this excellent meat I may add. What have you planned for our journey Ferrax?'

'We shall leave here when we have eaten and then travel north. Our journey will take us two, maybe three days, but comfort and shelter shall be provided each night. As well as Perris and Buldan our party consists of two other warriors from our village; they are currently tending to our horses and readying them for the journey.'

'I am grateful to you, and Lord Sisal for your consideration and can only hope that our business can be conducted in such a spirit of friendship and harmony' said Corillun.

'You will find our father to be a fair man sir. Hard in business it is true, but a man of his word.'

'I can ask for no more.'

Hours later and the small party were ready to set off, Ferrax and Corillun mounted on horses, Perris. Buldan, Forrun and the two others walking alongside. Before they left, Forrun had returned to the ship and brought with him two leather bags which were now slung across the horse ridden by his master. Ferrax had reckoned that it would take them until sundown to cross the crest of the chalk hill and was gazing at the way ahead when he heard a shout and the sound of running feet to one side.

Seven men came screaming battle cries from the trees, their swords drawn and their intentions clear. Ferrax acted quickly and dismounted, grabbing the reins of Corillun's horse as he did so, but if Ferrax was quick, Perris was faster, quickly taking command of the situation.

'Buldan! With me! Ferrax, stay with our guest. You two' he called to the others 'to the flank.' Perris looked round expecting to see Forrun staying with Corillun but was surprised to see the big man, a wolfish grin on his face, standing alongside himself and Buldan, his sword drawn and an evil looking dagger in his left hand, its blade curved and the edge glinting in the sunshine.

There were seconds until the attackers were upon them and yet Perris was ready and confident in his ability, secure in the loyalty of his men. One of the attackers was faster than the others, and perhaps sensed that Forrun was an outsider, he veered towards the big man who effortlessly stepped aside and allowed the thrust of the sword to swipe at thin air before he slashed, just once with that vicious dagger and opened the man's throat. Blood sprayed around as the man fell to the floor writhing and Forrun stilled him with a stab from his sword through the spine. By now the other assailants were upon Perris and Buldan and the close quarter fighting was harsh and brutal. A blade nicked Buldan's arm and he roared with the pain as he pushed back against his assailant. This provided the space that Perris needed to drive his own sword forward, straight into the mouth of a man, and Perris used such force that the thrust carried the point out through the back of the neck. The dead man slid off the sword and the stink of his blood reeked as the combatants stood in the growing pool that was staining the grass red. By now, not only was Forrun back in the fray but the two fighters that Perris had sent to outflank the attackers had charged into the fight; and with two dead comrades, the attackers had lost their numerical advantage.

The remainder of the fight was swift and decisive in favour of Perris and his men and all but one of the would-be assailants lay dead. The survivor, wild eyed and shouting curses upon Perris, had been pinned to the ground by Buldan who now had his foot on the man's neck.

'Get him up' Perris panted, the exhilarating exertion of the fight nevertheless had left him exhausted. Buldan reached down and grabbed the hood of the man's cloak and pulled him to his feet.

'Kill me then you brave warrior!' shouted the survivor. 'All of you, just to kill me!' He would have carried on save that Perris punched him hard in the face, feeling the cartilage in the nose break and yet more blood was spilled.

'I have heard enough, and I have seen enough of you to last me a lifetime' said Perris. 'What I want to know is who you are, and where you came from?' The man looked at him defiantly.

'Very well, play your games. Buldan break part of him.' The warrior drove a fist into the side of the man and everyone heard the sickening sound of a rib breaking. The man shrieked and tried to fall to his knees but he was held upright by the brute strength of his captor.

'Now then, I shall repeat my question, who are you and where do you come from to defile this land of my father?' said Perris. Through rasping breaths the injured man gasped that his name was Storril and that his village was on the banks of the inlet from the sea towards where the sun set. Perris had seen this place and knew of the village which he had passed by on one of his scouting trips three seasons ago. It was not a prosperous place, the ground was soured with salt from the sea that often flooded the land. It was no wonder perhaps that these people had turned to petty thievery for their survival, but it was essential that the rule of Sisal remain unchallenged and paramount.

'You have attacked Perris, son of Sisal the Lord of these lands and to attack me is to attack my father and that earns retribution upon you and your families. You have the choice to accept my punishment upon you or we visit your village and destroy it. What say you?'

'I am no coward' hissed Storril 'I am prepared and ready to die so do your worst my lord' he emphasised the last two words in sarcasm and spat on the ground in contempt. Perris looked at him and laughed.

'Death for you is too good. No, I want you to remember today for the rest of your life, to carry the mark of defeat so that all shall know not to defy me. So choose you runt, do you lose an eye?' Perris had drawn his sword again and pushed the tip towards Storill's left eye. 'Maybe something more valuable?' The sword lowered to

Storril's groin and circled his genitalia, Sotrril's eyes widened and he shook his head. 'No? Then a hand it shall be! Buldan, hold his hand out' and as Buldan complied, Perris sliced through the fingers of Storrils hand severing them at the knuckles. Storril collapsed on the floor, thrashing from side to side, bellowing in the excruciating pain, heedless of Perris leaning down to him, but he heard the words clearly enough.

'Go back to your dung infested hovel and sit there in fear Storril, and you quake at the day you ever met Lord Perris.' With a final kick in the ribs, that caused another agonised scream from the broken man, Perris walked calmly away. Ferrax and Corrilun were already mounted back on their horses and Forrun was wrapping Buldan's arm in a poultice of leaves and nettles.

'You should have killed him Perris' said Corrilun with humour in his voice 'all you have done there is made an enemy of his village for generations to come.'

'With respect, honoured guest, all I did was send a message, and I sent it very clearly. They will now fear us and will do so for all time.' The travelling group set off again as the birds began to land and peck and rip at the carrion that littered the ground. A crow flew past, a severed finger clearly visible in its beak and it was all Ferrax could do not to retch his lunch on to the grass. Buldan also saw the bird and took it as an omen from the gods that their enemies would be borne away and scattered to the four winds, and so, relying on such wisdom, it was a happy group that set out northwards.

For three days the seven men rode and walked in companionable mood, Ferrax waxing lyrical to Corillun about omens and auguries for the success of the Gaul's visit. For himself Corillun seemed content to keep his counsel, though truth be told, he had found Perris's mutilation of Storril distressing and slightly disturbing. He had sought the advice of Forrun who by a series of grunts and gestures had indicated that although he too had felt that Perris enjoyed the fate that had befallen Storril too much, nevertheless Perris was a fearsome warrior and a force to be respected.

three days later – Caer Sisal - a Hill Fort

It was the day appointed for *cwnsl,* where any man in the village could bring their concern to their Chieftain, and it had been this way for all the seasons that Sisal had held power; ever since he had usurped his own weak and frail father.

Sisal strode from his own dwelling at the exact moment of sunset and saw those of the elders and the warriors who would be sitting with him to give advice or opinion on the matters brought forth. Their village was unusual, normally only the Chief or Lord was allowed an opinion and a voice, but Sisal was said to have been born wise and knew that to allow men to speak was to know what was in their hearts as well as their minds, and to show the respect of listening would be repaid by their willingness to fight and die should he require it. Sisal saw the faces of Drullis and his supporters, Cwaenog the Outsider, and Berros looking at him expectantly, he knew they were plotting something simply because Drullis was an ambitious man and he always was planning ways to advance himself. He had no real fear of Drullis even though their ideas seldom matched, but he did fear the march of time that Drullis, much the younger man, represented. Looking around further, Sisal saw the unmistakable huge outline of Gargonstus the master builder; Beline his doting father and one of the revered tribal elders, and the robed figure of Morcant the druid.

Cwnsl was always on the first sunset of the new moon and as the light of the day faded quickly it was replaced by the intense orange glow from the fire built in the pit at the centre of the settlement. Sparks and embers rose in time with the music created by the crackling sap in the wood as it boiled and burned and Sisal looked round appreciatively, all was exactly as it should be as he struck the hilt of his sword three times upon the metal boss at the centre of his circular shield, left at the side of his chair by his slave. As Sisal sat, he smiled indulgently at the young woman, she had done her tasks well as she always did, never complaining but always seemingly content to serve her Lord and his Lady. She hurried away, back to Sisal's nearby home, as women were not permitted at *cwnsl.*

The fire was an integral part of the settlement; each home had a duty to maintain the flames, and each had an equal right in sharing the benefit. Only the druid was exempted from civic duties imposed on all others and it was as well that it were so, for many druids were itinerant, and a Chieftain that could honestly boast that his tribe had a druid of their own was regarded as having considerable power and influence. Sisal was such a man and he never shied away from reminding people of his influence.

The general hubbub of chatter fell silent as the men acknowledged the signal from their leader. Sisal looked around, every pair of eyes except one met his; the only person casting his gaze to the floor was Drullis and it was at that point that Sisal knew that the challenge he had been expecting was to come this very night. So be it he thought to himself, for he was ready and well prepared to deal with whatever the fates had in store for him. Sisal leaned forward in his seat; he looked like an old man, his beard matted with grey hair and his once luxuriant hair thinning at the back of his head. The eyes however remained clear, a striking blue that pierced into the very heart of anyone who dared to question the authority of his office. By custom, the Chief was the last of the men to speak and so as each man said his piece, Sisal bided his time.

Drullis, that wily and ambitious creature, spoke at length of the harvest and the requirement of storing food for the winter. Not only did he speak for his own household, but also for that of his neighbour for Poril had died that spring and his woman had not yet sought a replacement husband. Sisal suspected that plans were made in Drullis' mind to replace his own wife with the widow of Poril, but, as the Chief contemplated, maybe he wanted a second wife, a status or power that he, as Lord of the village had expressly forbidden. Not losing eye contact with the speaker, Sisal moved his leg slightly to ease the pain he was feeling and felt the grinding ache in his knee as he stretched the limb, it had been there permanently now for three summers and each winter it worsened.

Sisal listened to and adjudicated upon disputes over land, the grazing of animals, the ownership of water in the streams and arguments between neighbours. Sisal worked calmly without needing to raise his voice and invariably both sides to a dispute were happy with the outcome. On the rare occasions where a man disagreed with his Lord then he had the opportunity to place the dispute before the whole of *cwnsl* to adjudicate or to leave the Tribe. During the whole of Sisal's reign this had happened but once and the young family had elected to leave and try their fortune elsewhere. Upon their departure, Sisal had made them gifts of food and a small amount of gold and both he and the young warrior had held back genuine tears of sorrow as they had parted.

With the evenings business concluded Sisal stood to close the proceedings for another month but, as he expected, he was interrupted by a nervous-looking Drullis who rose to his feet. Sisal sat back down

'My Lord' began Drullis 'and my friend' he continued with a smile that was quite disarming 'we once again give thanks to the gods for their guidance to your heart in the way that you lead us with such wisdom and intelligence.' There was a murmur of approval from the men seated round the fire. 'We can only hope' continued Drullis 'that such wisdom continues for many more seasons and that we and our families continue to prosper in peace and friendship as we do at the moment. However my Lord, there comes a time when every man has to yield to the inevitable frailties of age and plan for the future, so Lord Sisal, please do not think me in any way disloyal if I ask what provision has been made both within the House of Sisal and for our villages future?' There was a silence the Chieftain noted, Drullis had perhaps tried to secure support for a challenge and failed and the Village now held its collective breath. Drullis spoke again. 'My Lord Sisal your leadership has been blessed by the gods of earth sun and water and it is only right and proper that the future should be so blessed too.' Finally Drullis sat down, allowing the Chieftain to stand.

Lit by the glow of the fire, Sisal spread his arms wide in a signal that all were included in what he had to say. Long ago he had learned the value of silence, of pausing for effect before he spoke so that everyone listened, and so as he stood there, he looked around him. Drullis was acting the innocent and had a wide smile on his face but the effect of his actions were shown by the fact that both Berros and Cwaenog the Outsider now looked at the fire and not at either Sisal or Drullis.

'My people, I agree with my friend Drullis.' There were a few gasps of astonishment from the gathering and Sisal snuck a look at Drullis who was sitting open-mouthed staring at his Chieftain. Sisal laughed easily and continued, 'Worry not however as I have no plans to die just yet!' Nervous laughter greeted this statement. 'What we must do is to secure the future of our village and the best way to do this is to create a way that all may have a say but where only one person bears the burden of leadership.' Sisal stroked his beard as if deep in thought.

'Over many years we have fought off our enemies, we have built our farms and created links with many merchants who know that it is both safe and profitable to trade here. We have welcomed new people to our village such as Cwaenog and his family, and they have added their skills and knowledge to our own. Our families grow strong and wise and none more so than my own two sons.' Sisal paused.

'Where are they tonight?' interrupted Drullis. 'Do they insult *cwnsel* by their absence deliberately?

'No Drullis they do not. It had been my hope and my wish that they would be here with an honoured guest, but alas it appears not to be. However, they will be here of that I think we can have no doubt and it is of them that I wish to speak. And of you Drullis' Sisal left his words hanging in the air, using the pause again for maximum effect.

'It is my intention to join the houses of myself and Drullis by a marriage between Caeryl, his daughter and my youngest son Perris. My elder son Ferrax will in time replace me as our Chief. Between the two of them, Ferrax with his wisdom and learning and Perris with his skills with the sword, it is my hope and my belief that we will all prosper in safety and harmony.' Sisal sat down to a storm of cheering and applause from the men around the fire. Such was the noise that a few of the women and children risked peering from their homes at the commotion. Even Drullis had a grin on his face, knowing that he had been outsmarted and out manoeuvred by the wily old Chief who sat and toasted his people with a horn of wine. All Sisal had to do now was tell his wife that he had married off her youngest son and that was a job he could put off until morning.

Sisal felt a presence next to him and looked up into the face of Drullis.

'A clever strategy my Lord' said Drullis. Sisal indicated that he should sit and Drullis, savouring the proximity to his Chief, made a great show of preening himself and gaining as much attention as possible before lowering himself to the ground.

'I take it you approve then Drullis?' asked Sisal.

'I would have preferred Caeryl to be with Lord Ferrax' said Drullis simply and without rancour 'they are already enamoured of one another it would seem.'

'I suspect at the instigation of our respective wives' nodded Sisal in agreement 'but no matter, they will do as we command and my friend, it will be good to welcome you to our family.' Sisal held out a hand and the two men gripped each other's wrists in a manner to seal the arrangement.

Where are your sons by the way?' asked Drullis

'They have gone to the harbour to collect an emissary from Gaul who wishes to trade and who appears willing to pay a levy providing we secure the land around the anchorage.

'I can see why you have sent them both then' laughed Drullis. 'The thought of Perris being diplomatic is like a goat trying to fly.'

'And the thought of Ferrax wielding a sword would make me worry for his own safety' agreed Sisal.

On the night of the third day, the travelling group approached the hilltop Village, their way lit by the amber glow from the fire pit. Ferrax knew it was the night set for *cwnsl* and was disappointed that they had not managed to time their arrival earlier. The prestige that would have come from Corillun seeing his father dispensing wisdom and justice could not have failed to impress upon the visitor that he was dealing with a man of substance and authority.

'Still!' called Perris, and obediently the group stopped.

'Perris...' whispered Ferrax, believing that what was to come would serve no purpose other than to delay their arrival still further. He was tired and he felt sure that Corillun would similarly appreciate the chance to rest. The only reply from Perris was a wolfish grin that showed his teeth white against the dark night.

'Stay here and let us see which of the men earns their meal eh?' Silently, Perris stole off into the night and was gone for a matter of minutes before there was a shout and a clang of metal on metal and Ferrax and Corillun kicked their horses on to find out what damage had been caused.

They need not have worried as Perris was pinned to the ground, giggling helplessly as he was held there by a huge man with arms as thick as most mens legs.

'That, my lord Perris was one of your more stupid attempts to catch us out if I may say so.'

'You may Gadrig, you may' laughed Perris. 'I am glad to see that not all of our village sleep beneath their women's cloaks.'

'You insult me Master Perris' replied the man without rancour. 'But yet I suppose that I should feel content that there was no way you were going to sneak round me this night.' Seeing the two riders, Gadrig hailed Lord Ferrax who introduced him to their honoured guest.

'Gadrig is our metal worker' he explained to Corillun 'which is why he is as strong as an oxen.'

'And smells like one too' said Perris only to have his face ground into the mud even more which he seemed to find even funnier.

Hearing the commotion, another of the sentries had roused Sisal who now came to the edge of the settlement to formally greet his guest.

'Corillun of Gaul, welcome to our village. I am Sisal, born of this place and Chieftain to my people as well as being father to these two.........Gadrig, let him get up.' Perris got quickly and agilely to his feet, a smile on his face.

'Greetings and felicitations to you Sisal, your reputation is known far and wide and will only be enhanced when tales are told of our journey' said Corillun.

'You have had trouble?' Sisal had taken in the silent meaning of Corillun's words, but was also aware of the injury to Buldan and the slightly exaggerated behaviour of his youngest son that usually followed a fight or a hunt.

'It was nothing Lord Sisal' said Corillun with a dismissive wave of his hand 'but I shall relish the telling of it on the morrow. For now, I confess I need my rest, as the journey has been long, though my gratitude to you Lord Ferrax for your witty and intelligent companionship.' Corillun made a small bow from the saddle to Ferrax who acknowledged this gracious compliment.

'Come dear Corillun and we shall show you to your bed. We keep a building ready and available for visitors and it is my guarantee to you that you shall not be disturbed until morning' said Sisal, leading the now dismounted Gaul into the village and showing him and Forrun to a small but dry hut where a number of beds with fresh straw and woollen woven blankets had been set out. In the centre of the hut, providing both warmth and light, there was a small fire, the smoke spiralling lazily upwards to a hole in the centre of the plaited reed roof.

'I am treated like a king rather than a merchant' said Corillun expansively. I bid you a good night Lord Sisal.' The villagers withdrew to give their guests peace and tranquillity.

the same night

Sisal strolled happily back to his own dwelling, his sons and his guest were safely within the village and it appeared that, a little bother aside, a good impression had thus far been made. Sisal's home was very similar to the rest of the dwellings within the village; a circular hut with walls made of wattle and daub and a roof of thatched straw, laid on a timber frame made from stripped saplings that rested on the wall and were bound to the stout centre post made of oak but with a hole kept open in the roof to allow smoke from the fire to escape. Alongside the hut was a smaller building of the same construction and used as storage, or occasionally when he was younger, and his wife had been in one of her rages, for sleeping.

Standing in the doorway was his wife of much time, still beautiful and striking, though it was true, more lined with age. Idon had always been a force of nature and time and age had never diminished the force of her opinion or the strike of her tongue. Time however lessens the challenge and whereas once upon a time, Sisal would argue and the two of them would stalk each other like warriors for time before usually reconciling in the best way a man and his woman can, nowadays he found the performance slightly amusing.

'What is he like then, this Gaul' asked Idon barring the door with her own body. Sisal considered for a moment.

'A courteous man, from the cut of his clothing I would say affluent and successful' and then to forestall any further questions 'but I don't know if he is joined or single, the name of his parents, whether he has a dog ....or his favourite food.' Sisal smiled, Idon glowered.

'You think yourself so clever Sisal, so powerful and mighty, but you just remember and you recall that before you met me it was never so much as 'Lord Sisal' but 'here comes Sisal the Slow' I made you powerful and don't you forget it.'

'How can I' answered the Chief easing his way past her 'you never stop telling me!'

'Lest you forget...... Get off me!' She struggled and beat her fists against Sisal who had leaned over and kissed her. Idon started laughing and Sisal soon joined in before taking her hand and leading her to sit near the fire.

'I take it our sons are safe?' she asked.

'It seems there was a little bother on the journey' replied Sisal 'Perris is his usual self after a fight. Like a bird that swoops and dives but never lands.'

'Poor Ferrax then if he has had to suffer that for days. What happened at *cwnsl*?' Sisal had known this question was coming, for Idon was in a way right about her assessment of him; prior to joining with her he had been regarded in the village as being strong but slow and a little simple. Idon had changed all that, a renowned beauty, she had the attention of every young warrior from all the local tribes, but somehow she had picked Sisal who had never even shown the slightest interest in her. Later as his wisdom grew, he had come to appreciate that Idon found power lustful, and it drew her in as the rain always ran down the roof of the hut. Nowadays, Idon always knew what was coming in *cwnsl* by the simple expedient of gossip from the other women of the village, she also always had an opinion on whether Sisal had made the right decisions or favoured the right family.

'You were right of course, that Drullis sought to clarify what shall happen after my death' said Sisal with a sigh.

'He's a dangerous one' agreed Idon. 'Ambitious and greedy, it is a nasty combination.'

'Just as you told me before *cwnsl*' agreed Sisal 'but I made a decision for the best and I think it will please you.'

'Tell me of this decision' said Idon, a wary note of caution in her voice, and Sisal went on to explain about his idea that Perris should become husband to Caeryl in order to effect control over the ambitions of Drullis, thus leaving Ferrax free to arrange a union with the daughter of another tribal chief to unite their peoples and prevent more battling bloodshed.

For a moment, after he had finished speaking, Idon said nothing, but the shaking of her head was a bad sign and Sisal knew it. When she did speak, it was not loud and that her husband knew, was a very dangerous sign.

'I think that you have just proven Drullis right my husband, your idiotic and stupid scheme ....' the volume started to increase 'would demonstrate to anyone with half a brain that you had lost all of your wits! What were you thinking, you stupid stupid limited fool of a man? And stop looking at me like that with your mouth open like a dead fish!' She was shouting now. 'Ferrax is close to Caeryl and you give her to Perris like she is a sow? Perris may be a brave warrior but he is a sullen and immature fool who knows no more how to treat a woman than you know how to use the small brain that the gods gave you! You stupid man, get out there and undo the damage you have done. Get out! Out!' She was advancing on him know with the stick she used to stoke the fire in her hand; her eyes were flaming in anger and her mouth set in a straight line grimace. Sisal made the mistake of moving towards her and she raised the heavy stick menacingly. 'One more step Sisal and I'll use this on that empty head of yours' she warned.

Sisal stood still, waiting for the explanation that he knew would come, once she had calmed herself a little, and sure enough, her shoulders slumped and she drew in a deep breath.

'Sisal, my husband, Ferrax and Caeryl have an understanding that they will be together, he has spoken to me of this and I have talked with her and her mother. Caeryl is a sensible and loyal girl and she will be good with Ferrax, giving him wise advice and stopping him from always listening to that fool druid you both set so much faith in. If you stand by your choice then you will set our sons against each other and you will set Ferrax against yourself. I fear he would never forgive you, and I know that I will not either. You are a wise Chief Sisal, and the man I chose to be with in life, but you are a foolish father who chooses to keep his eyes closed to all that goes on in this house.'

'Surely Perris will be good with the girl as well' pleaded Sisal.

'Perris is an animal, he would destroy the girl and that, dear husband, would make an enemy of Drullis and divide your tribe. Go and put right the damage you have done this night Sisal and don't come back until you have done so.'

'It's late, I'll.........'

'Go!' She pushed him. Nobody else would ever get away with anything like that but Idon was not a nobody and she knew it. She pushed her Chief and her husband out of the hut. 'Put it right' she said as he turned and walked away.

Sisal did not in fact walk far, at the bottom of the hill on which the village sat was the stream from which the people drew their water and Sisal, with an acknowledgement to the sentry on guard, walked to the bank and sat staring at the gurgling water reflecting in the moonlight. As he had done many times past, he reflected on the words Idon had used and the way she treated him. If what she had said was true, then certainly his plan was deeply and fundamentally flawed, but he could resolve that with Drullis in the morning. He was left more with a feeling of injustice and hurt that would simply not go away. Maybe he should revisit that decision he had made about taking second wives. Maybe a man could tire of the constant sanctimony, the volatile temper and the stubborn nature of one woman and maybe the solution lay in playing one off against the other. He sat for some time with the various scenarios running through his mind, after all what was the point in being Chief if there was no personal benefit?

With his mind full of positive possibility, Sisal eventually pulled himself to his feet, his aching knee protesting, and walked back towards his home. He knew that Idon would be awake and waiting for him with that triumphant smile upon her face and he resolved that he would not give her the satisfaction of victory and so for the first time in many years he wrapped his cloak around him, pulled the hood over his head and settled down in the storage space between the roof and the walls and was soon asleep.

the next day

Sisal awoke early and with a start, the noises around him were unfamiliar and the air felt different, it took a while for his senses to return and his memory followed shortly after enhanced by the view of the sloping roof. A prod in his ribs and a snort or derision from Idon reminded Sisal of the current state of her displeasure and the wickedness of the revenge he now had planned to disclose to her. On reflection overnight he had certainly moved far away from taking a second wife, and he recalled with a sense of horror the thoughts he had of even considering the widow of Poril. However, that did not mean that he was above scoring a few points of his own and one thought that had set itself in stone overnight was that his plan to marry Perris to Caeryl was the right one.

'Well?' spat Idon. 'What have you to say for yourself?' Sisal propped himself up on one elbow and looked at his wife indulgently. He nodded, his shaggy mane of hair moving as if it had a life of its own.

'I've been thinking' he announced. This was answered by another jab in the ribs from the pole that Idon held; the one that was usually used to herd the pigs.

'Stop thinking and start doing' ordered Idon. Sisal smiled, an act that he knew would infuriate her if he stayed silent. He stayed silent and she looked at him.

'So' she said 'you are determined to go through with your idiotic scheme?'

'I am' replied Sisal casually 'but it is far from idiotic. However I want to explain it to you, in the hope that you will understand and support me.' Idon remained silent and leaned on the pole she had used to jab at him. Sisal took it as a sign of progress.

'I do not trust Drullis, for the obvious reason that he cannot be trusted and should Ferrax and Caeryl join together then eventually the grandson of Drullis will become Chief of this tribe. That is not something that any responsible person would wish to see; the man will use every chance to exert influence and corrupt the child to his ways.'

'And you wouldn't?' asked Idon with a smile on her face.

'I would teach the child the ways I learned from my father, yes. But that is different, our family knows its responsibilities and acts accordingly. Ferrax will understand that when I explain it all to him' said Sisal.

'Sisal, my husband and my Chief, do you remember when I birthed Ferrax and you were at my side? Was that not against the wishes of your own father, the druid and the mother women of our tribe? Did you not stand up then and proclaim that the son of Sisal was more important than the passage of the moon across the night sky?'

'Yes, but....'

'And did you not seek to fight against the tradition of sending our son away to be raised by another?'

'Yes, but I was persuaded against the idea and now the other children are away learning to be adults. Only the other day I had news from Garron, son of Sterras, who says that our boy Merrad does well and is becoming a fine young man.' Sisal caught the look on his wife's face and fell silent, the mention of the other children was always a sore point. Idon, unlike Sisal, had never accepted the truth that children developed better away from their parents and it had been in truth her wish that he tried to defy convention with the raising of Ferrax and Perris.

'The point, my husband, is that in your dotage you are forgetting the very things that made you stand out as a brave and forward looking Chief to your people. You are becoming hidebound to the old ways and the words of that reactionary druid you seem to fawn over. Caeryl will marry Ferrax and that is the end of it, if you go against me in this Sisal then you will break this tribe and your kingdom will scatter.' Idon folded her arms.

'My mind is set' said Sisal.

'You stupid ignorant man' replied Idon with a shake of her head.

the same day – a meeting between Sisal and Corillun

'My only concern Lord Sisal, if I may speak freely, is the safety of the goods landing on your shore. We only have to consider the unfortunate events of my arrival to know that measures must be taken to protect our mutual interests.' Corillun spoke earnestly, but as Sisal acknowledged, truthfully. Over a morning, discussions had proceeded well in Sisal's opinion; Corillun was an experienced trader and negotiated hard but fairly and there had been much agreement on both sides. Corillun wished to expand his business across the sea and Sisal commanded an area that was both profitable and peaceful, in short the perfect trading partnership, for where a land was peaceful, men created wealth and wherever wealth existed, Corillun could trade to his own advantage.

The two men had agreed a system of tariff; firstly Corillun would pay a levy on each item of merchandise he landed within Sisal's lands, and secondly he would pay a sum out of each sale he made. In return, Sisal would allow the merchant and his men free rights of passage across his lands and provide an armed escort as well as introducing the merchant to the placid Chiefs of nearby tribes. For Sisal, there was the opportunity to make profit for little or no effort and for Corillun, he would capture the market before an of his competitors, and with luck his ships could return to Gaul laden with goods from these lands such as the fine woollen cloth they produced and the leather, iron and honey he had already marked out as being of superior quality to that found over the water. That slavery existed in this land, Corillun already knew, and he bided his time before broaching the subject. It was not that Sisal was averse to slavery, there was the attractive girl that served his own house, but slavery inevitably arose from conflict and the mere taking of slaves created embitterment and enmity that Corillun saw Sisal was anxious to avoid.

There only now remained the assurance of safe landing and departure and for a moment Sisal sat and considered the problem. Having seemed to reach a decision he turned and called for Perris to join them and in due course the hard-faced young warrior was summonsed and smiled at his brother who had been with his father and their guest throughout.

'Perris, join us' said his father, indicating a space where the young man would sit. Dutifully, but with an ironic smile on his face, Perris sat and looked round the small group that consisted of Sisal, Ferrax, Corillun and the druid Morcant. 'Lord Perris' began Corillun 'I seek your guidance on the matter of protecting my merchandise as it lands from the sea. I am mindful of the unfortunate incident when I arrived.' Perris looked at his father who inclined his head in a gesture that allowed the young man to speak his mind.

'it is my opinion sir' said Perris to Corillun, the tone of his voice winning approval from both his brother and father 'that there are two options available; the first is to attack and wipe out the people that were responsible for the insult to yourself; the second is to build a fort to protect the landing, to secure storage for your goods and to deter any future aggression.'

'I am impressed with your succinct assessment Lord Perris' said Corillun, clearly struck by the young mans grasp of the situation. 'Of course you maimed that poor man as a warning, but you still think that his village would attack again?' Perris shrugged his shoulders.

'If not them, then someone else' he replied 'after all rich merchandise left unprotected is an invitation to a fight is it not?'

'So you favour the building of a fortress?' asked Ferrax.

'I do' replied his brother, his steady gaze right into the eyes of his brother leaving no doubt as to his preference. Corillun, skilled as he was in negotiation and trade, readily caught the prevailing mood, and begged the indulgence of his host Sisal to excuse him while he took a walk to ease his joints and consider any alternatives. When he had walked away, Sisal leaned in to his younger son and spoke.

'Build a fortress? Have you any idea of the cost and manpower required? Not to say the length of time it will take to fortify the area.'

'Father' replied Perris 'you know the land of which I speak and if you picture it within your mind then you will see how a ditch and a wall can be made around the land to use the sea on two sides. That will cut down the time, manpower and cost. It will give you a new settlement on the coast that we can offer to other merchants as well as this Gaul and it will keep him in check as well.'

'What do you mean?' enquired Morcant, his deep and commanding voice giving him an apparent authority and gravitas.

'Merchants seek to make a profit druid. It is simple, they buy things to sell at a higher price and the driving force is wealth. Sooner or later Corillun or one of his acolytes will consider that if they held land on the coast then they can control the arrival of their goods. It will not only free them from the levy that they seem prepared to pay for now, but it will also, in time, become a threat to the authority of my father.' Sisal smiled indulgently at Perris, not only had the boy considered the trade benefits to be had from the arrangement with Corillun, he had also thought of the benefit of the tribe as a whole. In essence, Perris had been thinking like a Chief and Sisal swelled with pride. Maybe Perris was growing up at last and if only Sisal could combine Ferrax' intellect with Perris' prowess in battle then the village could be secured for the next generation.

'Father?' It was Ferrax speaking. 'I think that Perris is right and that we should build. There are already some people close by there living off the sea and we can use those men to help us dig the ditches and build the wall. But I also think that we should act against the other settlement, the one that tried to attack us. I will lead a group of our men to their village and provide them with an ultimatum, that either they join with us and agree to be subject to your laws and benefit from your protection' he looked round 'or we wipe them out.' Sisal thought for a moment, considering what he had heard.

'And you will send Perris on this task?'

'No father, I will go myself. To send the eldest son shows them respect and it is my hope that I can persuade them to agree to our terms. I took little part in the previous fight and they might be naturally, shall we say, distrustful of my little brother.' Ferrax smiled and caught sight of the grin on his brothers' face. He looks like a hungry dog thought Ferrax, ready to attack at any moment.

'Morcant?' asked Sisal.

'A sound plan' said the druid. 'If these villagers do not submit then Lord Ferrax has the presence of mind to eliminate the men while the women and children can always be sold as slaves. This provides us with goods to trade with Corillun thus showing our faith in him and our trust in our agreement. Lord Ferrax is to be congratulated in his clear thinking.' Perris snorted and stifled a laugh, the druid had always favoured Ferrax, and eschewed the old ways of settling disputes by force. Perris, much more the product of his fathers thinking, considered that you negotiated a peace from a position of strength having slaughtered your enemy in battle first. Morcant and therefore Ferrax, favoured the threat of battle to extract mean mouthed words of obedience that would never be honoured. A man, thought Perris, needed to know he would die if he disrespected his Lord. And a woman would live in fear of losing her man which would mean that she would undermine any sedition and opposition with her logic. Perris looked across at Sisal who had clearly reached a decision. The words of the druid were spoken as if they were the ideas of Ferrax, very cleverly contrived, thought Perris who mistrusted anyone who twisted words and meanings.

'Perris, you understand battle and the thoughts of men who wish to fight. It is for that reason that I will ask you to work with

Gargonstus to plan and build our fortress. I have my own ideas on that and will discuss them with you both later. With your knowledge my son, I want you to build a fort that will resist any attack and that will keep our people and our friends' a sweep of his hand indicated that he meant Corillun 'safe. Think like the attacker Perris and then defeat yourself with your own fortress.' He turned to his eldest son.

'Ferrax I agree with your plans for the settlement. Visit them, talk to them and make them see sense. Take Buldan and Gadrig with you as well as Morcant, and I hope that will combine persuasion with force.' Morcant raised his eyebrows at being commanded in this way, but he said nothing, preferring wisely to keep his thoughts to himself until he could get Ferrax alone and persuade him to his way of doing things. Slaves could be very profitable and if he could deliver women and children to Corillun then there may well be profit in it for the druid as well as Sisal. Respectfully, Morcant inclined his head in acceptance of his Lord's wishes.

Corillun was delighted with the plans, and leaving Ferrax to consider his approach to the village, he asked if Lord Perris had any plans to return to the harbour.

'I will discuss matters with Master Gargonstus our builder, but I favour riding to the coast in the morning, why do you ask?' said Perris.

'It is in my interests to return to my ship, to ensure that she remains safe, as much for my own peace of mind as anything else, and I would also like the opportunity to see your ideas for this fortress.' Perris considered for a moment, Corillun was not bad company but he was more intrigued by the wordless Forrun and would welcome the company of the Gaulish fighting man.

'I agree Corillun, let us travel together and enter into the spirit of co-operation and friendship as my father wishes. Our new fortress can only benefit from the insight and opinions of yourself and

Forrun.' The merchant hurried away to make his arrangements as Perris sought out Gargonstus and told him of his plans.

The following morning :

Finally, after months of unyielding cold and rain, there was warmth in the day; the sun was shining weakly making the fields and pastures steam as the dew evaporated. From the fortress is looked as if the very earth were on fire and smouldering as if after a fierce battle. Trees, still this early in the year without their leaves and silhouetted against the sunshine added to the image of destruction, looking as if they had been set to fire, their blackened branches standing stark against the light.

Ferrax walked the proud black horse he had chosen for the day to the entrance to the fortress and agilely leaped on to her back, he then turned to look at Morcant, perched uncomfortably on the donkey he habitually rode. The druid, looked sour and ill at ease, even with his favourite pupil as his companion.

'Druid Morcant!' proclaimed Ferrax cheerfully, 'it would appear that you were right once again' he shook his head, wondering how the Druid could be so knowledgeable. 'How could you be so sure that the sacrifice was what the gods demanded?' Morcant looked up, into the eyes of Lord Ferrax and smiled weakly.

'My Lord, it is my lot in life to know these things. The gods delayed the seasons change because the woman Palem harboured doubts in her mind. The only way to appease the gods was for her to make sacrifice and trust that the gods would provide and they duly have done so. As I said they would' he added pointedly so that his significance was not lost. The sacrifice had cost Palem the twelve ducks she kept and tendered for eggs feathers and meat. In making the sacrifices, Morcant had forbidden any person to touch the dead birds and instead had insisted that their carcases be burned as an offering. Palem's status within the village was ruined and the birds, a sign of her affluence, were gone accompanied by a stern warning from Morcant about not replacing them for fear of angering the earth goddesses. Palem was reduced to tending fields and helping others for meagre rewards of food until her man returned from tending Sisal's flock of sheep on the hills many days walk away. The fact that Palem had rejected Morcant's advances to bed her, were of course completely irrelevant to his pronouncements and decisions.

Ferrax saw the poor woman enter the fortress carrying the tools she had used to break the earth on the lower slopes.

'You must be joyous for the day!' called Ferrax, Palem kept her eyes averted and mumbled something neutral. 'Your sacrifice has gladdened the hearts of the gods and they smile upon us now Palem' continued Ferrax. The woman merely nodded her agreement, scowled at the impassive face of the druid and continued on her way.

'Well Morcant, let us be on our way, if we ride well we can be there by nightfall perhaps?' He kicked the horse on but she stayed obstinately still, and he repeated the action three times before drawing his sword and slapping her rump with the flat of the blade. The horse shook her head and shivered but remained immobile. Ferrax shouted at the animal and kicked her flanks harder but still the horse would not move.

'You should know better than to take my horse brother' called Perris walking towards the small group. 'You know she will only tolerate me to ride her, and you can kick and curse her all day and she will just ignore you.' The horse, hearing Perris' voice craned her long neck round to see him and her gaze followed him as he walked in front of her, stroking her face and offering her an apple which she readily accepted.

'This is not your horse' hissed Ferrax 'we do not hold possessions within the family as well you know brother.' Perris smiled.

'We don't' he said, emphasising the first word as he bit into a second apple from the store huts 'but she does' he said, meaning the horse. 'Still then, best of luck and safe journey' and he made to walk off. As he did so, the horse followed him, despite all of Ferrax's attempts to control her. Ferrax was in danger of being humiliated and he knew it, Morcant was whispering something that sounded like an incantation, whatever it was it failed to have any effect and eventually Ferrax jumped down and approached his brother.

'You have made me look foolish brother' he said, quiet and menacing 'and I will not forget this.' Perris smiled arrogantly and shrugged, continuing to bite into the apple as Ferrax stormed away, returning minutes later with another, smaller, beast to ride. With a look of scorn towards his transferred his possessions from one beast to the other, Morcant looking away, found something to occupy himself. Buldan and Gadrig, the warriors accompanying Ferrax were already mounted on horseback and waiting outside the fortress, and they saw nothing of the altercation between the brothers.

'That was a foolish thing to do Perris' said Sisal, walking towards his son with a slight limp and a look of pain on his face. The discomfort was not lost on Perris who asked what was wrong. 'Nothing that won't go away as the day warms me' replied Sisal. 'Now wait for me to speak to Ferrax and then come and discuss with me and Gargonstus how we go ahead and build this fortress.

***

'Ferrax, a small amount of your time before you depart' said Sisal, walking over to his eldest son. Ferrax stopped what he was doing and gave his full attention to his father, who drew him to one side so that they would not be overheard.

'One of the burdens of my position, is that I have to make decisions that are the best for the people, even if they are the worst for the individual. This' said Sisal, his voice sounding heavy and tired 'is something that you shall come to learn, and hopefully, one day accept. I have been thinking long and hard about the future for myself, for you as my eldest son, and for our tribe and I have decided that we have spent our days looking inwards, and that the world is changing. With Corrilun bringing us goods from afar and the prices we extract for our produce, we need to consider how best to ensure those profitable relationships.'

'I agree father' interrupted Ferrax, but he was silenced by Sisal holding up a hand.

'I have not finished, and this is already hard for me' said the Chief. 'I have decided that you will join with a relative of Corrilun. We have discussed it and he both agrees and has a suitable match in mind. I will arrange with him to bring her on one of his next voyages.'

'But father . . .' said Ferrax in confusion. 'It is settled these many summers past, Caeryl, the daughter of Drullis, will join with me? Surely the strength that gives us within the tribe validates the match?'

'I said this would be hard Ferrax, and so it is, for I suspect that it will get worse for you. Yes, there is a truth in what you say. Drullis is strong and has influence with our people; he spreads discontent and displeasure, and the way to stop that is to join our two families . . .' his voice trailed off as he saw the look of horror on Ferrax's face. The young man had readily worked out his father's meaning.

'You cannot do this thing father' said Ferrax, his voice hollow with a building anger. 'Not now and not ever. It would be wrong! And besides, what of Caeryl and . . .'

'And what Ferrax?' said Sisal calmly. Ferrax, his mind whirling, walked away to try to compose himself, but his mind what a whirlwind of conflicting emotions; duty to his father, the feelings he and Caeryl shared, the destiny of the tribe, and the revulsion he felt that his brother would join with the woman he loved. He turned and walked back towards his father.

'Do you think I loved your mother when we first met?' said Sisal simply, taking the wind out of Ferrax's emotions. 'Oh, you see us now as a devoted couple I am sure, but it was not always so, at least not on my part' admitted the older man. 'And in time, as I said, you will come to see and accept my wisdom.'

'You cannot do this thing father' said Ferrax. 'I will join with nobody but Caeryl.'

'I see' said Sisal sadly. 'This is a shame because my mind is firm on this. Caeryl will join with your brother and that is an end to it.' Ferrax knew his father's moods well enough not to attempt any further reasoning with him, and instead walked back to his horse, called to Morcant, and rode hard for the fortress gates, the druid bouncing along on his donkey oblivious to the tears of anger that streamed down the young mans face.

***

Sisal, Gargonstus the builder and Perris were crouched down near the fire pit and had used the ashes from the edge of the ever burning fire to draw a crude map of the coast on the ground.

'We build here' said Sisal pointing to the top of the hill that overlooked the harbour. 'It is an excellent defensive position and will give clear views over the surrounding lands.' He looked up at his son who grimaced.

'I do not agree' said Perris 'If we build here' and with a stick he pointed to the land by the water's edge 'then we can protect the ships and the goods as they land. It also makes storage easier. The main problem with your plan My Lord is that if we station warriors on top of the hill, we would be forever sending them to the water to protect the ships as they arrive. We might as well put them there permanently.'

'Gargonstus?' said Sisal inviting the craftsman's opinion. The builder had learned his trade at the hand of his father Beline and knew more about the strength of stone and banks of earth than any other man alive.

'My Lord, I agree with Lord Perris' said Gargonstus his slow voice deep and rich. 'In normal circumstances, the defensive position atop the hill would be the right place to site a fortress, but from what you have told me you require the fortress to do, we should build where Lord Perris suggests. There are other advantages as well.'

'Continue' said Sisal.

'Well Lord Sisal, if we build earth and stone walls here' he drew a line with the stick he took from Perris 'with a ditch in front then firstly the spoil from the ditch creates the earth wall as normal, but we only need to build on two sides, leaving the sea as a natural defence for the rest. Also my Lord, if for any reason the fortress is overrun then the warriors have a ready escape route if they keep boats within the anchorage. It will be much cheaper and quicker to build as well.'

What was being proposed went against all of Sisal's natural instincts. Forts should be built where they were able to command their lands, and to Sisal that meant they should be built on the highest land available.

'Alright you two, I sense that you have already discussed this and agreed' said Sisal with a wry smile. 'So tell me this; what do you propose to do if men land from boats? You are vulnerable and unprotected from attack from the sea.' It was Perris who replied.

'Father, Master Gargonstus has already given the answer, we use boats ourselves. The water between our new fortress and the sea is long and the journey will take the most part of a day. We can either attack an enemy ship on the water or we can set it afire by arrows.' Gargonstus picked up the narrative.

'Lord Sisal is correct again. In time we could site defensive posts here, and here.' Gargonstus pointed to the harbour mouth 'and the warriors sent here can either light a fire as a warning of attack or attacks the ships themselves.'

The three men sat in amiable silence for a while; Sisal considering all options as he made his decision, and Perris and Gargonstus confident that their Lord would follow the logic of their advice.

'Very well, I need to see this place for myself before I decide. We shall set off when the sun reaches the mid point' and with no further comment, Sisal pushed himself to his feet, clearly in some discomfort and limped away. Both Gargonstus and Perris knew better than to offer to help their Chief.

With Ferrax and Morcant

The four men rode on in tense silence, Buldan and Gadrig had the presence of mind to distance themselves from Ferrax and acted as guards to the front and rear of the small group, leaving Morcant to counsel and calm his protégé.

Thus far all of the Druid's attempts to engage Ferrax had failed. It had taken some time for Ferrax to slow his horse to a walk and allow Morcant to catch up. The druid's bones hurt from riding and the donkey was slow and ponderous which is why he preferred riding such an animal. Morcant tried another approach.

'My Lord. . .' he began only to be cut off by Ferrax.

'Why must he behave in such a manner? He seeks to shame me in front of our people Morcant and I shall not tolerate him much further! He is my brother but also my tormentor, never losing an opportunity to prove his arrogance, it will be his downfall.'

'My Lord Ferrax' said Morcant soothingly 'your brother is only half the man you are with your learning and your wisdom. Lord Perris is proficient with a sword I agree, but he lacks your leadership and your clear thought.' The Druid saw the young man's shoulders slump.

'Druid, I hate and love Perris at the same time. I love him as my brother and loathe him as a bramble tearing at my skin, constantly reminding me that if I am to lead our people then I need to become more like him not less.' They rode in silence for a while, the robed druid understanding that Ferrax was best left to his own thoughts. As the miles went by, Ferrax slumped deeper and deeper into melancholy.

+++++

The distance between the settlements was a long day on horseback, and Ferrax's desire to complete the journey in a single day was always going to be over optimistic. As the day passed it became increasingly apparent to Ferrax that the small party would need to make camp. The journey took Ferrax roughly south-west and the going was easy over the rolling countryside with open lands interspersed with copses of trees, their branches still stark and empty, awaiting the warmth of spring.

'Not long now my Lord before the goddess of fertility stirs from her winter slumbers' called Morcant amiably. Ferrax, starting to appreciate the day, and forget his brother, turned on the horse to look at the druid.

'You are our guide to such matters druid Morcant' he said simply, but earnestly, his faith in the power or the robed man on the donkey absolute. 'There is a small pond a little further on that I recall from a previous journey, let us rest there a while and water the horses that we may talk and plan our discussions with the villagers we are to subdue.'

Already in discomfort from the unfamiliarity with riding, Morcant was more than happy to agree to a break in the journey, but could not resist sounding a note of caution.

'I fear my Lord, that after Lord Perris's previous dealings we may face a hostile reception and we would be better planning for conflict than resolution.'

'What do you suggest?' said Ferrax, Morcant noting a hardening of his tone at the mention of his brother.

'I suggest my Lord' said Morcant calmly, that we plan for combat and hope for sense to prevail, after all I suspect that is why your father entrusted the delicacy of this mission to you and the mud moving to Perris.' The compliment was enough to secure the gratitude of the young man who laughed easily.

'My brother, the mud mover. I like the thought that such toil is all he is fit for druid' called Ferrax and Morcant, ever observant, saw Buldan at the head of the group visibly relax at the improvement in his Lord's mood.

Presently, after about an hour and a half riding at walking pace, the four men came to the pond. In fact there were two bodies of water, a small pond and a larger lake; Ferrax suggested letting the horses drink in the small pond and tethered them so that they had freedom to move. He, Buldan and Gadrig went to the larger water to see if they could catch fish and Morcant took himself away to gather plants and roots not so readily available at home.

Within a small movement of the weak sun across the sky, the three warriors returned with but one fish, speared by Gadrig who was boasting of his prowess. The three men stopped short when they saw the thunderous look on the face of Morcant who stood over the body of his donkey, its neck still leaking scarlet blood onto the green grass although its heart had already stopped. Whatever had happened had also unnerved the tethered horses who were skittish and nervous, pulling at their ties to get as far away as possible from the dead beast.

Gardig was first to react and although he never let go of his speared fish, he ran to his horse to calm the large mare and untie her and take her out of sight; he was closely followed by Ferrax and Buldan, the three men slowly walking back towards the druid once the horses were calmed and safe. Morcant was still standing by the donkey, his hands smeared in its blood, raised to the sky, muttering incantations in a tongue unknown even to the educated Ferrax.

The three warriors knew better than to interrupt and sat cross legged a respectful distance away, trusting and believing that the druid would approach them when he was ready. Nobody dared speak and instead they looked to the ground.

'My Lord Ferrax' intoned the druid solemnly 'approach the sacrifice we have made.' Not daring to look at the others, Ferrax rose and walked slowly towards Morcant who dipped his fingers into the drying blood and drew lines across the young mans face, still muttering as he worked. He then made Ferrax stand to one side of the donkey and called over both Buldan and Gadrig and repeated the anointing with them both, although with fewer lines than for his Lord. When finally he was satisfied, the druid's shoulders sagged and he seemed to slump down within his own skeleton. His three companions had seen this before, the almost trancelike state and the exhaustion when whatever spirits had taken hold then released him. Buldan and Gadrig moved forwards and supported Morcant under his arms before leading him to a dry piece of ground where they sat him down. Gadrig went to fetch the druid a drink of water, which the man gulped down and signalled for another which again he quaffed without a word.

Presently, Morcant seemed to come more to his senses and looked at Ferrax.

'This place, is guarded by powerful spirits' said Morcant. 'They came to me for this is a place where the earth can speak to one who knows the language.' He of course meant himself, a fact accepted without questions by the others.

'What did the earth goddess tell you druid' said Ferrax gently. 'Tell me and tell me truthfully.' There was more of an edge to his voice Morcant noted with approval; that was good.

'The gods revealed the future to me Lord Ferrax' said Morcant putting a quiver into his speech for effect. 'Our journey shall be profitable but not fruitful and we face many dangers on our way..........and, and' Morcant choked back the emotion at the loss of his animal, 'the gods demanded a sacrifice and I was powerless in the face of such power to refuse them. They are calmed now and know that we shall do what is right for them and for ourselves; we must allow ourselves to be guided by the spirits as they have revealed themselves to me.'

'What do they want of us druid?' said Gadrig in awe of the mans' power and influence. Morcant looked up his eyes catching and holding Ferrax' stare.

'The gods demand a human sacrifice at our journeys end.'

With Sisal and Perris

The known rule of the tribe was that the Chief was never to be kept waiting and so it was at the mid point of the short day that Gargonstus was waiting at the entrance to the settlement with Sisal's chariot looking around anxiously for Perris who was nowhere to be seen. From time to time the builder noticed the woman Idon peer out of the Chieftains dwelling, ostensibly checking on the fire or acknowledging someone, but in reality also looking for Perris.

Just at the point where lateness would become an insult Perris came striding through the fort, the big black horse walking alongside him. Perris hailed the builder.

'You are late Lord Perris' hissed Gargonstus. 'Your mother is anxious and has been looking for you so that you do not insult your father.' Perris looked calmly at his friend, said nothing but shrugged his shoulders and looked around him before leaping nimbly onto the back of the horse. As he leaned forward to whisper into the animals alert ears, Sisal came striding across the flat ground to the chariot, a broad smile on his face and his favourite hunting dog Avon loping along at his side..

'You completed the task I gave you?' he called loudly to Perris. There was no task and the call was merely a face saver, as a number of villagers had stopped their work to view the scene. Hearing the words of the Chief and thus being reassured that Perris was not challenging the authority of his father, they returned to their tasks as Sisal mounted the chariot behind Gargonstus who flicked the reins and the three men made their way cautiously down the hillside.

After crossing the stream, Sisal indicated that Perris should ride alongside and, trusting to Gargonstus' loyalty and discretion he spoke sternly to his son.

'Perris, I tolerate your insolence only because you are my son, and for no other reason. You goad your mother, you challenge your brother and now you seek to make me look a fool? You are thinking that I am too old and frail to lead perhaps and that your time has come? You are trying to issue me with a challenge to my authority?'

'No my Lord' replied Perris easily. 'I will fight to protect your authority as well you should know by now.'

'Even that has the ring of insolence.'

'That was not my intention father. If I fear anything then it is what will come after you during the time of my brother, he is too tied up in his learning and too much under the influence of Morcant. My brother relies too much on spirits and not enough on swords.'

'Be careful Perris, the gods have favoured Morcant as their mouthpiece on this land and they speak clearly through him, you cross him and you challenge them; and let me tell you, a challenge to a chief may be a battle you can win, but a challenge to the gods is one you won't. Take heed my son and speak no more of this foolishness.' Perris opened his mouth as if to speak but wiser counsel in his own mind prevailed and he deferred to his fathers' logic. The conversation over, Perris dutifully allowed himself to draw behind the chariot, the mere presence of which over this land demonstrated the Chiefs power and influence.

Like Ferrax and Morcant, the journey to the coast would take over a day, but unlike the others, this party contained the Chieftain of all these lands. For accommodation they would call to a small settlement they knew and demand shelter and food for the night. That would still leave them a morning of travel to reach their destination, and Perris, ever eager to show his plans to his father was longing to give his horse the freedom to run on, the exhilarating feeling of speed and power an intoxicating mixture of emotion linked to his growing status and influence.

Sisal stood in the chariot, knowing his sons feelings and he smiled for he too had once been impetuous and governed by his emotions rather than his brains. He called Perris forward and bade him check the way ahead over the next rise to ensure their safety. The boy needed no further encouragement and he kicked his eager horse forward and was soon cresting the rise and lost to view.

With a jolt, Sisal recognised the sense of freedom he felt when apart from Perris, that the boy's pent up nature exuded tension and stress that seeped into the sub-conscious more than the insidious pain in his knees. It had been that way since the two of them had been born mused Sisal. As a baby, Ferrax had been docile and slept when fed from his mothers breast, but by contrast Perris had been a fighter since before birth; Idon had long complained during her pregnancy that the monster within her was kicking incessantly and she swore that he turned this way and that trying to escape the confines of her belly.

It was common within society for the children of warriors and chieftains to be brought up away from the family so that they may learn more of the world while allowing their parents the time and space to deal with their responsibilities and of course create more children to ensure the continuation of the family power and influence. Ferrax had been brought up from his second year in a nearby settlement and there he had come under the tutelage of both the family that lived there and more influentially Morcant the druid who was in some way related to them. Morcant and the young Ferrax cemented a relationship that Sisal was keen to foster, it gave the young boy and future Chief an education that he himself lacked and Sisal was forward-looking enough to understand that the more you knew, the more you ruled well.

By contrast Perris had grown up on the coast and had learned the skills of boat building, fishing and sword-craft, but whereas Ferrax had stayed with his lodge family until recalled, Perris returned early to his family in his ninth summer, the head of the coastal village explaining that they could not hold him nor deal with his impetuous ways, prone as he was to seeking a violent and confrontational resolution to any dispute. Perris it seemed had threatened to drown the man's son, a boy older than himself, and had gone so far as to hold the unfortunate youth below the surface of the water until he surrendered any pretence of superiority.

Sisal could not hide the fact that he in many ways favoured Perris in whom he saw his younger self. Now in his fifteenth year, the boy had become the man, and he was powerful, strong and quick witted, able to out-think and out fight an enemy. Clever enough to know that Perris was a potential disaster for the tribe he gave thanks to the gods for Ferrax, knowing that the elder son was a better prospect to replace him and if he, Sisal, could engender the loyalty of Perris to his brother then the two of them together would be formidable opponents to anyone seeking to challenge the rule of the House of Sisal.

'Master Gargonstus, we shall rest here awhile' announced Sisal as the chariot reached the top of the rise that Perris had galloped over some time before. Sisal saw the builder look at the way ahead and smiled, Perris had that effect on the men of the village, they looked up to him, they would follow him and they protected him. 'Fear not for Perris, Gargonstus, he will come and find us when his guts rumble!' The old man, himself now in his thirty sixth year, eased himself from the chariot and sat on a skin placed on the ground by Gargonstus who stood guard while Sisal ate heartily of the bread and cheese packed in a woven reed bag by Idon's slave girl.

With Ferrax and Morcant

Morcant now rode behind Ferrax, his status as druid would prevent him from riding with anyone less, and he now pressed home his proximity to his Lord.

'You seem quiet Ferrax?' he said.

'I am searching my thoughts to understand the meaning of the gods wishes. Are we to sacrifice before we approach the settlement or after we have placed our demands before those people. It hardly seems fair or honest to offer them protection and then to insist that they give up one of their number for sacrifice. Equally I am not minded to forego the benefits of the protection of either Gadrig or Buldan both of whom are earnest in their devotions to the gods.' The three horses were travelling at a good walking pace and making fair passage across the open grasslands. As a rule, travellers avoided the woodlands that were dotted about the countryside, the closely packed trees offering security and sanctuary for any number of men that may wish ill to a traveller.

'My Lord' said Morcant as if deep in contemplation 'if we do not do as the gods of the earth require then we run the risk of their anger and it is possible that the grains will not grow, the animals will be poisoned by the very grass they eat and the water we rely on will turn brackish and stale. The gods test of our devotion has to be a difficulty to us otherwise it is no test at all.'

'As ever my friend and teacher, you are right' said Ferrax. 'Do you have any advice?

'It is my belief that in this situation my Lord, the gods are giving a message as well as an instruction; that we should forego offering this settlement our protection and should sacrifice the men.'

'What of the women and children?' asked Ferrax with concern. Morcant paused to give his words more gravitas.

'We could spare them I suppose.........' his voice tailed off. 'But then they would be easy prey for anyone passing by. No Lord, far better I think that we deliver them to Corillun to sell as slaves in Gaul, it would be a fine gesture to him and one that your father would be sure to approve.'

'You are sure that this would please the gods?' asked Ferrax.

'I am Lord' replied the druid.

+++++

As the sun began to lose its heat and settle toward the horizon, Ferrax called a halt for the night. The place was perfect for a camp as they were by a river that would not only provide water, and maybe food, but was also deep enough to provide a barrier to any would-be attacker. In addition to that a short ride away was a clump of trees that could provide fire wood, and Buldan was sent to collect sufficient to keep the fire burning through the night.

Gadrig meantime, spurred by his earlier success at the lake, waded into the freezing river to try his luck with his spear again; Ferrax settled the horses and Morcant faced the embers of the day and muttered his invocations to the spirits to guard and protect them.

Within a short time there was the start of a warming fire crackling away within a ring of stones brought up from the river bank. The horses were tethered and chewing contentedly on the lush grass and Gadrig had returned sheepishly empty handed from his endeavours. The meal was thus a simple one of bread from home, the one cooked fish from the lake shared between Morcant and Ferrax, and between mouthfuls they discussed how the following day would pan out. If the two fighting men were shocked at the apparent change of plan, they hid their feelings well, knowing that the druid was watching and rightly surmising who was behind it.

'I shall take the first turn' said Ferrax speaking of keeping watch over the camp 'then Gadrig, then Buldan. Wake me at first light and we shall be on our way as quickly as possible.'

As the others settled themselves, wrapping their woollen cloaks around their bodies and heads, Ferrax turned away from the camp, keeping the fire to his back so as to cast any light outwards and also so as not to destroy his night vision. It was not long before his hearing detected the slowed rhythmic breathing of his three sleeping companions and he steeled his tired body to stay wakeful into the dark night.

Ferrax felt his mind begin to wander, his thoughts turning to Caeryl, and then to his father and the future which meant to Ferrax responsibility without the guiding hand of Sisal that he had relied upon all of his life. A perceptive man this summer would be his seventeenth and he knew that in the natural order of things, life would move forwards. It was right that he should take a woman and create his own family, just as it was the natural order of things that his father would grow older until he either chose to die in combat or he was usurped by his son. That brought thoughts of Perris into consideration, and Ferrax knew that his brother would always be a problem. His constant challenge to authority would inevitably bring them into conflict. Ferrax sat quietly, he had already sought counsel from Morcant whose advice was typically robust and without compromise.

'You must exile him from the tribe Lord Ferrax. Your brother is a dangerous man who thinks of nought but himself and I predict that he will destroy you if you do not protect yourself and your people.' Easy to say mused Ferrax, but it would be impossible to cast aside the brother he loved.

Ferrax heard movement, his hearing attuned to the sounds of men and the snap of a twig was unlikely to have come from an animal, he was sure he would have heard it moving around in the darkness. Keeping low to the ground, Ferrax made his way as quietly as possible back to his sleeping companions. Gadrig, habitually a light sleeper, was already awake.

'Lord Ferrax?'

'Wake the others, there are men out there Gadrig.' Ferrax returned to where he had been sitting, his senses alert, keen and intent. He was sure he could hear something. Then there was a splash from behind him, and a shout and all of a sudden the air was rent with screams and Ferrax saw a huge warrior bearing down on him, mouth gaping wide, teeth bared as the man shouted his battle cry. Ferrax was dimly aware of noise behind him but his concentration remained on the man who was now mere feet away. Ferrax crouched, legs taut and ready to clash with his foe who suddenly stopped, his expression changing from one of aggression to one of surprise as he looked down to see the shaft of a spear protruding from his chest. With a roar the man fell forwards which drove the spear further into his body until he almost gracefully toppled to his side. Ferrax looked round to see a grinning Buldan who then drew his sword and stood by the young man's side.

Nobody else came towards them, so the two warriors turned and made their way back to the small camp. Gadrig was holding two men at bay, his sword sweeping in a wide but deadly arc. Morcant had gutted another man and was drawing his sword out of the mans belly when Buldan and Ferrax ran past and quickly dispatched Gadrigs two combatants, Buldan with one mighty sweep of his sword that neatly severed the mans head that bounced onto the grass with a sickening squelch.

Gasping for breath, the three warriors and the druid stood surveying the scene of carnage.

'Is everyone alright?' asked Ferrax, there were grunts and smiles all round, as each of them, wary in case there was a second wave of attackers, looked around. Ferrax knew he would never get used to the stench of death, the gut churning mixture of blood, gore, shit and vomit that inevitably followed a deadly swordfight.

Stillness and quiet returned to the scene and all four men rinsed their blades in the river, drying them on their woollen cloaks. If there were any more men out there, then they were wary of attacking, having seen what befallen their comrades.

'We can't stay here' said Ferrax speaking for all of them whilst looking around at the bodies. 'I'll get the horses.'

'I'll come with you' said Buldan, wary and watchful as the two men walked across the grass. As they approached the place they had left the horses to graze, they heard a sob, quickly stifled and the sound of someone running. Quickly, Buldan was after them, his sword drawn. The figure was quick on its feet, but slight and small, and also no match for Buldan who pulled his sword back and slapped the back of the runner with the flat of the blade. The runner sprawled on the ground, then struggled to get away but without success as Buldan grabbed the cloak and lifted them off the ground.

'It's a girl!' he exclaimed in surprise before more animal instincts took over and he began tearing at her clothing. The girl, probably eleven or twelve summers old, screamed and struggled, but Buldan, his blood up after the slaughter and with a thirst for revenge threw the girl on the floor and started pulling at his own clothes, his intention obvious. The girl scrabbled away on her back, her jaws snapping, threatening to bite anything that came near and Buldan in an attempt to subdue her, backhanded her across the face leaving a trail of snot and blood where her nose had broken. He was leering at her now, his breeches round his ankles as he kneeled down and grabbed the girls legs, forcing them apart. She screamed, thrashed and tried to kick but she was helpless as Buldan bore down on her, he was laughing now, sensing both her distress and his physical power over her.

'Buldan! Buldan! Enough!' Ferrax tried to drag his comrade off the girl but the warrior shook him off and sent him sprawling on the ground. The girl screamed as she felt Buldan pushing against her and she closed her eyes rejecting the inevitability of what was going to happen, when suddenly she heard a grunt and heard and sensed Buldan slump on top of her. Still trapped, the girl nevertheless realised that the immediate danger was past and she squirmed under the weight of her attacker clamping her legs together as strong hands rolled Buldan off her.

The girl opened her eyes to see three men, two fighters and a white-robed druid, all were blood spattered and all were staring at the unconscious man on the ground. The girl tried to get to her feet but was instead lifted up by the youngest of the three men and held firm.

'Who are you?' demanded the man holding her.

'Who are you and why are you on our lands?' she spat as a reply. The young man laughed.

'My name is Ferrax, though that would be Lord Ferrax to you, son of Sisal.' The girls' eyes widened, revealing that she indeed knew who he was. 'And now that I have introduced myself, I shall introduce my companions' he was being deliberately light-hearted she thought as he in turn pointed out Gadrig and Morcant, Ferrax released the girl and kicked at the prone body on the ground. 'This is Buldan.' The girl spat at the unconscious man.

'He killed my father and my brother!' She launched a frenzied and tearful kick at the prone body but was restrained by Gadrigs' strong arms. He looked desperately towards the fire where the dead could be seem in the flickering light.

'Your brother and your father attacked us' said Ferrax simply. 'There was no need as we were no threat to you.' The girl slumped in Gadrigs grip the grief hit her, her wailing and tears seemingly endless. 'Set her down Gadrig' said Ferrax gently.

'My Lord?' Morcant interjected. 'What do you propose is to be done with this female?' He stood stern and forbidding, almost challenging to Ferrax.

'Well Morcant' said Ferrax smiling 'we could just kill her, she could be that sacrifice you want, but my senses tell me that would be a waste. She's an interesting thing and I have an idea that she might be useful.'

'We could sell her' said Morcant.

'I think I have a better idea actually' replied Ferrax. 'Girl, what is your name?' he said sternly and with real authority in his voice, a fact not lost on Gadrig. The girl looked up at him, shivering probably from the shock of the nights events.

'Speak woman!' roared Morcant. Ferrax laid a placating hand on the druid arm.

'Morcant, Gadrig? Take Buldan and dump his head in the river till he wakes. How hard did you hit him?'

It was only a small rock, so I just used enough force to knock him out' said Gadrig matter-of-factly. Ferrax nodded and indicated that the warrior should set the girl down.

'Take him away then, I'll be alright here' said Ferrax, and reluctantly the druid and the warrior dragged Buldan to the waters edge. Ferrax crouched down to the girl and waited for the splash from the water before he spoke.

'I asked your name, and I am not in the habit of needing to ask twice' he explained kindly. The girl dried her eyes on a shawl she had pulled round her shoulders and looked Ferrax in the eye.

'I am called Ancastia' she explained 'I was named for the goddess Ancasta, at least that's what my father told me.'

'Very well Ancastia, you belong to me now' said Ferrax, a thin smile on his lips.

With Sisal and Perris

'Why did you bring that dog?' asked Perris. Sisal looked up at his son who was standing close by. The chief shielded his eyes from the glare and shrugged his shoulders.

'I like him.' Avon, lying on the ground near his master sensed that he was the subject of conversation and his tail thumped the ground.

'It doesn't like me' continued Perris. 'Look, I'll show you' and he took two steps towards his father. Avon, still lying on the floor bared his teeth and growled; the sound low and menacing, the dogs' ears pricked and alert. Perris backed off and the dog lay quietly.

'See!' said Perris 'that damned animal is a menace.'

'I like him' repeated Sisal neutrally. 'You brought your horse didn't you?'

'What has that got to do with anything' said Perris.

'Think of it as a lesson my son' replied his father patiently 'nobody can be all things to all people. We are indeed set to our destiny by the gods and they shall, and do, decree who we become. So just as I like my dog, you like your horse, but my dog doesn't like you. It's life, and the best you can do is accept it. What do you say Gargonstus?'

The big man who was sitting close by, pretending not to be there, smiled; this was typical of Sisal, a chief so powerful that he ruled lands as far as a man could see, yet he took time and trouble to respect his own people. The builder thought for a moment and then spoke.

'Lord, it is like building a wall, I can place a stone on top of another and they can fit together as if cleaved from the same rock face and it makes me look a genius, but then the next stone I set will not sit well and I have to shape it and make it fit. There are some stones however that no matter how much work you put in, will never sit comfortably with their neighbours. My job in building for you is to cast out those stones as they make the wall unstable and liable to topple.' Gargonstus looked to the floor but just caught the smile on Sisal's face.

'You see Perris?' Sisal waved an arm towards the builder, 'he understands the point I am making. Of course I knew that Avon for some reason does not take to you, but is that really important? Think of what having him with us does achieve; the companionship, the protection and the ability to hunt our own food should the need arise. When you have considered all that, you will be thinking like a man and not as a boy.' Sisal rubbed his hands on his tunic as he spoke. 'Now I think is right for us to be making more of our journey, here, pull me up.' He held an arm out to Perris who stepped forward. The dog growled and made to get up but a terse command from the Chief stopped him and he lay there, his large brown eyes watching the young warrior unblinkingly.

'Come on then' said Perris tersely. He felt something close to humiliation that his father should seek to teach him how to behave in front of Gargonstus. He took his fathers arm by the wrist and pulled him up, but as Sisal took his own weight on his legs, his right knee buckled and he fell to the ground, jarring and twisting the already painful knee in the process. Like the chief he was, Sisal did not cry out even though the pain was immediate and excruciating but as he sat back on the ground his difficulties were clear to all.

'Lord Sisal!' said Gargonstus who rushed forward and picked up the man as if he were a child and carried him to his horse that had luckily not been re-harnessed to the chariot. Once he was sat on the back of the beast all could see how the knee had swollen to almost double its normal size.

'My thanks Gargonstus' said Sisal simply 'could you do me the favour of concealing my chariot carefully until we can collect it on our return?' Gargonstus nodded in acquiescence and moved away, his huge strength easily dealing with the weight of the chariot as he dragged it towards a nearby copse of trees. 'We shall stop for the night at the next farm over there on the hill' called Sisal to the builder 'catch us up when you can.' Gargonstus waved an acknowledgement and Sisal turned his head and called to Perris 'shall we move on? Avon!' The dog, hearing his masters' call, rose to his feet and ambled along beside the horse. He had made no objection and no sound when Gargonstus had swept Sisal off the ground. Perris stared at the dog from his lofty position on his own horse and began to imagine accidents that could befall the loyal Avon.

'Ride alongside me my son' said Sisal, and Perris dutifully brought his horse alongside his father. 'I have been giving thought to the future, not mine, but yours and Ferrax's.' Sisal looked at his son to gauge his reaction but the boy looked blankly back at him. 'It's about time that we considered what will happen when I go to meet the gods' said Sisal as matter-of-factly as he could 'and I want to make arrangements for the future of my children, of your mother and of the tribe.'

'Well it is clear that Ferrax will become Chief' said Perris, an answer that told Sisal much about the mindset of his second son. He was about to remonstrate with the boy but thought better of it and decided to let him have his head.

'Of course' said Sisal calmly 'that will be the way of our people unless Ferrax is challenged under our laws. Will you support your brother?' Perris rode along in silence for a time that was in danger of becoming insolent. Sisal was about to speak when Perris answered.

'As I have said before father, I fear the time when you are gone because I have no trust in Ferrax' ability to stand up to Morcant. Our druid takes too much on himself but he is feared of you and bides his time waiting for my weak brother to inherit.'

'You see your brother as weak?'

'Weak is perhaps the wrong word, he is too much under the influence of the druid and spends his time trying to please the gods. If he puts the gods above the people then our tribe will suffer and I am not sure I want to be part of that' explained Perris.

'You trouble me son. We support the gods and they provide for us; they send us the sun and the rain, the beasts that feed and clothe us and the crops that we harvest. It is right that we please the gods surely?'

'Of course father' replied Perris 'but I think that sometimes Morcant sees himself as a god and Ferrax spends time trying to keep him happy, content and provided for.'

'What would you do my son?' Sisal was genuinely interested in the thoughts of the young warrior.

'I would not preclude the visits of other druids and priestesses father. I would welcome their teachings and their wisdom to augment and counter the influence of Morcant.' It was a clever answer thought Sisal; it enhanced the influence of the gods and diminished the influence of the man. Sisal decided to move the conversation on.

'I have decided that you should live like a man with a woman of your own, and she is chosen announced Sisal with what he hoped was a definite tone.

'You have always brought me and my brother up to think independently father, and yet now you decide my future for me?'

'I do, and I do so for the benefit of the future and of the tribe.'

'I see, well, who is the woman?'

'Caeryl the daughter of Drullis of our village. She is...what?' Sisal stopped in mid sentence, interrupted by the laughter of his son. 'What?' he repeated.

'And you have talked this through with my mother have you?' said Perris with incredulity.

'She known of my thoughts on the matter' said Sisal.

'Which is very different from her agreeing with you...I expect the argument was violent?'

'Your mother's thoughts on this subject are irrelevant.' Sisal was sounding irritable now. 'I am the chief of this tribe and I am entitled to some respect for my decisions and opinions.'

'Indeed you are my father, but my mother has a fierce temper, like a mad dog and she has a bite much worse than her bark' explained Perris in a manner that drew a wry smile on his father's face. Perris pressed on.

'Father, you know that Caeryl is spoken for by Ferrax, the two of them understand that they will be together, certainly my mother favours this and I am sure that Drullis and his wife feel the same way. You ask me to support my brother and then in the next breath you give me the woman he wants as his wife?'

'I have my reasons Perris.'

'Father, you always have reasons but I wonder if this time they are sufficient' said Perris warily.

'So, you defy me in this matter do you?' Sisal tried to turn but winced as the pain shot through his injured knee

'Certainly not. She is a fine young woman and one that any man would covet.

'So covet her' growled Sisal.

Later when Sisal and Perris reached the farm, they were resting with the men and eating heartily from a bowl of mutton stew, prepared with a rich and aromatic sauce, flavoured with herbs grown within the farm lands. Perris noticed how attentive Sisal was to his people; how he listened intently to their concerns and how he deflected away any obsequiousness given out of duty as he was their Lord. Perris reflected that his father had a natural authority that came out of his character, his reputation and his age.

It was well past the setting of the sun when Gargonstus arrived and was admitted to the room. The locals seemed surprised when

Sisal rose from the table, despite his obvious discomfort, and embraced the builder giving thanks to him for his ardour and loyalty. Truly they reflected, this is a man we are proud to serve, which in part of course was the objective of Sisal's behaviour.

That night was spent in the shelter of the headman's hut, curled on the floor wrapped in cloaks and under skins provided by the farmers. Sisal made only one concession to the offers of the farmer, and that for his aching knee, in that he accepted the offer of a straw bed that provided both warmth and comfort. Avon the dog slept in the same place as the horses, fed and tended to by the people of the farm.

+++++

When Sisal awoke next morning he asked Perris to summons the men of the farm and by the time they were assembled outside the hut, the Chief had dressed and belted his heavy sword around his waist. Sisal was determined to walk out of the hut himself, to demonstrate his powers of recovery and he gingerly took a few steps across the packed earth floor. Satisfied that he would not make a fool of himself, he strode outside into the daylight and was surprised to receive a spontaneous but rousing cheer from the men and women who were gathered. Sisal abandoned his planned words and spoke spontaneously.

'When I arrived last night, I was tired hungry and weak. Through your kindness you have fed me and restored me to full health. I am proud to be one of you, proud to be your Chief' he paused and smiled at the farmers wife 'and happy to be very well fed by your kindness. Good people, my son and myself are on our way to the coast to discuss the building of a fortress that will protect our new links with traders from across the seas. Such trade will make us all richer and more comfortable and to show my gratitude to you I give you this token and tell you that if ever you are in trouble you may present this to my house and you will be protected and cared for.' Sisal unclipped a brooch from his cloak, it was a small circle of gold, and he presented it to the blushing farmer's wife with a smile.

'And now we must leave you but we shall return as friends and as your proud Chieftain.' There was another cheer and the two horses were brought forwards, they had been groomed and clearly stabled and fed overnight. The dog Avon had not been touched, clearly his demeanour kept even the bravest of the farm boys away. Gargonstus stepped forward to help Sisal, but the Chief waved him away.

'I shall ride behind my son' he explained 'you take my horse.' Shortly thereafter they walked out of the farm and made their way south, towards the sea.

With Ferrax

Morcant was in a foul mood, and it showed no sign of improvement. Ferrax was clearly taken with this girl Ancastia and he, the druid to the most powerful Chief in the land had been reduced to rising behind the stinking hulk of Gadrig. The mixed aromas of sweat, blood and dirt assailed the more sensitive nose of the druid who had argued that his status alone should allow him to ride the horse, making Gadrig and the still groggy Buldan walk. Instead Ferrax had directed Gadrig to ride and to hold a binding to Buldan who stumbled along as best he could, frequently falling to the ground and scrabbling to regain his feet as he was dragged across the grassland.

Ferrax seemed oblivious to all this, riding out in front with the girls arms wrapped round his waist.

After the fight nobody could sleep, and in any event nobody wanted to remain close by the dead bodies that lay bloodied and still on the ground. Instead, Ferrax had decreed that they would make an early start on their day and had made his decisions accordingly. Now, having been walking slowly for some time, the sun was risen and they were walking along the banks of a wide and fast flowing river. Ahead in the distance they could see that the river opened up into the sea but that they were approaching a small settlement of huts on the river bank. Drawn up on the bank were three small round boats, overturned to keep rainwater water out, the huts were clearly occupied as a wisp of smoke rose from each. Ferrax reigned in the horse and jumped lightly down to the ground. Ancastia made to get down as well by Ferrax held a finger to indicate she should stay.

Foolish youth, thought Morcant with a roll of his eyes, with Ferrax on foot now there was nothing to stop the girl from riding away. Surprisingly however, Ancastia sat still and immobile and if anything looked disappointed that she was not walking with Ferrax towards the huts.

'Hello!' called Ferrax but was greeted with silence. He repeated the salutation and began to look around. 'Gadrig! With me' called the young man and the warrior smoothly dropped to the floor and drew his sword as he walked cautiously to his Lord's side.

'Something is wrong Gadrig' whispered Ferrax. 'The boats are ashore, there are no animals, no sounds and no people. I am going into this hut, grab my belt and if I call out, pull me out of there.' Gadrig did not speak but Ferrax felt his huge hand grab the leather belt round his middle.

Ferrax pushed aside the woven curtain that covered the door and immediately cried out in revulsion and fear. Immediately he felt himself propelled backwards out of the hut as Gadrig responded and pulled hard on the belt. Winded. Ferrax lay on his back on the ground where he had landed, Gadrig standing guard over him, protecting him from whatever danger lay within. All he could hear was a low hum.

'Gadrig, here help me up' said a winded Ferrax. 'We have nothing to fear in there.'

'The noise, Lord?'

'Flies Gadrig. Thousands of them, feasting on the bodies within. I couldn't see much in the gloom but there are at least three people in there, all dead. Check the other huts, I suspect you will find the same. Gadrig moved away as Morcant sidled over to Ferrax.

'We must leave this place Lord' he intoned. 'I sense the spirits and there are bad omens for anyone here.' He drew himself to his full height of around six feet. 'Lord, the spirits tell me that the girl is a powerful force of evil, for wherever she goes, death is never far away, waiting and always ready to take those she wishes harm to.'

At that point, Gardig returned and with a shake of his head, indicated that everyone in the settlement was dead. 'All slaughtered Lord' he said dispassionately. Morcant turned back to face the young girl.

'You!' he bellowed. 'Release your evil hold on this land' and he drew from the folds of his robe a knife whose sharpened blade glinted where it caught the light. Morcant raised the knife and took a step towards Ancastia who was clearly terrified and screamed.

'Morcant!' called Ferrax. 'Stop this nonsense.' The druid paused and turned to Ferrax.

'Lord I cannot be held responsible for the evils to come if we do not rid ourselves of . . . '

Morcant, her mother was a priestess and was training Ancastia to the same calling. The girl has dreams, powerful visions of the future and she is no more the harbinger of evil than I am. If anything she is a seer.'

'She has entrapped you in her lies and deceit' cried Morcant. 'I see the black shroud over her soul and it will damn us all.' The druid was wide-eyed and recognised that he was appearing slightly deranged. He made a play of shielding his eyes from Ancastia who smiled at Ferrax as if this were all a game. Ferrax walked over to Morcant and held the man's shoulders as he looked into his hooded dark eyes.

'Morcant, for many years I have relied upon your guidance and wisdom and now I ask you to trust mine.' The druid shook his head

'I am sorry Ferrax but I cannot. I can see only evil around her and the only thing to do is end it with her death. Put her to the blade Ferrax and appease the gods who will smile on your wisdom in ridding their lands of a dark force.' Morcant stood, proud and tall and it was clear to Ferrax that either he believed what he was saying or it was the best performance Ferrax had ever seen.

'Very well Morcant. I will consider your words over time but for now Ancastia remains my prisoner and therefore under my protection. You understand? This means that to act against her is to act against me.'

'I understand Lord' growled the druid as Ferrax turned away and called to Gadrig.

'Untie Buldan, and then the two of you put this place to fire, at least we can give these wretches a decent send-off to the afterlife.' Gadrig nodded in approval at the decision, it showed respect and decency on the part of the young man. Indeed it was yet one more action that showed that Ferrax truly was deserving of being called Chief when his father joined the spirits.

By the time the sun was edging towards the middle of the sky, there was a pall of smoke from the funeral pyre now behind the small group that moved slowly along the coast. The river had opened up to become the sea, though the far bank could still be viewed in the distance. It had been the unfortunate and disgraced Buldan who had tasted the water and pronounced it fouled with salt as Ferrax had already known it would be because the trees no longer grew to the shoreline. After ordering the setting of the fires for the unfortunate dead, Ferrax had decreed that the five of them should ride and walk on to find the settlement they sought, and face whatever befell them there. Ancastia said she knew of the place and had even been there once with her father, the village she described was poorly defended due to the flat land that surrounded it and relied on raiding surrounding tribes for the majority of its wealth.

'It's round that next headland' she announced, pointing towards a spur of land that jutted out into the sea, a sort distance away, she smiled at Ferrax who drew himself to his full height, almost as if consciously acknowledging that his skills of leadership, diplomacy and persuasion were about to be tested. He would be judged by his father and the rest of his tribe on the events of this day.

'Lord Ferrax? I beg you release me' pleaded Buldan. 'What if we encounter armed men with evil intent, I can be of no service trussed up like this, and if I am to die then at least let me go with a sword in my hand?' Ferrax held his hand aloft to signal a halt, and turned the horse to face the hapless man.

'Buldan, you disgraced me and my father by your actions and by your weakness. If I am to succeed my father as it is intended then I have to be fair to all the peoples of these lands, not just those that serve close to me.' Ferrax looked away as if making a decision and the determination on his face when he looked again at Buldan showed that he had made it. 'Normally' said Ferrax calmly 'I would pass you to Morcant to stand accused and to be punished if found to have failed our laws and those of the gods, but in this case I am going to make an exception.' He paused and Morcant moved forward as if to speak but once again a raised hand stilled him.

'The innocent in this is Ancastia and it is to her that we must turn initially for your fate Buldan.' Before Ferrax could continue, Morcant blustered his way into the conversation.

'The justice of the gods, and of men, is and always shall be a matter for the druids for it is our function to understand and interpret the gods wishes and to impart our wisdom in the matter of recompense and settlement. Have I not administered justice fairly in the service of both the gods and your father? And yet you now insult me by usurping me with this wench!'

'Morcant, you know I value, and always will value your wisdom' said Ferrax soothingly 'and as for usurping your authority I ask what have you to fear from myself? I am no threat to you because I have been taught by you, but Buldan is a warrior under my command and it is right that I decide his fate.'

'The woman shall have no say in matter of justice' retorted Morcant.

'My decision is mine alone' said Ferrax tersely and he turned his head to speak to Buldan.

'On your knees' he commanded quietly. Buldan, wide eyed, looked around at the others, Gadrig looked away, Morcant looked as if he wanted to remonstrate again with Ferrax and the young lord smiled indulgently and indicated that Buldan should comply. Slowly, the warrior sank to one knee and then the other. He looked downcast and beaten.

'Look at me' said Ferrax calmly and Buldan raised his head to look into his eyes. 'What do you think would happen if every man that met every woman acted in the way you did? Here is my punishment for this man' announced Ferrax speaking loudly so that everyone in their small group could hear. 'Buldan shall serve Ancastia with loyalty and on his promise to protect her body, her sprit and her mind as if it were his own. He shall never touch her and never have or own her unless she shall choose so, and if he should break the vow that I demand of him then he dies at the hand of the druid in sacrifice to the gods to wash away his wrongdoing.' The pronouncement was greeted with a stunned silence

'Morcant?' said Ferrax.

'You show great wisdom for one so young my lord' admitted the druid grudgingly. In truth he was impressed with Ferrax' quick-witted solution, for he had in one move allowed Buldan to live, but ensured not only his binding loyalty to the girl, but also her own safety as few men would take on Buldan in combat. 'I think that the gods would favour your demands as fair and reasonable in all the circumstances Lord Ferrax.'

'Buldan. What say you?' said Ferrax.

'Your brother, my lord, would not favour a wench over a warrior. He understands the ways of fighting men and the favours to be bestowed on the winners in battle.' Ferrax looked down from the horse at the kneeling man.

'My brother is not here and my brother has no say in this matter. Your future is now entirely in your own hands and either you agree to the just settlement as approved by our wise druid' Morcant inclined his head in acknowledgement of the compliment 'or we kill you here and now' finished Ferrax.

'You want me to serve her?' said Buldan.

'No, the gods demand it of you' said Ancastia lightly. Buldan looked around but found no support. He shouted to the skies, screaming oaths to the spirits of his ancestors before submitting to the will of the gods.

'Swear it!' said Ferrax. 'Swear to honour these terms even if it shall kill you!'

'I swear on the spirits of my father Stronam to protect you from harm from myself or others to the end of my life' said Buldan reluctantly to Ancastia. He was still on his knees, the top of his head reaching her chin.

'Give me your knife Gadrig' said Ancastia and held out her hand. When Gadrig hesitated she flicked her fingers in an impatient motion and the warrior handed over his sharp honed blade. Ancastia walked to the sea and put the blade into the water, muttering an incantation over it. Gadrig, fearing that the blade would be blunted moved to stop her but Ferrax stopped him with a word of command. Ancastia walked towards Buldan and cut the ties that bound his hands but before he could stand she grabbed his left forearm and cut a small incision into the soft flesh. She did the same with her own arm and joined the two cuts together so that the dripping blood mixed as it fell to the ground.

'Buldan, we are now bound and our blood joined and shared. This seals your promise and your devotion to me for evermore. Do not fail me.' Ancastia turned and walked back to the sea and washed the blood from the blade, dried it on her skirt and returned it to a stunned Gadrig.

Morcant was the first to speak and break the spell of silence.

'Where did you learn such powerful spirit girl?'

'I have no learning druid other than what my mother taught me and that was not very much apart from the use of herbs and roots. All I did with Buldan was what I thought was right and what I felt guided to do.' Morcant was himself becoming reluctantly enthralled by the enigmatic young woman and like all of her sex he both feared and respected them. This Ancastia was potentially a challenge to his standing within the tribe and he felt she had to be dealt with but he realised now with a start, that if he laid a hand on Ancastia, then Buldan was duty bound to kill him.

With Sisal and Perris

The rise in the land was gentle but long and for some time the two horses had walked determinedly onward and at the top of the hill Sisal called a halt and in some discomfort had dismounted. He limped to the summit and looked at the land beneath him, his son and the builder soon joining him. Spread out beneath them was the land and the sea that Perris coveted.

'It is as if we were birds looking down' said Sisal, the wonder evident in his voice. All of them shielded their eyes for the sun sparkled on the sea, the waves making the glare flicker and dance, but beneath them they could see clearly the lie of the land. To the east of them was a large island, with only a small creek between that at the mainland; to the west of the island was a huge body of water fed by a river that ran from the right hand side and beyond that was a spur of land that between it and the island created a huge natural harbour. Below them was another spur of land that Perris was pointing to and Sisal could see that it too created yet another harbour within the larger one. It was, as had been claimed, a safe and secure anchorage for ships that could be well defended.

'You see father?' said Perris. 'Create the fortification around that land and you can defend yourself against any attacker. Sisal looked around and remained unconvinced, his hand absent-mindedly stroking his dogs head. The gentle slope of the hill they had just walked up was wooded and would offer cover for any attacker and, the Chief figured, the advantages to be had from such a commanding position on top of the hill potentially outweighed the benefits of proximity to the harbour. The views were stunning as well as commanding and Sisal, being a man of his time, naturally favoured defending the high ground.

'Gargonstus' said Sisal 'we should build a fortress here, on the hill. It holds all the advantages; a gentle slope on one side and a steep one facing the sea, trees for building material and therefore also a good soil for digging earth banks, a lofty position from which we can see our enemies and it would be easy to hold with comparatively few men. If we build down there' he pointed to the inner harbour 'then we run the risk of being taken by surprise. Men can approach through the trees, hidden and dangerous.'

'Father' protested Perris but was silenced by a look from the Chief.

'I am discussing matters with Master Gargonstus, but never fear, I shall hear you as well my son.'

'Lord Sisal, in normal situations I would agree that this is the best place to build but respectfully not this time' said Gargonstus. He hurried to carry on lest he would be interrupted. 'If we build at the coast the works will take less time, will cost less in terms of labour and manpower and would be just as easy to defend. There is also one major advantage Lord.'

'Which is?' demanded Sisal.

'As we know from your own successful fights, a fort on a hill can be surrounded and the inhabitants starved until they come out and fight, and once they do that they have lost the advantage of their defences. Down there, the sea can provide a number of things; a natural defence, a source of food, and the means to go around and behind any attacker and cut them off.'

'Father' repeated Perris only to be silenced again.

'How long would it take you to build here on the hill Gargonstus?' said Sisal.

'To finish completely? A full four seasons Lord, and that is if the gods are kind and keep away the storms and the snow.'

'And down there?'

'With the right men, it would be finished by the end of the coming summer' said Gargonstus confidently. Sisal looked around the land for a moment.

'Very well' he turned to his son. 'Show me this place, let us go there and see for ourselves.' Sisal turned and immediately felt a pain in his knee, but refused to show it and instead walked slowly but carefully to where Ferrax's horse stood patiently grazing. Within a short time they had picked their way on horseback down the steep slope and were approaching the sea.

'Father' said Perris again, and patiently, 'this is where I say we should begin to build our ditch and wall.' Perris was standing at the water's edge, a gentle swell running the sea up and down the shore. Sisal remained on horseback and indicated that the three of them should trace the proposed course of the fort, and with Gargonstus walking on one side and Perris leading the horse they walked the land.

As they moved along, Gargonstus pointed out the natural features to Sisal; the trees that could be used as both building and defensive material, the soil that could be cropped and of course the sea, with all its uses. Walking in a rough curve they soon reached the other shore; they had gone from the west to the south and as Sisal looked around him he could see that what Gargonstus proposed encircled a large land area for relatively little effort.

'Perris, fetch wood and make a fire' ordered his father pointedly. 'I will talk with our builder.' Petulantly and feeling that he was being sidelined, Perris did as he was ordered but hurried the job and fetched damp wood that was impossible to light. This incurred the anger of Sisal who complained bitterly about how spoilt his son was becoming and sent him to mind the horses while he built a fire himself. When the wood was crackling and the smoke rising, Sisal could not help but be pleased with his efforts. Being Chief was all well and good but sometimes, achieving something as simple as a fire was a task that took concentration away from the bigger picture and consequently made decision making easier when the time came.

Gargonstus and Perris knew Sisal well enough to leave him to his labours; they knew that he was thinking subconsciously as he worked to build his fire and sure enough a while later he called them over and indicated that they should sit with him.

'Everything I know says we should build on that hill' said Sisal quietly 'but everything I feel,' he emphasised the last word 'tells me that this place is right. We shall build your fort Perris and we shall build it here by the sea.' Perris grinned and clasped his fathers arm then slapped Gargonstus on the back. Sisal smiled ruefully and made his second pronouncement. 'I have decided that we shall know this place after the man who wanted it built. This shall be Caer Perris.

With Ferrax and Morcant

Coming round the headland indicated by Ancastia, Ferrax saw the settlement; their destination. It was in fact a motley collection of no more than ten huts, some of them in better condition than others, but all apparently occupied. The village was surrounded by a thin fence of wooden stakes, each about the height of a man's waist, punctuated by many gaps where the wood had been broken, or rotted, and never replaced. A dog barked and the chickens that had been pecking at the ground scattered in a flurry of feathers and squawking noise.

A man, stooped and by the look of him, quite ancient came out of one of the huts as the women and children ran inside. It was clear that this was a place that feared strangers rather than welcomed them and the man hesitantly shuffled to the nearest gap in the fence and waited.

Ferrax told the others to stay where they were, and then dismounted and walked forwards with Morcant, his hands outstretched and open as a sign that the man had nothing to fear from him.

'I am Ferrax, son of Sisal, a powerful Chief within these lands, and I have travelled for two days to be here' announced the young man. 'And this' he half turned to Morcant 'is the druid to our tribe.' Mentioning that his tribe had their own druid was a status symbol, designed to impress anyone and from the expression on the old mans face, it had clearly worked.

'You are welcome Ferrax, son of Sisal, though our hospitality is meagre, what we have is yours.' It was a standard greeting but non the less welcome. 'We have not seen a holy man here for many seasons and some of the children remain unblessed by the gods.' The tone was hopeful, as if Morcant would resolve this situation. The druid looked unimpressed.

'We would discuss much with your Chief or leader' called Ferrax hopefully. 'I am here for my Lord and father to offer your people our protection and seek your loyalty.'

The old man wheezed a laugh, his mouth a festival of gaps and rotten teeth. 'We have no King, Lord, Chief or head man here my Lord' he said. We are a simple people living however we can, using the resources of the land and the sea.'

Ferrax saw, out of the corner of his eye, Gadrig making his way slowly towards the trees. He turned.

'Where are you going Gadrig' he yelled.

'I need a piss' shouted the warrior who waved a hand but kept on walking. For some reason this agitated the old man, whose gaze kept breaking away from Ferrax and darting towards the place where Gadrig had entered the small wood.

'Where are the men of your village?' demanded Morcant sounding more severe than Ferrax would have liked.

'Hunting sir' replied the old man subserviently. 'I cannot go on account of my poor breathing, they say the rasp of my breath scares the boars away.'

'So they hunt swine in these parts do they?' said Morcant, looking around.

'Yessir' the old mans head bobbed up and down in agreement and he smiled his rotten smile again as there was a shout and Gadrig emerged with one massive arm around the neck of another man that he was half strangling.

The captive man only had one hand, the other arm ended in a stump, bound and wrapped in a poultice of leaves. He was struggling and shouting but for all the good it did against Gadrig's strength he might has well have been singing a lullaby. He caught sight of Buldan who was striding towards him and renewed his efforts to pull away from Gadrig. Buldan began laughing and turned to Ferrax.

'We are in the right place Lord Ferrax' he called 'remember this dog turd?'

'Storril wasn't it?' said Ferrax. Gadrig pushed the one handed man to his knees as Ferrax approached, the wheezing old man from the village limping along behind calling for Storril not to be harmed.

'Lord, please' the old man called. 'Storril is the only able man we have left in the village, without him we shall all perish.' Ferrax stopped in his tracks and turned to face the man who was now leaning forward, hands on his knees as he gasped for breath.

'Old man, we have met Storril before, he attacked us and yet was allowed to live. The rest of the men, who I assume came from this shit hole were cowards and are now food for the birds.' Ferrax was losing his temper, as he was irrationally prone to do from time to time; fast and furious, he looked again at the old man. 'You lied to me.'

'My Lord . . .'the old man said, still having difficulty breathing as Ferrax took a step towards him.

'You seem to have difficulties with your lungs. Here let me help you breathe more easily.' Ferrax drew his sword and thrust it deep into the old mans chest. Bright red, aerated blood bubbled down the blade as the pierced lung collapsed and the man died silently and slightly pathetically. Ferrax attempted to withdraw the sword but it had stuck in the flesh so he kicked at the corpse until the red blade was extracted. Storril renewed his struggle for freedom and was punched hard by Gadrig for his trouble. He slumped to the ground, unconscious. Gadrig spat on him.

'Pathetic.'

There was a keening wail from the village, quickly cut short, presumably as a hand was clamped tight over a mouth.

'Bring that' said Ferrax looking at Storril, and he turned and walked back to the fence. He stood at the gap where the old man had spoken, legs apart and hands on hips. He looked everything he was, a man of power and not afraid to use it.

'Hear me!' called Ferrax, his voice loud and commanding. 'Do as I say and you will live, defy me and you will all die by fire.' He looked at the shoreline, the tide was on the way in and was not far short of the seaweed line. 'I will allow you til the height of the tide to decide your own fate. After that your village will be destroyed.' Ferrax turned to his warriors. 'Gadrig, drop him there.' Storril hit the ground with a soft thud. 'You and Buldan take the horses and go round the other side, if anyone makes a break for it, kill them.' He looked at Ancastia, her eyes wide and fearful, here was a man she thought, who was entirely unpredictable and she began to understand that her own survival was a matter of luck rather than design. She spoke a word of thanks to her own named goddess, Ancasta.

'Morcant? You approve?' said Ferrax.

'Yes Lord. It is how the gods would wish it; these people are verminous predators and should be removed from the land.'

Eventually and just as the tide reached its high point, a woman came out of the village and stood at the fence. She cast her eyes to the ground, too afraid or too subservient to look at Ferrax.

'Do you guarantee our lives if we do as you say? asked the woman in an accent that was clearly not local.

'Lord Ferrax is a man of honour' snarled Morcant, how dare you question his word woman!'

Ferrax replied calmly, 'I stand by my word, and that word is that anyone in the village that surrenders to me will live.'

'Do you guarantee our freedom?' asked the woman.

'No' said Ferrax bluntly. 'You will all belong to me to dispose of as I wish and it is my wish that you all be taken to Gaul and sold to slavery. The woman seemed to accept this calmly, as if an inevitability. She risked a look and saw Morcant grinning at her, sensing his own share of any profit no doubt.

Without another word the woman turned and walked back to one of the dilapidated huts. She called out something unintelligible as she walked and Ferrax could hear and sense movement from most of the rest of the dwellings. Shortly after, seven women and nine children meekly walked towards Ferrax, each clutching a pathetic and small bundle of belongings. Ferrax stood still as they passed him by and sat huddled in a small group near where Ancastia sat.

'Is that all do you think?' he asked Morcant. The druid who could not know the answer shrugged his shoulders. 'Very well. Fire the place' Ferrax ordered and turned away, just as an old woman cam out of her hut; the same one as the old man had lived in. She stood in the opening, defiantly staring at the men.

'Buldan!' roared Ferrax, and quickly the warrior came into view. 'Burn this place' said Ferrax. 'And anyone too stubborn or stupid to leave.' He looked the old woman in the eye. 'Anyone' he repeated. She spat on the ground and turned her back on him, walking back to the hut.

A while later and two huts were ablaze, the salt dried grasses and timbers almost eager to be consumed by the flames; and the fire was spreading, a gentle breeze fanning tongues of orange from one roof across the gap to the next where the old woman sat. As the fire took hold she barely seemed to notice but pulled a shawl around her head and mouth to keep the smoke out. All the while she sat there, she stared unblinkingly at Ferrax, her hard stare designed to unnerve him and unsettle him. The small home was by now well a seething mass of fire and the flames began to reach out towards her, yet still she sat, immovable despite the shouted pleas and cries of the women who had walked out of the village.

'What is she doing?' whispered Ferrax to Morcant.

'She is dying' replied the druid, respect in his voice. 'She has chosen her path and is demonstrating that she is stronger than you my Lord. This is powerful, and the gods favour her. She deserves our respect.' At that moment the old woman's hair caught fire and almost immediately the shawl turned from the ochre red of the dyed wool to a writhing orange. Slowly and clearly in agony, the woman stood, now alight from head to foot. Ferrax could smell the stench of scorched and cooking flesh and gagged at the sight before him as the woman raised one arm and pointed at him before turning and walking slowly and silently back into her disintegrating and fire ravaged hut. As she passed from sight into the consuming flames, there was a resounding crash and the hut caved in on itself to lie on the floor as a ruin.

Momentarily, Ferrax was deafened, not by the sounds from the village, but by the hammering sound of his own heart in his chest. As he began to breathe again and the world returned to normal he heard screaming and wailing from the women and children behind him, all of whom had witnessed the same as he had.

'Shut up! roared Ferrax. 'Be quiet or I will feed all of you to the goddess of fire.'

'He doesn't mean it' said a mother soothingly to her daughter. She looked Ferrax in the eye. 'If he did that then there would be no profit in coming here and that's all he understands.' Ferrax was numbed by fury and temped to separate the womans' head from her neck but a restraining hand came from Ancastia.

'Be a Lord and not a warrior Ferrax' she said calmly. 'You have no need to prove anything more this day and these people are your captives and now your slaves.' Ferrax looked into the young girls eyes and then pushed her roughly to one side. He walked to the mother who was squatting on the ground, her young child held close to her breast, he drew his sword, still red from the blood of the old man, and held the point in front of her eyes.

'One more word from you, just one' he moved the sword point to the child 'and I will cut her eyes out.' The child whimpered, although probably too young to understand the language, the meaning was all too clear. The mother glared at Ferrax and held the child tighter.

'Buldan!' called Ferrax, 'tie these women and children together and they are in your care.'

'Lord' acknowledged Buldan sullenly, not wanting to become a nursemaid to a group of women and children, but seeing no alternative.

'We shall set off immediately and be home within two nights' announced Ferrax.' And Buldan?' Ferrax looked the woman in the eye

'Yes Lord Ferrax?'

'I won't hear anything tonight.' As he turned he caught sight of the horror on the face of Ancastia and the quickly hidden smirk of Morcant.

With Perris and Sisal

The decision made, it appeared to have taken years off Sisal who announced that he would walk a while by the sea. Corillun's boat had departed, either back to Gaul or further along the coast to meet its master who had been intent on meeting other tribes and forging new links for trade, and of course, profit. As long as the goods came ashore and left the land here, thought Sisal, I shall not mind what the merchant gets up to. The Chief approached the waters edge and kept walking, the cold and the wet penetrating his leggings and shoes; a sensation not unpleasant to the old warrior. When the water was to his waist, Sisal ducked his head into the sea before emerging seconds later spluttering and rubbing his eyes.

Perris and Gargonstus were at the shoreline, laughing at the discomfort of Sisal and he had the presence to grin back at them before wading back to dry land.

'We thought you were going to drown yourself' called Perris as his father approached.

'Don't get too hopeful' called the Chief happily. 'I intend to be around for a while yet you young hound!'

Gargonstus stood a little apart from Perris, a smile on his face, but too respectful to join in with any word play. Mischief took hold of Sisal and he scooped water in his hands and splashed the other two who recoiled from the water. It dawned on Sisal that the pain in his knee was reduced and that he no longer felt restricted or infirm.

'Perris!' Sisal shouted to his son. He nodded towards Gargonstus. 'Throw him in here, let's mark this day.' Perris looked at the builder, he was huge, his muscles like tree trunks, but Gargonstus was backing away, his hands held out, palms outwards in supine defence. Perris grinned, Gargonstus was weakened by his loyalty and he grabbed at the builders clothing. Gargonstus tried to pull away, but Perris was strong too and this left Gargonstus with only one defence. He grabbed at Perris and lifted him easily above his head and with a roar, walked into the sea, passing the laughing Sisal, and threw Perris into the water. The young man landed with a tremendous splash, arms and legs flying in all directions.

Like his father before him, Perris stood spluttering, water dripping from him as he beat at the rippled surface of the sea with his fists, calling oaths and insults at his father and Gargonstus who, despite his reservations of status was laughing uncontrollably. Perris strode forward.

'Pull me out you ox!' Perris called to Gargonstus who in loyalty held his arm out to the young Lord. Perris seized it and yanked hard, pulling Gargonstus off balance and face first into the sea. Slowly the huge man rose, the grin still on his face as he put his massive arm round Perris's shoulder and the two of them walked back to dry land where Sisal was already waiting, the dog Avon at his heel barking at the two younger men

'Our land' said Sisal. 'Our sea.'

'And our fortress' finished Perris.

The three men sat smouldering round the fire, the steam gently rising from their clothing that tightened as the woven cloth dried.

'We need men to build the walls and ditches' said Sisal.

'There is a small village at the head of the harbour father, you can just see the smoke rising over there.' Perris pointed and true enough a small wisp of smoke could be seen. 'There will be men there who can work when they are not fishing and we have Gargonstus and myself. If we need others we can go to other villages and take men from the land.'

'Very well Perris but don't let your ambition ruin lives. Only take what a man can afford to give and not a minute more else that man becomes dependent upon you for his food and shelter.'

'Yes father' responded Perris dutifully.

'We shall return home shortly' said Sisal, 'Gargonstus can you ready the horses.

'I can Lord, but will you allow me to stay and make arrangements for the build? I can approach the villages and seek the men in your name?'

'You may Gargonstus, and may your work be fruitful and fast.'

'I thank you Lord' replied the builder simply.

'Father, may I also. . . '

'No you may not Perris' interrupted his father. 'For a start it would not do for a man of my status to travel without a guard and secondly I need you and Caeryl together, and' he added ruefully 'to get your mother and brother used to the idea.'

Perris saw the sense in both of these matters and acquiesced without further objection, though his mind was working furiously as to how to best use the situation to his own advantage.

The journey home was uneventful and good humoured although Gargonstus was even quieter than usual, possibly reflected Sisal, because he had a new project to dwell upon. Once again the three men stopped at the small farm and if anything the welcome they received was even more effusive and, learning of the new fortress plans, the head man of the farm agreed to provide two men, one of them his own son, to help with the work. The son was a well muscled youth of about twelve summers and Sisal, always astute, cemented his place in the affections of these people by appointing the boy as apprentice to Gargonstus for this building. The status conferred on this family would never be forgotten and it created a bond of loyalty that would be hard to break.

On the afternoon of the second day of travel, having collected the chariot from its hiding place to the north of the farm, Sisal re-entered his hilltop fortress and was greeted by Drullis. Perris took the horses away and spent the next hour grooming them and tending them after their journey

'Welcome home my Lord Sisal' called Drullis, as he stepped forward to take hold of the horse and steady her so that Sisal could alight.

'My greetings to you Drullis!' called Sisal.

'You seem in good spirits, your journey was productive?' enquired the man.

'It was but you seem to have the weight of rocks on your shoulders Drullis, what ails you?'

'I would beg a discussion with you in private Sisal if I may' asked Drullis. This was a very unusual step as most matters within the fort were discussed in cwnsl or with Morcant for his pronouncement. Sisal arched an eyebrow and pointedly glanced at the direction Perris had taken.

'Is this a . . .family matter?' said Sisal and Drullis nodded in relief at his Chiefs understanding of the situation. 'I see' said Sisal, and then, raising his voice made it clear that he was tired after his journey and needed water, asking Drullis to accompany him to the stream at the foot of the hill. It would be an uncomfortable walk back up the hill again, but the benefit was the privacy to be able to talk in private.

As soon as the two men left the fortress, Drullis made to speak but Sisal held up a hand to stop him.

'Drullis, be patient, I really am thirsty and let us wait until we are well out of the hearing of our friends?' said Sisal. Drullis fell in step beside Sisal and the two men walked companionably together down the hill. When they were seated on a rock next to the bank of the stream, Sisal drank his fill and then, smiling asked Drullis what was the problem.

'Lord, while you have been away I regret to say that our work has been undermined by our women.' Drullis tried to look offended but, as Sisal understood, it was only an act.

'Go on' said Sisal.

Your woman Idon and Caeryl's mother Eilas have been plotting and have announced the building of a new home for Lord Ferrax and my daughter as if it has been decided and agreed upon by you. Idon has announced that you will approve her change of arrangements.' Drullis sat with his head bowed.

'I see' said Sisal simply. 'Thank you for your candour Drullis, I know that this new arrangement would suit you better, but I am determined to be right in this matter and Caeryl will be with Perris.' He patted Drullis' knee as he stood. 'Let us be getting back home' he announced simply.

With Ferrax

Buldan sat and scowled at his charges; the older women protected the younger, and for the most part the younger women had children of their own. In any event Buldan was in a bad mood; celebrating after battle was one thing but burning a village and an old crone could hardly be called a fight and there was no honour in marking the event. He spat on the ground, his disgust at his responsibility self evident.

With the village dying away to embers, Ferrax had called on the people to move and the growing band had trudged resignedly northwards. At least, considered Ferrax, they were going home. As they travelled, Ferrax considered the future; he thought of the responsibilities he would take on and the status he would seek to earn and maintain. He was proud of his ability to out-think his brother, for where Perris was skilled with the sword, he Ferrax considered that he had other talents equally worthy of respect. The only matter that Ferrax could see causing a problem was his desire to make Caeryl his wife and his father's seemingly implacably opposition. Ferrax had known the girl since they were children and they had grown together into an understanding of their future. That this could be undone on a whim both confused and hurt Ferrax who resolved to bring the matter up with his father before it was too late.

For that reason, Ferrax made the decision to take Morcant with him and leave the warriors and the new slaves to make their slower way home. Morcant was pleased to be freed of what he regarded as the incessant and inane chattering of the women, and the two men, having given instructions to Gadrig, rode away.

After a while on the journey, Ferrax stopped to give the horse a chance to rest and took his chance to engage Morcant in earnest conversation.

'Druid, you know of my father's plans with Caeryl?' The Druid remained silent which the younger man took as permission to continue. 'They trouble me, both as a son and as a loyal warrior. I thought it was understood within our village that Caeryl and I were to be joined and yet my father seems not to care for the distress caused when he announces that Caeryl will share her life with my brother Perris. I wish to challenge my father's decision Morcant and I seek your wisdom and guidance in the matter.' He turned and looked at the Druid expectantly, and Morcant sat still for a moment and considered the situation.

'Master Ferrax, you are a good man and shall grow into being a great one. The taking of counsel in one so young is a good thing and to be encouraged for this is the way that wisdom is learned.' The druid paused, whether it was for effect or to gain thinking time Ferrax did not know, but he sat on the ground expectantly, hoping to hear words that would provide comfort to the pain he felt at his dilemma. Morcant smiled. 'Your father is a good man, but also a wise and powerful one and he will have his reasons for making his decisions. What those reasons are, I can merely guess at but I suspect that he fears Drullis' ambition. Perhaps it would be more truthful to say he fears the scheming of his wife Eilas for she would seize whatever power she could grasp, and having her daughter married to the next Chief would give her the influence and the status she more than craves.' He paused again. 'Women may not wield swords young Ferrax, but they have weapons that are much stronger and can cause wounds just as deep. They play with your head and your heart until you have no idea what you are doing or why and I suspect that your father is acting to protect you, and at the same time, protect the people he has long promised to defend. Of course if you and Caeryl have an understanding this will cause you hurt, especially if the mothers are in agreement with the plan, but your fathers wisdom is great and in choosing to join Caeryl with Perris he not only keeps

Drullis and Eilas close and therefore loyal, but also frees you to learn to make your own decisions in your own time.'

'Would you have chosen the same Morcant?' asked Ferrax quietly. The Druid looked up at the young man, the pain clearly visible in his eyes.

'No. No I would not, but that is not to say that I disagree with Lord Sisal, I am merely not as strong as he is. If Eilas seeks to tell Perris what to do, she is likely as not to have a sharpened sword to her throat for your brother has neither the sensibilities not the intelligence that you thankfully possess. It is to my never ending gratitude young man that you were born first.' Morcant smiled and hoped that Ferrax would take some relief from the lightening of the mood, but he merely inclined his head and wandered away, deep in thought.

Eventually, still with a troubled expression the young man approached the druid.

'Advise me Morcant, on how to change my father's mind.'

'I regret Lord that I cannot do that, for firstly to do so would be to undermine a man that holds both my loyalty and respect; and secondly you must find your own path to resolve the problem you face.'

'Then we ride on now until we arrive home and I will ask to speak with both my mother and father together' said Ferrax.

'As you command my Lord' said Morcant hauling himself to his feet and making towards the horse that had been contentedly grazing nearby.

The two men followed the path of the River until it petered out into the water meadow at the base of the hill upon which stood Caer Sisal. Ferrax halted for a moment and spoke to the Druid.

'Morcant is there nothing in the laws of our people and our lands that I can use at cwnsl to challenge my father?' The druid was silent and Ferrax jumped down from the horse's back to be able to look at the older man. With a wry smile on his face the druid shook his head.

'Lord Ferrax, I commend you for attempting a peaceful means of resolving the problem, though I am not sure your father would see it in that way. However most of our laws concern possessions and rights and until you are joined, Caeryl is not your possession and you have no rights over her. Only her father may properly decide her future, so I would suggest you direct your efforts in talking with him.'

Ferrax considered the advice for a moment and seeing at least some hope, thanked the druid for his counsel and helping the man down from the horse, the two of them walked to the fort in comfortable silence.

With Sisal and Idon.

Sisal had entered the Chiefs hut to find his wife sat in earnest discussion with Eilas, the mother of Caeryl. Idon, wise to the ways of her man, suggested that Eilas leave and return to her own home, but Sisal stayed where he was blocking the entrance.

'Eilas, I am glad you are here for it saves me having to repeat myself later. You two know of my wish that Perris shall live with Caeryl and yet despite this you plot and plan behind my back to suit your own ends.'

'Sisal' said Idon, rising to move towards him.

'Don't' ordered the Chief, the bitterness in his voice all too clear. 'You stay where you are woman, and for once in your life, you listen to me. The same applies to you Eilas for I have already spoken with Drullis and he knows my mind on this matter. My decision in the matter of Caeryl and Perris is final and any desire in your part to reverse that decision shall be disloyal to me for which the punishment, yes even for you Idon, shall be banishment from this place.' Both women stared aghast at the angry warrior standing before them. Sisal now in full flow, continued. 'Eilas, it is the right of Caeryl's father to approve or reject her partner and he has given his approval of Perris. This is all that needs be said on the subject.' Sisal turned on his heel and strode out of the hut in time to see his eldest son and the druid walk into camp.

'Ferrax! Where are Budan and Gadrig?'

'Worry not father, they are safe, but Morcant and I left them to bring our new slaves back here.' Sisal grinned, his heart and mind approving of the capturing of slaves.

'What have we got?' he enquired.

'Women and children sadly' replied Ferrax 'and one man, injured and probably useless.'

'But a lesson given nonetheless?'

'Yes my Lord.' The three men stood in a slightly awkward silence until Ferrax asked to be excused and made his way towards Drullis' hut. Sisal raised an eyebrow at Morcant.

'He is troubled by your decision to let Perris have Caeryl, he has talked of little else during our short time away' explained the druid.

'That bloody girl is more trouble than she is worth' muttered the Chief, more determined than ever to resolve the matter as quickly as possible.

'Morcant, please put the word around that I call cwnsl together this night.' It was unusual but not unheard of and the druid made to hesitate, but seeing the determined look on the Chief's face, decided against it and hurried away to call on each of the families.

At Drullis' hut however, Morcant stood awhile to listen on the conversation within.

'Why is my father so against me?' Ferrax was talking low and angry.

'Your father will be made to see sense and reason' said Eilas, her voice, though quiet, still possessed of a strident quality, that frequently made her sound aggressive and demanding.

'Lord Sisal seems intend upon his plan, and we are placed in some difficulty. We have always wanted the best for Caeryl, as would any parent, and what is proposed is still a joining with the Chiefs' family. With that comes additional status and power.............' Drullis was cut off by his woman.

'Perris is a pig, everyone knows it and if you are weak enough to agree to this farce then you are sacrificing your daughter to the life of a slave.'

'Ferrax?' said Drullis.

'My brother is not a beast' replied Ferrax dully 'but Caeryl is the woman I planned to spend my life with and.........and I don't know what to do. My father seems immovable.' Morcant thought he heard a stifled sob but could listen no more without attracting attention and so called from outside the hut to announce his presence. When Drullis, as the man of the family, came to the entrance, the druid passed on Sisals message and then moved on to the next dwelling.

When the men of the village were settled near the fire, Sisal took the unusual step of standing to address his tribe.

'I have called you together here for a happy and joyful event' he announced, 'the joining of my youngest son Perris with the daughter of my friend Drullis. There was a murmuring around the fire as people turned to their neghbours, some were concerned about the advancement of Drullis, some were supportive of Ferrax' claims over the girl and some just wondered what the fuss was to call a special meeting of the cwnsl. As the initial conversation petered out, focus switched to Ferrax who sat close by his father, the scowl on his face open and unhidden. Suddenly Ferrax looked about him, he stood and shouted.

'Where is Perris?'

At that very moment a piercing scream ripped not only the tranquillity of the night, but also the heart from Ferrax chest. The noise was that of a woman in pain. Ferrax had heard that kind of scream before when the women birthed and he knew then that his father has deceived them all. In calling cwnsl, Sisal had sent Perris to take Caeryl and this he had clearly done. Ferrax stood, silent and mute, his mind a maelstrom of emotions and indecision.

'It is done' announced Sisal simply and made to leave. He froze as he heard the sound of a sword being drawn, and turned slowly to see his eldest son bearing arms within the village. A serious offence against the laws of the tribe and a definite challenge to his authority as Chief.

'Put that away boy' snarled Sisal. 'You offend me and our people.' With a sound that was half like a whimper and half like a scream, Ferrax turned away from his father and strode to where the scream had come from.

'Ferrax! Stop!' The voice was that of Morcant and Ferrax paused so that the druid could catch up with him.

'Did you. . . ?'

'Did I know?' said Morcant. He shook his head 'no I did not, but even if I had, it would make no difference. Your father is the Chief and his word is law and to fight that puts you outside the law. You understand what that means?' Ferrax did not respond but continued to look to where he could hear Cryl sobbing even though he could not see her.

'Come back to the fire' said Morcant gripping Ferrax' arm. At that moment however, Perris came into sight, his outline clear in the dim light and the grin on his face one provocation too far for Ferrax. With a snarl and a cry he launched himself at his brother who drew his own sword and within seconds the two of them were fighting, the clash of metal on metal ringing through the village like a bell announcing that the end of the world had arrived.

The fight was evenly matched. For all that Perris was a more skilful warrior, Ferrax had the strength brought on by the pain he felt and he drove his brother back with an onslaught of blows.

Perris remained emotionally detached, parrying the cuts and thrusts of his brothers' attack which infuriated Ferrax still further. There was a sound of running feet and the men of the village gathered and were about to put an end to the fight when the voice of Sisal cut through the night.

'Leave them' he ordered. 'Ferrax has taken arms against his brother and must face the consequences. This fight shall be a judgment upon my decision.

Morcant made to speak but was silenced by a shake of the head from Sisal. Ferrax renewed his attack but he was weakening and Perris as the stronger was coming into the ascendancy. He began to goad his brother..

'Poor Ferrax, father decided he wasn't man enough for Caeryl, so he gave her to me. And I took her Ferrax, I had her just there behind me. She's still there now, waiting for me.'

Ferrax renewed his attack, feinting a strike with his sword but pulling it away at the last minute so that Perris' arm was across his body. Ferrax used the lack of defence to smash his fist into his brothers' unguarded face and the feeling of victory made his careless. Perris' sword arm came back in a viscous arc so that the flat of his blade smacked into Ferrax' head knocking him to the ground. Dizzy and battered, weakened by his exertions, Ferrax spun round and tried to kick his brothers' legs. He was rewarded when Perris landed with a thud on the ground but seconds later was pinned to the floor by his brothers powerful arms and he looked up into the leering face of Perris who spoke very quietly so that only the two of them could hear.

'She wasn't very wet you know. I had a hell of a job doing what I had to, but by the gods, she was worth it! It was like riding an unbroken horse. She bucked and fought and struggled and tried to push me off, but I was just too strong. I rode her brother, I rode her until I could hold on no more, but there will be other times and who knows, even know she may be with child. Mine!'

'Enough!' called the stern voice of Sisal who had heard nothing of the words spoken. Strong hands pulled a laughing Perris off his brother who lay dejected and defeated in the mud of the village. He was disgraced not only by his fathers' decision but also by his failure to beat his younger brother in combat, and to add to that he felt the humiliation of Perris' words playing over and over again in his mind.

Ferrax sensed people moving away, the excitement of the night over, and he lay there, tears coursing down his face as he cried for his loss, repeating one word over and over again. 'Caeryl.'

'She is gone to you now Lord Ferrax' said a resigned and weary voice eventually, and Ferrax looked up to see Drullis looking down on him. 'That battle is lost my Lord and my daughter is now joined with your brother.'

Defeat was not a natural ally for Ferrax. He had grown up in the house of Sisal, the most successful Chief in these lands and one who never backed out of a challenge.

'We can go away together' said Ferrax quietly, but Drullis shook his head.

'No Lord, Caeryl is joined, and Perris is now her man to do with as he chooses. She will no more go with you than fly like a bird. It is over.' Drullis made to walk away but gave one final thought. 'You have a good heart Ferrax and Caeryl loved that in you, but you fight with your heart and not your head and that was your undoing this night.'

Ferrax was left alone with his thoughts and his pain.

The next morning when the village awoke, Ferrax was gone. Sisal questioned the sentries, who told him that Lord Ferrax had taken a horse and said he was going to ride to find Gadrig and Buldan and help escort the slaves, but when the two warriors returned they denied having seen Ferrax since he left them with Morcant, the day before. Sisal sent search parties to scour the countryside for his eldest son, but to no avail.

Three Years Later

The sea fort was built, finally finished it represented all that Perris and Gargonstus had planned it to be. Stout and strong, it provided both shelter from the weather and a stronghold to be able to defend the land.

Perris stood with Gargonstus and admired the work of the builder. Looking toward the sea, the young warrior was confronted with a deep ditch and a high earth bank making the fortress seemingly impregnable to any attacker. The earth bank was topped in places by a wooden palisade that afforded protection to the defenders against missiles such as slingshot, spears or even arrows. There was a narrow passage across the ditch that allowed an entrance to the fortress, and this was easily guarded by two wooden towers that gave the advantage of height to the defenders. The sea itself provided a natural obstacle to any warriors wishing to attack from the south or east and a stout wooden wall made any seaborne landing both impracticable and illogical. The heavy and fortified gates in the wall, allowed access to fishermen and women, and others who had cause to leave to the seaward side.

Perris sniffed the air, it was clean with a tang of salt and felt very different to the close confines of his fathers' hill top fortress, many miles away. The young man shook the builder by the hand.

'Gargonstus, you have achieved all I asked of you, and as reward you shall pick the place for your own dwelling.'

'My gratitude for your kindness Lord' replied Gargonstus 'but my place is not here and with your leave I shall return to your father's place.' Perris' features clouded fleetingly at this implied snub but he knew the builder well and knew he spoke from loyalty.

'Very well my loyal friend, but you are welcome here at any time.'

In the time it had taken to construct the fortress, trade with Gaul had flourished, as Corillun the Gaul had promised it would. The tribe had prospered and a small settlement had grown up around the place the trade ships landed their wares. The fact that the settlement now had a fortress to defend it was not a hindrance. At first every ship that landed goods paid its dues and those dues were sent to Sisal, but of late, Perris had been hoarding the coin and sending payments, minus a healthy commission, only at full moon. His father was powerless to object.

Sisal had never got over losing Ferrax, for many seasons he would make excuses to travel his lands, always searching for the whereabouts of his first born son. Always in vain. Although too proud and too stubborn to ever admit that he had made a mistake, Sisal regretted his decision to let Perris have Caeryl for it had effectively lost him two sons.

Caeryl was not a loyal and obedient woman to Perris, she denied him her bed, her company and her counsel and a man without the wisdom of his woman was alone in the world thought the Chief. Sisal had aged, the vibrant colour in his hair and beard now dulled by a steel grey and the eyes, once so alive and vibrant were now clouded and avoided contact with other people. Sisal also had Idon to contend with, for she blamed and continued to blame the loss of her son on Sisal's decision and she never let him forget his culpability for her pain.

Idon had accepted Caeryl into her home as a daughter, and defended her right to reject Perris. This in turn drove Perris to spend much time away from the village, mostly in dealing with his fortress on the coast. Sisal therefore felt isolated and could not reach out to Perris for he was never there.

Not even the advice and guidance of Morcant was able to rally Sisal, and in any event the druid was preoccupied with the woman Ancasta whom he suspected to have the powers and wisdom of an Ovate. If so then hers was a talent, a gift and a power to be nurtured and crafted. When Gadrig and Buldan had returned to the village with the slaves, Morcant had spoken with Sisal and told his Lord of his belief that the girl was possessed by the spirits and could speak with the gods. Sisal, fearing such power had readily agreed that the girl should be tutored and guided by Morcant. The druid however had rather different plans and one night had crept to the hut in which Ancasta slept. He got three paces into the dwelling before he felt the point of a knife press against the skin of his neck and heard a curse muttered that was so powerful and so terrifying that from that night he considered the girl as possessed and from then on he focused his efforts on her education in the ways of the gods and the laws of men. Ancasta, for her part, rather enjoyed the power she was able to wield over Morcant, for she knew that he feared her.

Perris walked on the path across the ditch and into the fortress. Outside his hut in the centre of the settlement a dark-haired girl sat with a baby sucking contentedly at her breast. She smiled coyly at Perris who watched fascinated as his son drifted away to a happy sleep on his mothers' tit.

'Inside' ordered the warrior, and the girl quietly obeyed, taking care to lay the baby down on the skins in the corner, where he would sleep undisturbed. The girl turned to face Perris who, as she knew he would, bent down to her and fixed his mouth roughly on her nipple and sucked hard. She had learned to pretend that she enjoyed the attentions of her Lord, though in truth she was thinking of how to get Perris to acknowledge her as his woman, rather than just the mother of his son. She gasped and moved in the ways she knew he liked and Perris, oblivious to the subterfuge gorged himself on her milk until there was no more. He pushed the girl away, lay down and was soon snoring contentedly.

A while later he was woken by a small hand shaking him. His sleep addled brain slowly registering the words his ears were hearing.

'Lord! ......My Lord! A ship approaches.' The girl Halen, smiled as Perris returned to consciousness. 'A ship, Perris. A Gaul I think.'

Perris smiled and grabbed the woman who giggled as he planted a kiss on her lips and strode out of his round house to see the new visitor. Walking through the wooden gates that were opened as he approached, Perris saw the square sail of Corillun's ship and ordered that a pig be slaughtered and roasted for the night meal. Corillun was always most exact about paying his landing dues and the goods he traded in were always of the finest quality. Perris hoped there were jars of his favoured wine, the ruby red liquid from Gaul that tasted as if the gods had made it.

Later, as the power of the sun was waning, Corillun, slightly larger round the middle than when he had first set foot on this land, waded ashore, his greeting as effusive as ever it was.

'So! It is finished and you are now Lord of your own lands?' Corillun looked round appreciatively. In truth he could find no flaw in either the plan, or construction of the fortress and he was impressed. 'Where is master Gargonstus?' Corillun looked around for the builder who was usually present every time a boat landed.

'Gargonstus has decided to return to my father's side' announced Perris, 'I suspect he makes preparation for his journey' he added offhandedly.

'But surely he will join us for a meal tonight to celebrate his achievements?'

'What he does is his business and not mine' replied Perris, his uncaring tone slightly jarring with Corillun who knew of the effort put in by the builder to achieve his Lords' ambition. Wisely Corillun decided not to press the matter further but mentally noted that Perris was becoming too powerful and too uncaring of those that served him. Corillun, for the first time on British soil, felt uneasy and hoped that his own warrior, Forrun, was not too far away.

'You, and your men are welcome to our hospitality Corillun' intoned Perris. 'I have ordered a beast slaughtered in your honour' he added.

'Your kindness is well known Lord' replied Corillun in the manner expected of a guest.

After the sun had set and the only light was from the fire pit, Perris was sat with Corillun, his warrior Forrun, and Gargonstus who had agreed to stay the extra night to be with men he regarded as friends. Also present was Perris' loyal servant. A man with one hand who had developed a loyalty to his master that was so devout that he was oft compared to a dog.

'Storril!' called Perris. 'Feed our guests and see to their drink you lazy little man.' Perris laughed, others smiled politely, not wishing to offend the young man who wielded power in this place. Storril scurried to do his masters bidding, smiling dutifully as he hacked meat from the carcass of the pig and carefully poured wine into horn goblets.

Storril has proven useful to Perris; he had approached him after the fight with Ferrax and reminded the young man that his hand was missing because he had been bested in battle. According to the traditions of his own tribe, this meant that his life was at the gift of his victor, and instead of dismissing the man's offered subservience and freeing him from obligation as most would have done, Perris opted to enslave Storril. Although hindered by his lack of a hand, there was nothing wrong with Storril's hearing and many was the time over the preceding years that a man would be punished for making an adverse comment, overheard by the one handed man and relayed back to his master. Within the fortress there was thus a tension that led to mistrust and enmity. Perris, as Lord of all he surveyed, was oblivious to the tensions within his community and dismissed any warnings given to him, especially by Halen and Gargonstus.

As Perris had hoped, Corillun was indeed accompanied by Forrun and the two warriors shared tales of fights, of rumours and of deeds they yet hoped to accomplish. It was clear however to most people present, that Perris did most of the talking, and Corillun would sometimes interject to deflect Perris from a conversation, so as to protect Forrun. Perris however was merry with drink, and so taken with the company that his normally acute senses deserted him.

The feast to celebrate Corilluns' arrival developed into an event to mark the completion of the fort and wine flowed, a lot of it toward Perris. It was well into the hours of darkness when Corillun and Forrun begged leave to depart and made their way to the guest hut next to Perris' round house. Perris was left alone, inebriated and melancholic.

'Storril!' there was silence. 'Storril you useless piece of goat dung' hollered Perris uncaring of his duties as host to let his guests sleep. There was a shuffling noise and a clearly exhausted Storril stood before his master.

'There you are. More wine!'

'Lord, perhaps moderation would be a better plan for the night?'

'I said more wine, and I meant more wine' said Perris dangerously. 'Or perhaps you'd prefer to be the slave with no hands?' Storril had seen these moods before and knew that Perris was not joking in his threats, and so hastened away to do his masters bidding.

When he returned he saw Perris swaying on his feet, a burning branch from the fire held in his hand.

'Who's there' called Perris turning and causing Storril to move backwards to avoid being burned.

'Lord, it is I. Storril.' Perris slumped back to the seat he had occupied.

'Yes it would be. It's always you isn't it Storril. Plain, dull, unexciting Storril. My shadow.' Perris let the words run down to silence but then started shouting again. 'It should be him! What is the point of success and victory if there is nobody there to humiliate by it. Tell me that Storril? Tell me that. What is the point!'

Wisely Storril refrained from speaking and kept the stoppered jar of wine hidden behind his back.

'Storril, you are a good weasel but a lousy, awful conversationalist. Do you know that? Where is he and where did he go?'

'Who Lord?' asked Storril in genuine confusion.

'My brother you oaf!' roared Perris who once again leaped to his feet. 'My perfect brother, the favoured son of my mother and the cleverest boy ever taught by that fornicating old goat Morcant. My brother Ferrax, that's who.' He paused. 'Sometimes in this life Storril you get one chance to win. My father gave me that chance and I took it and then my brother disappeared, taking a lifetime of humiliation with him. My father was stupid and clever at the same time. He wanted Ferrax to be hungry, not to have everything he wanted for he thought that was the way to create a good Chief. Ha! Well my mother never forgave him, my so called woman Caeryl never forgave him, or me, and my brother ran away like a trail of shit down a chicken's arse.

'Look around us Storril, what we have is what I have built. This place is mine and I shall fight to keep it so, free of interference from meddling druids and their laws, from moaning women and their plots, and from stupid servants who don't bring me my wine when I demand it!'

'Here it is my Lord' said Storril nervously bringing the jar from behind his back and unstopping it. He made to pour the contents into the horn goblet but the jar was snatched from his grasp and he was sent sprawling to the ground as Perris upended the container and drank deeply.

'Storril, I hate you' said Perris, slurring his words 'you are an odious little turd, obsequious one minute and thinking of killing me the next........'

'Lord! No! It isn't true' interrupted the servant, struggling to rise. He was felled by a savage kick to his face.

'Shut up you rat' spat Perris 'and hold out your hand. Put it on the tree stump, there. Perris indicated what Storril should do and, with tears in his eyes, the man complied as Perris drew his sword and two handed raised it above his head to deliver the savage and maiming blow. Storril shut his eyes as Perris roared in anger, and then there was a thud and silence.

Storril dared to look round, it took him a while to realise that his hand was still intact and that Perris had passed out and lay on his back, unconscious, his sword still in his hands. Almost tenderly, the servant eased the weapon from the hands of his master and laid it beside him. He then went to his own meagre hut and brought his woven blanket which he placed over Perris and sat to keep vigil over his Lord.

The Next Morning

Spring was giving way to summer, the warmth seeping from the sky almost as soon as the sun rose into view. As the village woke, Storril urged the men and women to caution as Perris lay still, but he knew that there would be a raging temper when he regained his wits.

As tradition demanded, Corillun and Forrun, the only two of the visitors to spend the night inside the fortress, were duty bound to remain within the guest accommodation until the Lord had awakened and welcomed them to the new day. Storril however considered this to be impractical and begged permission to have conversation with the honoured guests. Corillun for one could see the sense of Storril's suggestion that he and Forrun pretend to have returned to their ship the previous night for this would have the advantage of allowing them to move freely about the place without delivering an insult to the unpredictable young man.

Corillun took Storril to one side as they were leaving.

'Does his father know how Lord Perris behaves?'

'I doubt it sire' replied the servant, looking over at the prone figure of Perris. 'I have not seen Lord Sisal here these past ten seasons. He came here once, in the early days when the ditch was just started, but that was it.'

'How was he?'

'He looked like a great man that had been broken Lord' replied Storril with sorrow in his voice. 'He tried to make a few suggestions, all of which were ignored by my master, and I once heard him mutter "what have I done?" to nobody in particular before he rode away. We have had few other visitors, but those that have passed this way from Caer Sisal have all said that the Lord prefers his own company and often rides or walks the countryside, sometimes he can be gone for days.'

'Sisal is a good man Storril, and he has always been fair with me, abiding by our agreements as I have done. I think it is time I paid my friend a visit. Can you arrange horses for myself and Forrun?

'Gladly sire. I am always most pleased to help.'

'Good. We shall leave at once.'

By the time Perris roused himself from sleep, the sun had moved across the sky to its highest point. Groggily and with croaking voice he demanded water which Storril dutifully provided.

'By the gods, my head has evil within' he muttered, drinking heavily from the water jug and demanding yet more. 'Where are our guests' he asked looking towards the guest house that had its entrance open and the fire was doused.

They slept aboard their ship last night sire' answered Storril carefully, 'and departed early this morning on an errand.'

'Did you attend to their needs' growled Perris.

'Indeed Lord, the reputation of your house is intact.' Storril busied himself, fussily tidying the area where Perris had slept and recovering his blanket in the process.

'Go away Storril, you annoy me.'

'As you wish sire.'

Perris rose and walked to the wooden gates and ordered them open. Riding at anchor in the protected harbour was Corillun's ship, a stout vessel but with her hull encrusted with weed and barnacles. Perris shielded his eyes against the glare from the water and walked into the sea. The stinging cold was both painful and refreshing and Perris, as he had done so years earlier, dipped his head under. He stayed for a while, blowing bubbles through his nose and wondering if anyone was watching, not that he cared. When his lungs were emptied he stood, emerging from the water more alert and feeling more able to face the day. He glanced back at the ship, there was no sign of life on her decks and turned to walk back to the shore.

Striding towards him was Halen carrying the baby. The infant gurgled happily and held a chubby arm out towards his father. Perris took hold of his son and looked at Halen.

'We have not named this child?'

'No, Lord. We agreed to wait until the druid visits so that we may seek his guidance and make the appropriate sacrifice.'

'We have no need of druids and their ways' replied Perris. 'This is my child and I claim the right to name him.' Perris held his child up to the sun.

'Hear me, for I am Lord Perris, master of these lands' he called, walking back into the water. 'Gods of the sun, gods of the lands, and gods of the seas, I call on you to know this child and to protect him as you protect me. I call on you to know his given name as Perran.' With that pronouncement Perris once again dunked himself in the sea, taking the baby with him who emerged blinking mere seconds later and bawling in his shock while reaching out for his mother who protectively took him back. Perris strode past the woman. 'See that all know his name and address him properly' he said.

'You are quiet Forrun?' said Corillun, impervious but not insensitive to the fact that the man was mute, as the two men walked along the grassland tracks. 'You were quiet also last evening. What is it?'

By a series of grunts and hand gestures that only Corillun would have comprehended, Forrun explained his quandary.

'I see' nodded Corillun, 'and how long have you known this?' Another grunted communication and a raised eyebrow from the trader in reply. 'And you never thought fit to tell me?' Forrun looked troubled until Corillun said 'no never mind my friend, but do you trust me to use this information where I see fit?' There was a nodded agreement. 'Thank you' said Corillun and the two men rode on until they came for a halt at the river that ran to the foot of the hill atop which stood Caer Sisal. Sitting on the riverbank was a man, hunched over the water, his feet dangling in the river. Nearby a horse was tethered on a long rein, contentedly chewing on the grass, and next to the man was a dog, lying in the grass.

The man looked up, his hair and beard streaked with grey and matted with food, the eyes misty and without recognition, he turned back to look into the river once again. Corillun put his hand out to stop Forrun and indicating that the warrior should remain with the beasts, he dismounted and walked towards the man.

'Sisal, my friend?' asked Corillun. The man looked up and the dog gave a low, warning growl.

'I am Sisal' he replied simply. There was none of the pomp or swagger that the man used to possess, instead he looked and sounded like a worker from the fields.

'Sisal, it's me Corillun' said the Gaul 'may I sit with you?'

'Corillun my friend, forgive me, I was lost in my thoughts.' Sisal made to get up but clearly thought better of it and indicated that the trader was welcome to sit next to him. Corillun, unsure that Sisal had indeed recognised him, removed his boots and dangled his feet into the clear cool water. The dog, apparently satisfied that his master was under no threat, lay down to sleep

'I have not seen you for so long' said Corillun. 'What troubles you?' Sisal sat silently for a time before sighing deeply.

'It is my son' he said. 'I cannot find him no matter how hard I look and I fear that he has been taken from us.'

'Which son have you lost Sisal?' asked Corillun carefully. The question appeared to confuse Sisal who answered as if he only had the one child.

'My son Ferrax. He was here . . . and now he is gone. He has been gone for so long Corillun, will you help me look for him?'

Corillun glanced over at Forrun, silently praising the man's loyalty and trust.

'Ferrax is not lost dear friend. He is alive and well and prospers in Gaul. He has built a life for himself and' Corillun took a leap of faith 'he wants you to know this and be happy for him.'

'Ferrax is safe?'

'Perfectly' answered Corillun with certainty, and saw with some humility that his friend was weeping uncontrollably. Corillun became more and more concerned the longer this went on. It was as if a tree that blocked a stream had been removed and the waters flowed freely. The trader bided his time however and eventually there was a break in the tears during which Sisal announced that he was tired and wanted to sleep.

'Shall I help you up the hill my friend?' asked Corillun. Sisal looked around and then upwards as if seeing the feature for the first time. His mouth opened as if in wonder and Corillun began to seriously worry.

'Forrun! I want you to stay here and protect Lord Sisal' said Corillun. 'I am going to the fort to collect Morcant, be gentle with our friend and see no harm comes to him?' There was a grunted response from the warrior and Corillun mounted his horse and rode slowly to the settlement on the top of the hill.

One of the sentries at the fort's entrance was Gadrig, who recognised Corillun and welcomed him appropriately as a friend, taking the horse as the trader jumped down to the ground.

'Gadrig, is Morcant here?' asked Corillun quietly.

'Yes sire, over there.' Gadrig had pointed to a hut outside which sat the druid and a young girl in earnest conversation. Corillun set off, leaving the sentry to hold on to the horse.

A quick but muted conversation between trader and druid followed resulting in the two men and a curious Ancastia making their way unhurriedly out of the fort so as not to cause any alarm. When eventually they approached Sisal they could see that he was soaked to the skin and Corillun asked Forrun for an explanation.

It seemed that the Chief had inexplicably thrown himself into the small river and the warrior had pulled him out. Sisal was sitting weeping again, but somewhat differently as his eyes were wide and wild as his gaze darted over everyone present and the surrounding countryside.

Morcant sat beside his Chief and tried to give him time to settle, but Sisal was too antagonised to speak and too upset to listen. After a while Morcant rose and beckoned Corillun over.

'He is possessed it would seem by a spirit' said the druid. 'It is a strong and powerful force that is controlling him and it will take much time and skill to cure him.'

'But it can be done?' asked Corillun out of concern for his friend. Morcant looked around, seemingly wrestling with a problem. He took in the blue sky, the lush green vegetation, the nearby trees and the sight of rabbits feeding contentedly on the grass before he spoke.

'It can be done, yes, but I fear there is a problem. For me to be able to speak with the spirit and persuade it to leave Lord Sisal I will need time and peace and tranquillity and I fear that we will not get that here.' He glanced up towards the hilltop.

'Why?' asked Corillun. Morcant took a deep breath.

'I fear that Idon, Sisal's woman, has been taking power and influence to herself these past few seasons. She has men loyal to her and permits no objection to her decisions from our Chief who has been weakened by the loss of Lord Ferrax, as have we all' he added with sadness in his voice.

'But Lord Ferrax lives' said Corillun who went on to explain what he had learned from Forrun much to the evident joy of the druid who clapped his hands together, but was restrained by the hand of Corillun on his arm.

'Look!' said the trader and Morcant followed his gaze to see Ancastia in earnest conversation with Sisal who was sitting with her hand in his, listening intently to everything she was saying. Nothing of which could be heard, so quiet were the words. As they watched, a smile stole across Sisal's features, a sight so rare recently that Morcant looked at Corillun and raised an eyebrow. Morcant made to move towards the two of them but Corillun held him back.

'Whatever she is doing, it is working, let's leave them to it?' Morcant, always concerned with his own status more than the benefits to others was about to resist the suggestion when there was a sound of horses approaching and Idon rode up followed by Cwaenog the Outsider and Buldan. She looked down imperiously from the back of her horse and addressed Morcant.

'What is going on here and why is Sisal treated in this manner?' She was referring to him as if he were not there 'And why is that girl with him?' She clicked her fingers and Cwaenog, with a nervous glance at Gadrig rode forward and drew his sword.

If Sisal noticed anything he did not react but Ancastia leaped to her feet as the horse and warrior came on and held an arm out, flat of the palm of her hand raised against Cwaenog. The dog Avon ambled to her side and sat next to her. Ancastia muttered words and the man reigned the horse in immediately and stopped, not daring to move any further forward. He looked round at Idon who glared furiously at Ancastia.

'What did you say girl?' shouted Idon. Ancastia silently glared at Idon. 'You would do well not to defy me!' threatened Idon and still Ancastia remained silent with her hand raised.

'My lady . . .' began Morcant only to be cut off at once.

'Silence druid. When I want your advice or opinion I shall ask for it and as I have never asked, that should tell you how high my regard is for you. She kicked her horse forward and rode slowly towards Ancastia who stood her ground, muttering an incantation. Morcant visibly winced, alone among those present able to understand the words spoken.

'What did you say child?' said Idon with bitterness in her voice. Ancastia continued her muttering. 'Druid, what did she say?' asked Idon.

'I think it best that you remain still my Lady' called the druid. 'The child has an understanding, and a power far beyond my teaching and I cannot speak for your safety.' His voice rose in volume at the end of the sentence as if he were going to shout a warning. Idon halted her progress, the horse and rider both seemingly of fixed gaze with the young girl. Eventually Ancastia lowered her hand.

'I thank you my Lady' she said. 'I regret that Lord Sisal is not well and needs rest and care.'

'What would a girl like yourself know of such things' said Idon haughtily.

'I know enough to help, my Lady' the girl responded simply. 'I need you to entrust Lord Sisal to my care.'

'And have you steal him from me! You will have to do better than that to outwit me.'

'If you do not trust me my Lady then Lord Sisal will fade away, his spirit will leave and his body will die.' Ancastia spoke simply and without emotion in her voice. Corillun, looked from the girl to the woman and then to Morcant who cast his eyes to the floor.

'I think' began Idon 'that I know what is best for Sisal. Stand aside girl.' Ancastia complied without a murmur and Idon nodded to Cwaenog who rode forward and dismounted so he could help a compliant Sisal onto the back of the horse. Sisal looked plaintively at Ancastia as the small procession passed her by on its way back up the hill.

'Druid, you would do well to control the girl' spat Idon as she passed by. Morcant looked at Ancastia who was about to speak and shook his head in warning. She smiled a curious half smile and obeyed, lowering her eyes to the ground.

With Sisal gone, Corillun turned to the druid and asked his advice. Morcant called Ancastia over.

'What troubles our Chief my dear' he asked kindly.

'His own spirit is weak master druid' she responded simply. 'He has not the energy to fight the minds of others and without regaining himself he will fall prey to the evil around him.'

'And do you really think you could save him?' asked Corillun. Ancastia looked at the small group climbing the hill.

'I could have, but now, I could not. Lord Sisal is lost to us.' She shrugged her shoulders, her certainty beyond doubt in her mind and speech.

Master Corillun,' said Morcant 'I sense, as I suspect do you, that this place is no longer safe for Ancastia. Idon fears her knowledge and power over the mysteries of life, for this is not the first time that they have been in conflict. My place is here with Sisal and I shall continue to serve him and help him for as long as I might, but will you take the child with you and protect her? She has the ways of a priestess of great power and can be both difficult and demanding as can all those who are truly touched by the gods.'

'If the child is willing then I am happy to help' agreed Corillun. 'But where shall I take her?'

'If Ferrax is truly alive, then take her to him and may the gods protect both of them.'

Sisal

Idon looked at the pale face, the scared and sunken eyes that stared at her seemingly without recognition. Sisal had been paid on the bed of furs and skins that he had not shared with her since Ferrax' disappearance, and apart from a sigh he had made no sound.

'Sisal, you must regain yourself' said Idon 'you are the Chief of this tribe and unless you rouse yourself and start to rule like the man you were, then you will shortly face a challenge and you will lose.' Sisal said nothing and Idon carried on talking without even looking at him. 'There are men within this tribe that covet all you have and you could lose everything.' Still Sisal said nothing and remained still on the bed.

'Get up!' shouted Idon. 'Don't just lie there like a vegetable waiting to be picked.'

'He's alive' whispered Sisal to nobody in particular. His eyes were open but he was not aware of what he was seeing. Sisal was lost within his own mind. Idon became aware that Sisal was speaking and bent down to him. She heard him repeat the same phrase over and over again. 'He's alive.'

'Who is alive?' There was no response. 'Sisal!' she shouted, her anxiety reaching a crescendo, 'who is alive?' The Chief turned away from her, still mumbling to himself.

Idon became aware of a presence outside the round house and waspishly called for whoever was spying on her to enter. The tall figure of Morcant bent to enter the dwelling, and Idon was caught between her dislike of the druid and her need for advice.

'Druid, I cannot reach Lord Sisal, he just mutters and stares into the sky in his own head. He keeps saying "he's alive." What is this nonsense?'

'My Lady, Lord Sisal has just heard the news that your son Ferrax is alive and well, and I regret that the relief of this has overcome his mind. He is quite outside himself.' Idon's hand flew to cover her mouth and stifle a small sob. Her other hand gripped the sleeve of Morcant's robe.

'Ferrax is alive?'

'Yes my lady. I am told he prospers across the sea in Gaul.' Hearing this news, Idon sank to sit on the bed next to Sisal, and without any other form of comfort she cradled his head in her arms as she leaned over him, whispering that everything would be alright and that Ferrax would come home. Morcant made to leave but was called back by Idon.

'Druid, much as it pains me to call upon you, I need your help. Sisal is stricken with this illness in his mind and will soon face a challenge to his leadership......'

'Indeed he will my Lady, there has already been a certain amount of discussion amongst the tribe' replied Morcant. In talking over Idon, the druid had displayed a great deal of rudeness, but his move was a calculated one to demonstrate his lack of care for Idon and his own power within the new dynamic.

'Who? Who plots and plans against Lord Sisal?' said Idon, her manifest paranoia working overtime.

'There is no specific plot Lady' replied Morcant calmly 'but there are talks about who should succeed Sisal should his health fail.' In point of fact, the only discussions had been of concern for the man who had led with tribe with wisdom and compassion, though there was a hint of fear that Idon would seek to exert her own influence. Idon was not universally admired, unlike Sisal, her temperament was mistrusted and her fiery temper led her to wild accusations and even wilder condemnations of those she fell out with. There was not one of the women within the village that Idon had not fallen out with one time or another.

'We must act druid, and you must be guided by me in this matter.' Idon spoke offhandedly as she rose to her feet and walked restlessly alongside the bed.

'Lady, I am guided by the gods and by my bonds with Lord Sisal. I need no other to show me that path I must take.' Idon stopped pacing and fixed the druid with a stare.

'Very well Morcant, you play both sides and keep your precious body and mind safe, but at least advise me as to what you think I should do now?'

'My Lady, I would send for Lord Perris. Tell him that his father is gravely ill and his own ambition to succeed as Chief will bring him running here. His presence and his power will subdue any talk or discussion of appointing a new Chief. In the meantime, word needs to be sent to Lord Ferrax so that he may return and, in time, succeed his father.'

Idon stood for a moment and eyed the druid as if she were considering all the angles to his advice, including any way in which Morcant's plan would benefit himself. Eventually she bowed her head and spoke.

'I wronged you druid, and for that I apologise, you truly have the best wishes of the tribe in your heart and I am grateful to you for this advice. I cannot leave Sisal and so will entrust the arrangements to you. Who do you plan to send as messenger to my sons?'

'My Lady, I shall send Buldan on a fast horse to Lord Perris and I propose that we should send the girl Ancastia, under the protection of the merchant Corillun, to Gaul to seek out Lord Ferrax.'

'The girl?'

'Yes my Lady. She will attract much less attention than a warrior, she has intellect sufficient to discover the whereabouts of Lord Ferrax and she has the gods with her to detract some of the more unwelcome attention that a woman may face.'

Idon had no liking for Ancastia, and no time for the druid that fawned over her every moment and thus, seeing the opportunity to be rid of the girl and her distractions, she readily agreed to the plan. Morcant turned and left the round house, calling for Buldan as he went.

Sisal lay on the bed, staring at the ceiling with a half-smile on his face, the loyal dog putting his muzzle in his master's hand for both attention and reassurance.

With Buldan and Perris

With the authority of both Idon and Morcant, and with fear of being too late, Buldan rode the horse hard and within the day the exhausted beast, white with sweat, had deposited the warrior at the gates of Perris' fortress. He was immediately challenged and told to state his business, and he in turn demanded to speak to Perris. There was a lengthy delay during which Buldan saw various faces appear at the wall before the gate opened and Perris strode out.

This was a very different Perris to the man that Buldan had last seen. His eyes were bloodshot and seemed to dart left and right as if searching for something, or fearful of an attack; there was a nervous twitch in a finger of the left hand, and Perris had put on weight. He looked somehow slower.

'Buldan! It is you' greeted Perris.

'Lord' acknowledged Buldan simply. 'I regret that I bring sad news of your father, and I am required by your mother and the druid to hasten you to his side.'

'I see' said Perris simply. 'Will he live?'

'In the hands of the gods sire, but if it were not felt to be urgent I would not have been sent.'

'True. Come in while we make preparations then. I will show you what we have built.' Perris turned and hollered for Storril who came at a run to do his masters bidding.

'Storril, prepare my horse; see to it that Buldan's animal is rested and fed. We leave at first light tomorrow for my father's home.'

'Yes my Lord' said Storril 'er...........'

'What?'

'A man of your status Lord should travel with at least one servant. To fail to do this would demonstrate weakness' said Storril. Perris considered this for a moment.

'A good and loyal observation Storril. Bring a third horse and prepare to ride with us.'

'Very good my Lord.' The man hurried away while Perris put his arm round Buldan's shoulders and led him into the fortress. Gargonstus had said that the fort was his masterpiece, and once inside, Buldan could see why. The fortifications were strong, the round house imposing and substantial and there were other huts and barns for the storage of food and goods. The warrior in Buldan tried to imagine taking the fortress in battle and eventually had to admit defeat. Without an army of thousands he could not see a way of overrunning the defences.

'Very impressive Lord Perris' said Buldan appreciatively. 'When Gargonstus told me..............'

'Gargonstus may have dug holes and cut timber but I designed the place and had it built' said Perris, cutting across the conversation.' This is mine, this is Caer Perris!' He threw his arms wide and turned on the spot encompassing the whole construction. Buldan saw a mother and child approaching Perris, the child, a babe in arms, was swaddled in fur; the woman small, dark and attractive.

'Perris? Bring your guest to our home' she said simply before turning and walking back the way she had come.

'My woman Halen' explained Perris simply, 'and my son' he added.

'But Lord, you already have a woman' said Buldan forgetting himself in his confusion. 'Caeryl still lives and dutifully awaits you at the home of your father.' There was a rasping sound and instantly the point of a sword was at Buldan's throat.

'Here, I am Lord and Master, Buldan, and my word is the law for these people. Don't ever question me or my actions again or your head will be the first on my walls.' Perris, for all his appearances belied it, had lost none of his speed or his aggression. Buldan swallowed loudly and nodded an acquiescence. The sword was withdrawn and sheathed and Perris stalked away from a shocked Buldan who remained rooted to the spot. He had no doubt in his mind that Perris would have killed him without a moment's hesitation.

Buldan was only half aware of Perris shouting and gesticulating and the hapless Storril rushing to do his master's bidding. He saw Perris approach the woman, kiss the child gently, and talk with her in low tones so he could not overhear what was being said before the two of them went into the round house. Storril came walking towards Buldan.

'All is ready for us to leave tomorrow morning' he said, his eyes cast to the ground. 'I have seen your horse turned out into one of our fields to graze and rest, he is a fine animal and will be ready to ride again by the time we leave. My master has his own beast of course.'

'Can you ride?' asked Buldan pointedly looking at Storril's missing hand

'I can' said the man simply 'but I cannot ride and fight, so I am gladdened that you are with us.' Storril walked away.

'You weren't that good a fighter when you weren't riding' muttered Buldan wondering why Perris kept the man at all. Seemingly left to himself, Buldan wandered around Caer Perris, admiring what he saw, and inhaling the clean, salt-laden air on the seaward side. Walking through the gate he saw a ship in the harbour unfurling her sail which caught the wind with a crack as the material pulled taught. With the keen eyesight of a fighting man, Buldan could just discern the slim figure of a girl on the deck; a figure familiar to him, yet denied him. The girl turned to look at the land and Buldan recognized the face. Ancastia was leaving for Gaul and she grabbed the wooden rail as the boat leaned over with the force of the wind. Buldan spat into the water and hoped she was gone for good.

The night was comfortable, the guest house warm and dry, and in the morning Storril brought a dish of dried berries, a flat bread and a wooden beaker of milk. Storril told Buldan that his master was still asleep but that he intended to wake him shortly and they could be on their way.

Sitting up on his bed, Buldan began to appreciate the efficiency of Storril but was neither surprised nor terribly amused when he heard Perris bellowing in complaint at the poor unfortunate man. There was a sound of crashing and Buldan could imagine breakfast being spread all over the round house. Then there was the piercing sound of a child crying and finally Perris hollering for Halen to tidy the mess and for Storril to fetch the horses. Seizing upon this as his cue to depart, Buldan emerged into the weak grey light that marked the start of the day.

'We leave now' said Perris as if any delay had been Buldan's fault.

'Yes Lord' acknowledged Buldan, keen to keep the peace as Storril lead the three horses towards them. Buldan looked over his own horse with a critical eye but he could find nothing to complain of. The horse was fed and rested and its ears pricked forward, listening intently. Perris still had his favourite black horse who stopped and patiently waited for his rider. Perris threw himself on to the animals back and with a shout he kicked the beast into a canter leaving Buldan and Storril to follow behind. Once clear of the fort, Perris let the horse gallop and the three men rode hard towards the north and the fading Chief Sisal.

Ancastia stood at the rear of the ship watching her land recede from view. Corillun had wrapped her in a cloak of leather to both keep her dry and warm and she appreciated the consideration. The trader has also appointed Forrun, his warrior, as her protector and she had already noticed the lascivious looks of one particular crewman enough to hope that this sea journey was short. She heard footsteps on the wooden deck and turned to see Corillun standing next to her.

'Fear not child, you shall soon return. Forrun will help you find Lord Ferrax.' When Ancastia did not respond, he continued as realisation dawned. 'But it is not this voyage that troubles you?'

'No. This land faces danger, for where Sisal has brought peace and prosperity, his passing will bring bloodshed and battle.' The young woman spoke simply and without emphasis, she was simply stating facts as she saw them. Corillun looked at her for a moment.

'But while Sisal lives there is hope?' Ancastia smiled, a gesture that did not reach her eyes and one that managed to convey pity rather than joy.

'Lord Sisal is as good as dead already. The gods that could have saved him will not go to that place while the evil spirit prevails.' She walked away, leaving Corillun to look at the grey green sea churned by the passing of his sturdy ship.

With Perris

A light drizzle fell, insistent and incessant, gently soaking everything and making the ground slippery and dangerous. Buldan, who loved this kind of weather slowed his horse to a trot, and Storril did likewise. It was a sensible precaution but Perris, for a short time at least, rode on, pushing his horse to its limit, heedless, or maybe just uncaring, of any risk to beast or rider. Eventually however, even the young Lord, sensing that he was alone, pulled the horse up and sat waiting for his companions to join him.

When they came within view, Perris began shouting.

'Why do you stop?' Buldan looked at the young man, his hair and beard were wet; droplets of water clinging to the matted hair that grew on his face, his expression a mixture of anger and confusion.

'We wish to arrive safely and in one piece my Lord' responded Buldan. 'We are no use to your father if we injure ourselves and require care' he added.

'And if he is dead by the time we get there?' snapped Perris. 'What do I care for your safety or the needs of others? We must make haste to hear what my father has to say!' He turned and kicked on, the black horse responding immediately.

'So that's it' said Buldan to Storril. 'Perris once again thinks only of himself and the desperate need to hear his father pronounce him to be his successor.'

'My Lord Perris is a strong man' said Storril simply 'he deals in making things definite.'

'Lord Perris is physically strong, but emotionally he is still a child, with a child's liking for pleasure before everything else. Come on we had better try to keep up.' Buldan and Storril both urged their mounts forward to try to keep the dwindling figure of Perris in sight.

The three men took an enforced break to allow the horses to rest. Freed from the burden of carrying, the animals walked to the lush wet grass and bent their heads to graze. Perris, Buldan and Storril walked to the comparative shelter of nearby trees. There was, they knew, no danger of the gods sending lightning and Storril, somehow started a fire, using kindling he had brought with him and kept dry. The damp forest wood sizzled as it burned, sending plumes of smoke into the sky.

'What food do we have?' demanded Perris. Storril did not speak but from somewhere produced a package tightly wrapped in leaves and then kicked at the fire until he could place the item in the embers. Perris grunted, a sound it would appear of satisfaction or acceptance, and Storril withdrew a short distance away. Buldan ambled over to his young companion, a man with whom he had shared much and fought and killed beside.

'Does Caeryl or your mother know of your woman and child?' Buldan asked. Perris did not respond, and Buldan sat on the ground, leaning against the same tree as Perris. 'I should like a son one day' he continued 'and some land to grow food so I can get old and comfortable and let my son do the fighting.' He smiled and turned his head to look at Perris. 'It seems as if you are ahead of me again my Lord.'

'If I wanted you opinion or your company, I would have requested it Buldan. I want or desire neither.' Perris too turned his head so that he held the warriors gaze. 'Go away and if you ever show me such disrespect again with your familiarity then you will never have sons, or daughters, or land. Do we understand each other?' Buldan scrambled to his feet.

'We do' he said through gritted teeth, as he walked away to join Storril.

'He's changed' announced Buldan simply.

'Of course he has. He now bears responsibility for his family, his land and his people' replied Storril 'whereas we have none of those burdens.' Storril spoke with such simplicity and such certainty that it took Buldan time to collect his thoughts.

'Sisal had all those troubles and more and still remained a good man'

'Had?' asked Storril. 'You said Sisal had those troubles?' Buldan could not help but think of the pronouncement of Ancastia, a woman who he remained infatuated with and who would forever remain out of his reach. When Gadrig and Cwaenog had returned to the hill top fort with Sisal and Idon, they had spoken to Buldan of Ancastia's words and actions and fearful of her power, they had tried to seek out Morcant, but in vain, as he attended to the frail and sick Sisal.

'Sisal is a changed man' said Buldan. 'His strength leaves him and he is fading.'

'All the more reason that the tribe shall have a new Chief then' said Storril, looking pointedly towards Perris. 'I shall return' he announced as he strode off in the direction of the fire.

Storril stabbed at the blackened package with a stick and withdrew the leaves from the fire. Carefully unwrapping them he handed a perfectly cooked fish to Perris who took the food with no visible appreciation. Storril handed over a skin of wine that had been attached to his belt, and Perris fairly snatched it from his hand and drank deeply until the dark red liquid trickled into his beard to join the raindrops. He stoppered the skin and used his fingers to pick the fish from its bones before he put it in his mouth.

'Soon Storril eh? Soon you will be the slave to the Chief of a tribe. How about that. A position of power and influence for Storril the cripple.' Perris chuckled to himself. 'You are a walking reminder to everyone not to cross me Storril, for everyone knows why you only have one hand, and everyone knows that your miserable pointless and pathetic life is in my gift.' Storril knew better than to speak and withdrew from Perris' presence.

'What do we get to eat?' asked Buldan.

'Nothing' replied Storril quietly. Buldan looked at him, and then at Perris, not wanting to believe what he was experiencing. Just three summers ago that young man sitting under the tree would have done anything for the men under his command; he was the one who made sure the men were fed before himself; that they had shelter, water, wine and even women. This Perris was a stranger. He was dangerous, petulant and unpredictable and Buldan began to see a future for the tribe that was bleak and rife with conflict and uncertainty, if Perris were ever allowed any more power than he already had. Buldan had loved Perris as a fighter respects a good commander; he had also despised Ferrax for the same reasoning plus the fact that he had never forgiven the humiliation over Ancastia. But he knew now that he could never serve this version of Perris, he could never fight again alongside the man who now thought only of himself and he was sure that Drullis, Cwaenog, Gadrig and the others would feel the same.

When Perris had eaten enough, he threw the rest of the fish to the ground and called the other two men to him.

'We ride on' he announced. 'Buldan I want you to lead so that the dumb guards at the fort see you first. Storril, you will ride behind me as befits your place in life.' Neither man made a sound, but instead turned and prepared their horses for the rest of the journey. Perris' horse, Buldan noted, tolerated Storril and he began to develop a respect for the strange, subservient one-handed man.

The rest of the journey was uneventful save that a group of men were seen riding on the horizon. They were no threat to the small party and Perris paid them no heed. Buldan kept a watchful gaze on them until they were out of sight and the sun was fading from the sky as Buldan heard the familiar and welcome challenge from the guard on the fortresses lower gate. Although he was recognized, it had long been accepted that if a warrior did not respond to a challenge it meant that there was danger, but Buldan, recognising the voice as Gadrig responded formally that he was escorting Lord Perris to see his father. As the three horsemen approached Gadrig he was about to say something, but the icy look from Buldan stopped him and Perris ignored him completely as he rode towards his father's house.

With Ancastia

The sun rose, its light muted behind low clouds, but nevertheless sufficient for Ancastia to see that the small ship had been moored offshore during the night. The Captain, clearly experienced and knowledgeable, had known enough to bring the ship to this point but his understandable and natural caution led him not to try to make landfall without sufficient visibility.

There were shouts on deck and the sounds of feet running along the wooden planks, the creaking of the mast and then movement as the anchor was hauled inboard and the ship began to move toward the coast of Gaul. Ancastia peered forward and saw a low lying spit of land with a steep hill rising behind it. There was a small settlement at the water's edge and a fort atop the hill with what she assumed would be a commanding view of the land around. There was not much wind and the ship's sail hung limply and the smoke from the fires ashore rose almost vertically into the sky. Ancastia wondered how they would approach the coast and hoped it would be soon. Travel by sea was very uncomfortable and privacy was non-existent.

There was a shout from the Captain, and the crew, to a man, groaned for as Ancastia watched, they unlashed oars from the side of the ship and fitted them into pegs inserted into the bulwark. In a timing called by one of the men, the sailors pulled at the oars and the craft began to move inexorably towards the shore. Ancastia was surprised to see both Corillun and Forrun pulling on an oar, the two men grinned at each other and Ancastia understood that they were in competition with the rest of the crew to drive the pace and prove their worth.

Eventually there was a splash as two of the crew jumped into the shallow water and took ropes ashore that they tied round large rocks that seem to have been placed on the beach for such a purpose. As the ship held fast, the Captain gave a flurry of orders that Ancastia could neither follow nor keep pace with. Corillun and Forrun, their faces red and dripping with sweat approached her.

'Gaul, my Lady' said Corrilun, indicating the land. 'I am going to get you ashore and then you and Forrun can begin your search for Lord Ferrax. He knows the places to look,' he said jerking his head towards the silent warrior 'and he knows to guard your safety with his life.' Forrun nodded and smiled as if such an implied threat were a minor matter, he reached and held his hand out for Ancastia and then guided her to the bow of the ship. He held up a finger to indicate that she should stop and then jumped overboard into the water and held his arms out indicating that he would catch her. For many reasons the young woman was none too keen on jumping and instead climbed down into the strong arms that easily carried her to the land.

Excusing herself, Ancastia took herself off into the nearby trees and took care of private matters before returning to Corillun and Forrun.

'I have asked of my people here my Lady' said Corillun giving a title to Ancastia that he knew would be adopted. She smiled demurely at him, knowing that even a small gesture such as that gave rise to respect, and that respect provided protection. 'They say that there is a man from across the water who trades from the other coast and that may well be Ferrax. It will be a few days ride from here and I will for provide horses for you. Can you ride?' Ancastia nodded her head. When her father was alive she had often sat astride the horse he kept for pulling the chariot he used to transport her and her sister around in.

A plump, friendly-looking woman came strolling down the beach and Corillun's face split into a grin as he held out his arms and embraced her, planting kiss after kiss on her cheeks. The woman laughed and pushed him away.

'Ancastia, this is my woman Karne' he said it with pride, and the woman made to hug Ancastia who was initially hesitant but allowed herself to be hugged, and was then led up the beach to the huts, as Karne prattled on about clothes and supplies once Corillun had told her of the quest to find Ferrax.

As the women departed Corillun turned to Forrun and spoke in low, earnest tones.

'My friend I fear that unless we can find Ferrax then the lands over the water will become Perris's. That boy is trouble and if the land of Sisal falls into conflict then our trade and all we have built will disappear. Find Ferrax and get him across the water and to his father before it is too late.' Forrun grunted his understanding. 'The sooner you are gone on your search my friend, the sooner you can help bring peace to that land.'

By the time the sun had cut through the morning haze and its warmth was felt, Ancastia astride a pony and Forrun on a grey mare were ready to leave. Karne had taken quite a shine to Ancastia and provided her with bags of food and clothing that she had sourced from within their small village. Forrun had loaded his horse and a pack animal with more food, water, wine and animal skins and furs for warmth and shelter.

'May the gods protect you on your search' said Corillun, surprised to see Ancastia close her eyes and mutter something. He arched an eyebrow and she explained that she had placed a protection over their village, much to the apparent amusement of Karne.

With a wave, Forrun led the small party away and towards the steep hill behind the village as Corrillun stood with his woman and watched the horses and riders get smaller and smaller as the distance increased until, eventually they were lost to view. Karne looked at Corrillun who stood, still staring at the last place he had seen them.

'You are troubled?'

'I am' replied the merchant.

'Pah, there are other places to trade and more deals to be done than to be lost' she said lightly and with a smile.

'It isn't that, it's the girl Ancastia. There is something about her.' Rarely had Karne ever heard Corillun talk of another woman, and she was both secure and comfortable in her relationship with him her trust in his was total and so her surprise that he should voice concern for another woman was genuine.

'You have feelings?'

'What? No, stay your mind on such matters. It is something that the druid Morcant said to me, for he believes Ancastia to have powers far beyond his own. He thinks of her as a priestess, able to communicate with the gods and in turn, they can speak through her.'

'This is great power for one so young' said Karne, clearly impressed. 'I could sense that something was special about her of course' she added knowingly.

'Of course you could' replied her man with tolerance as his hand slipped down to her plump rear. She smiled and let him guide her towards their home.

Ancastia meantime was actually enjoying herself; first she was glad to be back on land, secondly, although the accent and intonations were different, essentially the language spoken here was one she could understand and be understood in if the people talked slowly enough, thirdly she had a purpose and a sense a responsibility and freedom that came with it, and lastly, she snuck a look at Forrun sitting comfortably on the back of his horse, lastly she admitted to herself, there was no other man in the world rather be with on this journey.

Forrun caught her looking at him and smiled, it was a genuine smile that went into the eyes, and she quickly looked away, lest he get the right idea. There were some things a girl wanted complete control over.

The horses walked easily along a clearly defined path and when they reached the summit of the hill they saw the wooded land for miles around them. Forrun called a halt and using sign language and the occasional grunt, he indicated to Ancastia the direction in which they would travel and also the time he expected each part of the journey to take. After a drink of water, the two travellers set off again, downhill this time and to the south west.

With Perris, Idon and Sisal

When he arrived at the summit of the hill, Perris handed his horse over to the care of Storril and strode towards his fathers' house. Dutifully he waited at the threshold until his mother approached and then tried to push his way in. Idon stopped him with a fierce glare and ushered him outside. This had all taken place the previous night and Perris could still feel the ringing rebuke in his ears from the old woman as she berated him for never having visited for the past four seasons and his clumsiness at just trying to barge in and see his father who was a very frail and sick old man.

Perris had been denied access to Sisal and told to return in the morning. In the meantime, his mother stressed, he had other duties and responsibilities, and she looked meaningfully at the hut that had been built for himself and Caeryl. Perris snorted in derision and asked for use of the hut kept for guests but his mother would not countenance such a snub from her own flesh and blood and she stood her ground until Perris, biding his time for any fight that may come, agreed to see Caeryl.

He had approached the hut and at first all seemed well. He entered what was of course his own home and saw Caeryl busy preparing some kind of food.

'Welcome' she said with a voice as welcoming as winter ice, and thereafter doing her best to ignore his broody domineering presence.

'You are well?' asked Perris, trying to sound neutral. In truth, though Caeryl was a beauty, the only attraction she had ever held for him was that his brother wanted her. Once that challenge was won, she held no fascination nor interest for him.

'How long will you be staying?' asked Caeryl. She was keeping her tone neutral so that he could never know whether she wanted him there or not. He guessed not.

'I have come to see my father and that will take as long as it does' he responded. Caeryl nodded her head

'I have forgiven him' she announced.

'Who?'

'Your father. I have forgiven him for giving me to you like some kind of sacrifice' said Caeryl, looking directly at Perris as if daring him to say anything against her.

'I am sure he sleeps better for it. No actually, I am quite sure he doesn't give a watery shit what you think woman' responded Perris with bitterness. 'Who do you think you are, spreading your forgiveness as if you count for something.' He stood up and strode towards her. She slowly rose a glared at him. 'You think you have status, an influence?' He laughed, 'yet you are nothing, not much better than a slave and you should be on your knees when I am before you.' Although a head taller than Caeryl, Perris somehow found himself looking into her eyes, and he saw strength and defiance there.

'On your knees I said' commanded Perris through gritted teeth and he grabbed her hair and pulled her down.

'Get off me you pig!' shouted Caeryl and she spat at him, the saliva hitting him just above the left eye so that it trickled down causing him to blink. With his right hand, Perris slapped Caeryl across the face and then began to fumble inside his clothing.

Caeryl looked on as Perris's semi hard cock appeared before her face. She spat at it and he laughed, pushing himself towards her, still holding her hair tight in his left hand.

'Do what women should' said Perris. 'Or do you want a repeat of the first time?'

Caeryl, in apparent compliance opened her mouth and felt him touch her tongue. She was surprised how much he grew so that he filled her and then he began pushing himself in and out of her, the tip of his prick hitting the back of her throat and causing her to retch and gag. Eventually she spat him out, but he was not satisfied and laughing, he forced himself back in only to scream as Caeryl bit hard, her teeth gripping the shaft and holding tight. Perris had nowhere to go, he was too close to her to hit her. He dare not pull out because of the pain and injury it would probably cause and he bellowed in pain as Caeryl reached up and grabbed his balls, squeezing hard. Eventually as he felt he was falling, Caeryl released her grip and herself fell back. Perris sank to his knees with hatred on his face as Caeryl began to kick. She kicked him indiscriminately, not caring where the blows landed, and she put all of her strength into each kick. One caught Perris between the legs and he doubled over howling like a pig stuck by a spear, one caught him in the face and his lip split, but eventually Caeryl tired, her energy waned, though her hatred of the man cowering in front of her did not. She slumped to her knees, she felt dirty and defiled and she regarded Perris with something below contempt.

'Get out of this home. It is not yours and it never will be. I am not yours, and I never will be, so Perris, son of Sisal get it into your head that you are not wanted here today, tomorrow or any other day.'

Perris struggled to a sitting position and regarded her coldly. His pride and his ego were hurt and he had fought many battles both in training and in earnest and had never been so humiliated.

'I want you to know I hate you' said Caeryl. Perris nodded in apparent understanding and then launched himself at her.

It was easy to knock Caeryl off balance, Perris had double her body weight and as she sprawled on the floor Perris was on top of her. With an instinct of self-preservation Caeryl crossed her legs and clamped them together. She had been here before and knew what was in his mind, she knew that he cared nothing for hurting her and that what he wanted to do was humiliate her and break her spirit in that way. She also knew that she could expect no help from anyone else. Within the tribe what went on inside the home was the private business of the family and would never be interfered with.

Perris was pulling at her legs now, his intentions clear and obvious, but Caeryl was fit and strong enough to resist.

'Pathetic, you failure of a man. You cannot make me want you so you have to try to take me like a thief!' She had brought her legs up to give her added protection as she curled into a ball

'I am entitled to take what is rightfully mine' grunted Perris as he tried to turn her over. She struggled but he was too strong and she felt his fingers begin to probe along her buttocks. She brought her legs down to deny him and he seized on the opening and punched her hard in the stomach.

Winded and battered, Caeryl gasped for air, the pain excruciating and Perris seized the chance he had created and stood over her. Viciously he kicked her legs apart and ignoring her protests and pleas he knelt between her thighs and savagely drove himself into her. Caeryl screamed, just as she had done the first time and through her tears all she could see was the savage look of triumph on the face of Perris as he thrust ever harder into her.

When he was finished he wiped himself on her face, the act of final humiliation, immune to the tears that were running freely down her cheeks.

'By rights I should throw you out into the night' he said 'but it would not be right for the new Chief to be in dispute with his woman, so keep your mouth shut and you will stay, but breathe one word of your defiance of me and I will kill you with as much remorse as when I wring the neck of a chicken.' He turned from Caeryl and walked out into the night in search of drink.

All of that happened the night before and just as Ancastia awoke in a new place, so Perris found himself waking in the warmth of the guest house that he demanded he be able to use. His head hurt and he knew he had drunk too much. He recalled his argument with Caeryl and he could remember thumping someone in his drunken stupor to get access to this hut and the warm bed that it afforded him. Slowly as his wits returned he recalled that he was here to see his father and to ensure that his succession as the new Chief went uninterrupted. He sat up on the furs and the world swayed slightly before returning to normal. He bellowed loudly for help and when Storril tentatively peered into the hut, he demanded water. He drank, refilled the horn cup and drank again and again before staggering out of the hut and relieving himself close to the fire in the centre of the village.

Morcant was watching Perris with Gadrig and Buldan, the three of them offended by what they saw and heard. All three had heard Caeryl's screams the night before and were powerless to intervene, but all knew that the young warrior was out of control and that their only hope lay with finding Ferrax and bringing him home.

As they watched, Perris strode over to the round house and noisily proclaimed his presence. Swiftly Idon came outside and pushed her son away accompanied by a verbal dressing down and a wagging finger in his face. Aggression was written large in Perris's eyes, but despite what he was clearly feeling, he held himself in check, for not only was Idon his mother, she was also the woman of the Chief and to lay a hand on her was to invite banishment at best or death at worst. Held in check, and largely by his own fear, Perris stood facing his mother as she called Morcant and the two warriors to her.

'You two' she said to Gadrig and Buldan 'are to guard this house, and he' she pointed at Perris 'is not to enter without my permission. If he orders you to let him past then you are to ignore him. If he tries to fight his way past you then you may use whatever means you can to stop him. You understand? Any means.' Nervously the two warriors assumed guard of the house and Perris, looking at them with contempt, turned and left. 'Morcant' continued Idon quietly, 'Lord Sisal fades, can you help?' The druid considered for a moment. That Idon had asked for his assistance was one thing but her admission that Sisal was not responding to the infusions and herbs that had thus far been used was quite another and more worrying development.

'May I see him?' the druid asked. Idon thought for a moment, then stood aside to let him enter the round house. As Morcant stooped to enter the hut, his sense of smell was assailed by the conflicting and pungent aromas from whatever medications Idon had been using. It was clear that she had sought advice from more than one healer thought Morcant as he carefully examined the remains of whatever had been ground or fired nearby. Morcant stood for a moment and looked at Sisal who lay on his back, staring as if into the stars in the sky. His skin was a pale and almost translucent white, the veins standing out as ribbons of colour; his hair had been falling out and now he only had patches and his teeth had blackened and one or two had even fallen out.

'My Lady' began Morcant respectfully, 'I fear that the time for medicines is past and that Lord Sisal is in the hands of the gods. We can only ask that they are merciful and keep him with us.'

'Your suggestion?'

'A sacrifice to the gods, but the choice is difficult... '

'. . . You mean a person' whispered Idon. Morcant made a calming gesture.

'No my lady, we have rarely indulged in such things and the gods would I fear be angered were we to act in such a way. We need an animal that matches the status of Lord Sisal, this will be a suitable offering to the gods to release the hold they have on him, but even then' he stole a glance at the seemingly helpless old man 'it may already be too late.

Idon ushered the druid outside and away from the two guards. The two of them continued their conversation in hushed but urgent whispers.

'Have you a suggestion?' enquired Idon. 'Do you suggest we slaughter our bull? The ram?'

'No my Lady' said Morcant indulgently, and was about to continue when he was interrupted by Idon, her intensity palpable.

'A stag. The Chief of the animal kingdom.' She looked into Morcant's eyes. 'It would have to be the head of the herd. . .'

'My Lady' said Morcant defying her wrath for his interruption. 'The gods may be pleased with your ardent fervour but I fear that the suggestions you make are too remote to convince them to spare your husband and our Chief. The animal needs to be of value to Sisal, and in that, there really is only one suitable.' The druid looked pointedly back to the hut, where outside the door as if on guard with Gadrig and Buldan, lay Sisal's loyal hound, Avon. As if armed with a sixth sense, he seemed to feel the gaze of Idon and the Druid upon him and his ears pricked up. Idon turned back to the Druid, a smile on her lips.

'We are in accord then Druid. I am of one mind with you on this issue. Make your preparations and create your incantations for I shall call cwnsl this night and the deed shall be done.'

'I agree my Lady. We have no time to lose if we are to have any chance of saving Lord Sisal.' The Druid made his leave and went to his own hut on the edge of the village. Idon stood for a moment and then slowly walked back to see Sisal and tend to his needs. For herself she was determined to do all she could to save Sisal; he was her status, her passage to influence and power far beyond the norm for a woman, even a high bred one such as herself. Under her guidance, her simple minded husband could be bent to her will and together they had forged a tribe of strength and durability.

Sisal was trying to speak, Idon crossed to him urgently, but his whispers were too faint. She leaned over him so that her ear was almost touching his mouth, and could make out the words he spoke.

'Fetch. . . my . . . son. . . and . . . his . . . woman.' Sisal closed his eyes, exhausted with the effort of speech and consciousness and for a moment Idon feared the worst. She stood back, Sisal's chest still rose and fell as he breathed, and she hurried from the hut to find Caeryl and Perris.

***

Caeryl was in her hut, weaving, a favourite pastime of hers. She stood immediately as Idon entered.

'Where is Perris?' she demanded.

'I suspect he is with the pigs as they are the only beasts that will keep him company' replied Caeryl.

'I have no time for your squabbles' said Idon. Normally she and Caeryl got along well, but her fear and her lack of sleep made her irritable.

'I apologise, my Lady. I have not seen him since he tried to gain admittance to my Lord Sisal.'

Idon sighed, 'Forgive my manner child, but Sisal calls for Perris and I fear the worst. Take Buldan and find him, as fast as you can.' Both women hurried from the hut, Idon issuing new orders to the warrior to help Caeryl.

Buldan took charge and having considered matters for a moment, decided that one person above all would know where to look.

'Storril!' bellowed the huge man. 'Storril you animal turd, where are you?' There was a scurrying sound and Storril almost ran toward Buldan. 'Where is my Lord Perris?' shouted Buldan, stopping the servant in his tracks. Storril pointed with his good hand.

'He is with his horse Master Buldan.' The warrior strode purposefully towards the field where the animals were kept, out of sight behind a cluster of homes at the edge of the village, but his way was blocked by Storril. 'I cannot let you go to my master' he said pushing against the muscular bulk of the warrior.

'Get out of my way Storril' growled Buldan, but the servant stood his ground.

'My master is indisposed and not of fit mind to . . .' Storril went flying as Buldan pushed him out of the way and strode on. Storril clambered to his feet and hurried after Buldan but was stopped by Caeryl, who placed a hand on his chest. Storril pointed uselessly.

'But he's. . . my master is . . .'

'Drunk?' finished Caeryl. Storril hung his head and nodded. 'Storril, your loyalty does you credit, but Lord Sisal has called for Perris and whatever state he is in is not important now.' She was cut off by a bellow of rage and the sound of a scuffle. Voices were raised, indistinct and one of them almost animalistic. Before she could approach however, Caeryl saw Buldan coming back round the side of the Druid's hut half carrying a struggling Perris. He continued past the impressed young woman, half dragging a nonsensical Perris and she was sure she spotted Buldan getting one or two punches in for good measure. She followed until Buldan approached Idon waiting at the entrance to her home; she looked at Perris with thinly disguised contempt, and Storril bustled away, eager to be somewhere else.

'Buldan' commanded Idon, 'release Lord Perris.' Buldan complied and Perris crumpled to the floor like a sack of grain, groaning, but whether from the drink or the treatment he had received she neither knew nor cared. Idon carefully considered her position, and knew that she had no choice. She knew that Sisal was to name his successor and to retain her status and influence she had to ingratiate herself with the man who was likely to be her new Chief. Against all protocol she knelt down next to Perris, and to the surprise of all present, but particularly Caeryl, she cradled his head in her lap, talking softly.

'Caeryl, you must stay, but the rest of you leave us.' A small group of people had gathered. If asked they would have feigned concern for Lord Perris but in reality they were looking for gossip at the state of the young Lord. Buldan ushered the people away and then took station at a respectful distance.

'My son, my son' said Idon gently, rocking Perris and stroking his hair. 'Your father has called for you and Caeryl.' She let the words sink in, knowing that Perris was astute enough, even in his befuddled state, to work out the importance of what was being said. She felt his body tense and knew that he had heard her. 'For the sake of your father, your Chief and your Lord' she continued 'rouse yourself and regain your wits and show him the respect due to him.' Perris lay still for a while and then made to get up. Idon helped him and he stood swaying a little, but the focus was returning to his eyes. Caeryl moved forward, but Perris shoved her away and staggered off away from the hut. Idon and Caeryl watched him walk towards a trough of water kept for the animals and then bend to stick his head in. Perris straightened up, vomited copiously on the ground, dunked his head once more into the trough and walked back to his mother, a cruel smile on his face.

Idon turned and held back the skins that covered the entrance as first Perris and then Caeryl entered and walked over toward the recumbent Sisal.

'Father' said Perris gently, 'I am come as bidden. I come to hear you pronounce me as your heir, and to rule in your place.' Caeryl looked at Idon who rolled her eyes. Sisal stayed still save for a twitch at the corner of his mouth that could have been the ghost of a smile.

'Father' said Perris, louder now but still respectful, for all he had ever wanted would happen within the next few moments.

Sisal's eyes flickered for a moment and then opened.

'My son. He lives' he gasped, his voice weak. He held put his hand in a gesture unseen by Perris. Caeryl, knelt by his side and took the bony hand, its skin as brittle as tree bark, in her own. Sisal turned to look at her.

'Are you with my son?' he asked. Caeryl nodded, too overawed to speak. 'I wronged you girl' said Sisal, turning his head away. 'I tried to come between you and Ferrax, your union was blessed by the gods but I thought I knew better . . . I am glad if all is resolved. . .' his voice trailed away. Caeryl looked to Idon, her face displaying the uncertainty she clearly felt. Idon gestured that she should speak but Perris leaned over his father and shook him by the shoulder.

'Father. Father it is I, Perris, your son. You must name me your heir, the gods demand it and the people need certainty at this time.' Sisal stirred.

'Perris? Too ambitious Perris, too strong for your own good. No, my heir shall be my son who lives and that is my final word.' He slipped easily into unconsciousness. Perris turned on his mother and Caeryl.

'You heard him, his successor is his son that lives. Me. I live and I am his son.' He turned to walk out into the daylight, presumably to pronounce himself the heir to the fortune and lands of the great Sisal.

'Your brother lives too Perris' said Idon quietly. 'Across the sea it is true, but he lives.' Perris stopped in his tracks and slowly turned to face his mother.

'You heard what he said, did you not? My father asked if Caeryl was with his son? Well she is with me, a union of his choosing lest it be forgotten. He named his successor as his son who lives. What do you think he meant by that? Lives in Gaul or lives in our own lands?'

'Sisal lives, and while he lives he remains Chief. He did not name you as successor, but the point is irrelevant while he still has breath. You will not defy me in this Perris, for to do so will see you banished and never rule this land. Tonight there will be a ceremony, a sacrifice to the gods so that your father, your Chief, may live and be restored to health. You will play the part of the dutiful and subservient son or I shall denounce you and your claims and shall claim the right to speak on behalf of Sisal.'

'You have no such right . . .'

'Do not tempt me to test the resolve of our people Perris.' Idon spoke quietly but forcefully. 'We shall await any further words of your father, in the hope that he clarifies his mind and speaks his will. You may leave' she added ominously to preclude any further argument. Perris stood for a moment in confusion, then turned and left the round house. When he had gone, Idon turned and looked at Sisal, the unspoken hope and fear both clear in her expression.

With Ancastia

With Forrun's guidance and protection, Ancastia now stood looking down over the coast from a small rise. She could see the smoke from cooking fires rising over two settlements. She turned to the warrior and pointed at one of the villages. He shrugged his shoulders as if the decision were without logic or thought.

'That village has a moored boat and another on the beach Forrun' she said with patience, 'and where there is a boat, there is likely to be a trader.' Forrun smiled, he was exhausted and tired of being constantly vigilant. Ancastia had driven the two of them hard, only resting where necessary, intent solely on finding Ferrax. 'Come on' she said and was about to kick her horse forward when Forrun grunted and she stopped. He indicated that they should rest for a while, using the signs and sounds that they had developed to indicate that the best time to approach the village would be before nightfall, for if they went now and Ferrax did not want to be found, he could easily put to sea and disappear.

'You are weary Forrun?' He nodded and she understood. 'Constantly alert and watching over me. I apologise.' She jumped from her horse and started to collect firewood as Forrun sat with his back against a tree and closed his eyes and was soon asleep.

As the daylight waned, side by side the two travellers made their way carefully down to the sea and approached the village, stopping to hail the sentry that stood by the wooden palisade. After a brief explanation by Ancastia they were escorted to the centre of the village where they were met by the Head Man. Standing to one side was Ferrax, but etiquette needed to be preserved, and the first problem was that the Head Man addressed himself to Forrun and was discomfited that Ancastia spoke in reply. She explained that Forrun was mute and asked permission to speak in his stead and that she be allowed to converse with Master Ferrax. She avoided use of the term 'Lord' as she was not aware of what status he held within this community or even what he had told them about himself.

'Ferrax is a loyal and trusted ally of this community' said the Head Man, his deep voice one that would command respect. 'He is neither here as a captive, nor as part of our tribe and your request is properly addressed to him. All I ask however is your word that nothing you have to discuss will damage our community, and that any weapons you hold are left with me. They will be returned to you when you leave.' This was expected, and Forrun, with a display of courtesy elaborately removed his sworn and handed it hilt first to the Head Man who took the weapon and weighed it in his hands.

'This is perfectly balanced' he said with some admiration in his voice. 'Such a weapon speaks well of its owner.' Protocol was being followed, compliments exchanged and trust built. Ancastia spoke next.

'We come to speak with Master Ferrax on a matter of interest to himself and I can assure you of no harm to you and your people.' Ferrax responded at the invitation of the Head Man that he was happy to speak with Ancastia and that he knew her to be kind and possessed of a wisdom far beyond her years. The three of them were afforded the use of the communal hut where they could talk undisturbed.

When they were alone, and without preamble, Ancastia told Ferrax of her mission, of his father's health and his mother's desire that he should return home at once to claim his birthright. Ferrax fell silent for a moment and looked to the floor, Ancastia caught Forrun's eye and smiled reassurance to him.

'What news of Caeryl?' asked Ferrax, his voice filled with a mixture of apprehension and hope. He slowly raised his head and fixed Ancastia with an unblinking look into her eyes.

'My Lord,' began Ancastia 'I do not know much, but she lives, she is well and is a support to your mother.'

'And my brother?'

'Your brother lives mainly in his own fortress, away and apart from everyone.' A hint of a smile crossed Ferrax's face. 'Yes Lord' said Ancastia uttering the words Ferrax longed to hear. 'Lord Perris and Caeryl live away from each other. She is one of your people my Lord, and they need you.'

'Wait here' commanded Ferrax as he strode from the hut. He returned later and announced that the boat on the shoreline was his, that he had paid the Head Man of the village for stores and provisions and that his crew were even now readying the vessel to put to sea. They would sail at night as his crew knew these waters and would be home within five sunsets. Ferrax was animated and even enthusiastic under the surface it was clear, but he maintained a solemn disposition out of respect to the threat to the life of his father.

Forrun, looking, on felt a pride towards Ancastia, and a need to protect her that outweighed all other loyalties he had ever felt. He was surprised when a small cool hand slipped into his and gave it a squeeze. He looked down at the girl who looked into his eyes and nodded.

As the moon rose, casting a silver dappled light on the water, the boat's sail rose and she turned as the steering oar bit into the gentle swell. Ferrax was going home.

The Fortress of Sisal

As night fell, the whole village was gathered around the fire pit. The occasion was solemn as befitted the giving of a sacrifice to appease the Gods to spare the life of the once powerful Lord Sisal. For most of the villagers, Sisal had been the only Chieftain they had known and his reputation had spread wide among the chalk hills as a wise and noble ruler who was never afraid to use force, but only when necessary.

In truth, most of the gathered people assumed that Sisal's time had come and that it was inevitable that he would leave this place and take his seat among the gods for all time. However, they retained the spark of hope and this, together with their belief in the power of Morcant the Druid, created an air of expectation bordering on excitement, as parents pushed their children to the front of the small crowd gathered round the bright flames of the fire.

Standing with his back to the Chiefs' hut, in stark white robes, stood Morcant, his arms outstretched for silence. Behind him, with heads bowed, stood Idon, Perris and Caeryl. When all attention was on the Druid he spoke, his voice slow and clear.

'We gather this night to call on the gods to release our Lord and our friend Sisal from the demons that afflict him so terribly, and so that the gods may be pleased we offer a life in exchange for that of Sisal.' Morcant paused for a second and then reached down to an earthenware bowl at his feet. 'To clear our minds so that we may better feel the presence of the gods, I have prepared this potion and all must drink of it. Mothers, be assured that it is safe for your children but only a wetting of the mouth will be necessary.' He passed the bowl, as tradition called, to idon and she drank and passed it to Perris who in turn passed it to Caeryl. Morcant retrieved it and asked Buldan to take it round the assembled villagers.

Idon felt her head go light and became slightly unsteady on her feet. Her eyelids were heavy and she craved sleep. The words of the Druid bored into her consciousness.

'Gods of life and gods of air. Gods of land and of water and gods of fire. Come together and witness the life of Sisal. See the wisdom and understand the benefit of this life to the people before you, all ask you to release Sisal from the bounds in which you tie him.'

At this point one of the women began wailing, the cry was soon taken up by others and was quite a normal reaction to the potent potion of fermented fruit and the paste formed from the caps of the brown mushrooms [*panther caps – cause hallucinations*] Morcant stood silently, arms outstretched beseeching the gods as the ululations swelled and fell back in volume. Morcant had the people in his hands and he slowly turned around to take in Idon, Perris and Caeryl. All were showing the signs of intoxication that he desired as he called for the sacrifice to be brought forward.

Idon pulled the frightened dog by a strip of leather tied round its neck and handed the animal to Morcant. The Druid once again raised his arms to the skies and called upon the gods to accept the life of this loyal servant of Sisal in exchange for the man. Morcant began to sway from side to side, knowing that his audience would do the same thing, the motion enhancing the effect of the potion. The bowl had been returned and placed at the feet of the druid who now encouraged the dog to drink the dregs, where the ground mushroom was more concentrated. The dog sat, and then as its eyes glassed over, it lay on the ground, panting.

Morcant withdrew a knife from inside his robes, a ceremonial double edged blade reserved for sacrifice that shone gold in the dancing firelight. The Druid could feel the heat building within the metal as he thrust the blade into the fire and turned to the prostrate animal.

Morcant stood upright and turned towards the dog but stopped, his mouth agape in shock and surprise, his arm with the viciously sharp blade, still raised aloft. Sisal stood at the entrance to his hut, an accusatory arm raised with a finger pointing at the Druid.

'Stop!' bellowed the Chieftain with power that his voice had not held these past two summers. The noise and the movement stopped and all eyes turned to look in awe at Sisal. 'You will not harm my animal. This is my command as your Chief' roared Sisal in fury, the finger still pointing at Morcant. 'Druid, you presume a power that is not yours to take! You will leave this place and you are banished, never to return. Be gone!' It was one of those moments where everything stops; not a sound could be heard and Morcant stood, his features flickering in the firelight, but his expression of absolute terror fixed as his power and influence ended with the command of Sisal.

Idon was the first to react as with a subdued scream she threw herself towards Sisal who stumbled into her arms where he died without uttering another sound. Idon gently lowered Sisal's body to the ground as everybody pushed forward and the situation was descending to chaos as she slowly stood upright and held her arms out commanding the people to stop. They obeyed, sensing the power and affording her the respect due to her status.

'Sisal is dead' she sobbed. 'His last command was that Morcant should leave this place and that command will be obeyed without delay so as not to offend the gods where the spirit of Sisal now sits.' She fixed a stare on the Druid. 'Be gone from this place. Buldan, you will ensure that Sisal's wish is carried out.' Morcant made to speak but was silenced with a glare from Idon, who addressed the people present.

'Sisal named his successor before he died and even now our new Chief will be returning home. Ferrax, the first son of Sisal will rule these lands.' Her words were a deliberate and calculated affront to Perris who stood close to his father's corpse, impotent and enraged.

'Gargonstus? Help me move my Lord Sisal and in the morning we shall begin construction of his tomb.' The huge man moved forward and gently picked the body of Sisal from the floor and, muttering a brief word of excuse, pushed past Perris and took him into the Chieftain's hut.

There was another moment of silence before the babbling of voices filled the night. Buldan was standing next to Morcant as Perris drew his sword and screamed as he went to strike the insensible Avon lying on the ground. There was a ringing of metal on metal and sparks flew as Perris' sword clashed with Buldan's. The warrior had acted with speed and on instinct and the two men were locked in a contest of strength.

'Do not do this my Lord' grunted Buldan. 'The dog is protected by your father and that is powerful magic to be offending.' Buldan looked into Perris's eyes and saw the fear, the loathing and the hatred and thanked the gods that Sisal had named Ferrax.

With a growl, Perris pushed Buldan away and as the warrior stood over the dog, Perris pointed his sword at the man and spoke

'You will regret getting in my way Buldan. You exceed your authority and your power.' He spat on the ground, turned and strode away calling for Storril. The people watched him go and soon after the drum of hooves on the ground announced his departure, the hapless servant walking slowly away behind him.

Buldan turned to Morcant; the druid looked somehow shrunken and smaller.

'You have no choice Morcant' explained Buldan gently. 'Sisal spoke his last commands and Idon is duty bound to follow them, no matter what her loyalties and no matter what her own feelings may be. Go quietly and in time there may be a chance of return, but make a stand and I am bound by my honour to my Lord Sisal to strike you down.' Morcant looked beseechingly at Buldan but understood and accepted the words he heard.

'You will allow me a small time to collect some possessions?'

'Of course' replied Buldan 'and I will see you safely away from this place.'

'The girl, Ancastia. . .' began Morcant. 'When she returns, her powers will have increased and she must be made to stay and serve our people.' They were interrupted by the soft thump of the dogs tail on the ground as he regained his wits. It was taken by the people with an audible gasp as a sign of approval from the spirit of Sisal.

Part II

Ferrax

The Next Full Moon

Sisal was buried in his chamber beneath a grand mound that befitted his status. To settle his passage through to the gods he was provided with everything he could need and for the full passage of the moon, as was the custom of the tribe, a fully armed warrior would stand guard day and night.

Idon, both by the power of her own personality and by general consensus, had assumed day to day control of the people and the fortress, and there was as much a feeling of relief that Perris had stayed away as there was anticipation that Ferrax would return and assume his rightful place.

An astute woman, Idon had rejected the suggestion that she adorn herself with the accoutrements of a Chief and instead she dressed simply and unobtrusively, standing quietly as the men of the tribe rolled a heavy stone over the entrance to the mound that held the remains of Sisal, and covered it with earth. Members of the wider tribe, from settlements all over the land had travelled to the Fortress to pay respects and mark the death of the great man. A crowd far larger than had ever been seen during Sisal's life attended upon him now in death, and all, naturally looked to Idon for leadership and guidance.

Before the procession from the Fort to the burial ground, Idon had confided in Caeryl that she was tired and that she longed for the return of her eldest son when she could live a simple life. The death of Sisal had knocked her hard and she had not realised how much she had relied upon him, even his presence, as a force for good and stability.

Caeryl now, standing at the burial ground, instinctively understood Idon's need for solitude and called for the people to return to the Fortress. Animals had been slaughtered for a feast, and drink was brewed and fermented. This night songs would be sung, lamentations made and the memory of Sisal would be honoured with stories and verse.

As the crowd turned, almost as one, a group of men on horses rode into the burial ground. There was an audible gasp of shock as not only did the men not dismount but they carried weapons and shields; an affront to the dead Chief and the tribe. The leader of them men, an unmistakable figure, held up an arm to signal his men to stop and, pushing people aside with the flanks of their horses they fanned out in a semi-circle behind him.

'You are not welcome here with arms' called Idon, her voice clear and strong.

'I will act as I choose' replied Perris 'for I have come to claim my rightful place as the head of this tribe.' He spoke loudly enough that everyone present heard the proclamation.

'Your father named . . ' began Idon.

'My father named his son as his successor. Look around you mother, do you see any more of your brood?' Perris paused for effect and then turned his horse to face the people. 'My father named his son as his successor and as his son I claim that right unless any here shall challenge me?'

There was a movement within the crowd who parted to let a youth stand in front of them. He stared at Perris with an unblinking gaze before he spoke, his voice young and high

'You defile this place with your lack of respect and yes, for my birthright, I will challenge you.'

Perris laughed and looked down at the boy, dressed as he was in a fine wool cloak. 'And who might you be my little egg?'

'I am Marrad, son of Sisal' called the boy in his thin voice. 'If leading our people is your birthright, then it is also mine, and in defiance of you, I claim that right.'

'You are not armed boy' said Perris.

'I respect our laws and traditions' called the boy. 'Just as you insult them.' It was a calculated insult designed to enrage Perris, but he looked down at the brother he hardly remembered and spoke kindly.

'You realise what you are asking? That we fight to the death?' The boy nodded, his stare once again unblinking. 'And you realise that you won't win. You would be better served swearing your allegiance to me now before this gets out of hand.'

'I came here to pay respect to my father, a man the people admired and respected. If I submit myself to your rule then I dishonour him and I condone the disrespect you show.'

'You make a grave mistake, but that is to be expected of one so young' said Perris. 'Withdraw now and no harm will come to you. I do not fight children.'

'Gadrig!' called Idon, and the man came forward. In truth he, as guardian of the burial, should have been the only armed man present. 'Stay at my side' she commanded as she strode over to Perris.

'This will stop now' commanded Idon. 'There has been one death that has caused untold grief and there will not be another. Perris you are a fool if you think you can enforce a rule on the people that they do not want. You may kill a few of us, but the numbers here will drag you and your men from your horses and rip your arms from your bodies.' She turned to her younger son and her tone softened somewhat 'Marrad, you spoke well and with dignity, but this fight is not yours and you will walk away with the rest of our people.' Marrad made to object but a glare from his mother stopped him.

'Go Perris. Leave this place and we can part in peace for you have outgrown our tribe and you become a stranger to us. You could strike me down now but it would get you nothing.'

'I will gain my destiny mother, one way or another' said Perris. 'It will spill much less blood if you yield to me now and acknowledge me as your new Chief.

'It will not happen Perris, not today, not tomorrow, not in my lifetime.' Perris made to draw his sword but saw Gadrig's hand move to the hilt of his own sword and thought better of it.

'Tell my snivelling brother that if he ever decides to show his weak face again, I shall be ready and waiting for his challenge. Until then you may keep your fortress but the lands and the rewards are mine and mine alone. If you value life then do not seek to overrule me.' He kicked his horse and, followed by his men, left the burial ground. Gadrig walked to the boundary to stand guard, leaving the grieving and angry Idon who remained outside Sisal's tomb, tears streaming down her lined face repeating the same words over and over.

'Sisal, send him home, send Ferrax to me.'

The Coast

The sun was setting as the tide reached its height and Ferrax jumped into the shallow cold water that lapped at the shore of his homeland. He heard the splash as the immensely strong Forrun heaved the anchor stone over the side of the vessel. Ferrax turned to start collecting wood to build a fire, but his attention was drawn back to the boat as a cacophony of good natured whistles from the crew accompanied the sight of Forrun very gently carrying Ancastia to dry land. He put her down on the ground and turned to the crew, bowing low with a huge smile splitting his face. The voyage home had been a happy trip, fuelled as it was by Ferrax's eagerness to return and by the blossoming relationship between the girl and the warrior.

Ferrax stood for a moment, his feet wide apart, his hands on his hips as he took huge a lungful of air. Now that he was in his own land there was a steadily dawning realisation that he would be the Chief of all the people and that recognition was tinged with the sadness at the likely demise of his father.

One by one, Ferrax's crew dropped over the side of the boat and waded ashore. Very soon a fire was built and lit and in celebration of the homecoming four fowl were taken from their wooden cage on the ship and were soon killed gutted and plucked and were now turning on a wooden spit over the crackling flames. Ferrax sat in contemplative silence until Ancastia knelt beside him.

'Lord Ferrax, we give thanks that you are home safely' she said somewhat formally, 'and when your family learn of your arrival they too will celebrate.' She paused, but Ferrax knew there was more she wanted to say and waited. 'When I left this land my Lord, there was division and anger in the eyes of men. These people that live here Lord need you, your wisdom and your strength. Do not let anything divert you from that cause Lord Ferrax.'

'I was thinking of Caeryl' replied Ferrax with a diffident smile. 'As I often do.'

'When I last saw her she was well Lord' replied the girl simply. 'She has no love for your brother and hates him as much as she loves you.' Ferrax laughed, not a pleasant sound but a hollow, pained bark.

'She is gone to me, she was given to and taken by my brother, a man I loved more than any other but who is now a stranger to me. I can never forgive what he has done, yet . . .' The words tailed off and Ferrax looked up at Ancastia whose attractive open face, free of guile and subterfuge made men speak and act as they never would around anyone else. 'Yet' said Ferrax with more energy in his voice, 'I do not blame my father for his idiocy that led us here. Is that strange, or wrong, or even the attitude of a mad man?' Ancastia smiled, reached out and held his hand.

'You understand that your father's actions were influenced by his need to do the right thing. I believe' she said earnestly 'that he knows he did wrong by you and Caeryl. Your brother on the other hand is influenced by all that is wrong with men and in your heart this is why you cannot forgive him. It is not a bad thing Lord Ferrax.'

'My gratitude to you Ancastia' said Ferrax nodding his head 'you are wise beyond your years. Tell me, what are your plans beyond our present journey?'

'You are a true leader of men Lord Ferrax' announced the girl 'to be weighed down with responsibility and yet concerned about the fate of one woman.' She smiled at him and diffidently he grinned back and shrugged his shoulders, the man coming out from the shadow of his destiny. 'My future and my fate' announced Ancastia 'is tied forever with Forrun. Wherever he goes, I shall follow, not from duty but from love.' She turned to look at the warrior and when she looked back the reflection of the flames shone in her eyes. She smiled at Ferrax and in a parody of him shrugged her shoulders and the two of them laughed together.

By the time the light of the day subsided to darkness the attention of the small group on the shore was drawn to the rhythmic beat of horse's hooves on the soft ground. Ferrax looked and saw that his boats crew and Forrun all had swords drawn and had formed a line facing the direction of the sound. Ancastia went to stand beside Forrun but he shook his head and gently ushered her back to the fire. Taking command he indicated to one of the crew and Ferrax that they should guard the rear in case there were more horsemen working their way around them. Listening carefully Forrun held up four fingers to indicate the number of horses and shortly that number of warriors rode along the beach, initially at a canter but slowed to a walk when they saw the men facing them.

'Identify yourselves!' commanded the leader, a large, dark haired man, so confident of his own ability that his weapon remained in his belt. Absentmindedly he patted the neck of his horse.

Ferrax walked slowly through the line of his crew and stood facing the four horsemen. 'My name is Ferrax, son of Sisal!' he called.

'What is your business here' said the man, much to the consternation of Ferrax and his crew. Collecting his wits, Ferrax laughed but to no visible effect on the horsemen.

'I repeat, I am Ferrax, son of Sisal and named by him as the new Chieftain of this land.'

'This land is ruled by Perris, and he slaughters all who oppose him. We saw your fire and came to collect tribute.' Ferrax listened and then spat on the ground.

'Tell my brother,' he paused and pointed to the ground, 'that is all the tribute he will get from me.' There was clear consternation between the four men before the leader spoke again.

'That was an unwise affront to my Chieftain, Ferrax son of Sisal.'

'Lord Ferrax to you.' The leader laughed and spat on the ground himself, a direct insult to Ferrax, before wheeling his horse round and riding away, followed by his companions. Silently Ferrax indicated that they should remain vigilant and his caution was proved prescient when three of the horsemen crashed through the line of trees and charged towards the group around the fire. They never got close and were efficiently hacked down by Forrun and the boats crew. Ancastia stood still and unmoving by the fire, never flinching at the sound of the terrible screams of the dying men.

Ferrax turned and saw the remaining warrior standing by his horse. Sword drawn, Ferrax walked slowly towards the man who stood his ground. 'Tell my brother of this' said Ferrax, 'tell him how his men died needlessly for his pride and his dreams of power.' The man nodded, uttered no words but climbed on to his horse and rode off into the night.

Having arranged a guard, Ferrax sat with his boat's captain and Forrun and made plans for the morning. Unusually the sea gave a double high tide and their boat was still afloat, and so it was decided to spend another night aboard and offshore. The fire was doused and when everyone was aboard, and the anchor stone recovered, the boat was poled out into deeper water where she remained until morning.

***

Ancastia opened her eyes and pulled away from Forrun, blearily she made out the shape of the lookout who was shaking the crew awake. Forrun and Ferrax were instantly alert, a smile of mutual respect passing between them.

'First light Lord Ferrax' whispered the lookout, 'you asked that the crew be woken.'

'Thank you' said Ferrax. He called to the captain, 'take us as far upstream as you can go and the three of us will leave you and make our way to my father. Ferrax looked around him, they were in a wide body of water with both banks just becoming visible. Originally they had landed just north of a river, a place Ferrax knew from his previous visits. If his memory was right then this open water soon narrowed and divided and a decision would be made when they reached that place. The crew, well-practiced and well led, soon had the sail set and the boat tacked its way upstream against the prevailing wind.

As the sun was rising over the horizon, the boat reached the point where the water divided and Ferrax directed the captain to take the right hand course. 'We'll go as far as safety permits and you can land us on the left bank' explained Ferrax. He received a nodded acknowledgment and shortly after the captain leaned on the steering oar and gently guided the boat to the bank explaining that they had run out of room to tack the boat. Ferrax, Forrun and Ancastia said their farewells and the captain agreed to return within four sunsets to the same place to receive further orders. Ferrax knew his man and knew that within those four days he would find something to trade with someone and wished him luck in his endeavours.

'And now we walk' announced Ferrax, setting off on a path that led towards the fortress of his father.

Caer Perris

The exhausted warrior stood in front of Perris; he had ridden through the night and explained his meeting with Ferrax and the slaughter of his men. Perris sat in front of his impressive abode and glared at the man in silence. The warrior was nervous as well he should be, Lord Perris brokered no failure and his retribution on those who failed him was swift and harsh.

After a lengthy silence, Perris called for his horse. 'You will show me where this took place' he announced. The warrior was about to remonstrate, but a glance from Perris made the words stick in his throat.

'Yes Lord' murmured the man asking for a fresh horse that, grudgingly, Perris agreed to provide.

'I warn you it will go bad for you if you are lying' growled Perris.

It had been some time since the death of his father and Perris had instigated a harsh rule on the land. He had paid for armed bands of warriors to enforce his will, collecting tribute and dispensing a violent justice in his name. The method to be used, he left to the men, knowing that they would care nothing for the people and everything for their own reputation and the glint of gold. Quickly, dissent and unrest was dealt with at the sharp end of a blade and Perris gained control over the land and its people.

Perris ordered his men to stay away from both his father's fortress and his burial chamber. It appeared however that his mother and her warriors had confined themselves to the same places, probably out of some misguided respect to the dead Chief, or, more dangerously, to await the return of Ferrax. If Ferrax was to be the catalyst of opposition, then he had to be dealt with swiftly and mercilessly. Perris paused mentally to consider the path he had chosen, that his enemy was his own brother, but just as quickly he dismissed the familial link. Ferrax had run away as Perris saw the situation, and that made him weak and unfit to rule. To Perris, removing Ferrax, however he did it was necessary for the future of the people and more importantly the prestige and prosperity of himself.

Perris looked around and saw Storril leading his horse towards him; the animal's black coat shone, a testament to the work of the hapless one handed man, and Perris grudgingly acknowledged the fact to himself. Not that he would ever admit such a thing to Storril, a man after all that he had defeated in battle and whom he regarded as barely human.

'Why do you take so long to do everything?' growled Perris as Storril approached.

'My apologies Lord' mumbled Storril, his gaze directed to the ground so that he did not see the fist as it clubbed him to the ground, but he both heard the snort of derision for Perris and felt the kick to his midriff that left him doubled in pain. Perris stepped on the prostrate body to heave himself on to the horse.

'Get up and do something useful for once Storril you waste of life' snarled Perris as he kicked the horse's flanks. Storril has the presence of mind to roll away to avoid the hooves as the animal leaped forward. The sound of a second horse told the man that the other warrior was following his Lord out of Caer Perris and along the coast.

Perris rode hard, neither sparing his horse nor the man with him who had not slept. The two men passed settlements where men busied themselves and women hid their children at the sound of their passing; they rode through open country and forest until the horses could take no more and Perris called for a halt. He ordered the warrior to water the horses at a nearby stream and took a skin of wine and a cooked chicken from a bag Storril had sung over the horse and sat on the ground to enjoy his meal. He offered nothing to the other man.

Perris decided that there had been sufficient rest and the journey resumed, at a slower pace now. He sent the warrior ahead as a scout to assess any danger on the route and kept himself alert, his body conditioned to the effects of wine through his frequent excesses.

Eventually the two men came across the beach where just the day before three of his men had died. Their bodies lay where they had fallen, the wounds black with dried blood and encrusted with flies that fed on the corpses. Apart from the buzzing of insects, the only sound was the gentle lapping of water on the shore, and the scent of death was masked by the salt of the water and the mustiness of the nearby woodland. Perris dismounted and approached the body of a man which lay face-down and used his booted foot to turn the cadaver over. The cut to the head was deep and vicious, slicing through bone and eye to expose the now sand-encrusted grey brain matter within the skull.

'This was not the work of my brother' muttered Perris, 'he fights too nicely and does not possess the strength to leave marks like this.'

'It was the work of a powerful silent warrior My Lord'

'When I want to hear from you, I will ask you' snarled Perris who sat on the sand, his knees drawn up and his elbows resting on them, his bearded chin cupped in his hands The disturbed flies swarmed but he ignored them, thinking as hard as he was about the inevitability of a fight with Ferrax.

'Do you have a brother?' called Perris to the warrior whose name he had never known, nor cared to ask.

'Yes Lord, I had two, but one now lies at your feet.' It was the man Perris had turned over. Perris grunted in acknowledgement.

'So how come you live and he died?'

'The three of them charged at the group of men; they were well organised and well-armed Lord' explained the man. 'I was told to stay out of the fight Lord and to watch and learn.

'How old are you?'

'I have seen sixteen summers Lord.'

'So, as my men were slaughtered, you did nothing but stand and watch' said Perris, his tone dangerous to those that knew him. Sensibly the warrior remained silent. 'I doubt you will see your seventeenth summer you coward. We passed a settlement a while back, three huts and an enclosure for animals. We shall spend the night there.'

By the time the sun had set, Perris was sitting in the Headmans' abode, drinking some fermented concoction brewed for the Head Man, the inhabitants thrown out to sleep elsewhere and the warrior acting as servant to his Lord.

***

Ferrax, Ancastia and Forrun walked for as long as they could along the bank of the river, the water running downstream in the opposite direction. Ferrax had walked ahead of the other two, partly out of a sense of wanting to give them some privacy and partly through his greater sense of purpose in needing and wanting to return home. He was mentally gnawing on a problem that had been troubling him for some time, when he heard a splash and a peal of laughter behind him. He looked round to see Forrun rising from the river, a look of confusion on his face that slowly turned to a rueful smile as he saw Ancastia laughing. Ferrax stood smiling as he watched Forrun wade to the bank and hold a hand out to the girl as if he wanted pulling up the bank. She took it and in one swift movement he grabbed her and pulled her towards him. Her laughter turned to a shriek as she wriggled and struggled to set herself free. Forrun ignored her completely, but did catch Ferrax's eye and winked before he let himself fall back into the water, taking Ancastia with him. Ferrax could not help himself laughing as the two of them emerged from the water, Forrun grinning and Ancastia looking thunderously angry as she now made her way to the bank. Once again Forrun caught hold of her and turned her round, but this time planted a kiss on her forehead and then lifted her as easily as if she were a feather and put her on the low bank. Forrun stood in the water, unmoving and now looking confused. Ancastia turned towards Ferrax to apologise and the new Chief saw Forrun's problem. The water had made Ancastia's robe translucent and almost transparent, leaving nothing to the imagination. Ferrax laughed gently at Forrun's embarrassment, knowing what the warrior was trying to hide, and explained it gently to Ancastia who immediately crouched low to the ground to hide herself, it being her turn to look shocked. Then she seemed to make a decision and walked back into the water towards Forrun who tried to turn away but was held back by the girl. Ferrax was sure that he saw her hand reach out to the man, and before he left them together he saw a look of surprise on the face of the warrior as the outstretched hand clearly found its target.

Later, when Ferrax was resting, the two of them caught up with him, Ancastia explaining carefully, that they had never let him get out of their sight and that Forrun was feeling a sense of wrong over abandoning his duty to protect Ferrax.

'I can look after myself against most men' said Ferrax, 'but I thank you for being close by in case we were set upon. I think however that I am glad you have dried your clothes' he added carefully, failing to make mention of the grass stains on the back of Ancastia's robes. The two lovers looked away for a moment and then the three of them dissolved into a fit of inexplicable but happy laughter.

Later still, as they walked on, Ancastia fell in step beside Ferrax. 'I can see you are troubled again Lord' she said. 'I am sorry if Forrun and myself were the cause.'

'You are not' said Ferrax kindly.

'Then share the burden with one who is good at listening; it was a joy your father found with me before I departed.'

Ferrax did not break stride but turned to face her. 'Very well, I have lands and people that I can rule over. I was born to it and it is my destiny. It may, if my father already sits with the gods, now be my life. That does not trouble me in the slightest. But my heart is ruled by another and I cannot release the pain within me.'

'Caeryl?'

'Yes.'

'Lord, seeking to control that which you cannot is a waste of energy. You cannot know what either of you will feel until you are together, for it is not just about you, but her as well. For all you know she may be just as . . .'

'Terrified?' added Ferrax hesitantly.

'Yes, terrified, that you will not want her, just as you are fearful of her rejection. Put it from your mind and leave it to your feelings my Lord, for they will fly straighter than any spear you can throw.' The two of them walked in silence for a while before Ferrax spoke again.

'Your age and beauty defy your wisdom Ancastia. The wisest women are normally the ugliest and most broken through all they have lived through.'

'I have lived Lord, and now I have loved in a way I never thought could exist. I merely wish that for you too.'

***

As the sun began to move toward the horizon, the three travellers approached the hill atop which sat the fortress of Sisal. It was a very different place than when either of Ancastia or Ferrax had left, and both immediately noticed the burial mound.

'Wait' commanded Ferrax and strode off towards the tomb where his entry was barred by the imposing bulk of Buldan, sword drawn against whoever approached.

'I am Ferrax, son of Sisal' he called and saw the immediate and welcome recognition on the face of the warrior. A huge grin split the man's face before he knelt at the approach of his new Chief.

'Get up Buldan, by the Gods I am pleased to see you.' The two men embraced and both felt a keen sense of relief. For Ferrax it was that the proper respect had been and was being afforded to his father; for Buldan it was because the tribe would now have leadership, direction and strength.

'Lord, there is much to tell you . . .' began Buldan.

'I am sure there is' replied Ferrax, 'but before that would you grant me some moments alone here?' Buldan made to withdraw and Ferrax called out to him. 'You will find Ancastia and Forrun waiting on the path to the Fortress, please see that they are well cared for and treated as my honoured guests, and please bring my mother to me here. She and I have much to discuss.'

Buldan left to carry out his Chief's wishes and Ferrax heard the murmur of voices recede as the three of them walked away, leaving him to commune with the spirit of his dead father. By the time his mother arrived in a flurry of noise and movement, Ferrax was sitting calmly, his knees drawn up under his chin, at peace with his world and his new place within it. He leaped to his feet as his mother ran across the grass to him.

Idon threw herself into her son's arms with a wail and a sob that cut itself off as she remembered that others were present. With a visible effort she restrained herself and regained her composure.

'It is good to see you my son' she hesitated 'and my Lord' she added deferentially. Ferrax looked at her, she seemed to have aged so much since he had last set eyes upon her, the hair was streaked with grey, and the face was lined where once there had been beauty.

Ferrax was momentarily lost for words, for although he had assumed that one day he would succeed his father, it was only his mother's deference that finally and irrevocably forced his tired mind to accept his new position as the Chief of these people.

'Mother I must call cwnsl, and we must do it this night.' Idon nodded her head in agreement. It was the way of the tribe that if any man should challenge the new Chief then it should be done at the first calling of the cwnsl. Ferrax was not prepared to wait for the full moon, but instead wanted his authority to be known and unchallenged from this night.

Ferrax sent a messenger that night to meet with his ship, to release the captain and crew to trade and bring profits to what was now his fortress at the height and low of the moon in the skies.

***

As the sun set, the village was lit by the orange flames of the fire in the centre of the settlement. The logs crackled as an accompaniment to the voices of those who sat in the places of honour and influence, and of those who stayed back in the shadows either because of their lowly status or gender.

The skins across the entrance to the Chiefs hut were drawn back and Ferrax walked slowly but purposefully towards his allotted place. Instead of sitting down as was custom, he remained standing and the hubbub of voices died away leaving and expectant silence.

'My people' began Ferrax, 'I cannot begin to tell you how good it feels to be home, and yet how sad the reason for being here is. I have called cwnsl this night, as it is right and proper to do so, and to take my place as your Chief and to make my solemn promise to you, my people, that I shall serve you, as did my father with loyalty, compassion and justice.

'If there be any amongst you who dispute my claim to lead this tribe, or who seek to challenge my authority, then let them come forward now . . .' Ferrax looked around, some men looked at the ground, others at the fire, and one of these was Drullis, the father of Caeryl. Was it pain he saw in the other man's eyes? Or maybe defiance? Feeling some nerves, Ferrax steeled himself to announce that as no challenge was forthcoming, he now assumed the duties of Chief.

There was a murmur of assent and then Cwaenog the Outsider stood. For a brief moment, Ferrax' heart felt as if it would burst out of his chest, fearing that here was a challenge to his authority. He indicated, as he had seen his father do, that Cwaenog should speak.

'My Lord' began Cwaenog, his accent strange and yet mellifluous. 'We give thanks to the gods that you have returned to us, that you are safe, well and clearly prosperous.' There was a murmur of assent at this last statement. Prosperity was associated with intelligence and achievement and that augured well for a new Chief.

'As you will see though Lord Ferrax, one of your father's most loyal and devoted servants is no longer with us. I refer of course to the Druid, Morcant.' So, thought Ferrax, this is the challenge, and clearly Morcant is still around and has the ear of some of the tribal elders.' Cwaenog has paused, and Ferrax indicated that he should continue.

'Your father was not in his right mind at the time of his death and your mother was obliged to act on his instruction.' He paused again. 'Our tribe need the favours of the Gods and we lack the knowledge of the spirits that Morcant possesses. Will you allow him to return as the people desire Lord Ferrax?' There was another murmur, seemingly of agreement, but less pronounced than before.

'Morcant will not be allowed to return to this fortress' announced Ferrax, concentrating on keeping his voice strong and loud to silence any dissent. 'Unfortunately, Morcant forgot his position as the servant of the Gods and took decisions for himself and his own interests. This is my final decision on the matter.'

'But the Gods will not look favourably on us Lord' persisted Cwaenog, and he was about to say more when Ferrax raised a hand and brought silence.

'You have had among you, a remarkable guide and someone truly touched by the spirit of the Gods. I have found their guidance invaluable and invariably wise over the short time I have known them.' Once again the murmurs started and Ferrax could see heads turning as men questioned their neighbours about the meaning of these words spoken by the young Chief.

'Who do you mean?' said Drullis gruffly. Finally the man had broken his carefully managed silence thought Ferrax, understanding that he had only remained silent so as to judge the mood of the others before deciding whether to challenge or not.

'Drullis' said Ferrax, 'my respects to you and your family. I am surprised however than any of you need to ask the identity of the person. To me their talents shine like the light from the flames.'

'You mean the girl?' said Drullis in a low growling voice, redolent with insulted anger.

'I do, and I see and hear that you recognise her in my description' said Ferrax simply.

'I recognise her trickery and her magic over men' said Drullis to the accompanied agreement of Cwaenog. 'I recognise her desire to rule this tribe alongside your gullibility and your foolishness for falling under her spells!' shouted Drullis in a clever attempt to whip up a protest against Ferrax. It seemed to Ferrax, and his mother watching from the shadows that it might work. The men of the tribe grew agitated and a few got to their feet, hands on the handles of swords, though none drew their weapons.

And at that moment, the very time when Drullis raised his arm to point accusingly at Ferrax, the sky was ripped apart with a bolt of lightning that flashed and burned across the retina of every person present, leaving a green streak across the vision of everyone. Women screamed and men looked around in confusion as the thunder banged the eardrums and the wind blew strong, bringing with it the promise of rain.

Into this maelstrom of noise and emotion walked Ancastia to howls of protest from Drullis and his supporters, as she stood before the fire. As the roll of thunder died away she spoke simply and clearly.

'You know me, I am Ancastia.' She pointed at Drullis. 'You wrong me, I have given my body and heart to a man, but it is not your Chief whose love for another is pure and untainted. I serve Ferrax for his wisdom, for the benefit of you all, and will pass on the voices of the Gods as would a Druid. I did not choose these gifts, they were given to me by the Gods and all I ask is to serve them, serve my Lord Ferrax and live among you with the man I love.' Dramatically there was another flash of lightning and the thunder came much sooner with its portent of the rainstorm to come.

Drullis, Cwaenog and the other dissenters were cowed by the display of power from the skies. They had seen lightning before and seen its power to split and set fire to trees, but they had never known anyone able to harness that power, to bend it to her will.

Ancastia stood in her simple white robe as the men muttered their agreement and remained standing as the first of the big fat raindrops fell, making the fire smoke and sending men running to cover.

With Perris

Perris awakened, his mouth was dry and his head ached. He took a moment or two to understand where he was, and then tried to stand, striking his head on a beam above the bed. He bellowed a curse to the gods, sank to his knees and only then began to take in his surroundings.

The warrior had heard his Master and came dutifully to serve.

'Where have you been?' growled Perris. Your duty is to serve me, not your own pathetic needs.' He took a swipe at the servant. 'You are worse than Storril and he is lower than life should ever be.' The youngster beat a hasty retreat and returned moments later with a cooked chicken and a bowl. Perris gnawed at the fowl and absentmindedly took a drink from the bowl which he then spat on the floor.

'What is this?'

'Milk, my Lord, I took it from the cow myself.'

'Get out of my sight and never let me set eyes on you again, you miserable excuse for a man! You are not fit to serve me, you are a maid, not a warrior. Be gone, and if I ever see you again you will suffer.' Perris pushed the warrior hard in the chest and the young man stumbled backwards before falling. Perris kicked at him in rage until the youth could escape from the hut. He stood in utter desolate confusion until reaching the only decision open to him.

For a warrior, the membership and protection of a tribe was paramount, for his was a life of servitude without production. It was true that in later life many settled with a woman and took up a gentler life of growing food and hunting the wild beasts, but for now the youth was faced with the stark choices of seeking a new master to serve, or roaming the land living on his wits and ability to take food and shelter by force, until the inevitability of an early death intervened. The man, tears stinging his eyes, rode quickly away from the settlement.

Perris heard him go and dismissed him from his mind, which was, in any event, ruminating on the events to come within this new day.

Ferrax was back, and that meant a challenge to his authority. Perris had taken influence over the lands through a combination of bravado, guile and brute force, but even he knew that legitimacy lay with his brother. The only way therefore to rule these lands was to drive his brother back across the seas; and if Ferrax refused to leave, then he would have to die.

Death in battle was honourable mused Perris; the fact that the intended victim was his brother, to whom he had once been so close, was immaterial when measured against the potential rewards.

Perris began shouting and the settlement's Head Man nervously entered the hut.

'See to my horse, I shall leave you as soon as all is prepared.'

'All is ready Lord' said the man. 'Your warrior had everything done, he would not let any of us tend to your horse.' The man paused 'a beautiful animal . . .' If he had anything else to say, then it was lost as Perris swept past him and out into the grey light of the day. Without another word, he threw himself over the back of the horse and was gone, heading towards the north and the former fortress of his father.

***

Perris felt his innate anger subside and slowed the horse to a walk. In turn it allowed him time to think; something that he rarely bothered with, preferring to trust to his instincts that had served him well thus far in life. Thinking was however a relative term, for he wasted no time considering the wisdom of his desires, merely the best way to achieve the outcome that he lusted for most.

What Perris wanted, he would take and he cared not whether that would be by force or guile. He knew and understood that Ferrax would be with their mother, going through the stultifying formalities inherent in becoming the new Chief of the tribe. It was the right time to show his face and extract something of the deference due to him.

Perris was by now a wealthy man; the port that his father had long dreamt of was serving him well and his fortress controlled the port meaning that he could levy a duty on all those passing through with goods, be they slaves, wines, furs or food. For those duties, merchants bought safety for their trade in the lands controlled by Perris; for those that refused payment or tried to circumvent the settlement and port of Caer Perris, his roaming bands of warriors brought death.

Ferrax on the other hand had nothing. A fortress to be sure, but very little in the way of land, no trade and no income. His domain was moribund and teetering on the brink of extinction, suffocated by Perris. There was no thought in Perris's mind of sharing power or fortune with his brother; that had ended with his taking of Caeryl and the stupidity of their father playing his games with his son's lives. Perris would never have forgiven his brother had the situation been reversed, though he doubted Ferrax would have had the balls to take Caeryl from him. Perris laughed to himself absent-mindedly, congratulating himself on being strong enough to know what he wanted and to take it without regret.

'Halt and identify yourself!' A shout from the road ahead, and Perris looked up to see a mounted warrior, bearing his marks, sitting confidently and comfortably on a large horse, sword drawn and shield pulled forward.

'I am Perris, the ruler of these lands. You will stand aside.' The horseman spat on the ground and laughed.

'You are Perris? Very good. So tell me Lord Perris why would you be on your way to the fortress of Sisal contrary to your own orders that nobody should be allowed to pass? And why would such a great Lord be travelling alone?' He pointed the sword at the still distant Perris. 'I think you are lying.'

Perris stopped his horse about twenty paces away from the warrior and glared at him. It was true, that he had set patrols to stop men and goods getting to Sisal's fortress; and though that were an impossible task, it created a risk for travellers that few were willing to take. Perris sat upright, his chin jutting forward as he shouted to the warrior.

'If you serve me, then you have failed, for my brother Ferrax, is even now at his mother's side, plotting against me! Unless of course you have captured him?' This was said sarcastically, but the warrior made a gesture with his arm and four men came forward on horseback, a fifth was running along, being pulled by a trip of leather that was bound tightly round his wrists.

The warrior leaned forward, and looked at Perris earnestly. 'If this is your brother, then we have served you well it would seem' he called. 'We stopped this piece of shit this morning.' He made another gesture and the tied man was brought forward. Perris could see, it was the young man whose services he had dismissed that morning. He slid off his horse to the ground and walked towards the others.

'This is not my brother you fools, but he is a piece of shit as you say. Tell them who I am' he said casually to the youth who did not reply. TELL THEM WHO I AM!' roared Perris, the transition from calm to furious as instant as a bolt of lightning.

'You . . . you are . . . Lord P. . . Perris' stammered the youth. 'I served you loyally until this morning, my Lord' he continued. The mounted warrior and his companions looked at each other in apparent confusion as Perris walked to the youth and kicked him hard between the legs. The youth crumpled to the ground crying out in pain. Perris spat on him.

'You were useless to me, and seeing how easily you were captured, it seems you were useless to yourself. Where were you going?' The youth, gasping for breath, did not reply. 'I SAID WHERE WERE YOU GOING?' Spittle flew from his lips as he screamed at the youth, his eyes bulged and he indiscriminately kicked out again and again at the prostrate form on the ground.

'He was heading for the fortress my Lord' said the leader of the warriors who now got off his horse, as did his men. Perris nodded and walked around the youth, shouting down at him.

'So you would betray me would you? Run from my side to fight with my brother?' He looked at two of the men. 'Pick him up and hold him between you.' He turned his back on them and heard the youth grunt as he was lifted up, and then drawing his sword he turned back to the youth who raised his head to look at Perris.

'Lord . . .' was all he said before the point of Perris's sword pierced his left eye with a sickening squelch and a stream of blood jetting out soaking the bright metal of the weapon. The youth screamed and shook as if trying to free himself.

'This is what I do to those who are disloyal to me!' screamed Perris as he rammed the bloody sword into the boys gut and heaved upwards tearing through skin and organs as if they were grass. The youth died on the sword, his body falling limp and lifeless onto the ground in a pool of blood and offal. The warriors all looking nervous at the frenzy of explosive violence they had witnessed against an unarmed and defenceless boy.

'You' said Perris to one of the warriors, 'clean my sword. And you' he said to the leader 'come with me.' The warrior hesitated for a moment but obeyed and was both amazed and fearful of the serenity that seemed to have come over Perris. They walked a short distance, and talked of patrols, of the traffic and trade that the men had seen nearby, and then with the insects beginning to feast on the dead body, Perris sat with his men and shared their lunch, drinking his fill from a skin of wine that one of the men produced, explaining that he had taken it from a trader who could not prove that he had paid his duties to Perris.

'Ah, then it is mine!' said Perris with a laugh as he drank. He did not offer to share.

Later that afternoon, having slept soundly as the sun made its way to the horizon, Perris mounted his horse and looked at his men. 'Leave that there' he said nodding towards the body. 'It will serve as a reminder to others not to cross me. I leave you to go about your tasks.' He kicked at his horse and the animal reared up and galloped away in what Perris hoped was a dramatic departure that demonstrated his skill as a rider. Satisfied with his day, he continued towards the hill fort, arriving just as lightning ripped the sky apart.

At the Fortress of Sisal

As the rain began to fall, and the men ran both for cover and to escape the magic of Ancastia, Ferrax looked up and saw Caeryl. She was lit by the dancing light of the fire, the red and orange hues flickering in her eyes; he had long wondered about this moment, the reunion between the two lovers that were never allowed to be. For all his thought, all his hopes, the reality was more intense and disabling than he had ever thought it could be. Ferrax, the Chief of the Tribe was struck dumb, immobilised through his own emotions. For her part Caeryl stood, and seeing no discernible reaction from Ferrax, she turned and walked away into the rain.

Too late, Ferrax got to his feet and made to go after her but was halted by a shout from the gate. Caeryl could wait, or maybe he thought as he hastened over the wet ground, he was relieved that he could put off the moment of meeting.

'What is it?' Ferrax called to the warrior on the platform overlooking the entrance to the fort. His voice barely reaching the other man over the wildness of the weather

'You had better come up here' came the shouted reply. Ferrax clambered up the wooden ladder to the platform to find himself with Marrad, his younger sibling who had achieved a status by standing up to Perris at the time of their father's death.

There was another ripping sound as the sky flashed with lightning and Ferrax saw the reason for Marrad's summons. Perris sat astride his horse calmly awaiting the arrival of his elder brother.

'What do you want Perris?' shouted Ferrax. The younger man grinned and spread his arms wide.

'To welcome my brother home of course.' The horse moved underneath him, unsettled by the weather.

'You come to pay tribute?' shouted Ferrax. 'I think not.'

'You know me too well to think that. But we do need to talk brother.'

'I agree.' Ferrax signalled for the gates to be opened, and as he reached the ground, Perris rode in at a walk. The symbolism was not lost on either man as Perris remained on the horse and looked silently down on Ferrax; his height emphasising the dominance he believed he held over the tribe.

'Do you not have servants to tend to my beast?' Perris finally dismounted and waited for Ferrax to approach him.

'I will see to your horse' said Marrad, taking the reins and leading the animal away to shelter. The two brothers stood some distance apart and Perris held out a hand, Ferrax held out his and it became a test of nerve as to who would move toward the other. Neither did and Ferrax shrugged his shoulders and dropped his arm, Perris laughed and did the same thing.

'Come under cover' said Ferrax leading the way to the Chief's hut. The man following him was, he realised, a stranger. Gone was the ready smile, replaced by wary and distrusting eyes. Also gone was the self-conscious way Perris used to lope across the ground; he now walked with bearing and confidence, projecting an image of the warrior, the Lord and the man.

Inside the hut, the noise of the rain was muted, but the sharp intake of breath from Idon preceded her words of hatred.

'You! You defile this place and are not welcome here.' She spat at him, and Perris ignored her.

'Mother' said Ferrax, 'this must be done and it might as well be done now as at any other time. You are welcome to stay and bear witness to what has to be done.'

'I agree' said Perris. 'You should hear what needs to be said.' The three of them sat, Perris refusing an offer of refreshment.

'I repeat my question then' said Ferrax. Why are you here brother?' Perris chose his words carefully.

'I have come to claim that which is rightfully mine' he said simply.

'By which words you mean what?' asked Ferrax. The younger man leaned back and spread his arms.

'I control all the land, from the sea, the rivers, the forests, the settlements and the hills. All except this one. I levy duty on the merchants, the farmers, the herders and the fishermen. I am a wealthy man and what I have, I have taken by the strength the Gods give me. I have warriors who serve me, and I can call upon armed men to do my bidding.'

'But you lack the one thing you crave most' said Ferrax with a smile. 'For all your wealth and power, you are not the Chief of this Tribe. I am. Our father saw your greed and your ruthlessness and knew you to be unfit to rule and so he called me back from my exile, named me and I intend to fulfil my destiny.'

'It will be a short life' snarled Perris. 'If you will not give with humility, then I shall take by force.'

'Perris, keep your wealth, keep your fortress by the sea. I have no wish nor desire to demean you. All I ask is that you swear allegiance to me as our father wished.'

'I can never do that' said Perris quite calmly and Ferrax shrugged again and smiled.

'Then it seems our destinies are set by the Gods does it not brother?'

'To the death' said Perris.

'Agreed.'

'Very well, I shall send word' said Perris, 'and now I shall take Caeryl with me. Have her fetched and brought here.'

'No' said Ferrax. 'She goes nowhere.' Perris roared with laughter

'You are a man of low honesty for a Chief, Ferrax son of Sisal. On one hand you claim to do the will of our father who no doubt you will say, sits with the gods, and yet on the other, you defy him. He gave Caeryl to me and the Tribe to you, and yet you cannot see the sense in being parted from either.'

'You arrived empty handed and you leave in the same manner brother' said the Chief of the tribe. Perris stood, glared at Idon who had come forward to stand at her eldest son's shoulder and looked down on Ferrax.

'I shall return to take that which is mine, but I will give you a period of grace so you run away and keep breath in your body. Leave this land Ferrax, it will be the only thing that saves you.' Perris turned and strode into the night shouting for his horse to be brought to him. His departure left Idon and Ferrax sitting silently for a while before the woman spoke.

'Kill him' she said quietly. 'I know he is my son, but he will destroy everything unless he is stopped.' Ferrax nodded his head slowly.

'There is no other way' he agreed.

***

Ferrax walked out of the hut and into the night; the embers from the fire still smoked but the heat and the light had been extinguished by the rain that fell unabated. Ferrax ignored the water that ran from his hair, soaking his face, his beard and his clothing and strode purposefully towards the one place that he knew he could avoid no longer. At the entrance he hesitated, but called out and Caeryl answered the only way that she could.

'You should not be here.' She spoke, as he remembered, with a voice that was both kind and caring. He felt his heart beat increase as he asked for permission to enter. How different he was from his brother she thought as she told him that as Chief she could not deny his right to be wherever he chose. He walked inside and she sat lit by the flames of a small fire, the smoke from which curled upwards to a vent in the roof. She made to stand up but he placed a hand on her shoulder and sat beside her.

'You should not be here' she repeated.

'And yet, here I am' he shrugged diffidently and smiled. Caeryl looked away, the light from the flames reflecting from the tears that ran down her face.

'Your father kept us apart and that is the way it must be' she said with a tone of finality.

'My father appointed me his successor to make the rules and the laws as I see fit' replied Ferrax 'and as much as I can bind people together, so can I separate them.'

'Your father sits with the gods and would be displeased if he hears such words.'

'Possibly' agreed Ferrax. 'But he would also trust me to make a judgment in the interests of the people.' Caeryl wiped her eyes on the sleeve of her tunic.

'And what is your judgment my Lord?' she asked in a whisper.

'That the people need two things; some good news and a future. Good news brings a celebration and a feast, and . . .'

'Say it Ferrax, say what you really mean.'

'The future comes from a Chief taking a woman and making her with child, it creates the bloodline, the next Chief after me.'

'I cannot be with you Ferrax' said Caeryl, her grief evident in her tears and her sadness. 'I am tainted by your brother who forced himself upon me many times. He was himself; rough, cruel and uncaring and he tore me apart.' She wept, the tears now unrelenting. 'I cannot carry a child Ferrax!' She turned to him in her anguish 'I cannot, I cannot . . .' her voice faded to a whisper as she hid her face in her hands.

Ferrax knew her better than to bully his way into her thoughts, and instead sat quietly until her energy was spent, and, as he knew she would, she lowered her hands to look at him.

'Do you see? I cannot be with you.'

Ferrax reached out and held her hand, so small in his, and keeping his eyes on her hand, spoke quietly. 'Do you not see Caeryl. I cannot be without you.'

'I will serve you Lord Ferrax as will any loyal and devoted woman of this tribe, but I can be no more than that. The men here need to respect you and they know I have lain with your brother, that he has had me, used me, abused me and come back for more. And they did nothing. Cross them, my father included, and their stupid and pathetic superstitions, and they will abandon you Ferrax.' She was about to go on when he leaned forward and very gently kissed her eyelids, tasting the salt of her tears. She sat, mouth open in surprise but her insides were a tumult of feeling; pain, confusion, desire, horror, fear. She felt them all in a split second of indecision which was when Ferrax picked her up and lay her down on the furs and skins she used as a bed and kissed her, unleashing all she had ever felt and kept hidden for this man.

Through the night she felt pain as old wounds were revisited, she clawed at Ferrax breaking the skin of his back and his chest, her spirit alive and free; but she also felt a sense of belonging; that she would gladly give herself, all of whoever she was, to Ferrax for as long as he lived and she could be with him. After the storm of passion he slept and for a time she lay, listening to his breathing, feeling his steady heartbeat in his chest as her own demons left her and she succumbed to a deep untroubled rest.

With Perris

Perris rode away from the settlement, partly in anger and partly feeling a satisfaction that he had brought matters to a head. Here was the solution to the problem caused by his interfering father, to take his rightful place as the leader of his people, he had to kill his brother and better that it be done cleanly in battle and with honour than by subterfuge and underhand means. He and Ferrax had agreed that a fight to the death was appropriate and to die in battle with a sword or axe in your hand was a good thing. He spat on the floor; his fool of a father had died trying to save a dog, only steps away from his bed. He spat again, feeling only contempt for his family.

He wondered whether he should have insisted on taking Caeryl. He had no real desire for her other than as a trophy, and had no care for her looks, preferring the woman who had borne his child. He smiled lasciviously as he recalled to his mind, the heavy milk filled breasts that he had greedily fed from leaving the child to wail in its hunger until it had been removed by other women from the settlement and quietened at the breast of a woman whose own child had died. He laughed as he rode on, conscious of his power over the people and satisfied with his feeling of self-worth.

The night was filthy with rain, pitch black as the stars and the moon were covered with cloud and Perris knew that he was merely guessing the direction of travel. He had wanted to ride through the night, to be home to Caer Perris by morning to begin his plans for battle, but he knew that this was a futile endeavour and he would need to secure shelter as much for the beast he rode, as for himself.

Perris had the senses of a warrior and could smell the scent of a fire somewhere nearby. That had to mean a hut or other shelter, for there was no way to keep a fire lit in the rain that teemed from the sky. He scanned the surroundings for the tell-tale orange glow and found it, hard to his left. He wheeled the complaining horse around and rode hard towards the source of the light which indeed turned out to be a rather dilapidated and seemingly abandoned hut. Dismounting the horse, Perris unceremoniously thrust the skins over the entrance aside and walked in, leading the horse behind him. He expected the usual screams and anxious challenges, but instead saw that the only occupant was an elderly looking man hunched over a pot from which came the delicious aroma of a cooked rabbit and herbs. Intrigued as to who this man was, in his dirty, mud encrusted robes, and why he seemingly had no fear of him, Perris took another step forward only to be held in check by the horse who was wide eyed in fear and distrust. Perris drew his sword and held it before him, the metal glinting orange in the firelight

The man looked up from his meal and spoke. 'Hello Perris' he said.

***

'Morcant!' said Perris with some surprise. 'I thought you dead or banished?'

'Still very much alive Lord Perris, although you astutely perceive my banishment by your brother and vindictive mother. Hence' he spread his arms wide to indicate the ramshackle hut 'my reduced circumstances which you, Lord, are welcome to share.'

'From other men, druid, I would just take and not be interested in any consequences; from you however, I gratefully accept your offer. Your food smells delicious.'

'Sit and eat your fill Perris, for we have much to discuss.' Over the next few hours, Morcant told Perris of the last days of his father, of his attempts to appease the Gods and of his fall from power. For his part, Perris felt as if a treasure had been unearthed to him; his fortress had lacked one thing, a source of inspiration and guidance from the Gods to the people; and a man who could talk to the spirits could legitimise his hold on power and his challenge to his brother.

By morning, Morcant was again a man of influence, even though he knew his new Lord was a man of mercurial temperament and bouts of extreme violence. The two men travelled back to Caer Perris slowly, each forming their own plans on how to gain the most advantage.

Upon arrival at the coastal fortress, Perris was impressed with Morcant's words of approval, his appreciation of the defences and the way in which they were challenged by a band of mounted and armed warriors. Perris called the inhabitants together and introduced them to their new druid, and felt that the final piece of his settlement had come together.

Caer Perris now had everything it needed; trade, warriors, wealth and approval from the gods.

Caer Sisal

It started with a look, it was not a look that demanded much in the way of perception on Ferrax's part, for the look was from Drullis, Caeryl's own father and it was one of utter revulsion, as he watched the young chief emerge from his daughter's hut. Ferrax made to walk away but was called back by the other man.

'I will speak with you Ferrax' called Drullis.

'When the time is right' responded Ferrax.

'The time is right.'

'You forget yourself Drullis' said Ferrax 'and more importantly, you forget who I am perhaps?' Drullis walked over to the younger man.

'I do not forget a man, no matter who he may be, who dishonours my family. Caeryl was given to your brother, a union sanctioned by one who now sits amongst the gods, and you have no earthly powers that will undo that.'

Both Ferrax and Drullis were painfully aware that everything being said between them was heard inside the hut; the skin covering the entrance twitched and moved as Caeryl listened intently.

'I have feelings for your daughter that I have never had for anyone else' said Ferrax. 'I cannot deny such powerful sway on my character, and more, I will not deny it.'

'Then you have to be prepared to face the consequences' answered Drullis, pulling himself to his full height as if to intimidate.

'Such as?'

'Such as a challenge to your position, maybe even your presence within this place. A challenge brought by one who respects our ways and our laws.'

'You mean yourself? Don't bother hiding it Drullis, I see the lust for power in your eyes. My father always knew it was a matter of time before you sought to challenge him, but you never quite had the stomach for it did you?' Ferrax prodded the other man in the chest. Come to my hut when the sun reaches its highest point in the skies and we shall settle this once and for all.' Ferrax strode away whilst Drullis stood for a moment, glaring at the departing back of a Chief he could not respect, before pushing his way into his daughter's hut. The remonstrations were long, loud and not particularly private.

***

'Fetch Ancastia' ordered Ferrax to Buldan and he watched as she made her way across the settlement. Others averted their eyes so as not to catch hers, the tribe tacitly acknowledging that she held the power of communicating with the gods. Ferrax entered the hut and waited on her.

'Lord?' she said as she entered.

'I spent the night with Caeryl' blurted Ferrax. Inwardly he wanted to shout with joy about the event, but that would be unseemly and wrong, but the genuine grin that spread over the girl's face showed that she understood and shared in his happiness. 'Drullis has already sought to castigate me for my actions and I need to know the opinion of the gods. He will come here at the middle of the day.'

'I understand Lord' replied Ancastia simply. 'I shall need you, Drullis and Caeryl to be here, and nobody else' she added pointedly. Ferrax nodded his head.

'It shall be as you require' he replied.

At the appointed time Drullis approached the Chieftain's hut but was asked to fetch and bring his daughter. He complied reluctantly and it was noticeable to all present how the two of them neither looked at, nor spoke to each other.

If Drullis was surprised to see Ancastia present, then he hid it well, but contented himself standing leaning against the hut's central pillar, the trunk of an ancient oak.

'I have asked you here Drullis, to allay your fears, to ask Ancastia to speak to the gods and to let us all present have their determination. For myself, I shall abide by whatever the gods decide.'

'As shall I' said Drullis gruffly.

'I have prepared a potion' announced Ancastia 'that enables the gods to speak through me. It is a recipe given to me by Morcant. I am not aware of my voice or the words that the gods use, the time with the gods is limited and the risks to myself high if we incur their displeasure.' She bent forwards to a horn of grey green liquid that she held in her hands and drank deeply; thereafter she sat quietly, her hands in her lap, her eyes closed. Drullis and Ferrax had seen Morcant behave in a similar way and were untroubled when she started to sway and moan in a low undulating tone. Caeryl, who had no such experience, made to move towards the girl but was held back by both men.

'Who seeks the guidance of the gods?' called Ancastia in a voice unlike her own. It was deeper, and somehow older than her natural light tone.

'Ferrax, Chief of this tribe and Drullis, the father of Caeryl also present.'

'Welcome daughter' intoned Ancastia 'I am glad to be able to right the wrong done to you.'

Caer Perris

'And you think battle is inevitable Lord Perris?' asked Morcant.

'I predict that slaughter is more likely' said Perris, taking a deep draught from a skin of wine and speaking in a tone that was redolent with confidence in his own ability.

'Is there perhaps not another way?' said Morcant with some hesitation. Perris stopped drinking and sat up, glaring at the druid.

'There are two other resolutions as well you know' said Perris, 'the first is that Ferrax submits to my terms, he keeps his lands but I lead the tribe; the second is that I submit to him and that is something that will never happen.'

'I recall a time, years ago . . .'

'Do not pester me with your reminiscences druid' spat Perris, the mood between the two men changing in an instant. 'My brother grew weak and ran away, whilst I remained and through hard work I built this place and kept peace within these lands. I care not which of us is the elder, but think far more as to which of us is the more deserving. Perhaps that is where your thoughts should also lie?'

'I can understand your. . . .'

'You understand nothing! You cook with your herbs and see things in smoke and the people adore you for it Morcant. That is why you are here, to give the people what they want, and to educate them that what they really want is me as their Chief. You were banished from one fortress druid, don't make a habit of it. Begone and think well on my words.' Perris waved a hand and Morcant, taking his cue, rose and left the hut.

A few days later, the druid was in his own dwelling and the air was suffused with the heady aromas of plants striving to outdo the nauseous stench of a sheep skull boiling in water over a fire. Without seeking leave, Perris entered and sat across the fire to Morcant.

'As you remain here, I take it you accept the terms I set out?'

'I would prefer a different course, but yes, I accept' replied the druid quietly.

'Why does it matter to you whether Ferrax lives or dies?

'Of itself I suppose it does not, but my loyalty was always to the legacy your father created. True' Morcant waved a hand to silence the inevitable interruption from Perris 'in his last seasons, your father lost some of his sense. He drove a barrier between the two of you which was unwise. He always understood that each of you possessed strengths that the other lacked and it was his intention to join those strengths to mask the weaknesses.'

'What say you about my father's intent?'

'He understood your impetuosity Lord, he understood it because in his youth he shared it, and it was only the guiding hand of your mother that calmed him and made him think before he drew his sword. It is my belief that this led him to the greatest mistake of his life, but made for the best of reasons.'

'Careful druid, you slur my father, and I will slay you.'

'Understand Lord Perris, I do not demean your father, but rather seek to explain to you the nature of his wisdom. His greatest mistake was to believe that by putting you and Caeryl together he would recreate the solution he had found within his own family. He thought she would teach you an inner calm.'

'He was wrong!'

'Yes, he was, and I believe he regretted his decision until the day he joined the gods. The damage he did is probably incapable of repair for he broke your brother's spirit' Morcant looked into the eyes of the younger man. 'And the only way Ferrax can recover that is to defeat you in battle.'

'So you agree with me then? A battle is inevitable.'

'A battle has many losers Lord, not just the dead. Think on this, are you not more powerful with a broken and beaten brother as your servant in all but name?'

'The people would think me weak.'

'Or they would think you loyal both to your brother, and your father.'

'You speak words that are either wise or foolish. I cannot decide.' He gestured towards the pot with the bleaching sheep head. 'What is this foul matter for?'

'I asked the gods to give me a sign, if the meat clings to the bones then it is a sign to act in haste, if the bones bleach white, then it means the gods tell you to wait and consider your moves.' Mocant sat back while Perris peered through the steam.

'The bones are white' he stated.

'Yes Lord' replied the druid.

Caer Sisal

Ancastia continued to sway as she spoke. Ferrax and Drullis listened intently, Caeryl stared with wide eyes and rapt attention fixated on the woman in front of her, completely caught in the intensity of the situation.

'My son' intoned Ancastia in a voice much deeper and older than her own, 'you have returned to claim what is rightfully yours and in this you have my permission. Let the gods cast aside the union I created and let right come from wrong.' There was a long pause.

'Drullis? You are also present?' The older man was startled to be so addressed.

'I am here' he replied in a quivering voice, doing his best to mask the fear he felt in such powerful company.

'You will serve my son with better loyalty than you served me.' It was a statement and not a question. Drullis looked around him, his mouth agape.

'Lord, I . . . I' he stammered

'I see not only men's faces but also their hearts. You have greatness in you Drullis but you have ambition beyond your talent. Be content with your place at my son's side, give counsel and put my words into action.' Drullis said nothing but bowed his head, a sure sign of his supplication.

'My son, it is to you that I must give the most painful advice. You must act swiftly to protect your rule over your lands and you know he who you must challenge. Do not delay for he grows stronger and know that the gods are with you.' Ancastia heaved a huge sigh and collapsed forward onto the table, spent and exhausted.

Drullis made to move towards the girl but was held back by his own daughter.

'You have other matters to attend to' said Caeryl. 'Do so immediately.'

'Our first call must be to my mother, she must know what we have heard' said Ferrax.

'No need' said a voice from the shadows at the walls of the hut. 'I heard all and am glad that Sisal is once again strong.' She walked forward and looked down on the unconscious form of Ancastia. 'I wronged you girl, we all did. You are truly touched by the gods. Drullis, do you accept that these were the words of Sisal from beyond his tomb?'

'I do' murmured the man, still in awe at what he had witnessed.

'Then the way forward is clear. You and I as the parents must tell the people that which we have heard and cast aside the union between Caeryl and Perris.'

'We must call cwnsl' said Ferrax

'No, for then only men are present' said Idon. The chattering is done amongst the women. We must call a feast to celebrate the return of Ferrax and will address all matters at the same time.'

'You speak with wisdom' agreed Drullis which brought forth a thin smile from the widow.

***

At the same time therefore as Perris was peering at the boiling sheep's head, the entire population of Caer Sisal was gathered around the fire pit as Ferrax cut lumps of cooked and charred meat from the slaughtered ox that was the centrepiece of the feast. At the appropriate time, Drullis stood and called for quiet. He then spoke in hushed and reverential tones of the scenes he had witnessed when Sisal had spoken through Ancastia, and told the people of the words he had heard, his devotion to Sisal and now to Ferrax and of his support for the union of his daughter with the new Chief. It was powerful oratory such as had rarely been heard and coming from Drullis who was known to be a force for challenge and self-advancement it carried a powerful message. Ancastia was accepted as being no mere whim of a dying man, but a powerful and wise vessel of the gods. She was revered until her death many years later and villagers from outlying settlements as well as visiting merchants and other tribal Chiefs would seek her wise counsel and approval.

While the festivities were progressing, Ferrax sat quietly, acknowledging the good wishes of everybody, but deeply immersed within his own thoughts. Both Caeryl and Idon understood. In the few days since the revelations from Ancastia the two women had acknowledged their differences and reached a deep understanding of the mutual benefit to be had in working together. Caeryl nodded her head in understanding at a look from Idon, and the elder woman approached her son.

'You are brooding Ferrax, thinking of your brother.'

'I am. You understand me so well, as I suspect does Caeryl which is why she lets you approach me. The thought of Perris still causes her anguish.'

'It does. And it is right that it does, for her pain means that she has a better life to look forward to.'

'If I live you mean' said Ferrax with a sigh.

'Yes' agreed Idon. 'You lack belief in your strength even after the words you heard?'

'The time is all wrong. I had planned to journey back to my home across the ocean, to return with men loyal to me, and to crush Perris until he begged for mercy. Now it seems we few must confront him.'

'It is better this way' said his mother 'challenge him when he least expects it, before he has time to prepare.'

For a moment Ferrax sat quietly, Idon was concerned that he, her eldest son, upon whom so much now depended, would seek to argue her opinion, but he knew she was right. He closed his eyes and spoke quietly.

'Mother? Have Caeryl's possessions moved into the Chief's hut.'

'Of course, I shall move to her dwelling . . .'

'There is no need.'

'It is only right and proper that it be done this way.' Idon bustled away leaving Caeryl sitting with Ferrax.

'We are joined, as we always should have been' he said.

'Yes' she replied quietly.

'Make ready and I shall join you. If we are to have but one night then let it be shared together, for Idon is right and I shall rife to challenge my brother when the sun rises.' He turned to look at his woman, there were tears in her eyes as she leaned forward to touch his lips with hers.

'There will be many nights together, the gods have decreed it' she said as she turned and entered her new home.

***

The following morning promised to be a fine day; the early morning mist hung over the meadows and the sun that would burn it away was already climbing into the sky as Ferrax addressed his small band of warriors. He looked around; there was Buldan, sat on a log, his powerful arms using a stone to sharpen the blade of an axe; Gadrig standing with the horses that would carry them to battle; Forrun smiling easily with Ancastia as she fussed around him unnecessarily; Drullis, looking somewhat hesitant in the midst of the powerful younger men; Cwacnog, clearly only there because he had to be; Gargonstus possible invaluable if they needed to break into the fortress he had built, and last of all Ferrax's young brother Marrad, clad in a warriors garb, a sword sheathed at his side. In addition there were twenty or so other men from the settlement, all armed with various weapons of war, from spears to axes and swords.

'Marrad, Drullis? To me please.' The older man and the youth looked at each other and approached. 'I need you two to stay here.' Marrad made to interrupt, but a look from Ferrax stopped him.

'I cannot leave this place without protection and it would be just like my brother to attack our homes and our people while we were away.' Drullis nodded his head, partly in agreement, and partly in not being able to believe his luck that he would likely survive this day. 'If I fall in battle then I shall be with the gods but Marrad I charge you to protect Caeryl with your life.' These were the words the youth needed to hear; that he was given a charged and meaningful responsibility. The fact that in his adolescence he was infatuated with his brother's woman was of course completely irrelevant.

'Drullis' said Ferrax turning to the older man 'in the event of my death, I look to you to protect everyone from the worst of my brother's excesses. He will become your Chief, of that there is no point in resistance, but use your skills and the influence of my mother to stop him exacting any revenge.'

'Yes Lord' said Drullis with genuine respect.

'Remain with us until we are gone.' Drullis turned to his small band and addressed them. 'We ride to confront my brother and there are too few of us to mount a battle, we would be outnumbered and overwhelmed and therefore we have to make our individual strength and skills count. I have already instructed Marrad and Drullis to remain here and guard our homes and the woman and children.' Ferrax felt sure he saw a look of relief pass between Gadrig and Buldan; they knew as well as he did that the two to be left behind would be more of a hindrance than a help. 'With the help of the gods we shall return victorious and safe!' called Ferrax. There was a cheer from the men as was to be expected before each of them mounted a horse and the war party rode out of the gates. Although small compared to the force under Perris' command, it was nevertheless the largest war party to have left the settlement since Sisal was a young man and it stirred the blood of those left behind who were convinced of the invincibility of their men.

Caer Perris

'You seem troubled?' Halen sat with her son on her knee. He had grown to be a chubby healthy child, the younger image of his father who sat across the cooking fire from them, scowling into the dancing orange flames.

'Do not trouble me with your prattle. And keep that whelp silent' demanded Perris. Perran gurgled and threw his arms around at the sound of his father's voice. Perris was drinking more each day, and no longer confined to evenings such as this. His moods varied from sullen to violent, the bruises on Halen's arms evidence of his roughness. She put her son carefully in the fur and skin lined basket woven for him with her own hands. She knew he would be safe and warm there, and she retreated to the shadows. Perran cried for a while, but just as his father's rage was growing to breaking point he sighed and fell asleep.

'Talk to me' said Halen. 'We share so much, so why not this trouble that afflicts you so?' The woman was being somewhat economical with the truth; whatever Perris wanted, Perris took, including her, but it was true that they had talked and shared and made plans like all people did. She had known fear of him in the beginning, then she learned to trust him as well as respect the security he gave her and the boy. But now, the predominant deeling was fear, it was as if he could slice through her neck without a whim, killing her as she had seen his despatch so many others.

'Come here' said Perris quietly, almost gently. Dutifully, she rose and walked toward him. Halen was sixteen summers old and was aware enough of herself to understand that she turned the heads of men, and made the older women envious. Having Perran had changed her both physically and mentally; she had a full figure, and her breasts were still heavy with the milk that her son fed upon. Before becoming a mother, Halen would look to herself, consider nothing beyond her desire for another fur or another brooch with the dull yellow gold and stones that shone in the firelight. Now such things were just a passing fancy and she gave no more thought to them than she did of the next meal she had to prepare. Her time, and her devotion were given to the boy and she would fight like a beast to protect him, even to the death.

As she walked towards Perris Halen, dropped her fur to the ground and stood in a simple soft leather dress that she made to untie. Perris shook his head and she stopped.

'Soon, I shall fight my brother and it shall be to the death. He is the one person that knows me well enough to anticipate my fight.'

'You fear him?'

'No.'

'Then why this talk?'

'Had I been the elder son, then none of this would be necessary. I grew up with Ferrax, I know his weaknesses and his way of thinking. Fighting him will be difficult but no more than that, I just regret the need for it.' Perris stood up, 'if he had stayed over the sea, if he had the sense to understand the strength needed to rule these lands . . .'

'If, if, if my Lord' said Halen softly. 'These doubts you have are because he is your brother and you love the man, but he represents a challenge to you and you are not a man to be subservient to another. You must ignore who it is that you fight, and focus on what it is that you are fighting for.' Halen reached out and took his hand. She knew she had him now, knew that look in his eye that only came when his mind joined hers and she had persuaded him to believe in her words. Slowly she pulled his hand until he sat down next to her and then gently she put his rough calloused hand on her soft breast, feeling the nipple harden and grow wet as he squeezed and teased her, the milk dribbling and wetting her clothing.

***

'I want each man to collect firewood, and each man to start a fire of their own' ordered Ferrax.

'Lord?' questioned Gadrig.

'A simple enough ruse Gadrig' explained Ferrax. I want my brother to think an army has come to slaughter him. I want him to piss himself in fear.

Ferrax and his men had travelled through the day, they had come across the patrol placed by Perris near their own settlement and had slaughtered them, Buldan having taken a man's head off with a single strike from his axe. It left them in good spirits, convinced that, with not even a scratch suffered, they were protected by the gods. Wary in case of other patrols, Ferrax had sent two of his best hunters ahead of the others to warn of any dangers, but either Perris had become lazy or was supremely confident because even here on the slopes of the hill overlooking Caer Perris there was nobody except themselves to be seen.

As the sun set, the smoke from twenty six fires curled lazily into the still air. Ferrax and his men sat together for protection and Buldan organised both sentries and patrols to tend the fires so they did not burn out. Those without a duty, wrapped themselves and settled down to sleep.

***

There was a commotion outside, and Perris, his mind instantly clear of the mental haze caused by wine, threw Halen's arm aside and rose from the place where they fornicated and slept. He emerged into the twilight and demanded to know why he had been disturbed.

'Lord, look at the hillside' said a warrior. Perris looked and saw the smoke and the tiny lights emanating from the fires.

'So, my brother has come to me' he said to himself. 'Fetch Morcant!' he commanded and was gratified to see that his words were instantly obeyed. Moments later the Druid appeared, his calm demeanour hiding the panic evident in his eyes.

'Lord Perris?' he enquired.

'Look Morcant, look!' said Perris pointing to the fires on the hills. You advised that we wait before battle but it seems as if my brother has other ideas. The gods sent you a sign but it seems as if the decision is out of my hands. Advise me.

Morcant closed his eyes and remained silent for what must have been a fleeting moment but felt to those watching like an eternity. 'Lord, the gods advised what you should do, not how you should react. The circumstances have changed.'

'And?'

'Firstly can you be sure that this is your brother? Secondly how many men has he, thirdly . . .'

'Leave the battle to me druid' snarled Perris. 'You just tell me the omens.'

'Lord, the gods show pleasure with you' claimed Morcant obsequiously. 'Is this not a land of plenty, with food from the sea and the land, with trade growing and making you rich?'

'Yes. What of it?'

'Why Lord, is this not the way in which the gods provide their favours? For another man the outcomes might well have been different.' Morcant smiled at Perris who stood, considering these words and then without further comment turned to the two men nearest him.

'You and you' he said, pointing at them, 'get out there and find out how many men side against us. Do it quietly, I do not want them to know you are there.' The men departed.

'Morcant, I fear no man, but it never hurts to have the gods smile upon you when you go into battle. What do you suggest I do?'

'The best way of securing their favour Lord would be through sacrifice of course.'

'Take whatever beast you feel will please them. Say it is upon my behalf.'

'And your plan Lord Perris?'

'I intend to wait and hear what the men say upon their return.' Perris strode back inside his hut and lay fretfully on the furs next to the slumbering Halen.

With Ferrax

An experienced warrior always knew that no matter what your plans, your weapons, your men and your position, luck played a part in whether you lived or died. Just as it was a truth that you made your own luck, so it was also acknowledged that sometimes the gods favoured you. And sometimes they did not.

The two warriors sent by Perris had decided to remain together, they were both experienced men, well versed in battle, and well known to each other. They rode horses to the lower slopes of the hill, then dismounted and walked slowly and steadily towards the fire on the farthest end away from the fort. It was their plan to work their way along the line, gathering information on the forces opposing them. As they approached the first fire, there was nobody to be seen and slowly and quietly the two men made their way around the fire, shielding their eyes so as not to leave the dancing pattern of the flames in their vision, but still they found nobody. They conversed in a whisper and agreed to move to the next fire, but if they again found that site deserted one of them would ride back to Perris with the information.

Silently they crawled back down the slope, each of them aware that the stillness of the oncoming night was both a curse and a comfort. Any sound from friend or foe would carry which made it all the more surprising when they heard a whisper telling them to remain still. Both men froze and looked at each other, understanding that anyone else on that slope was an enemy. Hurriedly they both got to their feet and were both felled by vicious blows to the head, neither man got to call out as hands were placed over their mouths before they were gagged and hauled back to their feet. Both swayed as they struggled with the after effects of the assault, but they were quietly taken into the presence of Ferrax.

'I am Ferrax, the ruler of these lands' he said simply. 'You serve my upstart brother and I assume are sworn to him?' One of the men was senseless but the other retained his wits and replied.

'We are sworn to the service of Lord Perris until death' he announced.

'Good' said Ferrax with a smile, 'because Lord Perris as you call him, should swear allegiance to me, and that means you are mine does it not?' This was a concept that seemed to confuse the man who stood dumb.

'How many men does Perris have under oath?' The captured man stood his ground and jutted his chin forward in a manner of defiance. Ferrax sighed. 'You clearly need some persuasion. Gargonstus?' he called. Gargonstus here' continued Ferrax almost casually 'is one of my men who captured you. I take it you felt the force of his hand?' The captive murmured something indecipherable. 'Gargonstus, kill the other one' ordered Ferrax. 'Break his neck.' Still the captive stared silently only wincing as a sharp crack and a sigh of breath signalled the demise of his companion.

'Do you want the same fate?' asked Ferrax. 'I ask you for the last time how many men have sworn loyalty to Perris?' Still there was silence and Ferrax turned away, and the captive died as a spear pierced his back and protruded from his guts. For a moment the man looked down at the sharp metal point of the weapon, red with his own blood before letting out a tortured scream. He would have fallen to the ground were his corpse not impaled, but as soon as Gadrig let go of the spear the man toppled forwards.

'Tie them both to their horses and send them back' said Ferrax. 'My gratitude Gargonstus, you did great service to capture them and bring them to me.' Ferrax raised his hand in salute to the other man who had been sent to maintain the fires with the huge builder, then turned away and settled himself once more to sleep.

***

'Lord. Wake up!' Perris was conscious of being shaken and through his sleep, knew the voice to be that of Storril. 'Lord, please' pleaded the man. Perris roughly shoved the one handed servant away and he fell to the floor.

'What do you bother me with you wretch?' he shouted, Halen who was already awake then went to soothe Perran who was crying because his own sleep had been disturbed.

'The men you sent out to track Ferrax have returned Lord. Tied to their horses and dead. One has his neck broken and the other . . .'

'I don't need to petty details you fool' said Perris. 'But this tells us much. Summon the leaders of the men, then come and make sure my weapons are prepared and sharpened. We shall do battle this day Storril and maybe you shall be free of me eh?' Perris laughed and Halen cowered in the shadows of the hut with her son.

Perris acknowledged the arrival of the last of his summonsed men with a grunt. 'As you will now know, Ferrax has slaughtered the two men I sent out to gather information. He sent them back tied to their own horses. This tells us two things; that they are alert and that they do not want for beasts. I sense therefore that he has sufficient numbers of warriors to bring us to battle.' He smiled 'and this is good, because whoever he has gathered to his cause does not know these lands like we do and when we do battle we shall slaughter him and all those fools who dare to challenge me!'

'Lord, where has he got his men from do you suppose?'

'I neither suppose nor do I care' roared Perris to the approval of his men. His confidence was infectious and the men stood taller, and prouder as a result. Here was a strong man, a leader, that they could follow and one whose rule guaranteed influence power and wealth. At least for as long as he survived. 'I suspect however' said Perris more quietly 'that he has planned this and brought men from across the seas' he waved his hand dismissively. 'But they will have no loyalty to him; their only loyalty will be to gold and silver and they will not risk death as you will.' The roar of approval satisfied Perris that his men were prepared to die, even though he had other plans.

'Storril! Storril you worm. Where are you?' roared Perris and as the hapless man came into view he called 'fetch Morcant the druid, I want him here. Now!' Storril disappeared, scurrying between the huts. He returned with an unflustered and calm Morcant who strode calmly up to the assembled men.

'Lord Perris?' he enquired. 'You summonsed me.'

'I did, because I have a special job for you Morcant. I want you to go and see my brother and give him a message from me.' He drew a short bladed and vicious looking knife from his belt and held it in front of the druid's face much to the horror of his men who recoiled from this slur to the gods. 'And if you decide to be disloyal to me druid and give my brother information I promise in front of the gods you hold so dear that I shall cut out your tongue and feed it to my dogs.'

Morcant laughed, a hollow sound with no mirth attached. 'I have no loyalty to a man that banished me; who took my life away from me Perris. You need have no cause to distrust my loyalties.'

'I trust no man except myself druid' snarled Perris, 'but my brother is a weak-minded man who will listen to the words you speak. Prepare yourself and take a horse and I shall tell you the message when you are ready.'

***

'Look!' called Gadrig, pointing to a small shape moving across the landscape. Ferrax, came and stood next to the man and indeed could make out what he knew to be a man on horseback. The sun had climbed into the clear blue sky promising a warm day and as Ferrax looked around he could see the land around, dominated as it was by the fortress at the water's edge.

'Bring my horse, and yours as well' he said to Gardig quietly. The warrior went immediately to do his master's bidding. Ferrax looked at the lands and an idea came to his mind. From the slope on which he stood, the land fell down to the water. A boat, clearly a trader's ship, rode at anchor in the tranquil harbour. Beyond that there was a flat island over towards where the sun rose, and another spit of land protruding into the sea on the side where the sun set. Across a small strip of water stood another large island, a land with hills, shrouded in a thin morning mist that would soon burn away.

Ferrax' attention was called back to the man on the horse who was already on the lower slopes of the hill. Gadrig approached with the two horses.

'We intercept him' said Ferrax. 'Do you recognise him yet?'

'Morcant' replied Gadrig. 'So he has sided with your brother?'

'He had nowhere else to go except in the ground as a corpse' said Ferrax simply. He threw himself onto the horses back, grinned at Gadrig and rode at an easy pace to meet the druid, the warrior a respectful distance behind.

After a while and as protocol demanded, Ferrax halted and let the druid come to him. Morcant saw the two mounted men and turned his horse to meet them. He halted in front of them.

'Lord Ferrax' he called simply and without any feeling of respect or pleasure in renewing their acquaintanceship.

'Morcant' said Ferrax, acknowledging the other's presence but doing no more than that.

'Lord Perris sends me to you with a message.'

'Let us hear it then.'

'First I must have your assurance of my own safety' replied Morcant. Ferris laughed and leaned forward on his horse.

'You are owed nothing from me druid, though I shall promise that the skin on your back shall remain unbroken.'

'Fair enough.' The druid paused and his horse pawed at the ground for a moment, impatient to be moving again. 'My Lord Perris invites you and your men to join in battle there' he pointed to an area of flat land near the fortress 'when the sun reaches its height this day.'

'Tell my brother that I am no fool, and tell him that if he wants to talk to me to come himself and not send his dog.' Morcant bridled at this slur.

'I remind you that I speak with the gods and served your father loyally for many seasons. You would do well to moderate your words to me.'

Ferrax spat on the ground. 'You served yourself Morcant, and it serves your purposes to ally with my upstart brother. If there was one shred of loyalty or decency or even humility within you, then you would be nowhere near this place. You tell Perris that I will be here if he wants to talk and that I have a way to avoid bloodshed and maintain honour between us.'

Morcant looked shocked at this possible peace for all but quickly recomposed himself. 'I shall pass on your message Lord' he said inclining his head in a gesture of respect.

'Gadrig will accompany you back to your new master' said Ferrax. He turned to the warrior. 'Speak with my brother from a safe distance and keep the druid with you. If he resists, kill him. Persuade my brother to meet me, just the two of us.'

'Yes Lord' said Gadrig who rode slowly forward to join Morcant and the two of them made their way slowly down the slope towards the fortress.

'Was that wise?' asked Buldan when Ferrax explained what he had done. 'You slaughtered two of his men and now send one of your best into his hands?'

'It shows confidence' said Ferrax. 'And my brother knows the regard I have for Gadrig. He will get the message that I can send a warrior of his calibre into danger, and that must mean that I have many others of equal stature.'

With Perris

'The druid is returning' said Storril. 'He is accompanied by a warrior.'

'I shall see for myself' said Perris rising from his seat by the fire and walking slowly to the fortress wall, Storril trailing behind him as protocol dictated.

The two men on horseback came to rest within hailing distance of the earth embankment. Gadrig, appraised the fortress with a warrior's eye and was impressed. Gargonstus had built as well as he ever did, in a time before conflict. Gadrig also counted the heads of the men that appeared at the wall and was impressed with the force that Perris commanded. He knew that what he was seeing was only a small number of the warriors serving the younger brother, but even so just by those on the wall, Ferrax was outnumbered.

Morcant made to walk his horse on but stopped when Gadrig muttered that one further pace would result in death.

'My Lord Ferrax sends greetings to his brother, Perris' shouted Gadrig.

'Why is the dog not here himself?' was the reply.

'Lord Ferrax seeks audience with his brother alone' called Gadrig.

'You may approach without fear.'

'I prefer to keep distance.'

'Send the druid back and ensure he is unharmed.'

'The druid remains with me until we have concluded our discussion.' A spear flew from the wall and landed about the length of two horses in front of Gadrig. The warrior's horse, trained in the ways of battle, neither flinched nor moved apart from setting his ears back in a gesture of disapproval. As the spear quivered in the ground, both men saw that the shaft was a bright red colour

'Take this spear Gadrig and return to your cowardly master. When he is ready to talk to me in person tell him to bring this with him. It is his guarantee of safety during those discussions. I shall require a similar token from him.

Gadrig untied a leather and brass shield from his horse and let it fall to the ground. 'Here is your protection Lord Perris' called Gadrigm, favouring the younger brother with a title in a mark of respect because at least Perris was observing the proper traditions of the tribe.

'You see the single tree that leans towards the sun?' Gadrig looked and followed the direction indicated by an outstretched arm from the wall.

'I see it' he replied simply.

'Tell my brother to be there when the sun points the tree shadow to this place.' Later on that day in other words. That would suit Ferrax just fine thought Gadrig.

'It shall be so' he called and told Morcant that he could return to the fortress, but that he should take care to walk slowly. Both men kicked their horses forward, Gadrig to collect the spear, and Morcant to return to his new home.

***

Both the druid and the warrior were questioned in detail by their respective masters; each of the brothers wanted to know the strength of the opposition. Morcant provided little information, explaining that Ferrax had ridden to meet him, thus shielding the prying eyes of the druid from the force camped on the hill. Gadrig on the other hand confirmed that which Ferrax already knew; that their small force was significantly outnumbered and in an even fight would be slaughtered. Far from deterring Ferrax, this news seemed to increase his resolve, though he would not disclose his plans to anyone.

Ferrax was pleased with Gadrig and the arrangements made for the meeting. He explained, overriding the opposition of his warriors, that he would ride to the meeting place alone, but that he would go armed and prepared for a fight if necessary.

Similarly, Perris advised that he would meet with his brother alone. All present knew not to challenge this decision for once Perris had disclosed his thoughts then they would not be altered even if flaws were pointed out. Perris was not a happy recipient of criticism and men had been put to death for daring to find fault with this angry man.

The Brothers Meet

Ferrax had taken leave of his men, their reluctance to let him meet with his brother alone was evident, they all offered to accompany him, explaining their mistrust of Perris and eventually Ferrax had to resort to ordering them to remain behind or leave and return to their homes to be with the women and children. The shame of such a banishment was enough to remove any further objection and Ferrax set off for the meeting place in good time, clutching the red shafted spear as a token of his peaceful intent. He had also taken a skin of wine and the meat from a cooked rabbit to share with his brother.

As the shadows from the crooked tree lengthened, Ferrax saw his brother astride his black horse, come walking slowly towards him. He held the leather and brass shield aloft until acknowledged by Ferrax who drove the spear into the ground. The symbolism was appropriate, the weapon rendered useless whilst in the ground, it meant that there was no need for a shield which Perris correctly dropped to the earth near the spear.

The younger brother dismounted and stood by the horse.

'You wanted to see me?' said Perris.

'I wanted to see if we could avoid unnecessary bloodshed my brother' said Ferrax amicably. Perris laughed

'A little late for that is it not? We are bound on a course where both want the same thing and unless the gods visit us, the only way to resolve our differences is battle.' Perris looked around sniffing at the air, the tide was out in the small creek that ran alongside the land here, but still there was the discernible tang of salt in the air, mingled with the foul odours of the mud that lined the shore.

'There may be a solution Perris' said Ferrax quietly 'and one that provides honour for both of us, as well as remaining within our father's wishes.'

'I care not for what that old fool spoke' spat Perris.

'Be careful brother for he now sits alongside the gods.'

'Well let us hope that his wits are restored then, for he died a babbling fool.' Perris let silence descend between the two men before asking what his brother's idea was.

'You have built a fine fortress here Perris' acknowledged Ferrax 'but I have the builder with me and he knows the weak points as well as the strengths. A battle will weaken both of us and leave our tribe vulnerable to attack from others.' He paused 'and I have no doubt that I will win, just as you believe that you will.'

'Get on with it. I have no patience for your prattling, brother.'

'We join forces, and we take the island over the water. By reputation it has fine land, good soil, natural harbours and fresh water.'

'And then what?' said Perris sourly

'It is yours. You become Chief of that land, I remain Chief of the lands ruled by our father, but with you keeping your fortress here. You would control trade by sea, and I control trade by land. Your status would equal mine and we would exist together with honour and hopefully friendship.' Ferrax walked towards his brother who drew back. 'I have wine and meat with me. Why not sit and at least consider what I have said?'

I have no need to think on it brother' said Perris. You offer me that which I could take if I wanted, and take away that which I already possess.' He paused for a moment, his speech was friendly and for once without rancour. 'Let me ask you whether you would accept such a settlement?'

'In your position I believe I would' replied Ferrax.

'And there is the vast difference between us my brother' said Perris. 'For I am in a position of strength and can take anything I want, whereas you have to beg and barter to keep your lands. You are weak Ferrax, your whole life proves it. You should have fought our father when he disrespected you and should have taken what was yours, but instead you were so keen to prove what a wise man you are. You wanted to rule by agreement and not by force. It demeans both of us to be here Ferrax, you are no Chief, no leader and no man. Far better that we settle this in the ways of the warrior. In battle.'

So be it my brother, but just you and me. We fight and the winner takes the land, the people and the tribe. The loser . . . '

'Will be dead' said Perris with a chilling finality. 'We fight to the death, and yes I agree that it should be just the two of us. Here in this place at the same time tomorrow.'

'Agreed. I give your warriors immunity and pardon after your death' said Ferrax. His brother laughed and leaned forward.

'I will hunt down those dogs that are your men and put them to the sword or the flame. You can save them by running away as you did before when I had your woman.' He prodded Ferrax hard in the chest. 'She screamed as I took her you know. She shouted your name as I rode her and where were you? Cowardly hiding across the sea, running away, just as you should now.' He spat on the floor at his brother's feet. 'Look at the sun Ferrax, watch it set and watch it rise for it will be the last time that you can. This time tomorrow the flies will be getting fat on your blood and guts and I shall be riding to your home to take back what is mine.'

'Until tomorrow then brother' said Ferrax, walking away to his horse and riding back to the camp on the hill.

The Following Day

'These men have chosen combat to settle their dispute. May the gods guide what is right and just and may the victor have compassion to the vanquished. Let no man strike while the other is unarmed. Declare your weapons!' Morcant looked severely at each of the brothers. Perris held his battle sword in his right hand and a thin bladed dagger in the other; Ferrax too held a sword in his right hand and a spear in his left. Once the weapons were declared, no other could be brought to bear on an opponent during the combat. It was different in battle of course, but this was a feud, overseen by Morcant and watched by supporters of Perris.

There was no sign of any of Ferrax's men. He had explained to them what had been agreed, and told them of his fears for their homes and families if he should fall. He bade them return, all save for Gadrig who was to remain and watch from afar so he could report the battle to the settlement.

Forrun, Gargonstus and Buldan were vehement in their opposition to Ferrax's plans. Egged on by the mute giant, the other two explained their lack of faith in Perris; their belief that he would use any means to slaughter Ferrax and seize control of the lands. Ferrax calmly explained that he had made his decision and that they should show faith in him and that with the help of the gods he would prevail.

And now, standing on the flat grass alongside the stinking creek, it struck Ferrax that whatever happened, everything would change for this land. If he were to win then he would have to deal with this horde of warriors who were unruly and lawless, chosen by Perris for their violence than their brains. If he were to lose, then all that his father had created was likely to be swept away in an orgy of destruction.

His mind was still in a turmoil when Morcant called the two combatants forward to face each other.

'Does either man wish to settle this matter without bloodshed?' he asked the two of them quietly. Ferrax shook his head and looked into his brother's eyes. Perris smiled grimly and said he did not. The two men backed away from each other and began to circle, each looking for an opportunity to strike. Morcant withdrew to the side of a rough circle formed by the watchers, none of whom would dare break the code by which they lived; this was a fight between these two men and neither would receive assistance from any other until one was victorious.

***

As the two brothers crouched and moved, the warmth of the day was waning and clouds moved across the sky reducing the light. Morcant pronounced it a sign from the gods that they drew a veil across the land so they could not see. It was, he said, a sign that neither man was favoured and that the contest was just and fair.

Ferrax jabbed with his spear, the thrust was effortlessly knocked aside by Perris, but as this exposed his chest, Ferrax lunged with the sword. Perris nimbly stepped back and the heavy blade did nothing except strike the air. Perris grinned and put the dagger in his belt, concentrating on the sword, and holding it two handed. Ferrax continued to jab with the spear, as much to keep his brother back as an attempt to cause injury.

Ferrax hoped to annoy his brother into losing his temper; it had been his favourite trick when the two of them fought as children, for an angry Perris lashed out, casting all caution to the wind and in doing so left himself exposed to an attack. Perris was however alert to his brother's intention and with all the time in the world, contented himself with knocking the spear aside with his sword, time after time, much to the obvious discontent of the watching warriors who grew bored of this repetition.

The crowd played more on Ferrax's mind than that of Perris. The younger sibling was content to let Ferrax tire himself, biding his time for when he would strike.

Suddenly in a flurry of activity, Ferrax jabbed with the spear and Perris slashed at the shaft, his intention to snap it in two thus depriving Ferrax of one of his weapons. Instead of snapping the shaft however, the blade became stuck in the wood, and though Perris was able to wrest the spear out of his brother's grasp he could not free the sword. Ferrax saw his chance and lunged with the sword. Had he controlled it with two hands, the chances are that he could have inflicted a mortal blow. As it was Perris bellowed as the tip of the sword pierced the skin of his left bicep, causing the metal to turn red as his blood ran down the blade. Ferrax shouted in triumph and raised the sword, two handed this time above his head, intending to slice his brother's head, but Perris was too quick and side stepped the strike and in one swift movement, stood on the shaft of the spear and wrenched his sword free.

Ferrax used the momentum of the overhead strike to swing the sword blade round to attack Perris's side, but the younger man was fast and brought his own sword round to parry the blow. Metal struck metal with a hollow clang, and sparks flew as the sword blades impacted. The watching warriors cheered as the fight ignited into savage combat, both men swinging the heavy blades at each other and both defending with all their strength.

Shadows were lengthening and Morcant ordered that torches be lit and placed in the ground so that the fighters had sufficient light to see. The dancing flames casting eerie shadows even though the evening light was still sufficient for all.

'Is that all you have brother?' sneered Perris, looking at the sweat coursing down Ferrax's face and launching another attack, this time it was Perris's turn to hold his sword above his head and repeatedly rain blow after blow down upon Ferrax who defending with his own sword, absorbing the strength and energy of each strike. Ferrax was however trying to lure Perris into a mistake and on the seventh blow, he withdrew his blade, sidestepped the attack, bent down to the ground and picked up the broken spear which he then jabbed viciously into his brother's thigh. Perris bellowed again in pain and dropped his sword, staggering away from the fight. Ferrax, conscious that his brother was now unarmed, restrained himself from further attack but stood almost bouncing on tip toes waiting the chance to strike and deliver the final blow.

'Pick up your sword!' shouted Ferrax. 'Pick it up!' He walked over to it, picked it up and threw it at his brother's feet. 'Pick it up!' he yelled again. The crowd were silent in anticipation of the next move. 'Fight or forfeit' shouted Ferrax, looking towards Morcant for support or a word of censure to Perris. None was forthcoming.

'What are you waiting for you coward?' snarled Perris, still without his sword in his hand.

'I will not kill an unarmed man' said Ferrax.

'But I am not without a weapon you weak fool' said Perris, snatching the dagger from his belt and advancing with a limp towards his brother. 'Come on, let's see if you have the guts to have a real fight' he said as he slashed the blade left to right in front of himself. Ferrax laughed, and believing himself to be on the verge of victory slashed out towards Perris's wrist. Perris twisted, again sending Ferrax's blade harmlessly into thin air and then he punched Ferrax in the face, using the full force of his considerable strength and sending his brother sprawling on to the grass, blood pouring from his broken nose.

'Come on!' shouted Perris. 'Come on Ferrax' A shout taken up by some of the crowd 'Come on Ferrax' they shouted egging the prone man to his feet. Ferrax scambled away and was trying to rise when Perris, howling with pain, took his weight on his injured leg and delivered a violent kick between his brother's legs. Ferrax doubled over in agony and writhed on the ground, his sword out of his hand and lying on the ground as he tried to cope with the pain.

'Up!' commanded Perris. And he picked up Ferrax's sword and dropped it next to the man. Perris took a few steps back, picked up his own sword and then advanced.

'See, he has his sword' he shouted, now raising the heavy blade as if to strike.

'Stop!' commanded Morcant in a voice that boomed across the open ground. Perris hesitated, but no more than that, however that hesitation and the tone of Morcant's voice was enough to allow Ferrax time to grab his sword and parry the blow that was aimed at his head. Again iron rang against iron and a piece of metal flew from Ferrax's blade leaving a 'V' shaped nick in it half way along its length.

Ferrax used the follow through from Perris's strike to stagger to his feet. He had tears in his eyes and could not see properly. He wiped his vision clear with the back of his hand as once again Perris advanced slowly because of the injury to his leg, but nevertheless inexorably.

'Brother' said Ferrax. 'Enough surely?'

'Never' snarled Perris and keeping his blade level, slashed at Ferrax opening a thin but stinging wound across the torso that produced beads of bright red blood. Ferrax staggered back and as he did so, the watching crowd moved back as well, but the woollen cloak he wore over his shoulder caught one of the torches in the ground and lit. Flames singed and burned the material, Ferrax struggled to free himself from the fire and made to hurl the burning garment at Perris, but as his arms were over his head, Perris thrust his sword into the belly of Ferrax and quickly withdrew it. It was the telling wound and had Perris heaved upwards would have been a mortal blow, but he had other plans and as his brother sank to his knees, the burning cloak dropped and forgotten, Perris kicked his head and rendered him to unconsciousness.

There was a moment of silence, before the watching warriors began cheering the victor, the new Chief.

Perris however, held his arms aloft in a call to silence, for he was not done, and as his men fell quiet, he turned to Morcant.

'Revive him. Give him a potion or use your words, or whatever you do, but revive him and when he is conscious, tie his hands and have him bound to that branch' he said, indicating a strong mature tree close by. Morcant made to speak, but Perris silenced him with a look.

***

Later, and once his own wounds had been cleaned and salved, Perris limped to where his brother hung by his arms from the tree branch. His feet barely touched the ground and Ferrax groaned as he breathed. He lived as Perris had commanded he should so that he could now deliver the final humiliation.

'This man' called Perris loudly so that all could hear, 'this man defied me and lost in battle.' There was a ragged cheer that Perris quickly silenced. 'Though he lives, his life is forfeit to me! I get to choose the manner of his death, and what I have chosen means that he goes to the gods incomplete, so that for all he may want their welcome, he cannot be with them and will forever be cast out.'

'Perris, you cannot . . .' began Morcant, but he was silenced by the new Chief who shouted him down, spittle flying as he raged at the interruption.

'Be silent you interfering old woman Morcant! I alone hold power in this land and from this moment I alone hold the decisions over the life and death of everyone. And anyone, anyone who defies me shall die like this wretch will die at my hand.' Perris took the knife from his belt and walked over to his brother and sliced across his forehead, a thin bead of blood tracing the path of the viciously sharp knife. Satiisfied with his work, Perris ran the knife down from the bridge of Ferrax's nose, and thenaccompanied by a keening whimper coming from the bound man, gently pulled the skin from his brothers face. Morcant once again made a move forward to intervene but Perris brandished the knife at him.

'Druid, tell them what I am doing and why.'

'You are rendering your victim unwhole so that he is unworthy to be seen by the gods' said Morcant quietly.

'Louder Druid. Tell them all and tell them clearly' shouted Perris as he continued to butcher the tied man.

'Lord Perris renders his victim unworthy to be with the gods!' called Morcant to the gasps of those watching. Death in battle was honourable and worthy of lament, but mutilation was reserved for those that stole from the tribe or attacked and mutilation meant humiliation and that any peace after death would be rendered impossible.

The man who was once Ferrax bellowed in rage as the stinging pain found its way to his numb brain. Whatever medicament Morcant had administered was wearing off, though Ferrax had no energy to fight and merely stood, tied and immobile as he was flayed alive.

'Enough Perris!' hissed Morcant, alarmed at the zeal the new Chief showed in his chosen task. Perris was now slicing into the shoulders of Ferrax who still, somehow, pathetically still lived, barely clinging to a life that he had no hope of continuing.

The watching warriors looked on, there was a rumble of discontent as they felt the savage butchery metered out to Ferrax defiled both his status and the bravey he had shown in fighting Perris, but the younger brother was impassive and focused on his task until with a shuddering groan Ferrax's spirit mercifully departed his body and his mortal remains slumped against their bindings. The crowd, having witnessed an execution the like of which they had never seen before, slowly drifted away, though Perris remained until he had removed all the skin he could from the corpse which he left for the birds to feed upon as he walked back to the fortress.

After the Death of Ferrax

Gadrig was too far away to see clearly. He saw one man fall to the ground and saw the assembled crowd surge towards the victor before he heard the faintest of sounds of jubilation. He believed then that Ferrax was dead and he had the sense not to stay where he was, having witnessed what he thought was the slaughter of his Chief. Fortunately he did not remain to see the mutilation of his Chief for he knew he had to ride to warn his comrades of the death of Ferrax; he knew that Perris would exact revenge on all those that opposed him, and he knew that he could not abandon the life that he had so carefully built and that he would stay and defend the people he cared about, to the death if needs be.

Gadrig, walked slowly to his tethered horse, untied the leather rein that held the beast, and threw himself over the back of the animal before riding hard northwards.

***

The next morning, Perris acknowledged the somehat muted plaudits of his men and did his best to cover the wounds to his arm and leg. In truth he had not expected his brother to put up such a fight, but instead of a grudging admiration he nurtured a growing and illogical hatred for the man who had caused him pain. Perris had believed himself invincible and had previously settled disputes with others by means of violence. Ferrax had inflicted injury and had drawn blood and that made Perris weakened and he feared that he was vulnerable. He knew he needed to assert authority to show these men that he feared nobody. He held his arms aloft and called for silence; the message took a short time to reach those at the back of the throng surrounding him but eventually all fell quiet.

'Cut his head off' ordered Perris clearly referring to Ferrax's corpse, 'and bring it to me at the fortress.' There was a murmuring of dissent, that initially Perris made to ignore as he walked away, but the rumbling grew and he turned around and glared angrily. The men were not happy and with good cause, for although they shared the joy or Perris's victory, Ferrax had fought and died with honour and he had been a Chief of the tribe, at least in name. His body should have been afforded due ceremony, yet Perris ignored this, and did so at his peril.

'I said cut his head off!' shouted Perris. 'Or do any of you want that I should do it like some menial!' The men backed away, more than a few looking to Morcant who stood closest to Perris.

'Lord . . . ' began the druid

'Do you defy me Morcant?' growled Perris dangerously.

'I merely counsel caution' replied the white robed man obsequiously.

'And I counsel obedience' said Perris. 'In fact, for your temerity druid, you shall do it. You have skill in dispatching the animals of this world to the gods in sacrifice, so now you can work on something a little more challenging.'

'Lord?' implored Morcant.

'I command it druid' said Perris. 'And when I command something I expect and demand that it shall be done. Someone give him an axe?' A heavy battle weapon was held out to Morcant, who looked at it as if it were diseased.

'Take it Morcant and do that which I command' said Perris dangerously. Not a sound could be heard, the warriors too shocked to make a noise, so intent were they on watching the battle of wills unfold before them.

Morcant looked at the axe, looked at Perris and turned slowly to look at the body of Ferrax, still hanging in the near distance. Crows were already pecking at the entrails that lay spilled on the grass. Men moved away from Morcant. Normally a druid held an exalted place within any settlement, but Perris had challenged that convention and coming so soon after the decisive battle with his brother, the power lay with the new Chief. Morcant pulled himself to his full height, and dropped the axe.

'I am a druid, not a butcher. I follow the words of the gods, not the demands of men' he called. 'Your brother was a warrior and a Chief and deserved due respect so that he may join your father. To cut him up as you did violates our customs and our laws and should you continue, you risk incurring the wrath of the gods that I could not hope to prevent.'

Perris by this time was suffering with the throbbing pain of his wounds. He had lost blood and his head was light but he effected to lean on his sword in a casual manner.

'Very well' said Perris calmly. 'This is your counsel to me is it druid?'

'It is my Lord' said Morcant regaining an air of confidence.

'I see . . . Storril ! Sorril? Storril!' called Perris.

'Lord' said the servant bowing obsequiously.

'Cut the head off that body. Mount it on a spear and bring it to me.' He turned and limped away calling over his shoulder. 'And Morcant, never defy me again.' The warriors watched Perris limp back to his dwelling, leaving Storril and a forlorn Morcant standing together. The servant made to pick up the axe.

'Leave it' said Morcant with authority. Storril just stood for a moment and looked questioningly at the druid. 'We cannot disrespect the dead in the way Perris demands' said Morcant by way of explanation.

'We cannot disrespect Perris without ending up like his brother' said Storril with a simple finality and ignoring the protests of the druid he dragged the heavy axe with his one hand and set off towards the body.

Part III
Perris

At Caer Sisal

The news of Ferrax's death was met with a forlorn silence that quickly transported itself to fear. The people of the fortress had put all of their hope and faith in Ferrax but understood the risks and knew of the strength and ruthlessness of Perris. Some now feared retribution, chief among them was Caeryl who sought guidance from Idon and her father.

The fortress was alive with gossip and rumour. Already the first family had left; one of the shepherds who spent most of his time on the hills had packed his woman and children and had hurriedly left. Drullis tried to quell the worst of the gossip but he had no authority and was powerless, Caeryl was wracked with grief and unable to function as with good reason, she feared for her life, the warriors made plans to defend the fortress, filling every container with water and ensuring that grain was in plentiful supply. The only person who remained cold and detached was Idon, and it was to her that the people gravitated for security and clear thinking.

Idon's first act was to call cwnsl and to declare that for the first time that anyone could remember, it would be open to all. When what seemed like the entire population was gathered, Idon rose and spoke clearly.

'Whether we like it or not Perris is now the legitimate Chief of this Tribe.' There was a murmur of discontent that she quelled. 'It is not our choice but it is our law' she said with a finality 'and as such we must make ready to receive him as his status now demands. This does not however mean that we should not take precautions. Any who wish to leave shall not be prevented, nor unwelcome on their return and I urge all families to look to their own protection. A battle or siege shall not prolong our lives, Perris has too many men and is too strong and ruthless to show any mercy and therefore our survival depends on us being pragmatic.' She paused for a moment and looked around, a number of people looked uncomfortable at hearing her words and she caught a look between Gadrig and Buldan that told her they at least were prepared to fight.

‘There are two people I fear for and wish to send to safety; Marrad my son who Perris will see as a threat, and Caeryl, Ferrax’s woman who Perris will almost certainly seek retribution from. I am sending Marrad away, but I have no control or influence over Caeryl and can only urge her and her father to give though to my words. These are my decisions and each of you must make your own plans but this fortress will not resist Perris for that will result in the destruction of us all.’ There was silence for a short time and then Cwaenog the Outsider rose to his feet.

‘This is fine for you to say Idon, woman of Sisal and mother of Perris and Ferrax, but consider this. Everything that befalls us, the honest decent people of this Tribe comes from your family. Your eldest son is slain, your second son claims to rule and you send your youngest away to protect him. Sisal was a fair and just man but since he left us your family has brought nothing but destruction and loss to the people.’

‘And your solution Cweanog?’ asked Drullis calmly. ‘What would you have us do?’

‘Kill the woman idon, kill Marrad as sacrifice to the gods and send Caeryl to Perris in peace to tell him we have cleansed this place of the curse from the gods that afflicts us.’ There was a murmur of assent from the gathered people and the mood of the fortress was turning hostile to Idon, who began to feel vulnerable. She looked to Drullis who made to rise to his feet but the murmurs fell away to silence as a slight figure in a white robe walked to the centre of the group and spoke.

‘The gods are not angry with you and this is not a punishment’ announced Ancastia staring directly at Cwaenog. Ferrax was a good man, raised by a good woman to take his place at the head of the

Tribe but that is not to be. Perris has none of the wisdom of his brother or his father but for the moment he has strength, and that might has prevailed, but it shall not last for ever and for now we must endure what is to come. Idon speaks with the sense of Sisal who brought peace and prosperity to these lands, she speaks in the way he would have done and she is touched by him from beyond his tomb.' These were powerful words that won the argument that day and earned Ancastia the lasting respect and trust of Idon.

Plans were quickly made to offer tribute to Perris, discussions were held as whether it were better to send an envoy to the new Chief or wait for him to attend and quietly Marrad was sent, with Gargonstus as escort, to a safe place, far away from the influence of Perris.

The gates to the fortress were not closed that night, but sentries were posted and told to wake Idon Ancastia and Drullis on the sight of anything.

****

The following morning dawned with a thin drizzle, the sort that soaked everything, made fires difficult to maintain and hung heavily on trees and men. Idon emerged from her hut and took in the scene before her. Everything was still, there was no wind and smoke from the fires in each of the huts rose into the air. All except for two buildings; the first was the Chief's hut that still housed the grieving Caeryl, and the second as occupied by Cwaenog and his family. Idon moved towards the latter dwelling but was hailed by Buldan who was standing guard by the gate.

'They've gone' he called. Idon changed direction and walked toward the man. His hair, beard and cloak were covered in silver-like water, almost looking like spiders webs.

'Gone?' said Idon with something that sounded like resignation.

'Yes Lady, not too long since. They took their cart and all they could carry.'

'Why did you not wake me Buldan?'

'I figured it was for the best' replied the warrior. 'Cwaenog had no place here after his words last night and he knew it. Better that he disappear than stay here like a disease causing pain. Besides' Buldan spat on the ground in a gesture of dislike 'he did not belong here. He never fought with us, never served us and spread his words like bad water over the land'

Idon was about to reply when a scream of pain pierced the air. The scream came from outside the fortress and was the sound of a man. Idon looked Buldan in the eye and both knew what that scream meant.

'Fetch Drullis and Ancastia' ordered Idon 'and Gadrig!' she called after the retreating figure who was already running across the sodden ground. There was no need to call Gadrig as he was already emerging from his hut and running for the gate, closely followed by Forrun and Ancastia.

As the small group assembled at the gate to the fortress a solitary horseman came riding slowly towards them. The horse, a magnificent black beast threw his head around, perhaps impatient at the slow process over the land or possibly in reaction to the smell from the severed head on the haft of a spear carried by the rider.

Dull red tendrils, the remains of veins and arteries hung from the head where it had been hacked from the body. The eyes, wide and lifeless stared without seeing, and the skin, now a pale grey and drained of life giving blood seemed to almost shine through the drizzle.

Idon, stifled a sob in her throat but could not prevent herself from needing to turn around and vomit on to the ground, the stench adding to the horror appearing before them. She stood, mouth open in shock and disgust as the tears coursed down her face.

Perris pulled the horse to a stop and looked down at the assembled group.

'I am surprised' he announced loudly 'at your wisdom. Mother' he acknowledged with an inclination of his head before proceeding in an almost conversational tone. 'I defeated Ferrax in battle as you can see' he smiled and raised the severed head high so all could see it. More of the people were now making their way toward the gate. 'I know come to claim my rightful place as Chief of this Tribe, the Lord of this place and you shall all acknowledge me as such.' He looked around and sniffed the air.

'I confess I anticipated that you would resist me and that we would do battle. I am both pleased at your reception, but disappointed that I am denied my reason to slaughter more of you.'

'More of us?' asked Idon, knowing the answer before it was spoken.

'My men came across Cwaenog the Outsider skulking away earlier' replied Perris simply. 'He was a coward and was dealt with as such.'

'We heard' said Idon.

'Good!' said Perris grinning 'so now you all know what happens to anyone I deem to be disloyal.'

'And his woman? His daughter?'

'They belong to me. My men will have use of them and if they live they can be sold'

'You grew up with them' said Idon hotly, the mother in her asserting authority over a wayward child. But Perris was way past such things and leaned forward to speak to her directly, even though his words were heard by all.

'Be careful woman' he threatened 'and do not try me. Never question my decisions, never seek to disobey me and never avoid your duties in serving me as your Chief. In return I shall let you live.

That is a decision I might alter if it suits me. Now stand aside as I wish to enter.'

'Ferrax deserves a decent burial as a Chief' said Idon defiantly. 'Where is the rest of his body?'

'In the sea' replied Perris. 'I had Storril take him out into the harbour by boat and throw him out.' This news of yet a further insult to her dead son caused another sob that caught in the throat of Idon.

'How could you?' she whispered.

'I can do whatever I choose' said Perris. 'I will not ask again. Stand aside.' The people parted and the new Chief rode slowly into his fortress.

Caer Sisal

That things had changed became readily apparent. Perris called cwnsl for when the sun went down, and unlike the previous day, the women were barred from attendance. Before the gathering, and with a mother's eye, Idon had noticed that her son limped and that he favoured one arm over the other. So Ferrax had struck, and with satisfaction she understood that Perris would be feeling vulnerable. She asked with exaggerated kindness whether he was injured, and his dismissive answer gave her even more perverse pleasure, knowing that he was too proud and too stubborn to admit any weakness. He took himself and his men out of the fortress he said to hunt, but in reality, everyone knew he was planning to divide what he had taken, and was issuing his orders accordingly

At cwnsl, Perris laid out his terms. He would remain in his fortress by the water and would appoint another man to rule this place in his name. Any warrior that wished to would join his men. Any that did not, would be banished. Those men loyal to Sisal, Idon or Ferrax had to be ready to leave by morning. In future Tributes would be collected at each full moon; these would consist of grain, meat, skins and silver. The exact amounts to be one quarter of whatever the settlement produced. Perris would come and go as he pleased and the Chieftains abode was reserved to him and him alone.

The Chief then introduced the people to the man who would rule in his name. He was a dark-haired, one eyed warrior of around thirty summers by the name of Dran. He stared around, the empty eye socket puckered and closed and when he grinned he only had four visible teeth in his mouth. His language was crude, coarse, and he spoke with an accent that was not of the same tribe. He threatened retribution on anyone found hoarding food, wine or silver, and made it perfectly clear that he was looking for a woman, and if it pleased him, then he would take the one he wanted whether she was with another man or not.

Having concluded his speech, Dran stood back into the shadows and Perris, admitting no question of his decisions closed the meeting and strode away towards the Chiefs hut. Idon stood in his way.

'Perris... '

'Stand aside woman. I have tolerated you more than I should, but I am tired and have no time nor tolerance for your meddling.'

'Caeryl rests within. She is devastated by the loss of Ferrax.' Seeing his face, Idon immediately regretted her words, and Perris pushed past her, knocking her to the ground and stormed into the hut. Dran followed and barred entry to anyone else, a toothless grin on his disfigured face. Idon heard a howl she recognised as being from Caeryl and then heard the sounds of pottery smashing. Silence descended for a short time followed by a bellow of pain from Perris and Caeryl came hurriedly out of the hut, a streak of blood running from the corner of her mouth. Idon gathered the young woman to her and took her to her own dwelling, hoping that their privacy would be respected.

Such hope was however forlorn as Dran appeared at the opening and informed them that he was taking the hut for his own and that they had to leave immediately. Despite protests, Dran was immovable and explained that immediately meant exactly that and they could leave with dignity or be thrown out like ash from a fire.

The two women gathered together their few possessions and left the dwelling. They only stood in the open, the still-falling rain soaking them, for moments before Ancastia came to them and without a word, led them to her own hut and sat them before the fire to dry. A sound from without signalled the arrival of one of Dran's men who announced that he had chosen that hut for himself and his men. Caeryl and Idon looked at each other, their resignation to their new and lowly status plain to see. Ancastia however had other ideas and walked to the skins covering the entrance and explained in a loud voice that she would invoke the punishment of the gods should any man enter uninvited. The warriors who initially stood grinning with the power they wielded, but as Ancastia's calm words put fear in their minds, they slunk away, cowered with the threat of retribution. She turned and smiled at Idon and Caeryl and provided each of them with food and honeyed milk. Before turning to Forrun who sat, ever silent, his head bowed.

'Did he . .? asked Idon. Caeryl shook her head. 'I heard him shout in pain?' continued the older woman, and at last the ghost of a smile appeared across Caeryl's features.

'He is wounded in the leg and the arm. He made to kiss me like the animal he is so I bit his arm where he is hurt.'

'He might have killed you in his rage' said Idon simply.

'I do not care' replied Caeryl. 'My life is no life now.'

***

Ancastia gently raised Forruns' massive head and looked into his eyes, they were glassy with tears, and she understood. Although a warrior he was the most gentle of men and could not serve Perris, he fought when it was just to do so and not through savagery.

'I agree' said Ancastia. 'You must leave, but in time you shall return and I shall await you.' She took his hand and placed it on her chest so he could feel the beating of her heart. She smiled at him and he grinned back, pulling her into a hug that drew the breath out of her.

'Where?' she asked, and in reply Forrun used a stick and drew the crude outline of a ship in the earth floor. 'Corrilun?' she said, naming the Gaulish trader. Forrun nodded and grunted an affirmative, and Ancastia nodded, the decision was a good one. 'Be nice to Karne' she smiled 'after all she has to put up with both of you now.' And after that there was no more to be said and she lay down with Forrun and buried her head in his shoulder for what might be the last time.

***

The following morning, the people of the fort assembled as they were called to do by Perris. He stood, and as his side was Dran, grinning and looking at each of the women in turn. Most avoided his eye and cast their gaze to the floor. One woman met his stare and he licked his lips like an animal scenting prey until even she looked away. The people murmured to themselves, the reasons being readily apparent; Forrun, Buldan and Gadrig had gone.

'I see' said Perris 'that three cowards have deserted their people. Have run away find new masters.' He grinned 'it is of no consequence, for I have sufficient men at my command and posted patrols. I knew they would run and knew they would head for the coast. By now they will be dead.' Hands went to mouths in shock, but Ancastia stayed standing still and her lead gave others courage. She stood between Idon and Caeryl who followed her example. Perris stared at her and walked over to her then turned and addressed Dran.

'Be careful of this one Dran. She has powerful magic and Morcant tells me that she speaks to the gods, you would be wise to heed her words, and wiser to mistrust everything she tells you.' He turned to Caeryl and ran his finger down her cheek. She did not flinch even though every fibre of her being cried out the scratch kick and bite. 'And this one Dran. She is mine.' He raised his voice 'any man touching this woman dies at my hand, and that death will not be pleasant. The same goes for the old woman' he added referring to his own mother almost as an afterthought. 'Other than that . . .' he grinned at his men and shrugged his shoulders to signify he had no interest in what his men did. They laughed and one or two called out until silenced by a look from Dran.

'You people think you know me' said Perris, addressing the crowd. 'I assure you that you do not. The boy that grew here became a man elsewhere and what I want I take without question. To refuse me is to invite death. I shall be leaving this place today and you will obey the words of Dran who speaks in my name. I call cwnsl at Caer Perris once when the sun reaches its height in the sky, and once when it reaches its lowest place, and from this land one man may attend to pay the due tributes and be held accountable for any failings.' Any further oratory was interrupted by the sound of horse's hooves and Perris clapped his hands together. 'My patrol returns with news of your cowardly deserters' he announced as four warriors rode into the fortress.

'Are they slain?' called Perris to the men, who jumped down from the animals and walked towards him. Their demeanour was not of victorious fighters but of failure.

'No Lord, they got away and killed three of your men.' Perris's face turned red with anger and he drew his sword causing a gasp from the assembled people.

'Get after them, and if you don't find them, or don't kill them, don't ever return to my presence. Do you hear me?'

'Lord . . .' stammered one of the warriors hesitatingly.

'Do not fail me' shouted Perris 'and do not question.' The men hurriedly re-mounted their horses and left. The fact that Forrun Gadrig and Buldan had not only escaped, but had killed some of Perris's men had the instant effect of cheering the people of Caer Sisal who murmured and mumbled to themselves again. Only Ancastia, Idon and Caeryl remained silent, looking straight ahead.

'Silence!' roared Perris, his eyes blazing with anger, spittle foaming at the corners of his mouth. He was obeyed. 'Drullis, Gargonstus, you will step forward' he added more calmly as the two men did as they were bid. 'You two have shown loyalty by remaining to serve me and so Drullis, I appoint you as the father of my woman

Caeryl, to be the headman of this place. You will be responsible to Dran and it is your function to keep these people in order.' Perris did not give Drullis the chance to speak but instead moved on to Gargonstus. 'You have served me well previously, and will do so again as one of my warriors.'

'No Lord Perris. I am a builder, not a warrior.' The man's voice was clear and easily heard by all. 'I will create huts defences harbours and animal pens, but I will never again take up arms.'

'You defy me?'

'No Lord, I serve you in the best way I can' said Gargonstus simply. Perris stared at him and without breaking that stare called for Dran's sword that was put into his hand.

'Take this sword Gargonstus.' The builder did not move. 'Take it I said' repeated Perris and as if reluctant the man reached out and took the sword from him. 'There' said Perris, a note of triumph in his voice 'a man who knows the value of obedie . . .' There was a loud crack as Gargonstus snapped the iron blade in two and threw the pieces to the ground.

'I am a builder Lord Perris' he repeated.

'Very well Gargonstus' said Perris. 'If that is your decision.' He turned to his men. 'Kill him' he commanded and they drew their swords and advanced. The men and women of Caer Sisal shouted and screamed and moved away, one man threw a sword to Gargonstus who deftly caught it and parried a blow from a warrior before punching Dran and knocking him senseless. Momentarily stunned, the warriors paused and Gargonstus seized his chance and ran. He was at the gates when Perris took a spear from one of his men and hurled it at the fleeing figure. The spear struck the builder between the shoulders and he collapsed face first into the ground, writhing to release the weapon from his body. Calmly, Perris walked over to Gargonstus and heaved the spear out, ripping flesh and causing agony. Gargonstus rolled painfully over and tried to rise as

Perris hacked his sword into the mans neck sending a fountain of crimson blood spewing forth and ending his life.

'This is what happens to those who defy me!' shouted Perris. 'Learn this lesson well.'

***

Perris had summonsed both Idon and Caeryl, and they now stood before him, each fearing for her own life. For his part Perris seemed calmer, as if the bloodshed of the past two days had satiated that most violent part of his nature. Whilst the women stood, Perris was sat, a bowl of food in front of him.

'You will eat with me?' he asked.

'Not hungry' shivered Caeryl, still unable to look at this stranger before her.

'Nor I' agreed Idon who had no such qualms and looked her son in the eye unflinchingly.

'I see' said Perris. 'Well I have called you both here to decide what to do with you, and as I see it there is a trade to be made.' The women looked at each other, both had the same thoughts. If Perris was talking of trade then he meant to sell them into slavery.

'A trade?' said Idon finally.

'Yes' said Perris calmly 'between us. Oh, I apologise, did you think I meant . . . ' and he laughed. Unlike Ferrax, Perris's laugh could be cruel and sadistic, he genuinely found their fear humorous. 'What I had in mind' he explained 'was that in return for your loyalty to me, I not only let you live, but protect you.'

'Loyalty?' said Caeryl incredulously.

'Be assured woman that I have no false hopes about yours views on me. Your words and actions will be sufficient to lead these people into accepting my rule.'

'Actions?' said Caeryl nervously. Perris seemed to consider his words carefully before he replied.

'You two are so careful to respect the past and to honour the words of my father. Well, let it be so. It was he who decreed that you and I should be bound together Caeryl, and that is something I shall hold you to. You are my woman and nothing of these recent distractions shall change what was decreed. I shall expect you to serve me wherever and whenever I choose.'

'And your other woman?' asked Idon sharply.

'What of her?' said Perris dismissively. 'She is the mother of my son who will one day rule in my place. She lives in my stronghold and you live here. Should you ever meet then you will show each other due deference as equals.'

Idon sorted in derision. 'These are my terms mother' said Perris 'I am not known for being patient, or for negotiating. Agree to what I want or . . ' he shrugged and left the sentence unfinished. Idon looked at Caeryl.

'If we do as you say, then you remove your man Dran from our fort. You shall receive your tributes as you demand and all will be done as you require except I shall not share your bed' said Caeryl. 'Your mother and I shall rule this place in your name and with allegiance.'

Idon continued to look at the younger woman but her expression changed from one of concern to one of pride.

'And if I say no?' said Perris.

'Then you can kill me now' said Caeryl 'but I warn you Perris things have changed between us and shall never return to the time where I was something to be used or bullied as you saw fit. Try and force yourself on me just once and our truce is at an end. Kill me and see how your people respond. They will despise you and your only solution will be to raze this place to the ground and slaughter everyone here, and even then the people will tell the stories of the brave warrior who put women to the sword.'

'Dran stays' said Perris. 'And when I am here, we share this place so that the people see and know that you are subservient to me.'

'Dran is an animal. He goes' said Idon, edging closer to Caeryl. 'I do not like the way he looks at the women' she added. 'We are not the spoils of war Perris as other places may be to you.'

'You think you can keep the ambition of men in check?' said Perris with some amusement. 'Do you not think that even now Drullis, your father Caeryl, plots his way to taking this place? And do you not think that as soon as the other tribes hear of a village ruled by mere women, they will not strike?'

'Firstly my father though ambitious, is by nature a coward' said Caeryl, growing in confidence. 'He will be given due respect as is due and shall be made to feel important, that will be sufficient for his mind. Secondly Perris, the actions of others all depends on how fearful they are of you, doesn't it? We shall have warriors, pledged to your service of course, but living here. And' she smiled wryly 'if we are attacked and slain, why, your problems with us are solved. You can wail and cry false tears and honour us with sacrifices to the gods and then take your revenge on those who insult you in such a cowardly manner. As for you sharing this dwelling, I can agree the appearance but you do not lay one finger on me. I no longer belong to you and never shall.'

Perris stood for a moment and then roared with genuine laughter. 'Very well, our terms are settled' he announced clutching his mother by the shoulders and kissing her forehead before walking out of the hut. The two women looked at each other, the younger with a fierce determination in her eyes, the older with something akin to relief.

With what seemed great urgency, Perris summonsed his men, explained that they were all leaving, much to the evident regret of Dran, and had ridden out of the fortress. The people buried

Gargonstus and what remained of Cwaenog the Outsider. Of his wife and daughter, nothing was ever heard of again.

Part IV
Seven Summers Later

Caer Sisal

Idon sat with Caeryl as they often did these days; the older woman's face was lined and her hair almost white, her hands curled like claws that made gripping anything difficult. The toll of losing her husband and eldest son had been hard on her, though she had taken comfort in the companionship of the younger woman who had steadily but respectfully taken over the day to day responsibility for the fortress. Respect was still due and shown to Idon but she knew it was a fiction and played her part as a willing accessory to the charade. At times she would give gentle advice, but would never admonish if that were not followed.

Caeryl's first act had been to send messengers and seek the return of Gadrig, Buldan and Forrun. Of the first two, nothing had been heard, but, for Ancastia, one joyous day, she had been called to the gates and had thrown herself into the waiting arms of the grinning giant that stood there. He had brought Corillun with him and explained that he would not serve Perris, but travelled and traded with Corillun and would ensure he spent time with her whenever he could. That day was a happy one for the people, for they had taken Ancastia and her wisdom to their hearts and to see her tears of joy had spread the emotion throughout the settlement.

Since that time, Forrun had been as good as his intent and had visited many times, though Ancastia remained without child. As she explained it was her duty to serve the gods and it was their decision that her dedication should be to them and not distracted by the needs of a son or daughter.

Marrad, Idon's youngest son had returned, and had developed into a strong young man. At Idon's insistence he had travelled to Caer Perris to serve alongside his elder brother, though he soon returned, replete with tales of Perris's excesses and uncaring brutality.

Drullis had died three summers previously, struck down by an illness that not even Ancastia with all her knowledge of herbs and remedies, could counter. His skin had turned yellow and his body seemed to almost sink into itself before with a sad, final groan, his spirit left him.

Through all, the settlement prospered, new faces took the places of old, firstly as the young grew to be mature and secondly as incomers sought a place to live and raise a family. Trade blossomed, helped of course by the frequent visits of Forrun and Corillun, who had even once brought his woman Karne with him, much to the delight of Ancastia who, with joy, introduced the woman to Idon and Caeryl.

Tribute was paid as due and on time, and Caeryl was scrupulous about ensuring that this was done. She wanted to give Perris no reason to extract any more than that willingly given. His visits to the settlement of his father had been infrequent, chaotic and disturbing; his appetites for wine and meat for himself and his men always left the fortress reeling and counting the cost. On one occasion he had taken a liking to one of the younger women, a girl in fact, just blooming into maturity, and he resolved to have her until checked by the combined disapproval of Caeryl and Idon who reasoned with him that to publicly insult Caeryl in this way would undermine the people's trust in him. They had plied him with drink and had quietly moved the girl away until she was claimed by another and only returned to the fortress when swollen with her first child.

Perris had grown fat, lazy and self-indulgent; his strength had been sapped by his successes and his unending celebrations of his own power. And as Perris had settled to a life of idle pleasure, his men, notably Dran, had gained power and influence to the extent that they roamed the lands unchecked and doing what they wished, often exacting their own tributes on top of those demanded by Perris. Thus far they had left Caer Sisal alone, but if Caeryl had a worry then it was her fear that Dran would some day soon, seek to take what had been denied him previously, and that which would be forbidden by Perris.

'You look tired' said Idon one day as Caeryl entered her dwelling, 'come and sit by the fire and rest.'

'I will, thank you' and she sighed deeply as she sank her bones onto the furs and skins Idon had placed over a wooden bench. 'I've been with Marrad around the crop fields' she explained. 'We saw Dran' Idon stiffened, Perris's henchman had been seen far too frequently these past days.

'Did he speak?' asked Idon.

'In a fashion, he hurled insults at Marrad. Said he was tied to the breasts of women, and ought to learn to fight like a real warrior.'

'Pathetic' spat Idon with contempt. 'But I don't trust him and he is biding his time.'

'You suspect a challenge to Perris?'

'I do. He had men with him?'

'Many of them' said Caeryl, 'and I suspect more that we could not see.' Idon thought for a moment and then, with an almost maternal pat on the younger woman's knee she made her mind up.

'Send Marrad to me' she said.

'You are going to warn Perris?'

'The gods know I have no love for that man even though he is my son, but yes, for the good of all the people of this tribe I will warn him of my suspicions.' Caeryl eased herself to her feet. Idon smiled sadly, 'I am sorry my dear, your rest was short lived.'

'Even when I rest, I think mother' said Caeryl smiling and using the familiar term she had adopted seven summers previously. She left the hut and shortly thereafter, Marrad entered.

***

Taking Idon's advice Marrad rode away from the fortress and headed north until he came to a river that was about as wide as the height of five men, he then turned towards where the sun rose and rode along the bank before making a camp for the night. To avoid any detection he lit no fire and merely wrapped himself in his cloak and slept beneath the spreading branches of a beech tree. The following morning he rode south, starting as dawn was breaking, and paused at the burial mounds on the heath north of the great hill of Bryttes Oran.

He paused there for a while, using the comparatively high land to search the surroundings for bands of warriors but saw none and decided to ride on towards his destination. As the sun came down out of the sky Marrad rode to the entrance to Caer Perris and asked the guard for admittance.

Marrad was shown to the dwelling of the Chief, the largest building in the fortress, where Storril came out to welcome him.

'I regret that Lord Perris cannot see you at this time Master' said Storril calmly. Marrad peered at the man, there seemed to be the remains of a bruise on his face and he walked with a pronounced limp.

'Tell my brother that I have an urgent message from our mother' said Marrad loudly enough that anyone inside the hut would hear. Storril made to quieten the visitor.

'Please, not so loud, my Lord is in a fearful temper and liable to react harshly should he be disturbed.' Marrad, frustrated by the delay, the behaviour of the servant and the disrespect shown to his mother, tried to push past Storril.

'No-one may enter, these are the instructions of Lord Perris and if I permit it I shall pay with my life.'

'You would fight me?' asked Marrad incredulously.

'I would lose I am sure' said Storril with respect 'but it would be a better death than the alternative.' He smiled sadly. 'There are only two who may enter and speak with Lord Perris, excluding myself, Halen his woman over there' Storril pointed to a woman surrounded by a brood of young children 'and Morcant the Druid.'

'Morcant will listen to me' said Marrad, 'take me to him.'

Caer Perris

'Marrad, you have grown into a fine man, and you look so like your father. He would have been proud to see you standing here' said Morcant rising to his feet as Storril approached with the young warrior.

'Morcant' acknowledged the young man 'I need to see Perris on a matter of some urgency.' Marrad saw a look of anxiety pass between Morcant and Storril.

'That . . . er won't be possible for a time' said Morcant, sit down here by the fire you must be tired after your journey.'

'Will nobody tell me what is going on!' demanded Marrad, almost shouting. Storril had walked away as Morcant, like the servant before him, made to quieten the young man.

'Please be quiet Marrad' asked the druid patiently. 'Perris cannot see you as he is not well.'

'What is wrong with him?'

'He suffers from a fever, his skin is cold yet wet, and he shakes all over.'

'You mean he is drunk?' said Marrad resignedly. Morcant's eyes narrowed at the perspicacity of the young man, he thought he had been subtle enough. The druid seemed to slump a little

'Yes . . . yes that is exactly what I mean, only it has now gone on for days.'

'Thank you for trusting me Morcant, and in turn I shall repay that trust two-fold. Firstly I shall never speak of this conversation, but secondly I must entrust you with my reason for visiting.'

'Let me guess that it involves Dran' said Morcant wearily

'Yes' said Marrad with awe, 'how did the gods tell you . . . '

'Alas, it was not the gods, but the ways of men. The reason that Lord Perris is drunk is also Dran, he takes too much power and now abuses it.' Marrad considered this information for a moment; he was not without intelligence and guile, so that when he spoke, he knew what he wanted to achieve.

'Morcant, tell Perris that he is under attack' said Marrad calmly.

'I'm not sure . . .'

'Just do it. Tell him I have ridden in to tell him. You need accept no responsibility for the ruse, I will deal with any repercussions.' Morcant rose to his feet and walked slowly to the Chief's home, from where, moments later there was a bellow like a wounded animal would make and Perris emerged, unsteady on his feet and somewhat fatter than Marrad recalled. More than this Marrad saw that his brother's hair and beard were streaked with grey, and the eyes sunk into the flesh of his face. Perris staggered unsteadily to the water trough from which the horses drank and slumped to his knees. He plunged his head into the cold, filthy water, emerged and drew a lungful of breath before thrusting his head back into the mud coloured liquid. He repeated this four times before wiping his hand across his face and turning to Marrad.

'You say we are under attack whelp, yet I hear nothing!'

'Perris, brother, the attack is not here, but with your mother and your woman Caeryl. The attack is on your authority and on your rule. I am sent to seek the help of our Chief.' Marrad knew that if he appealed to the vanity of Perris, it would have an effect.

'Who dares question my authority in this way?'

'Dran. He is not loyal to you Perris and demands tribute for himself.'

'You speak truth?' Marrad nodded his head. 'He is well rewarded and yet he seeks more.' Perris paused. 'He is strong and leads many men.'

'The majority will desert him as they are loyal to you. I fear he plans an insult to you Perris.'

'He means to attack?'

'Yes, but not here. He means to attack Caer Sisal as that will have significance to the whole tribe, especially those that recall your father. And I fear he means to take Caeryl, to show the contempt he has for you.' Marrad knew that there was no love lost between Caeryl and Perris, yet he also knew that for Dran to take Perris's woman was an insult that could never go unchallenged.

'You are sure?' said Perris cautiously.

'I am certain' replied Marrad. Perris nodded his head.

'We ride' was all he said as he walked without any of his previous uncertainty, back into his home.

In about the same length of time as it took someone to kill and pluck a chicken, the two men, and Storril rode out of the fort but instead of heading north, rode towards the place where the sun set at night.

'Where are we going?' asked Marrad

'I have men at a fortress close to the place where two rivers join the sea' explain Perris. We will stay there overnight and travel onwards in daylight.'

Caer Sisal – that night

'I can see the light of torches, look! There.' One of the sentries pointed towards the pin pricks of light that flickered through the branches of the trees, lighting them in stark silhouette.

'How many men do you think he has?' asked Caeryl.

'If he wants an all-out attack, then not enough if we resist' replied the sentry. 'But he has enough to surround us and starve us out over time.'

'Close and bar the gates' ordered Caeryl.'We'll place lookouts around the defences.

At the height of its influence, during the life of Sisal, the settlement probably housed about two hundred people, over the past seven years that had reduced to about one hundred and fifty; and of those, over two thirds would be women, children and those too old to fight. This left Idon and Caeryl with just under fifty men who were able bodied and capable of handling a weapon. Unfortunately whilst the settlement lacked numbers it also lacked leaders; the warriors having left and not returned. Instead of calling cwnsl, Idon and Caeryl went to each home and explained what was happening. The women, the elderly and the older children all volunteered to share the task of keeping lookout, leaving the men to be armed and ready, but also able to sleep so that if there was an attack, they would not be exhausted.

All was done quietly so as not to arouse the suspicion of Dran and his warriors, there were no flaming torches lit and no signs of weapons on the forts defences. As she suspected would happen, and in the black of the night, Caeryl was awakened from her own sleep and told that Dran was at the gates demanding to be admitted. Caeryl made her way to the entrance and from the top of the earth bank looked over to where Dran sat on his horse, illuminated by the torches carried by three of his men.

'Must you wake everyone?' called Caeryl, attracting the warrior's attention.

'Open these gates' demanded Dran, his demeanour brokering no argument with the authority he took upon himself.

'Dran, it is the middle of the night and people sleep. Your men have been camped since before the sun went down. Why now do you seek to gain admittance?' said Caeryl, her voice carrying well in the clear night air.

'Do not question me or my authority' said Dran.

'What do you want Dran?'

'I come to collect tribute' replied the warrior with a sneer.

'Tribute has been given to Perris as is due. He is satisfied with our arrangements' said Caeryl wearily. She knew where the conversation was going and thanked the gods that she had closed the gates.

'I claim additional tribute for myself' called Dran

'You have no entitlement, and no authority' said Caeryl who sensed that Idon had also been wakened and now stood near in silent support.

'I have men who are armed and battle ready, and if you do not give what I ask, then I shall simply take it by force' said Dran.

'Come back when the sun rises Dran and we can discuss this then. I am too tired now.' Caeryl stood down from the bank so that she was out of sight.

'Woman! Open these gates!' Shouted Dran to the silent air. Caeryl and Idon grinned, knowing that the best way to anger a man was to ignore the noise he made, and that all Dran would achieve would be to tire himself out. Having given orders to the lookouts to stay out of sight but report any further activity, the two women went back their homes, to ensure they slept the rest of the night.

***

The following morning brought bright sunshine interspersed with the shadows of large white clouds that moved across the sky on the strong breeze. Idon and Caeryl were told that having shouted and raged for a short time, Dran and his men had winthdrawn. Now they returned, and by a quick observation it seemed that the warrior had brought many of his men with him this time and the settlement was possibly outnumbered, but certainly had less experienced fighters and fewer weapons. The heavy sounds of horses hooves on the dry earth leading to the fortress gates, that remained steadfastly closed, could be heard throughout the settlement.

Caeryl called one of the men over and told him to walk slowly round the earth wall, making sure that the lookouts were alert. She suspected that a small force would make an assault whilst Dran was at the gate demanding entry.

'Open these gates!' demanded Dran in a repeat of the previous evening.

'Dran, we have no tribute to give you, either by agreement or by force. Our loyalty is to the Chief of this tribe, Perris. Not to you' called Caeryl. 'If you seek to take what is not due to you, we shall resist.

'Do not defy me' shouted Dran 'or I shall destroy you and take that which is mine in any event.'

'And what of Perris? How will you explain the slaughter?'

'We got here too late to prevent the raiders who attacked and fled before we arrived.' Dran laughed and looked round at the men closest to him who joined in.

'Begone Dran and take your scum with you. There is nothing here for you.' Caeryl made to leave the earth wall.

'I will not ask again woman. I shall take' threatened Dran.

'Try it and you will die' said Caeryl lightly, though her heart was thumping with anxiety. She walked away and called Idon and the most capable of the men to her.

'If we agree to Dran's demands, then he will return again and again and with each plundering of our supplies we will lose families and the ability to survive' she said. 'I propose that we resist Dran and better a quick death than a long lingering one. Can we resist him?' She looked earnestly at one of the men whose opinion she valued. He was a good and honest man, but a farmer first and a fighter second.

'We can hold him off for a few days, no more' he said, confirming that which Caeryl already suspected.

'Get the spearmen to the walls' ordered Caeryl 'show him we have some teeth that can bite.' The man walked away to do her bidding. 'What are they doing?' she called to a sentry at the gates.

'They seem to be collecting firewood Lady.'

'Idon, they are going to try to burn us out, use some of the water and soak the gates, keep them wet if you can.' Idon smiled grimly and set off calling for some of the women to help her.

Caeryl looked up at the skies, 'Fyrris may you and the gods forgive me but I would be happy to see your brother this day' she muttered to herself.

***

The first attack when it came, in the middle of the day, was rather half hearted, a feint Caeryl suspected to draw attention away from the gates. A small band of about ten horsemen threw rocks and charged at the earth mound farthest away from the gates, and were easily pushed back. While the noise and commotion started, a further band of men rushed the gates carrying a sawn tree trunk that they clearly intended to use to batter the gates with. As they approached, the spearmen stood and aimed.

'Preserve your weapons' commanded Caeryl. 'Slingshot' she said and a few of the younger men and boys hurled stones at the warriors below. The lead man was hit about the head five times and collapsed to the ground, blood pouring from a cut over his ear, as he went down, he took the battering ram and the rest of the men with him. They were all peppered with stones and abandoned the tree trunk and scurried away out of range. A few of the men cheered and Caeryl let them, it was good for confidence. She called one of the boys to her. 'I am putting you in charge of collecting the stones to re-arm the others' she said. The boy grinned, happy to take the responsibility, and hurried away.

There was a lull in activity from Dran and his men until five spears, their shafts burning, arced over the defences and into the fort. Two fell harmlessly upon open ground, but three landed on or close to huts, one of which immediately caught light. The other two were quickly extinguished, but the burning hut threatened to ignite others close by unless something were done.

A woman and a young girl rushed from the building, carrying a few possessions and stood looking at their home as the flames took hold. A warrior ran from the defences towards them.

'Get back!' screamed Caeryl. 'Your family are safe.' The hut had to be demolished in such a way that it fell in upon itself rather than risk the spread of fire. As she was organising that, Caeryl heard shouts. Dran had burning spears hurled at the gates and the flames were working their way down the shafts towards the stout timber that stood between the people and carnage.

With Perris and Marrad

The two brothers, strangers, and yet bound by family, rode at the head of about fifty men. All were well armed and experienced fighters. Mercenaries paid for by Perris and while they rode in silence, Marrad took the opportunity to study the man who had brought so much division and destruction to his people. Perris had a reputation as a fearsome warrior; a man of incredible strength and physical prowess, yet this man sitting astride a proud black horse was running to fat, his face was soft and plump, the skin riven with thin veins that stood out against the pale colour. His beard was flecked with grey, and his eyes seemed dull and lacklustre, very much like the man himself.

Marrad had watched the previous night and marvelled how much Perris could drink and still remain conscious. Indeed it seemed the only thing the man was proud of, as his younger brother tried, and failed, to engage him in conversation.

'Will he fight?' asked Marrad.

'Dran? Yes, he'll fight for he knows that he has overstepped his boundaries and that I offer no second chances. Either he kills me or we kill him.'

'You could banish him?' said Marrad, and Perris laughed, a cold hard sound full of scorn.

'And let him run away to regain his strength so he can return to conquer? That is the path of weakness. He will die this day and we shall watch the birds feed on his guts.' Brave words thought Marrad, but somehow unconvincing and almost spoken automatically, as if said a hundred times or more already.

Smoke from fires could be seen in the distance and Perris called one of his men forward and bade him ride ahead and see what he could find. The man grinned and kicked his horse forward and was soon lost to view. The rest of the group moved on at a walk to preserve both their own and the horses' energy.

In the middle of the day, as the sun was its highest in the skies, Perris called a halt and with a groan eased himself from the horse to the ground. He stood for a moment as if to steady himself and then as his animal was led away to be fed and watered, he called for wine and meat and took himself off in isolation to feast. Marrad was neither invited, nor did he feel welcome to share with his brother. The peace was however disturbed by the thrum of horses hooves on the ground and the sight of a rider approaching at speed. Men grabbed their weapons and stood ready to fight until they recognised the rider as the man who had left them earlier; the fighting stances were replaced by good natured insults flung at the approaching man.

The warrior reigned in his horse and jumped to the ground asking where he might find Perris; his companions pointed and the warrior ran to his Lord to find him asleep on the ground. He hesitated for a moment before deciding that his words were more important that his master's reactions, and he shook Perris awake.

'Lord, there is fighting at the settlement' he explained. The gates are shut and bolted and Dran's men are attacking.'

'Are they winning?' asked Perris in a bored voice, still heavy with sleep.

'No my Lord, but it is only a matter of time. They outnumber the defenders and have greater experience and weapons.'

'All this, we know' said Perris. 'Take five men and do no more than watch. We shall follow on later.' The man walked away bemused and spoke to an older colleague, telling him that he did not understand Perris's lack of urgency. The man laughed.

'Lord Perris is no fool' he explained. 'He has no time for the fortress of his father and loathes his mother and the other woman who rules that place. He also now sees Dran as an enemy so why not let them both exhaust themselves fighting each other, then he can turn up and slaughter them all if he so chooses. Now be off with you and stop asking the questions of an idiot.'

As the sun moved across the skies, Perris and his men moved forward slowly and deliberately, but without seeking to hide their presence, relying on the fact that Dran's attention would be elsewhere than protecting himself from attack. As far as he knew Perris was still at the coast, and there was no reason to suspect that he was in any danger.

When the hill upon which his father's fortress sat came into view, smoke could be seen rising from within, and all men present knew that Dran was using fire to drive the inhabitants into surrender. Grudgingly, Perris gave Caeryl and his mother credit for holding out; they knew the fate that awaited them if they had given in to Dran's demands.

The five warriors sent to observe, came out of the trees, leading their horses, as Perris approached.

'Well?' he enquired.

'Dran is at the gates of the fortress, demanding entry Lord. He does this frequently and is refused each time. His men have tried battering the gates but were forced to retreat. He has tried fire but with no obvious success.'

'Have there been deaths?' asked Perris.

'A few amongst Dran's force my Lord' agreed the warrior. 'I cannot say what has happened inside the fortress.'

'I see' said Perris, straightening himself upright, and unsheathing his sword. He turned his horse to face the men behind him.

'I have been betrayed' he called loudly so that each man could hear 'by the scum called Dran. He seeks to take that which is mine and which you are all sworn to defend. Any man who defies me in this way shall meet death and must do so willingly for they know the consequences of disobedience and yet continue in the mistaken belief that they can defeat me. Not one of them is to be left alive and

I leave the methods of their deaths to you and your imaginations. No mercy! No exceptions! We ride!' He turned his horse as with a road or approval his men surged after him, the horses mains flying as the animals built speed, thundering over the ground towards their foe.

Marrad, caught up in the midst of Perris's men, was swept along both physically and emotionally as his senses were assailed by the noise, the scent and the pounding of his own blood in his heart as he raced toward his first, and possibly his last battle.

He told himself he did not fear death; but he knew the lie within that thought. Death was not the fear, but mutilation and pain were. Like all who lived he had seen the men who hobbled, those without eyes and those who pissed themselves at the very thought of another fight. Marrad was more afraid of showing his fear than of the fear itself, and so he whooped and shouted and screamed at the top of his voice along with the hard eyed men surrounding him.

The first of Dran's men had heard the approaching horsemen, and possibly made the mistake in thinking they were reinforcements, so stood casually, their arms raised in greeting as the sharpened stakes used as lances pierced their skin. The riders surged past and Perris spat at the writhing bodies that would be finished off by the last of his men to pass.

The noise was deafening especially to those not used to a fight. Men were shouting, horses whinnying even as those sounds were drowned by the hooves on the hard ground. Dran's men now knew there was a problem and some of them turned to face the new threat. Perris held up his hand to slow their advance to a walk and easily picked out Dran in the melee.

'Lord!' called Dran. 'We have trapped a band of marauders within the fortress. The women are sheltering them.' He looked around wildly, eager to see support from him men, most of whom looked sheepishly down at the ground.

The gates to the fortress opened and with a roar of noise, the men of the settlement, armed with whatever weapons they had surged down the slope towards Dran's force. Perris slid down off his horse and walked calmly towards Dran.

'See how even now they attack us, the dogs know they have no chance with you here, so try to escape.' He shouted to his men, and sword in hand turned to offer battle.

'Dran!' shouted Perris, and as the man turned, Perris hit him, hard in the gut. Dran doubled over and Perris savagely kicked him between the legs, Dran howled and fell to the ground, writhing. Perris continued to kick at Dran who alternated between using one arm to ward off the blows and another to protect his genitals. Perris was on the edge of control; he snarled, he kicked and at one point grabbed Dran's tunic and pulled the man upright and tried to bite him. Blood now began to stain Dran's clothing and all other fights had stopped, so horrible was the unfolding scene to behold.

Marrad, moved forward and tried to intervene, but was gently held back by one of Perris' men who shook his head. He knew that his master had the frenzy about him and needed to satiate that before any reason could intervene.

Dran was back on the ground, Perris still viciously kicking at the increasingly insensitive body when there was a perceptible crack as Dran's neck broke and he gurgled and gasped for air as Perris stamped repeatedly on his throat.

It was clear to all present that Dran was dead, but still Perris carried on, his rage unabated. Dran's men were perceptive enough to understand the danger to themselves and began to edge away from the fight. Most were restrained by the men who had rushed from the fortress, who held them, waiting for instruction and order.

The man who had restrained Marrad moved forward and tried to speak to Perris who back handed him, sending his sprawling to the ground.

'He's dead' called the warrior. 'Lord, Dran is no more and we have work to do.' This had no discernible effect and so Marrad drew his own sword and thrust it into the ground close to Dran's blood covered skull. Perris looked up, wild eyed and teeth bared, and stepped towards Marrad.

'Your instruction Lord. . . these men?' said Marrad hesitantly. Perris looked around, his long hair flying in all directions as he took in his surroundings and appeared to be returning to reality. He stared at the men being held and took no time to issue his order.

'Kill them, kill them all, every last one of them.' He drew Marrad's sword from the ground. 'And you shall release the first of them from this life.' He handed the sword to the younger man who walked over to the captives who struggled in vain attempts to free themselves and flee.

Marrad had killed animals in the hunt, he had imagined fighting men in the uncertainty of battle, where the frenzy overtook you and all you knew was that you were alive at the end of a skirmish, but he had never before killed in cold blood. Most of the men looked terrified, but one stood apart as calm and almost accepting of his fate. Marrad's inclination was to dispatch the smallest and weakest, but knew that to increase his standing both with his brother and the tribe it was the quiet man that he had to deal with.

'You are not afraid?'

'No.'

'You are about to die' said Marrad.

'I only ask that you make it quick' replied the man. 'And if you lack ability then I will do it if you give me a sword.'

'Why so calm?'

'We tried and we failed, death is our reward.' The man let out and groan as Marrad's sword pierced his belly and ripped up through his guts into his chest. His eyes widened and he staggered, clutching Marrad's shoulder, before falling to the ground twitching as life left him. The death of the man released a howl of fury from the men of the settlement and the remainder of Dran's force were dispatched in a savage assault as men were skewered on spears, hacked at by blunt swords long since used, and swiftly despatched by axes more commonly used to fell trees.

Perris waded in, swinging his sword, slashing at his victims, the blood once again rushing to his head as the fury of battle took over, before he stormed from the killing and stalked his way up the path to the fortress and the place he had grown up.

Inside the Fortress

Caeryl had maintained a constant vigil at the defences, ever since Dran and his men had first struck, refusing any suggestion that she might rest. Her eyes were now red with exhaustion, her skin sallow and Idon in particular was concerned for the woman she looked upon as a daughter. When she had sighted Perris and his men, Caeryl turned to Idon and grinned, then called to the defenders of the fortress and shouted.

'Arm yourselves, open the gates and attack! Kill the savages who defile and insult this place. Kill them!' And the men had run headlong to confront their enemy, had held Dran's men captive and had witnessed their demise with barely a flicker of remorse. They knew that had things worked differently it would be themselves lying there with the grass stained with their blood.

There was a sense of euphoria within the fortress; as if they had been tested and they had survived. As the men returned they did so with smiles on their faces, even those that had suffered minor wounds bore them with an element of pride, demonstrating as they did, that they had played their part.

Caeryl was however, prescient enough to know that what was to come would be harder than that which they had just endured, and she was determined to act once again in the interests of her people.

As the men returned, one stood out. His wild expression, the sheer bulk of his features and the haunted way he moved, made Perris seem apart from the others.

Caeryl stood and held her arms aloft to both draw attention to herself and silence the people before her. Slowly she got their attention and determined to use the situation to her best advantage.

'My friends' she said. She had deliberately avoided saying "my people" as that sounded possessive and would have put her in conflict with Perris, something she determinedly wished to avoid.

'We must stand together, as we did through our ordeal, and give thanks to our Lord Perris.' She left a pause, knowing that the murmuring would start. Perris was not universally liked, and the tributes paid to him cost the fortress much of its wealth. 'Without his arrival and his skills in battle, we would surely have succumbed to the scum that was known as Dran.' A cheer rang out, quickly taken up by the fortresses inhabitants. Like almost everybody else, Caeryl had seen the way that Perris had lost control as he killed Dran, and had been sickened by it, but her ends and those of the settlement were best served for the moment in appeasing Perris.

'Tonight we shall slaughter beasts and shall feast with our protector.' Once again a mighty cheer split the air. Idon, watching on the sidelines, nodded her head in approval, immediately understanding Caeryl's tactics and intent.

'Lord Perris' said Caeryl turning to him and fixing him with her smile, 'we give thanks to you, and the men led by your expertise of course!' Another cheer rent the air. 'Will you celebrate your victory with us?'

Perris leered at her, his expression a mixture of delight and something else that Caeryl could not define as he walked forward. She held her hand out to him but he pushed it away, grabbed the neckline of her garment and ripped it open, exposing her body underneath. Idon made to remonstrate as Caeryl screamed. Marred, drew his sword but was quickly grabbed and held by the same man as had stopped him previously, and Perris stared like and animal at Caeryl's breasts, licking his lips as if anticipating a feast. Caeryl tried to gather the material around her to preserve some element of modesty but the blood was raging in Perris so soon after battle and he grabbed one of Caeryl's arms, put the other arm between her legs and effortlessly lifted her onto his shoulder. He strode off towards the Chiefs abode threatening death to anyone who dared to intervene.

Idon shouted at her son and moved to try to get between him and the hut, but one of the warriors caught hold of her.

'Release her' snarled Perris 'and if she tries to get past you, cut her head off.' He strode on towards his destination and pushed his way into the hut before dumping Caeryl on her bedding, lying her on her back and sitting astride her chest.

Caeryl looked up at Perris, she knew him, knew his moods and his cruelty.

'You are hurting me you fat ugly pig!' she shouted. He grinned looking down at her lasciviously.

'I am sick of having to pretend' he said. 'You exist to serve me, yet treat me as if I am a disease.' He looked around, taking in the dwelling, the contents and the scent of the place. 'I arrive and save your life, and the lives of everyone in this stinking shit hole, and your gratitude was going to be to feed me? I think we can do better than that.' His hand reached behind him, and he fumbled in the folds of her remaining clothing as she struggled to push him off.

'I am stronger, and you know only too well, the more you fight, the more it hurts you.'

'I'll kill you!' screamed Caeryl. This brought a responding shout from outside as Idon fought with her guard. There was more shouting and Idon was clearly heard shouting 'No!' to someone, but Caeryl's attention was brought back to her immediate problem as Perris viciously backhanded her across the face, drawing blood from a split lip.

'Shut your noise' bellowed Perris, and half turning he shouted to whoever was outside the hut, telling them to be quiet or be killed. He returned to Caeryl and very calmly and deliberately put his massive calloused hand round her throat and began to squeeze. 'I am going to take what is mine whether you give it willingly or not' he began. Caeryl was fighting for breath, her hands alternately flapping uselessly or gripping the fur on which she lay. Perris gradually released his grip, leaving the woman gasping and drawing huge breaths, completely unable to do anything as Perris undressed.

Later that day.

Perris had departed, taking his men with him and leaving behind devastation and destruction. In the corporeal sense, the dead bodies of Dran and his followers lay where they had fallen, the birds already feasting on the detritus. One black bird, seen as a portent of doom, pecked at a corpse until with a sickening squelch it released an eyeball which it dragged until it severed from the body, and flew away. The people present watched in horror, transfixed and unable to respond until Ancastia reassured them that any message from the gods was for the man who had done the killing.

The corpse, looking vacantly at the sky from its one remaining, dead eye, was that of Dran, and the people were somewhat reassured.

The destruction however moved beyond the mere physical. Nobody in that settlement could possibly have doubted the events within the Chiefs hut. The screams, grunts and shouts that emanated from within left the people in no doubt that Perris was extracting a price for his presence.

The people were traumatised. In very quick succession they had been threatened, attacked, and then saved only now to be left with an empty feeling of violation that hung like a cloud over the fortress.

As Perris walked out of the hut, adjusting his clothing, he saw his mother, her eyes ablaze with anger, her mouth clamped shut and unable to even speak to this man.

'See to her' was all he said as he called his men and rode away, presumably back to the coast.

Fearfully, Idon entered her former home. It took some time for her eyes to adjust to the darker environment. Slowly, she advanced to the sleeping area and the inert body that lay there. Painfully, with every joint aching, Idon knelt down beside Caeryl who stared vacantly, seemingly lifeless into the distance.

Weeping, the older woman saw the blood on Caeryl's face and between her legs, and having risen back to her feet, she fetched water and tenderly cleaned the blood away, straightened Caeryl's legs and pushed them together, and covered her body. Throughout all, Caeryl made no sound and Idon feared that life had left her body until a sign, by way of a single tear ran out of her left eye.

Idon walked back to the entrance and called out for help. Marrad came hobbling over. Part of the scuffle heard by Caeryl had been Marrad's attempt to force entry and the subsequent beating he had received from Perris's men.

'Fetch Ancastia' was all Idon said. Marrad hesitated for a moment, explained that she was at the bottom of the hill supervising the burial of the dead, and hobbled away.

For a brief instant, sharp bright light broke into the hut as Ancastia entered. Idon winced and held her hand in front of her face. Caeryl did not react or move a muscle. As soon as it had flared, the light was cut off as Ancastia made her way, with her usual calm over to the prone form of Caeryl, ensuring to show the appropriate deference to Idon.

'Help her please.' Said Idon simply. 'Use your powers, and ask the gods to banish her suffering so she can return to us.

'Let me see her' said Ancastia as Idon moved aside to allow a full examination. Ancastia looked touched and probed where nobody should go and eventually moved away and called Idon to her.

'Physically she will heal' she announced. 'There will be pain and she may never be the woman she was before, but she will return to us in time. I have a salve that I can use to take some of the pain away.'

'But?' said Idon perceptively.

'Her spirit is broken and she has left her body.'

'Can it be found? Where do such spirits fly to in such times?' asked Idon, a note of desperation clear in her words and tone.

'Who knows' answered Caeryl. 'The spirit is unique to all of us and searches for a place of safety. If it is lucky and finds it then it may heal and she could return.'

'And if the spirit remains restless and does not find peace?'

'Then we have lost her' said Ancastia simply. 'I will do what I can but she needs peace and time.'

'Ask the gods. See what they demand, and they shall have it.' She touched Ancastia's robe gently. 'Bring her back to us however you can, but one thing is now clear.

'Perris must die.'

Part V
Caer Perris

Four Harvests Later

Idon sat as she often did, with Caeryl. As Ancastia had foretold, the woman's strength had returned and her physical wounds had healed relatively quickly, again thanks to Ancastias ministrations. Her mind was however still troubled and she never spoke, nor looked anyone in the eye.

On Ancastia's advice, those four long summers past, Idon had moved Caeryl into a newly built hut, keeping only those personal trinkets that were untainted by the bad sense of the past or present. The furs, skins and furniture from the Chieftain's dwelling had been burned and Idon had toyed with the idea of demolishing the hut, but held back as it remained a symbol of better times and strength to the rest of the people.

Idon had, for a short time, taken over the day to day running of the settlement, but her heart was no longer in it and she began to rely more and more on Marrad who over the past seasons had grown into the responsibilities heaped upon him by circumstance.

Marrad had forged close friendships with both Ancastia who treated him as a younger brother, and Forrun, who on his increasingly frequent visits, had taught the young man much about battle, hunting, and the ways of men and women.

Idon spoke to Caeryl as she always did, prattling on about the inconsequentialities of life, the gossip of the women, the fears of the farmers and upcoming events. She had learned to accept that the conversations were one-sided, but she suspected that Caeryl heard and understood everything.

Perris had never been spoken of by Idon, he exacted his tributes, often sending Storril as his representative; the one handed man seemed to like getting away from his master and rarely hurried to depart. In her few dealings with him, Idon suspected that her sons' emotions played large in his rule over the land, and those closest to him bore the brunt of his mercurial temperament. Though she tried to engage with Storril to discover specifics, she found that he was either determinedly loyal or thoroughly terrified.

Today however, a matter could not be put off any longer. Perris had decreed a cwnsl of all his peoples, and representatives from each settlement were required to attend. Idon, knowing that there was a risk involved wanted to discuss the matter with Caeryl. She had sought advice from Ancastia who had judged that Caeryl was as recovered as she ever would be unless some other life changing event occurred. Idon thus forced herself to speak.

'Perris has called cwnsl' she explained, fearing a reaction from the younger woman at the mention of his name. 'He demands attendance from the Headman of each settlement, and in effect my dear that is still you.' She quickly hurried on, explaining 'I suspect he wants to discuss yet more in the way of tribute that he can plunder. Of course we can sent Marrad but he is inexperienced in the devious ways of his brother and would have no authority nor standing to resist any further demands made of us . . .' Her voice tailed away as Caeryl lifted her head and looked into the old womans eyes. Tears were running freely down Caeryl's lined cheeks, her eyes widened still further and her body shook as she broke out into sobs. Idon made to put her arms round her but Caeryl shook her head and spoke the first words she had uttered in such a long time, her voice chillingly cold.

'We will travel together. And we will kill him.'

Idon and Caeryl

Idon sat for a moment, not sure that she had heard correctly. Had Caeryl just spoken or had she imagined it? And if she had spoken, had she really said the words Idon had heard. She looked intently at Caeryl and now saw a light in those eyes that had been missing since the death of Ferrax. It burned intensely, just as the look on her face was one of eager insistence that Idon agree to the task. And the more Idon thought of it, the more it made sense. Perris had been a force for destruction and damnation since he had taken power; settlements were poorer, fortresses neglected for want of men and weapons, barns and stores continually depleted by ever growing demands for tribute to feed, clothe and arm the warrior bands that roamed the country ostensibly protecting the people, but in reality bringing nothing but fear and loathing. Fights between the people and Perris's warriors were not uncommon, just as the outcomes were inevitable. Many had given up their farmsteads and instead had come to live within the limited protection offered by the fortresses; safety together as one woman had explained after her man and eldest son were slaughtered.

Such was Idon's devotion to the memory of Sisal, and her family, she had never considered all that had gone wrong and the root cause of it but now with those simple words spoken by Caeryl the conclcusion was inescapable.

Idon nodded her head, a quick, jerky movement as if she herself remained unconvinced either as to the wisdom of the plan, or to their chances of success. Caeryl leaned forward and gripped Idons gnarled hands tightly.

'We will kill Perris' she said with such devastating finality that there would never be any disagreement or dispute over the wisdom of such an act. She had birthed Perris, giving him life, and it was now hers to take away. There were however practicalities to be considered. She looked again at Caeryl who spoke the words she was thinking.

'We must consult with Ancastia, but give no word of our thinking at this time. We need her to speak with the gods and tell us the omens.' The two women looked at each other, bound together in a silent pact to do such a terrible but necessary thing, but both surprised as to how easily the decision had been made and agreed upon.

'How do you propose . . .'

'A knife in the heart. I have and hold enough anger within me to give me the strength to cut him like a beast' said Caeryl. Her eyes were once again cast down towards the ground and she was bent forward as if hiding from the world. It was as if the past minutes had exhausted her, and Idon feared that she would return to her previous silent exile.

'Where have you been to child?' asked Idon. 'I have longed for the day you returned to us' she explained simply. Caeryl looked up, a wan smile crossed her face as she spoke.

'I have been here all along, only I could not speak because all I could hear were my own screams inside my head. They only stopped when I knew I could punish he who had caused them.'

'Shall I fetch Ancastia?' suggested Idon.

'No, I shall go, let's give the people something to talk about shall we!' and this time Caeryl's smile was wide warm and genuine.

Caer Perris

Halen sat admiring the new bangle on her wrist, twisting it this way and that so that the gold caught the sun, She looked over at Perris and smiled at him. She was, he thought, a simple woman who loved him unconditionally, not for who he was but because of what he was. He represented safety to her and their children, for Perran was now an elder brother to a girl, a disappointment to Perris that he hardly had time for. Halen knew or rather suspected with good cause, that Perris would have fathered other children away from their home but she did not allow herself to be troubled by that. She knew of Caeryl though the two women had never met, and she knew that Caeryl had never borne a child. Of course she did not rely upon the word of Perris for that, but rather that of Storril whom she found to be singularly reliable in this place of thieves and liars. His devotion to Perris, Halen suspected was more in word than deed and she suspected that he harboured a deep seated loathing fot the man that had maimed him. He was, she felt, merely biding his time until he could get his own back. Perris eyed Halen with suspicion, for he believed her to have taken one of the younger warriors to her bed, quite without foundation or evidence.

'Why have you called cwnsl?' asked Halen. Perris growled his reply.

'I have told you to keep your prying out of my head! I do what I do for my own reasons and I do not need to explain them to the likes of you.' There was a period of silence where it became apparent that Halen was not going to ask again; a trick that she had learned early. She knew Perris wanted her to think him clever and masterful and he could only do that if he told her his plans.

'Why must you always question?' he demanded, and then immediately relenting and seizing the opportunity to explain himself, he continued. 'Very well, I shall tell you. It is my intention to increase our trade with Gaul and for this I need ships, and for ships I need more goods to sell.' He shrugged his shoulders.

'What is in this for the people?' asked Halen. 'You already exact tribute at a level way higher than your father and you need to leave the people with something for themselves and their families.'

Perris looked at her dangerously, searching for a hint of criticism, but over the years Halen had learned well to maintain a look of such innocence that he was wrong footed. 'The people' he explained through gritted teeth 'get that which their Chief gives them. And in case any of the people forget it, their Chief is me.' He stood up, using his height and his bulk to intimidate Halen, who had long ceased to be afraid, just as she had long ceased to love this bully that still shared her bed when he was sober enough to crawl to it. Instead of cowering, she smiled at him diffidently.

'You know best Perris.'

'Yes, I do' he replied as he turned and went outside into the morning, calling for Perran. The boy was always hiding thought Perris, but he knew where he would be and walked straight for the place. Sure enough there was Perran sitting with Morcant listening to the druids tales and stories; normally Perris held no objection to this as the recounting of famomus warriors and noble Chiefs instilled within his son the status of his father and the destiny that was to be his, today however Morcant was talking of plants and potions, of their power to heal and their strength in killing. Perris had no time for such matters, to him killing was done with a sword or a knife, or if no weapon were available, then brute strength and bare hands.

'Enough of this nonsense, druid' said Perris quietly, startling his son who had been so enraptured within the mysteries of the things that grew all around them. 'Perran, fetch your sword, it is time we practiced.' Reluctantly, the boy rose and with a smile of gratitude to Morcant he left to do as his father ordered.

'Do not seek to turn the boy away from his destiny Morcant, or you will be swallowing a sword, not a nettle.'

'Perris, I try to provide the boy with knowledge, and in these times that is no bad thing. To learn the ways of the gods and the riches they provide from land and sea is to enrich his life and can only add to the skills that you yourself impart.'

'Stop your pointless prattling' said Perris, walking away.

Perran stood waiting for his father, in his hand he held two wooden swords they used for practice; the boy was proud of Perris, but feared his moods and more than once he had fled his home and slept alone and afraid under the stars. He sensed that his father feared him and had thought long and hard about the conversation he needed to have. As Perris approached, Perran felt that the time was right.

'Father' he asked 'what do you fear?' The immediate look in Perris's eyes, caused him to back track a little. 'Everybody has something they don't like surely? Mother hates the mice and the rats, she says the way they move and scurry makes her flesh crawl. . .' The look in Perris's eye subsided and he took on the paternalistic role he was so unsuited for.

'You ask too many questions Perran, hand me that sword and defend yourself.'

'Is there nothing? Mother says that your father was a great and wise Chief who now is a god that looks after us. Do you fear not joining him?'

'Of course I shall join him' said Perris testily. 'That is my destiny just as it is yours to lead our people; but to lead them you must be able to defend our lands and yourself. You must learn to fight and make battle.'

'Tell me' persisted the boy.

'Why?'

'Because if you are afraid and yet you conquer it, then that makes you braver. If you have no fear then you have nothing to be brave about.'

Perris was taken aback at this, it was a point that he had never considered.

'Very well, sit and we will talk like old women. You want to know what I am afraid of?'

'Yes'

'I fear old age, of losing my strength and my power.'

'Do you fear death?'

'No. When I die I will be a god, why should I fear that?'

'Do you fear me?'

'Why on earth should I . . .'

'You killed your brother to take your father's place, and you have always said that Sisal died weak and old.' Perris sat quietly for a moment, something that Perran had never seen before. His father always portrayed himself as a man of action rather than thought.

'Dying old is no bad thing, it means that you are unbeaten in battle, but as you have asked a man's question I give you a man's answer. Yes I killed Ferrax and I did it because he was weak, I doubt that this tribe would have survived and prospered had he become Chief.

'In time my son, your strength will increase and mine will fade, and yes I fear that change, and I will promise you now that should the day come where you seek to take from me what is mine by force then we will fight and you will die. However should you learn that which I show you then we can arrange for you to take over when the time is right and when we are both ready.'

Perran sat, the words confirming what he already knew; that his father would have no qualms about killing him should he deem it necessary. The young man resolved to learn what he could in the sure knowledge that his life depended upon the unstable emotions of his father. Quickly he jumped to his feet and went to strike his father with the wooden sword.

Perris bellowed in anger demanding to know what the boy was doing.

'In our last time together you talked of using surprise. I was only trying to show you that I had learned that which you taught me' said Perran. Perris grinned, which relaxed the boy who let his sword drop, which was when Perris attacked, knocking the wooden sword from the boys hand and beating him with the flat of the blade about the body and the head until Perran curled on the ground. Perrris was about to kick the prone figure when a voice interrupted him.

'Master! The ship is in sight.' Perris froze, his leg drawn back, at which point Perran scurried away. Slowly, Perris turned to look at Storril, whose handless arm was pointing seaward. The trading ship was hopefully bringing not just goods but the rewards from the latest batch of slaves to be sold, and news from across the seas and Perris's plans for expanding his empire rested on that information.

With Caeryl and Idon

Caeryl's prediction that she would give the people something to talk about was absolutely right. Everyone had become used to her being in the company of either Idon or Ancastia, and her usual bearing was to be with her eyes cast to the ground, and of shuffling like an old woman. To see her, head up, eyes gleaming and with a smile on her face caused a commotion and numerous thanks being shouted to the gods that Caeryl, one of their own, had been sent back to them.

Ancastia had been tending the small patch of land that she cultivated for herbs and plants that she used in her salves and potions and upon hearing the tumult, she had risen from her knees and hurried to the centre of the settlement. She feared the return of Perris, knowing that any further damage to Caeryl, a woman whose inner strength she admired, and whose judgment she had come to trust, would likely prove fatal.

When she saw Caeryl walking towards her, she clasped her hands to her mouth to hide her surprise. Caeryl for her part could not disguise the joy she felt at seeing the happiness in the eyes of Ancastia and threw her arms wide. The two women rushed to embrace and tears flowed as they held each other.

'I . . . we all have longed for this day' said Ancastia.

'As have I from inside my head' explained Caeryl. And those were the only words she spoke before a crowd gathered round them, some cheering and shouting, some calling for thanks to be given to the gods and others just standing silently in awe and wonderment.

Idon quickly stepped in to protect Caeryl. She could see that although the young woman was moved by the reaction, she was also tiring rapidly. Fortunately she still carried enough authority to calm the people and lead Caeryl back to her hut, followed by Ancastia who made one of her rare proclamations. As she rarely spoke publicly, her words carried greater authority.

'My friends' she smiled 'the gods have granted us the return of our beloved Caeryl and she seems to be in good spirit.' That brought a cheer. 'It is right therefore that we should send our thanks to the gods with tribute and feasting to celebrate this wonderful day. I therefore call on each family to provide food, to build the fire so that the flames can be seen by the gods, and to give up one possession as tribute. That possession should be something that can be offered to the flames.' She turned and made towards Caeryl's home as the crowd dispersed, talking animatedly among themselves.

The sound of laughter from within Caeryl's hut was so unusual that it took Ancastia aback. She was used to coming here and sitting with Caeryl when Idon was otherwise engaged or unwell. Indeed she had sometimes slept here to keep the lost Caeryl company, and, over time, as she talked she had shared her own life, its past and its secrets with this woman. She saw Idon's gnarled and clawed hands held around Caeryl's and saw the two women smiling at each other, crying and laughing at the joyous occasion.

They both saw Ancastia standing there and beckoned her over as she explained the decision she had made regarding the feast and the celebration of the gods deliverance. Both approved and Idon glanced at Caeryl who subtly nodded, a movement seen but not yet understood by Ancastia.

Idon spoke cautiously at first. 'It is a day to celebrate is it not Ancastia?'

'Truly yes' agreed the Ovate, smiling at the two women.

'But we must ensure that the dark days we have endured are never repeated' said Idon. 'Do you not agree?'

'I do, yes I do' said Ancastia.

'Those dark days are brought about by one person Ancastia. My son Perris.' The mood in the hut changed, the smiles were gone to be replaced by looks of earnest intensity that Ancastia readily understood.

'I see' she replied. 'And you want to know the omens?'

'We do' replied Caeryl. 'I cannot tell you where I have been, for I do not rightly know myself, but each day I have been tortured. I have heard his voice, felt his stinking breath on my face and relived the pain he gave me and his weight on top of me. Each day Ancastia, every day and I can never go back to that so I must find a way to end this.'

'By killing Perris?' asked Ancastia.

'Yes' said Caeryl.

'But we must know the omens' pleaded Idon. 'Will you help?'

'I will tell you what it told to me' agreed Ancastia 'but I can play no part in the killing.'

'We do not ask you to' said Caeryl kindly, 'we only need to know the consequences of our action.'

'Very well, you had better tell me your thoughts and feelings so that I can listen to the gods. Are there any in particular whose opinions you favour?' Ancastia knew the answer before it was given.

'Sisal' said Caeryl.

'It shall be so.'

***

That night, the fire outside the Chiefs hut burned brighter and higher than anyone could recall. The glow from the flames were visible half a days walk away, and indeed one of the farmers made haste the following day to the settlement fearing that it had been attacked and set afire. As required by Ancastia, each family made sacrifice to the gods; for one it was a bowl from which they ate their food, from another it was a skin they wore as clothing. The most touching was a young girl who gave her prized possession, a doll made from plaited corn that her father had given her after the last harvest, and that she willingly held out to Ancastia, explaining that what the gods had given back was worth more than the sacrifice she made. All tributes were fed to the fire and the flames and ashes rose skyward in fitting gratitude.

Caeryl tired quickly, her body was not used to such exertion, and she retired to her bedding to sleep soundly and without dreams, whilst the rest of the people celebrated into the night.

The next day

Thunder clouds built their mass and rumbled angrily through the morning, obliterating the sun and causing people to rightly suspect that there would be a fierce downpour. Some suspected that the gods were not happy, that somehow they were displeased with the sacrifices made to them, but most were calmed by Ancastia explaining that the displeasure was directed at the acts that had led to Caeryl's illness. Nevertheless she was herself worried, concerned that the real reason for the anger in the skies was the act being planned by Idon and Caeryl.

It had been arranged that the three women would meet that afternoon to discover the omens, and as the allotted time approached, Ancastia grew ever more unsettled.

It had been agreed that they would meet within the old Chieftains hut where Idon still lived. That would afford them a measure of privacy and space and to Ancastia, troubled by the plans of idon and Caeryl, the privacy was of greater importance.

She was welcomed into the dwelling by Idon and the there women sat quietly for a moment; two of them afraid to speak in case the third told them things they would rather not hear and the third herself fearful of what she would find. Evenutally Ancastia spoke and the silence was lifted.

'How do you propose to do the deed?' she asked.

'A knife to the chest' replied Caeryl calmly. She sat, with her hands in her lap and spoke demurely as if she were discussing a trinket or a skin she wished to buy.

'Bring me the blade and place it here in front of me' asked Ancastia. Idon walked over to the cooking area and brought back a long bladed knife.

'It was Sisal's' she said, as if that would give the metal extra protection or power.

'I am going to do something I have never done before' said Ancastia with a resolution and certainty she did not feel. 'As you know, when the body dies the essence of the person goes to the other world, and when they die there, they come back here in a new body. In this way we live for ever. To look at the omens, we travel in spirit to the other place and consult the wisdom of the people there.' She looked up, the other two knew this and looked puzzled as to why Ancastia was explaining the obvious.

'What you wish to undertake is so extreme that I am going to take you on the journey to the other place with me.' There was a sharp intake of breath and Idon and Caeryl held hands and looked afraid. 'I cannot promise you that this will work' said Ancastia 'but it is worth the risk.'

'What risk?' asked Idon. Ancastia paused and looked each woman in the eye before responding.

'We may end up in different places, I may not be there to guide you in which case you will have to find your own guide, and discover how to get back here alone. The spirits will not harm you, but you may find such peace there that you do not want to come back and that will cause a very big problem.'

'Why?' Again it was Idon that spoke, her voice one of challenge. Again Ancastia paused as if choosing her words very carefully.

'When Caeryl was apart from us I knew that she lived' she explained. 'I went to the other place to look for her spirit and I could not find it, nor could any of my guides. If she was not there, then by rights she had to be here. And if she was here, then she lived.'

'So if we choose to stay in the other place, then what happens?' This time it was Caeryl who spoke and there was a tremor in her voice.

'It will be unnatural. Your body here will live, but be empty, yet your spirit will be in the other place though it should not be. We pass over when our bodies die, that is the natural course of events; should you choose to stay when you should not then you are trapped and your spirit will eventually wither and die as will your body and you will be lost for all time.'

'So we must come back then?' asked Caeryl.

'Yes, no matter what, or who you find over there, you must come back.'

Caer Perris

'I regret Lord Perris, there were some we could not sell.' Corillun shrugged his shoulders as he handed over a bag of silver. It was much lighter than Perris had expected and the trader caught sight of the fleeting displeasure on the face of the Chief. 'The market is flooded with slaves at the moment, a buyer can have their pick. The women and children you gave us were not top quality.' His voice tailed off.

'What of those you did not sell?' growled Perris.

'They went into the ocean weighted with stone. I am not a rich man Perris and they were costing me in food. The women were hags and the children too young and under developed to be of any use in field or aboard ship. I got you a fair return for what we could sell.' He nodded at the bag in Perris's hands. 'I have never cheated either yourself or your father' Corillun added.

'You have not' conceded Perris 'but it seems I shall need to change my orders to my men. No more captives for I too do not want the expense of feeding these vermin only for you to turn them into food for the sea. What of our other matter?'

'Not good news there either Lord, I am afraid. The terms you proposed were too onerous for the Gaulish tribe and I am charged to tell you that they are happy with the current arrangments and see no need for change.' Perris went dangerously quiet, his features reddening as his anger boiled. 'They also charged me with telling you that they do not want protection and that should any of your warriors arrive on their soil, then they will be put to death and all agreements between you will be at an end.'

'You told them all that I said?' demanded Perris.

'I told them most of it. I felt it prudent not to issue them with the warnings that if they did not agree then you would send your men into battle with them.'

'And why did you not do as I bid Corillun?'

'Because my Lord' explained Corillun as patiently as he could 'they are also my people, and they would neither be impressed nor afraid of your threats.'

'Really?'

'Yes Lord, they know their own lands and they have more men under arms than you do. To have passed on your threat would have made you, in their eyes, a man who plays tricks. You would not have been taken seriously.'

'I see' said Perris 'and what would happen my rich merchant friend if I were to gut you here and now for failing me?'

'You would lose your trade with the tribes across the sea Lord Perris. Nobody would trade with you if you touched a hair on my head.'

'There are other traders Corillun, be not so assured of yourself.'

'It is true, there are others, but do you not think we know each other and share information? And as much as you value our trade, you also value the information I bring you.'

'This is so' accepted Perris. 'What have you brought to trade this time?'

If Corillun was shocked at the instant change in attitude from the volatile young Chief, he hid it well.

***

An hour later and business was concluded to the satisfaction of both men, Corillun prudently proferred a skin of wine and watched as Perris greedily sated his thirst for the pleasing effects of the alcohol. As Perris looked at him, Corillun smiled indulgently but in his mind he was thinking that he would not return, that after all his years of travel and toil, he had never felt remotely threatened until this day. It was not so much the words that Perris issued but more of a look behind the eyes, a hint of the perpetual internal conflict within his spirit that at times left his mind and boiled over into action. There were other Chiefs and warriors with whom Corillun traded, but he feared none of the them, in truth he did not so much as fear Perris, as completely mistrust him.

With Ancastia

Both the druidess and Idon sat watching the inert form of Caeryl. They had regained their senses when the sun was at its rest and had compared their own experiences. As Ancastia had suspected, they had ended in different places; she with the lights and sounds that she assumed the gods to be; and Idon sitting in quiet silent contemplation with her beloved Sisal. It was an unspoken agreement between them that no conclusions would be spoken until Caeryl was also restored to them. The sun was now lighting the sky and apart from a few jerks and twitches, Caeryl remained apart from her body.

'Is this to be expected?' asked Idon with some concern.

'We are dealing with an unknown' said Ancatsia matter-of-factly. 'Caeryl has experienced much and is only just returned to us. It may be . . .'

'What? It may be what?' snapped Idon, her tone full of accusation.

'It may be that this journey was too much for her, or that she has found peace' said the younger woman calmly. 'You have been where she is, and you know how much you control your own destiny there.'

'This is true' agreed Idon, though with some reluctance. 'But why does she not return? Can you wake her?'

'No' said Ancastia simply. 'It would leave her separate and apart from her body, even if we could do it, which I doubt. We must wait for her, until she is ready.' Idon snorted in frustration and muttered something that sounded like always having to wait for Caeryl, but Ancastia remained unmoved. The sounds of the settlement coming to life reached the ears of the two women who looked at each other knowing that at least one of them must put in an appearance if people were not to start gossiping.

'I'll go said Idon' rising wearily to her feet. There was a gasp of air as Caeryl arched her back and breathed deeply before her eyes jumped open and she said, very calmly.

'Stay Idon, we have much to discuss as well you know.' The older woman, the mother of Perris and the slain Ferrax, stopped in her tracks. The calmness within Caeryl was chillingly unnerving. 'You know the same truth as I do' continued Caeryl. 'Our plan to use a blade on Perris is doomed to fail; the gods deem it impractical, yet they guide us do they not?' Idon, unable to speak, nodded her head. Her mind was a contradiction; on the one hand calm certainty that what she was involved in was right; but on the other hand the certain truth that she planned to slay her own son.

'It must be poison' said Caeryl, speaking that which the three women had known, but saying it with such finality as if to brook no argument nor dissent. Idon nodded her head; Ancastia merely inclined hers towards Caeryl, nevertheless a tacit agreement that she too had been taken to the same conclusion. 'We will go about our work as if nothing has changed' said Caeryl 'and when we next meet we must decide how and when, we kill Perris.'

Idon and Ancastia left the dwelling, Caeryl lay still for a few moments, looking up at the interwoven and intricate patterns of the wooden roof, wondering how her life had turned her into a woman planning murder. That Perris deserved to die was not in issue, her fear was that her nerve would give out and that she would be too weak or cowardly to do the deed. It never crossed her mind that the other two would administer the poison, in Caeryl's mind it had to be herself that saw to the demise of the man that had cost her so much. In her trance, she had been reunited with Ferrax, although it was more like a dream of him that she experienced. His voice, so far away, had sounded lost and confused. Part of her mind rationalised that he sounded that way because that was precisely what she felt, and she took to imagining what life would have been like with the man she had loved. Would there have been children? Would Ferrax have been a suitably strong Chief like his father had been in his youth? Would she have guided him and helped him or a shadow in the background like her mother had been to her father's ambition.

Her dream was a pleasant one but a dream nonetheless and Caeryl shook herself awake and stood upright, feeling a little light headed as she did so. She sat back down again heavily on the bed and waited for the hut to stop spinning, just as Ancastia came back into the building, a grin on her face and a horn cup of water in her hands.

'Here, drink this' she said, and held the cup out. 'After a journey like we had last night, I often feel a little unsteady on my feet. Water cleans the mind.' Caeryl gulped the water down. 'Another?' asked Ancastia and Caeryl nodded. Filling the cup from a skin tied to her waistbelt the druidess handed over the drink and once again Caeryl drank deeply. The effect was remarkable. The slight noise in her head like a swarm of angry insects stopped buzzing and her mind was restored to complete clarity.

'Thank you' said Caeryl, rising to her feet and smiling. Ancastia turned and made to leave the hut. 'The druidess stopped, and slowly turned. 'Only you can make the poison we need, we all know that' said Caeryl 'but only Idon and I have the right to administer it.' She paused. 'Idon to avenge the wrong done to herself and Sisal and myself to pay Perris for the suffering he has caused in my life. We will not ask you to come with us, or to be involved other than preparing the draught.'

Ancastia, who had been looking at the floor raised her head. 'Then you will fail Caeryl. Remember that Morcant serves Perris and he will know the signs of the poison and know that which you have done. He will also know the herbs and and potions that might save Perris. And if Perris lives . . .' her voice tailed off to a chilled silence.

'So?' asked Ancastia her voice clear and strong.

'So either Morcant dies as well or I help him prepare his potions and ensure I miss out the vital ingredients. Like it or not, we three succeed together or we die together' said the druidess. Caeryl smiled at Ancastia as she finished speaking.

'I always am in awe of your wisdom' said Caeryl.

'As I am of your strength' came the reply as Ancastia once again turned and left the dwelling.

With Perris

'Storril!' bellowed Perris, standing at the door of the Chiefs hut, causing a terrified screaming from a child within, the sound was hastily smothered lest Perris exact some petty revenge on the unfortunate and hapless infant. Fortunately the one armed man came running, eager to do his master's bidding. 'Where have you been?'

'Tending the horses as you required' said Storril obsequisously, his eyes cast down to the floor so as not to provoke a confrontation.

'You take too long and you insult me with your failure' growled Perris. 'Why I keep you alive, I do not know, you cripple.' Storril coloured at that. In his time with Perris he had endured many a beating and numerous insults but never once before had Perris demeaned him in this way.

'Lord' began Storril but his sentence was cut off by Perris drawing his sword from his belt. The one-handed man looked at the glint of metal in the sunlight and swallowed hard. He knew how sharp that blade was, as he was the one who had made it so.

'Well that shut you up didn't it?' proclaimed Perris roaring with laughter though nobody else joined in. 'What's the matter Storril, are you afraid your tongue will be next to go? Fetch me my cloak, and my horse, I want to look at the preparations for Cwnsl, and I want you with me so that people can see what happens to those who displease me.' Storril turned and walked away. 'Faster Storril, faster!' The man ran, returning a short time later with Perris's magnificent black stallion and his own, rather more modest pony.

'What is this?' enquired Perris, a note of heavy sarcasm dripping from his voice.

'Lord?' said Storril warily.

'Did I ask you to fetch my horse?'

'Yes Lord.'

'And what is this with it?'

'You said you wanted me with you so naturally I brought my own animal so I could keep up.'

'Come here Storril' said Perris smilingly. Storril knew that smile was dangerous and approached warily. Perris stood with his hands on his hips, the sword now back in his belt. 'Closer' said Perris as Storril inched his way towards his master. 'Closer, that's right, all the way here.' And just as Storril stood with less than the width of an oak leaf between them, Perris drew his head back and slammed it with full force into the hapless servant's face. Storril would have fallen to the ground anyway, but as he was going down, senseless, Perris kicked him and kept kicking the body as it hit the earth.

'You are a worthless runt of a man Storril' shouted Perris 'and when I want you to think for yourself I shall tell you' he continued, completely failing to see the irony in his words. Storril lay there like a corn figure so loved by the children at harvest, except their toys were not covered in blood. 'You!' called Perris to a warrior watching the beating dispassionately, 'bring me a leather binding, a long one!' The man ran to obey now fearful for his own safety.

Within the time it took to draw two buckets of water from the well in the fort, Storril hands were bound and the other end of the binding tied to Perris's wrist. 'Get up Storril, for it will be worse for you if you do not.' The servant groaned and made to move but the effort defeated him as Perris kicked his horse forward and the stallion walked slowly across the ground, dragging Storril with the binding held tight in Perris's hand.

Presently Perris reined the horse to a standstill at the hut where Morcant lived. He jumped from the animal's back and pausing only to kick at Storril once more, he entered the dwelling, still dragging the servant along the ground.

Inside was a scene redolent of his childhood, the scents of the herbs and other plants that the druid had used for decades, mixed with the more normal aromas of human and animal life. Sitting at a bench under an opening in the side of the dwelling to afford more light sat Morcant who slowly turned and rose to his feet at the sight of his visitor.

Perris looked at the druid intently. 'You age Morcant, there are grey streaks in your beard and your hair thins.'

'It is so Lord Perris' agreed Morcant, his voice slightly higher than it was when Perris and Ferrax were children. 'Can I be of service to you?' asked the druid.

'You know I have called Cwnsl from all those across my lands?' asked Perris.

'I do' agreed Morcant affably, nodding his head.

'I want to know the future Morcant. I need to know who my enemies are and who I should guard against.'

'I see' replied the older man, again nodding his head. 'Do you fear any man in battle?' he asked.

'No' retorted Perris as if the very question were an affront.

'And do you fear that men will join together against you?'

'Again no! I have enough loyal followers to defeat any alliance' said Perris. 'What are you meaning with these fool questions?'

'Simply this my Lord. If you fear no man, and you fear no army, then there is your question answered. The future is whatever you will make of it.' Morcant smiled at Perris who was taking a moment to consider matters. Eventually his face broke into a smile.

'You are right druid! I will create the future, like a god amongst my people. And this is the way that it should be.' With that simple logic firmly fixed in his mind and his mood considerably lightened. 'Druid, you are restored to me, and I have need of your wisdom' said Perris. Sit with me at my side in Cwnsl.' This was an honour that had been bestowed upon Morcant by Perris's father Sisal and one that he, so conscious of standing within the tribe, was only too happy to accept.

'My pleasure Lord' said the smiling druid.Storril let out a groan and vomited on the floor causing Perris to step aside as the contents of the servants stomach emptied adding their acidic stench to the already heady aroma. Untying the binding, Perris handed it to the Druid. 'Tidy that up and send it back to me when you have done your work' he said, inclining his head towards the man on the floor. The druid took the binding and went outside to fetch clean water as Perris too left the hut and remounted his horse.

***

Lifted in spirits by the simple, yet inalienable logic of the druid, Perris became a tour de force and to many a throwback to the days of his greatest strengths. He visited all parts of his fortress, demanding to know how the preparations went for the gathering, from the production of food, to the storage of wine; and from the housing of the beasts to the accommodations for the guests. Not a single consideration was left to chance, and at the end of the day, when the weary sun dipped below the horizon, Perris returned to Halen a contented man. For her part, she was as surprised as he when he kissed her, and even more surprised when she felt herself responding to him with an eagerness and a passion she had thought was long past.

***

Storril regained a modicum of consciousness not long after Perris departed Morcant's home. The druid handed him a horn cup of a foul tasting green liquid and bade him drink it all down. Storril struggled to even hold the cup and so, the druid, with gentle care, administered the draft and the pain Storril felt, soon numbed to a bearable level. The servant knew better than to accept the druid's offer to stay the night, for Perris would have forgotten his own brutality by morning and if Storril were not present to serve him, then retribution would be both swift and merciless. After sun down therefore, Storril staggered off into the night, but not before the druid had sat with him and advised him to leave the fortress and never return if his life held any value to himself. Storril had smiled both inwardly and outwardly at the druid's words. Morcant said that Storril had proven himself resourceful loyal and dependable in the service of his master, but that Perris' mercurial nature was such that not even those qualities could save him from the savage beatings he received with increasing regularity.

Morcant was right however, thought Storril. He was loyal, possibly to the point of stupidity, but he knew no other life than this one, even though he too understood that eventually it was bound to be the end of him. With this conundrum revolving in his head, he made his unsteady way back to his bedwarmed by the close proximity of the cattle, yet now, after these many winters, immune to their stench.

The day before Cwnsl

The three women sat astride docile ponies, preparing to leave for their journey to Caer Perris. Their luggage fastened securely to leather pouches slung over the haunches of their animals. Men of the settlement had offered to ride with them, but they had declined, reasoning that since the slaughter of Dran and his men, Perris reigned unchallenged.

However, the real reason was so that they could talk through their plans on their journey without needing to guard their words or tone in front of others. As the time came for their departure, Caeryl spoke to the people who had gathered to wish them a safe journey.

'Friends' she said, with a diffident smile, 'we shall shortly leave you to attend cwnsl with Lord Perris. How long this will take depends entirely on him.'

'Until the wine runs out then!' called a voice which let a ripple of laughter pass through the crowd.

'Probably' agreed Caeryl ruefully 'but while we are away, or if for any reason we do not return' she added with a darker overtone 'Marrad will act as Chief. You all know him as a son of Sisal, and a young man with strength in both body and mind. You are in safe hands.'

Faces turned to Marrad, who walked forwards until he was standing in front of the three women. 'Mother, Caeryl, Ancastia' he said, inclining his head slightly to each in turn 'I wish you a safe journey, protected by the gods, and assure you that all will be the same as you left it when you return, as surely you will.' He reached forward and kissed his mother's hand as she held it out to him.

'Your father would be proud of you Marrad' she said quietly as Caeryl kicked her pony on, and the three women passed through the gates of the fortress and were soon out of sight.

***

Fortified by the activity of the night, Perris slept longer and deeper than would normally be the case and it was only the mewling of his daughter that finally awoke him. He rose from the bed of skins and furs and saw Halen comforting the child as she turned from him, her woven tunic barely hiding the curves beneath. Perris mused that she was still a fine looking woman and no less than he deserved and with this positivity in mind, he gently touched her arm as he passed by on his way to face the new day. Halen flinched as she felt his touch but relaxed as he left the dwelling, her fears that his excesses of the previous night would spill over into the morning, as they so often had, proving groundless.

Outside the hut, the sun was already well into the sky, showing promise for a fine day to come; the warmth already feeling its way into his skin. Hearing his master, Storril came to do his bidding and was issued with a series of ordered tasks. Having neither expected nor received any comment on the previous day, the servant was merely happy to be of use and went about his masters business, seeking to disguise the pain in his belly from the kicking and his hip from being dragged across the ground.

On a whim, Perris fetched his own horse and left the fortress, riding fast to the top of the hill overlooking his land where he sat to observe all he could see.

Stretching beneath him was his fortress, named after himself and the centre of power in these lands. He could make out the trees that hid the animals he hunted, and the squares of earth that people toiled in to grow food. Shimmering like beaten silver were the waters of the natural harbour upon which sat the ship belonging to Corillun the trader. Safe from the raveages and storms of the open ocean, ships could anchor, load, unload or even effect repairs. And Perris got to thinking, wondering of the future and how his place would grow when his time on earth was finished. Of course in his mind, there was no doubt that he would be seated with the gods, and so would have a hand in the destiny of his people. He hoped that his son would grow to be strong like himself, a capable warrior who had the respect of the tribe, as he considered they also respected him.

Below him, on the lower slopes of the hill, Perris detected movement, and straining his eyes made out the shapes of people moving towards the fort. Some were riding horses and some were walking, but they were not acting like warriors; these were traders or villagers, come to make profit or give tribute and Perris felt heartened by their presence. He determined to surprise them and swiftly mounted his horse and rode down the slope towards the travellers.

***

Conversation between the three women was stitled at first, as if each were either lost in her own thoughts or scared to broach the subect in all of their minds. They had travelled far enough that their homes were lost to view when Idon spoke, finally, to Ancastia.

'What have you decided upon child?' she said. Her words acted like a collective sigh, releasing the tension in the women, as Ancastia replied, her words, so simple, their meaning so harsh.

'The blue flower' she said simply. 'It's taste is foul so I shall have to disguise it but the touch of it can make a man sick or even kill, and if we are to carry out our task then the poison needs to act with haste. It is the fastest that I know of, though I have never used it.

'Where do we get the flower?' asked Caeryl.

'It is wrapped in my cloak already' said Ancastia 'so neither of you must touch it. I cannot warn you strongly enough.' She spoke with a grim finality tthat left her two companions in silent contemplation for a short time.

'How will you mask its taste?' asked Idon.

'I do not yet know' said Ancastia 'I shall probably make a draught with honey and boiled nettles, that will both mask some of the taste and explain the residue.'

'And how will you handle the flower; you have already told us of the danger?'

'The gods will guide me as they always have done' replied Ancastia simply. 'We are all agreed on our course are we not?' she asked.

'We are' said Caeryl 'even if it shall be the death of me, I shall see that odious pig of a man suffering, as he has caused such pain for all, and the end of his days shall be a cause for such celebration as we have never known.' The two women looked to their third, Idon. Although Caeryl had spoken from her heart, fuelled by her loathing for all that Perris was and that he had done to her, she was still cogniscent of the fact that Idon was his mother. The older woman not only knew how Caeryl felt, but had long since waived away any restriction on what the woman could say, however both Caeryl and Ancastia knew that as a mother, she had different feelings towards Perris than did anyone else.

'My son is not a good leader of his people' said Idon, her voice quiet and almost frail. 'He has abused his heritage, his family and his father's wishes and brought shame on me for birthing him. As there is no power than can stand up to him, let the guile of three women be his undoing. He will die at our hands or we shall die at his, it is that simple.

The women rode on, determined to reach their destination by nightfall.

***

Perris rode south, towards the sea and the group of travellers approaching his fortress. He could see that there were six people, mounted on horses. As he drew closer, he discerned that one was older than the others, a second by the slender waist, was probably a woman, and a third rode a horse laden with leather bags that looked heavy. The rider of this horse and the three others were armed with swords, and also carried spears. The sounds of Perris's approach reached the warrior at the rear of the party and he called a warning and turned his horse to face the newcomer, drawing his sword as he did so. Perris, took in the skill of the rider and acknowledged in his own mind, the vigilance of the man who was clearly a guard. Perris reigned in his horse and held up his right hand to show he held no sword. He stopped a few yards away from the travellers and called to them. The man, sensing no danger put his sword back in his belt.

'A good day to you. Do you travel for cwnsl?' The man at the front of the group, lowered a hood from his head and turned his horse round to face his questioner. Neither man had laid eyes on the other previously.

'We travel for cwnsl, though we are not of these lands' said the man, his voice strong but deep with the years of his existence. He smiled at Perris. 'And you young man?' he enquired. Perris waved the question away.

'Why attend cwnsl if you are not under the protection of Lord Perris?'

'We bring tribute' said the older man 'as a means of introducing ourselves. We wish to trade, and hope to be able to discuss terms with Lord Perris. You know him?'

'I do.' Said Perris keeping his face straight, even though the encounter amused him greatly.

'His reputation is that of a . . . difficult man, shall we say?'

'He is not to be messed around, that is true. He drives a hard, but fair bargain.'

'I hear his temper is fearsome' said the man, becoming more confident in his companion.

'Do you? Well, I cannot comment on that, but he is a warrior of some skill and his enemies do not live long, that I can agree with' said Perris, his mood beginning to darken at the perceived insult. Perris thought himself a fair minded man and not someone prone to irrational anger.

'His skills as a warrior are not in doubt' said the man reassuringly, 'but as you see, I am well protected by my men.' He indicated his guards with a sweep of his hand.

'I see' said Perris, 'and are they any good?' He had walked his horse so that he was now alongside the small group, one figure remained hooded, the rider he had thought must be female. It intrigued Perris greatly for he was used to taking what he wanted, and for it to be provided without question.

'My men serve me well' said the merchant 'they are all proven in battle and have never let me down nor left me in danger.'

'And your hidden companion?' Perris jutted his chin towards the hooded figure.

'My daughter, she accompanies me everywhere I go.' The older man smiled.

'Does she not have a face to show to the world?

'She does, but it is her choice whether she shows it or not.' The merchant shrugged his shoulders as if to indicate that he had no say in the matter. This was a siruation alien to Perris and he moved his horse closer. Immediately, the guards drew swords and barred his way.

'What is this!' roared Perris. 'Who are you that you dare block my path in my own land? I am Perris, and all who travel these paths shall know it, and shall know me.' There was an infinitesimal moment of confusion by one of the guards, and Perris acting with the speed of his youth, reached over, grabbed the guard's spear and ran him through his gut. Instantly there was uproar as the other guards all tried to bring sword blades to bear on Perris, but they were all too close, and Perris, having wrenched the point of the spear from the fallen guard's body, jabbed at the rest of them.

One of the guards broke free and rode away before turning his horse and riding to attack. Perris judged his throw to perfection and launched the spear, catching the man in the shouler. He spun from the horse and crashed to the ground. That left two men to fight, odds that Perris would always take. He kicked the horse forward, and there were sparks as his sword blade clanged and clashed against those of the guards. The merchant had taken the bridle of his daughter's horse and was trying to flee, but there was only one way he could go as the fighting Perris blocked the route northward.

With a strong blow, Perris caught one of the guards on his head and the man, dazed and with blood pouring from a savage wound, fell from his horse. Swiftly, Perris jumped from his own animal and advanced towards the remaining guard on foot. Perplexed by this mistake, the guard advanced towards Perris, a war cry in his throat and his sword raised. Perris watched him come forward and thrust his sword deep into the horse's chest. The animal went down screaming in its agony and the rider, carried by the momentum went forward over the head and landed with a sickening sound as his neck broke. It was the work of moments to finish off the two wounded guards, retrieve his own horse and set off in pursuit of the merchant and his daughter. It was a hunt to the death and Perris was exhilarated, and realised he felt alive. All other thoughts were banished from his mind; only the hunt, and the necessity of the kill remained.

Ahead, Perris could see one horse, its rider cantering to try to gain the relative safety of the fortress. He kicked his own horse into a gallop, knowing instinctively that he would out-ride and out-run the other. As he drew closer, he saw that the rider was the merchant and for a split second he wondered what had become of the daughter, before he banished that thought and rode for the kill.

Seeing the chase, warriors had come to the walls of the fortress, and now, seeing who the hunter was, they cheered on Perris. Not because they had any special love or affection for the man, but because this was sport, and a game they all understood.

The merchant shouted for the gates to the fort to be opened, but they remained steadfastly closed and barred to him. He veered left and right, the blood punding in his head, his ears assailed by the sound of his pursuer. He could hear the heavy laboured breathing of both horses and above that a manic laughter of the man who was hunting him down. The merchant had hunted wild beasts, and now understoof how they felt as a growing sense of helplessness and finality came over him. He understood that his choices were limited to turning and fighting, or running until his horse collapsed with exhaustion and dying slowly.

Hoping that his daughter had got herself to safety, the merchant fumbled for his own sword, drew it and turned to fight.

***

Ancastia was singing, her young voice light and airy as she sang a ballad about a woman who became a warrior. She was going to sing her favourite about the girl who found the man of her dreams but in Caeryl's company, that would have been wrong. Idon and Caeryl had never heard the song before, and Ancastia, who had learned verse by painstaking verse as a child, lost herself in the simple melody as her voice soared.

The three women were climbing the shallow slope of a hill, and when the song finished and Ancastia had been suitably and justifiably praised for her talent, Caeryl explained to Idon that at the top of the rise they would see the sea. Idon was curious, she had never seen the ocean before and wanted to know what it was like. For a moment, a lightness of mood came over Caeryl and she was tempted to talk of monsters that lurked within the water, larger than the big fish in the rivers, but she held herself back and tried to explain how they would see what looked like a massive lake, with Perris's fortress that sat on a piece of land that jutted out into the water. She went on to explain that the land with hills they would see in the distance was in fact an island, though nobody she knew had ever been there.

'Forrun has' offered Ancastia, explaining that Corrilun traded with the people of the island who were, for the most part, friendly and peaceable. The chatter between the three women continued as they made their way slowly towards the top of the slope, where Idon let out a gasp as the view opened up before her. It was exactly as Caerly had described, yet to Idon it seemed to make the world look somehow larger. She could see the water, the land that appeared to be on all four sides of it, and in the middle of her view, she saw the smoke from the fires of Caer Perris rising lazily into the sky above. Idon, dismounted and let her horse graze, and taking her lead so too did Caeryl and Ancastia as the three women stood and looked down at the place where they planned to kill.

***

Killing was the only thing in Perris's mind as the merchant swung his horse around to fight. Sadly for the Chief of his people, whose blood was up, and who wanted to impress those that might see, the fight was short and rather one sided. The merchant swung his sword and Perris easily parried it, gauging if the merchant had any skills as a fighter. Sadly he did not, and on the second pass when the man once again brandished his sword, Perris not only knocked the sword away as one would swat at an insect, but grabbed the man's head, jabbing his fingers into his mouth. Fluidly he then gained a hold on the back of the merchant's head and twisted it violently to the right, both hearing, and feeling the vertebrae snap. The merchant let out a soft groan and gurgled as he struggled for both oxygen and consciousness whilst his brain died and he fell, lifeless, to the ground. Immediately,

Perris forgot him and wheeled his horse round looking for the one remaining member of the party, the daughter, whose face he had yet to see.

Perris pulled the horse to a stop and sat to listen. If she moved, he would hear her and know where to find her. But all was still and quiet. Slowly he walked the horse forward, keenly peering into the bushes and trees that grew all around, providing any reasonably intelligent fugitive with cover. Perris grinned to himself, the girl, whoever she was, had already proven to be more worthy than her dead father and his mind relished the hunt, looking forward to the inevitable chase and capture. Although he was alert, his mind flitted between possible outcomes, his imagination veering between slaughter and slavery as the elusive fugitive's destiny.

Perris pulled the horse to a stop, and sat, and listened. He knew his quarry was there, he could sense it, in exactly the same way that he sensed being watched by one of the boars he so enjoyed hunting. Those wily, vicious animals, would also stand in complete silence, waiting the moment to flee or fight.

His head whipped round, he had heard a sound away to his right, away from the fortress and back towards the rising ground that led to the northward hill. It was the sound of a horse, snorting impatiently. Perris kicked his horse forward and the animal broke into a gallop, its rider whooping and shouting and making as much noise as possible.

Ahead, the hunted prey broke cover, the girl riding as hard as she could, but her animal had been chosen for its placidity not its speed and the contest was an uneven one and Perris drew alongside, still not able to see the face of his fleeing victim as she leaned forward over the horses neck, urging the animal to speeds that were beyond its capabilities. Perris edged ever closer to the girl and her horse sensed the futility of the contest long before the rider was prepared to, and slowed to a walk. Perris rode ahead, swftly dismounted and restrained the frightened horse as the rider tried to jump off and run.

It was the work of a moment to grab her wrist and draw his sword, pushing her to the ground as he did so.

Irrational anger now came over Perris, feeling that this mere girl was taunting him and his prowess as a warrior. How dare she insult him and seek to humiliate him in this way? He roughly pulled the hood off her head, and grabbing her hair, painfully pulled her back to her feet, ignoring the inevitably crying and wailing that, in his opinion, women were so prone to.

'Quiet!' roared Perris, and stunned, the girl drew breath and stayed silent. Perris, still enraged, drew his fist back as if to strike the girl just as a voice spoke from behind him.

'Lord?'

'What do you want Storril' snarled Perris, his fist clenched.

'Your guests have watched your killing of these people, Lord,' said Storril calmly and yet with a quiver of fear in his voice. 'There is disquiet in the fortress and there will be yet more should you harm a defenceless woman.'

For the first time Perris looked at the girl. She was of about fourteen or fifteen summers, plain, dull and drab with no particular attractiveness about her. Perris lowered his fist.

'Who cares what they think' said the Chief, yet he yielded to the implied pressure of opinion and put his sword back in his belt. 'Take this thing, Storril' he said indicating the girl. 'We can get a price for her from Corrilun' he looked her up and down dismissively, 'it won't be much though.'

'Could I have her?' asked Storril diffidently. 'I am so busy and a willing pair of hands would be most . . .'

'Storril' interrupted Perris 'I doubt it is her hands that make you so eager, but if you wish to lie with her and rut like the beasts you are then yes, you may have her for as long as it pleases me. But' he paused 'she belongs to me and should you, or she, displease me, then she is sold.'

'Thank you Lord' said Storril and moved forward towards the girl, who seeing the mutilated stump of his arm, recoiled and cried.

'Deal with her Storril, deal with her properly and for the joy of the gods make her be quiet' called Perris as he walked away towards his horse who stood placidly nearby. Perris thought of swinging himself onto the horses back but decided instead to demonstrate his status and importance in front of this girl. He had no need to do this, her future was now clear, she would be his possession, but Perris was never rational and he called Storril over.

The servant, hurried away from the girl who watched with growing revulsion as the one handed man knelt on the ground so that his bully of a master could stand on his shoulders to mount his horse. He watched as he calmly walked his animal over towards her, take the reins of her own horse and ride away with it as a prize, a grin of triumph on his face as he did so The girl, who when she was hidden, had had the presence of mind to hide those few items of value bestowed upon her by her father, now resolved to make good her escape as soon as opportunity presented itself. For the moment she would have to be compliant however, and as Storril came towards her she forced herself to be calm and allowed herself to be led towards the fortress with the smells and sounds of civilisation masking the brutality that she had so recently witnessed.

She gasped and sobbed as she saw the body of her father, sprawled on the ground, uncared for and ignored as if he were a branch that had fallen from a tree His eyes, cold and lifeless, stared at her and she plucked at Storril's sleeve.

'My father' she said as he realised it was the first time she had spoken. 'He cannot be left there to be eaten by the animals. You must do something.'

'We are not in a position to make demands' said Storril simply 'but I will return later when my duties for the day are complete, and see what can be done for him.'

The girl got a glimpse into the dumb kindness of this man and said 'I must thank you for saving me back there. Would he have struck me do you think?'

'Yes' said Storril without hesitation, causing the girl to shudder. 'He is a very cruel and demanding man, so we must hurry as he will want feeding.' Storril walked on as the girl, revolted by violent death of her father, yet unable to take her eyes from his corpse, hesitated. Storril pulled her along. 'He was serious about selling you if you displease him' he reminded her, and then in a softer tone stated 'just as I am serious about helping you with your father later.'

Caer Perris

The sun was low in the sky, creating a golden hue over the land when three women arrived at the gates to the fortress. They were weary and Idon in particular in some discomfort as her old bones protested the discomfort she felt. The gates were opened and the women dismounted and walked their animals into the settlement.

Men approached and took the horses away, having first taken care to show due respect and deference to Idon in particular, and removed the travelling bags which were placed in a hut close to the sea border of the fortress. Ancastia, who had travelled sniffed the evening air, redolent with the tang of salt from the water that lapped gently to the shore. Idon and Caeryl looked about them, and despite their reservations about the man who had given his name to this place, they could not help but be impressed.

A solid and seemingly impregnable earth embankment, fronted by a ditch that was deeper than a man was tall, ran round the land border of the fortress and into the water that though gentle looked forbiddingly cold. The sea border had no defences as such save for a row of huts, that judging by the shields and weaponry that were on display, housed warriors. Within the embankment, Idon noticed, the large dwelling that would naturally be the home of Perris and, she concluded a woman, for he was not a man to have his needs go unmet. She also could see a fire pit in the centre of the fortress just the same as her own home where she had quietly observed Sisal giving wise counsel and settling disputes in his authoritative and decisive manner. There was also a smaller fire pit with flames rising into the sky, the orange colour burning to bright white at the base, showing the heat to be intense. She could hear the rhythmic beating of metal as skilled craftsmen prepared swords and shield frames as well as the more mundane items of domesticity.

Smoke rose from each of the occupied huts and nobody here looked underfed or without clothing appropriate for the season. On the journey, the women had seen abandoned settlements, and some that whilst occupied contained families living without the basic necessities; children with pale skin and sunken eyes. And here is all made sense.. This was where the wealth was taken, and this is where people prospered. She understood her son's method; to show his people, that he and he alone brought them riches, so as to keep them loyal and dedicated to his service. Anyone not immediately within the fortress could fend for themselves, kept suppressed by demands from Perris for tribute, meaning that there was no ability to buy weapons or pay warriors and wage war on the man who kept them in their hovels. It was not the way Sisal ruled his lands, but then Perris was not his father.

Idon could not help but notice the ship riding on the water of the harbour. It was a fine and proud vessel and instinctively she knew that it was the property of a successful merchant and suspected that Corrilun was present. That was a cause for concern, for if Corrilun were here, then so too was Forrun and that could unsettle and distract Ancastia, and she, and her knowledge, was essential to the task before them.

'There are so many people. We shall never get the time we need to do what we must. Someone will see us.' Idon turned and saw that Caeryl was looking anxious, biting her lower lip in concentration as her eyes darted here and there. She laid a hand on the younger woman's arm.

'Be calm my dear' she said, smiling. 'People bring confusion, and confusion brings opportunity. Besides' she said with an air of certainty 'would that there were only the three of us, we would be the only suspects. With all these people, most of whom will hate the ground my son walks upon, there are plenty who could be guilty if thoughts alone condemned you.

'Look over there' contined Idon, pointing towards Perris's long-suffering servant. 'Not at the wretch of a man, but the girl following him. I have learned that just this afternoon she watched Perris rip her father's head nearly off his shoulders so that his spirit left him and he was dead before his carcas hit the mud. She would want revenge if it were offered to her surely?'

'Look around Idon, there are warriors everywhere. I do not fear death, but I do fear pain.' Caeryl was losing her nerve, and once again Idon spoke calmly.

'I know men such as these, look into their eyes child, they are not here for the love of Perris. They are here because he rewards them well. Remove the rewards and they will drift away and look to serve another master. We have nothing to fear from them if we do our task well. If Perris survives . . .' she left the rest of the sentence unsaid, a rueful look on her lined and ageing face. Then she said 'opportunity will present itself, it always does. And when it comes we seize it with both hands and gratitude to the gods for providing.'

'Thank you mother Idon' said Caeryl. 'I was just a little overwhelmed.'

'We have the gods on our side, we will not fail. Where is our druidess?' asked Idon.

'Look there, over towards the shoreline.' Idon followed Caeryl's oustretched finger that pointed to a slight figure dressed in white that stood in the sea, the water soaking the skirts of her robe. Ancastia was staring at the boat in the harbour, clearly, to those who knew her, hoping to see sight of Forrun, but the deck was deserted and the ship showed no sign of life. The two women watched as a large shadow detached itself from the shade of a nearby tree and the unmistakable bulk of the silent warrior snuck up on the young girl before, in one swift movement, lifted her off her feet and twirled her round as if she were a leaf in the breeze. The distance was too far for the sound of laughter to carry, but the way in which Ancasstia threw her arms round Forrun and buried her hed in his neck told the whole story.

'You look sad still Caeryl?' said Idon. The younger woman shrugged her shoulders. 'You feel perhaps that your youth was taken away? That Sisal ruined happiness for you?' Caeryl knew Idon better than to criticise her dead husband, and anyway, he now sat with the gods and was beyond reproach. She opened her mouth to speak, but Idon cut across her. 'It's alright my dear' she said, 'Sisal did some great things in his life, and some really bad and stupid ones as well. Separating you and Ferrax was his one major mistake that I would dearly wish to put right. Alas, all we can do is avenge him.'

'And avenge him we shall mother' added Caeryl quietly.

***

Perris stood by the fire pit and looked around him. He had ordered the fire lit even though it was still daylight, and the wood smoked and crackled as the orange flame devoured it. The lighting of the fire had been a calculated decision on his part as it subconsciously told visitors and guests that he did not need to worry about something as trivial as a supply of wood, and that he had servants and men who would tend the fire and keep it burning. He also knew that the smoke would be seen from the hill and any traveller looking down upon the settlement would be suitably impressed, seeing not only the fortress, but the harbour and the signs of habitation.

A sudden gust of wind blew smoke into his eyes and mouth. He stood as long as he could, his eyes smarting and his chest heaving as he tried to draw breath. However, he began to cough and splutter, tears streaming down his face, and he crouched to avoid the stinging air that had driven the oxygen from his lungs. As he recovered his composure he spluttered a call to Storril that the man should fetch Morcant the druid to him, and he withdrew into his home where Halen washed his eyes with fresh water and made him sit and rest.

Perris continued to cough as his lungs expelled the smoke as best they could.

Presently Storril returned to say that he could not find Morcant and believed that the druid was away from the fortress collecting ingredients for his medications. It was well known that he had been seeking to prepare for every eventuality since Perris had called cwnsl. Perris flew into a rage.

'Find the old goat' he whispered hoarsely 'and tell him that if he does not tend to me at once then he shall be banished or tied to a stake for the boars to gut.' Storril hesitated.

'There is the girl if you would let her tend you?'

'I am not interested in your whelp Storril, I could trust her even less than I could trust you and that isn't much' he broke off into another fit of wheezing and coughing.

'Not that girl Lord, but the one they call Ancastia the druidess who lives at the home of your father Sisal and it is said is the woman of the warrior Forrun. She has powers of healing and can hear the gods.'

'Fetch her' commanded Perris between coughs that shook his body.

***

Storril had run from Perris and found Idon and Caeryl talking earnestly to one another. They turned silent as he approached, and looked at the floor as if concealing a secret. Storril in deference bobbed his head and announced that his master, Perris had summonsed Ancastia as he was in need of healing. Idon looked at Caeryl and Storril caught a flash of a smile that he did not understand, pass between the two women.

'I will go to him' announced Idon. 'Caeryl, you find Ancastia and bring her to us.'

'But my instructions were specific that I should bring the druidess' said Storril in some confusion. Idon drew herself to her full height and spoke in a tone that no mere man would counter.

'I am his mother. I birthed him and therefore I shall help in his healing. Now do not delay further and tell me what is wrong with him?' Storril who had never known his own mother was thus in awe not only of Idon's bearing and manner but also her assertion of powers and as he guided her, he gabbled away, telling her how spirits seemed to have entered Perris's body and were causing him to hack and cough in their drive to now be free.

Caeryl watched the two of them walk away, and went on her rather more difficult mission of finding Ancastia and interrupting her reunion with Forrun.

'These spirits of which you speak' said Idon imperiously 'they seek their freedom you say?'

'Yes Lady. My Master finds drawing breath hard while they fight to free themselves from his body. It is as if they clash inside him.' They had arrived at the dwelling indicated by Storril who stood, deferentially to one side, to allow Idon acces.

Idon walked into the gloom of the dwelling, the only light coming from a fire in the centre of the building. Her keen eye missed nothing including the woman sitting on a bed of skins and furs with two children held close to her.

'You are Perris's woman?' she asked, completely unable to keep a note of derision from her voice.

'I am Halen' replied the woman, her speech confident yet somehow reticent as if she were intimidated in her own home. 'And yes I am his woman, and these' she pulled the children closer 'are ours.'

'You keep a tidy and clean home' said Idon by way of praise, for in spite of herself and her genuine love for Caeryl, she saw in Halen, something of herself from so many years gone by. However before

Halen could speak, Idon had swept her way over to the wheezing man lying on the ground, his face angry and red, his beard flecked with spittle.

'You!' she commanded Storril 'move him towards the fire.' Storril held up his maimed arm showing the loss of a hand which caused Idon to snarl, more in frustration than anger at how useless he was. However, Idon was placated and reassured as she felt Halen beside her.

'Towards the fire?' asked the younger woman.

'Yes. If the fire spirits are seeking to leave his body then the fire will fraw them out and free him from their grasp' replied Idon. It made sense as so the two women with some assistance from Storril dragged Perris towards the fire. He was coughing and spluttering all the while, his body heaving with the effort, his eyes bulging as he fought the demons within.

'Turn him on his side so that his face is towards the heat' said Idon and the three of them eventually succeeded in pushing the bulk of Perris onto his left hand side, the reflected glow of the flames mingling with the redness of his face. The persistent coughing diminished and Perris began to breath more easily.

'The spirits are placated!' said Halen in joyful expression as the skin over the entrance to the dwelling was pulled aside and Ancastia entered. Idon smiled at the younger woman and stepped back, explaining to Halen that Ancacstia was a druidess and experienced not only in the ways of healing but also in hearing the voices of the gods. Halen, as Idon had planned, looked suitably awe struck that one so young could weild such power.

Another body entered the dwelling and Caeryl stared at the prone form of her tormentor before comprehending that Idon was speaking, pointing out Halen and the children. Idon's manner was quite clear; that there was to be no discord here and Caeryl understood instinctively.

Ancastia bent down and listened to Perris's breathing. The man himself was either asleep or exhausted and thus made no comment nor objection to the women around him. The druidess fumbled about in her robe,' clearly seeking something.

'You are Caeryl? Asked Halen. 'You by rights are Perris's woman and should be here with him. Caeryl looked at Halen but could find no artifice within her. There was an age difference Caeryl estimated, of between five and ten summers between them, and she looked at the younger woman who smiled diffidently. Halen was the interloper for she knew that Sisal himself had put Perris with Caeryl and she had no place here.

'This is your home Halen' said Caeryl 'and I will not put you, and your children out of it for the sake of myself. I was given to Perris, but I never gave of myself. What Perris had, he took. However, he chose you and that is the strength of your claim to him that I shall not challenge.' The two women had reached an accord and both stood aside to let Ancastia continue her work.

The druidess had produced a fired vial that contained a clear liquid that if held up to sunlight, had the merest blue hue. She removed the stopper and muttering an incantation, she tipped a few drops between Perris's lips. Satisfied that her work was done, she rose to her feet and spoke to Halen.

He will rest awhile and then be sick as the fire spirit leaves him. He will be weak and wretched so allow him rest, and I will see him again when the sun rises.'She moved away to leave the hut, followed by Idon and Caeryl.

'Thank you' said Halen simply and Idon turned and held her hand, the old woman's bony fingers like claws, gnarled and hard, but the gesture was as welcome as it was inclusive.

As the three women emerged into the sunlight Ancastia spoke softly. 'Not a word until we are alone' was all she said as the women walked along calmly and without hurrying.

Once inside the dwelling allocated to them, Caeryl let out a long sigh and slumped on to the bed she had chosen. ‘Oh for a sword and a strong arm with which to use it’ she said. ‘I would have gutted that pig without a second thought.’

‘And have been put to death for your effort’ added Idon. ‘Do you not see?’ she looked at the other two women, ‘that we have been smiled on by the gods? By my own dear Sisal, who has struck Perris down so that we may gain admittance to his home.’ She turned to Ancastia. ‘What did you give him?’

‘A very weak potion from the blue flower. Enough to make him vomit and convulse, but not enough to kill. It will leave him weak and lifeless, but nevertheless able to breathe and hear all that we do, even though he is powerless to resist us. The key is the woman Halen; she must have trust and belief that we are curing Perris, and indeed you are right Idon, this situation is truly a gift from the gods.’

‘Why not just finish him off when you had the chance?’ asked Caeryl

‘Your anger clouds your judgment child’ said Idon. ‘Look around us? This place is crawling with people who rely on Perris and his wealth. Yes they will abandon him eventually but if we were to poison him immediately then there would soon be four bodies not just one. No, Ancastia is right to win over the trust of this Halen. She will be our saving in this matter.’

‘Morcant will know what we have done’ said Caeryl ‘and we came here knowing our lives were lost anyway.’

‘I have something to live for’ said Ancastia simply, but pointedly, ‘and though I will not let you down, I will take every chance to live. She sat on her own bed of skins, here serene countenance untroubled by the murder she was an intrinsic part of.

***

Just as Ancastia had predicted, Perris was violently ill. His guts emptied over the floor of his home, and he was too weak and enfeebled to even shout at Halen to clear his vomit. His bowels also loosened and the proud Chief was helpless as, like a baby, he lay in his own ordure. The stench of vomit and shit was permeating everything and the the mighty warrior was reduced to a shivering, retching, sweating wreck. Halen, acting out of duty, ensured that Perris neither choked nor drowned, and cleaned where she could, only for another bout of vomiting to replace that which had been removed.

Halen marvelled at the powerful magic of Ancastia, both in terms of how she could produce so powerful a potion that drove spirits from the body, but also in her predictions of what would happen. She knew however that Perris required more care than her understanding permitted, but she dithered and fretted. On the one hand she should call Morcant for he was druid to the settlement and had the wisdom of both his years and his travels; yet conversely was it not Ancastia who had displayed her knowledge so proficiently thus far. Storril however was lacking in imagination and of his own initiative fetched Morcant who arrived as hurriedly as he was able, breathing hard and wheezing as he visibly recoiled at the sight of Perris lying forlorn and hopeless on the floor.

'Help me sit him up' commanded Morcant to both Storril and Halen, as between the three of them they pulled and dragged the recumbent form of Perris into a sitting position. Almost immediately, the retching started again though it was only able to produce a small amount of yellow bile that trickled into his beard.

'What has he eaten?' asked Morcant sniffing carefully at the pool of vomit on the floor. Halen told the druid of the smoke and the spirits and Perris's fighting for breath. She spoke of Ancastia's visit and of the potion given to Perris, Morcant questioned Halen very carefully as to the colour of the potion, establishing that it was an almost clear liquid.

'We need to move him outside' ordered Morcant.

'We cannot' countered Halen. 'The people cannot see their Chief like this, it would undermine him as a Chief, as a warrior and as a man to be seen to be so weak.' Morcant was about to remonstrate, but saw the sense in Halen's words and relented.

'I will ask Ancastia what she has administered' said Morcant and with a sweep of his hand that seemingly announced his departure, he left the hut, and walked into the light to be confronted by a group of warriors who were gathered outside the Chieftain's dwelling.

'What do you all want?' snarled Morcant, his mind working overtime as he tried to work out how to save and treat his master, mostly he admitted to himself, so that he could save his own skin.

'How is Perris?' called one of the men. Morcant noted the lack of respect in the voice, and implied by the omission of a title given to the man sat in his own vomit just a short distance away. 'Is he dead?' asked the same man.

'You would do well to guard your words' warned Morcant. 'Lord Perris of course lives for he is a strong man, and he can hear your doubts, and, knowing him as I do, he shall cause a reckoning with you.'

'So where is he?' the man persisted.

'Our Chief was taken by an evil spirit that has now left his body, but has also left him in need of rest so that he may return to full strength' said Morcant with more conviction than he felt. There was a murmuring within the group of men before another spoke.

'He owes us silver for our service, and we have come to collect it.' This was met with a general agreement from the others, Morcant drew himself to his full, and impressive height.

'Do you tell me that you doubt the word of Perris, the son of Sisal? The two men who have shaped these lands and brought such prosperity to all. Begone and away with you like the dogs you are' he added in imperious tone, 'and Perris shall deal with your claims at cwnsl if not before.' The men, partly intimidated by Morcants tone, and partly mollified by the prospect of payment, began to drift away. Morcant stood his ground until all had left, and then hurried away to find the druidess.

***

'I cannot agree with you' said Ancastia quietly but firmly. 'I have prepared the liquid and it must be handled with the greatest of care to prevent death. I can go through with what we agreed, for that is right. But I cannot accede to your demand, nor will I take the responsibility should anything happen to you.'

'You overstep your position child' said Idon angrily. Our purpose here is what unites us, and this attitude of yours places you above myself and Caeryl. And let me remind you that both of us have a far higher claim to wanting the end of Perris than you do.'

'You want to kill your own son' said Ancastia. 'Have you any idea how the gods will respond to that? You are revered amongst your people but if you do this thing then the gods will seek punishment, not just on you, but on all associated with you.'

'Yet you will walk away without a problem?' said Idon.

'I can talk to the gods and explain' replied Ancastia with disarming simplicity.

'Good, then you can explain my reasons and my actions. I will not argue this point any more.'

The three women were sitting in their accommodation, around the fire that crackled and smoked, but at least provided some warmth and light. Caeryl who had thus far stayed out of the argument, now spoke.

'For myself, I have been wronged twice by that pig of a man. Not only did he attack me, but he took away my chance of love and happiness. Were I a man, I would have challenged him to combat a long time ago and one of us would already be dead.' She paused, and looked at the two other women in turn. 'For what it is worth, I don't care who kills him, just that he dies, and preferably in considerable pain over a long time. However, I have listened to the two of you and I understand the arguments you both make, but' and here she looked at Ancastia, 'Idon should administer the poison. It completes a circle of birth life and death and the gods will see it as such. Before we do what we must however, we have much else to plan.'

'How do you mean?' asked Idon, still irate notwithstanding the support from Caeryl.

'When Perris dies, there will be bloodshed, unless a new leader steps forward quickly and establishes a legitimate claim that unites everyone' explained Caeryl.

'You mean Marrad' said Ancastia.

'Yes, I do.'

'It makes sense, save for the fact hat he is not here' added the druidess with a touch of irony.

'I wanted to ask if Forrun could ride and fetch him?' Caeryl looked at the other two. 'We should have thought this through, we should have considered the aftermath of succeeding . . .'

'Instead, we just thought of what would happen to us should we fail' interjected Ancastia cutting across Caeryl. She sighed. 'You are right, and we are foolish. I will ask Forrun to slip away and fetch Marrad, and Idon, forgive me for my selfishness born of my stubborn pride.'

'Come here child' said Idon holding her arms out. 'For one so young you carry a heavy responsibility and remain wise far beyond your years.' The three women were thus at peace with themselves, their task and each other when Morcant strode into the building.

'What did you administer to Perris!' he thundered at Ancastia who recoiled at these words. With anyone else she could have spoken soft words that would be believed but Morcant knew the secrets of the plants and the potions that could be made. Before she could speak however, Idon launched a tirade at the man.

'What do you mean entering this place without permission? You forget yourself and your place Morcant! Where you once held power you now have no position and no standing to make these demands. Get out and remain away from us until such time as you learn your place.' Idon moved to stand between Morcant and Ancastia, defying him by her very presence and challenging him to ignore her. 'Out!' she commanded but Morcant did not move.

'Lady, my esteem for you have never weakened, but my position here is with your son, the Lord Perris who rules this place with violence and intimidation. His temper, as you know only too well, is fearsome and I am charged with healing his illnesses. I know that you administered a potion to him that had an effect and I need to know what it is so that I do not either counteract its benefit nor do I combine it with my own remedy and create a poison.' He glared at Ancastia.

'Morcant is afraid' said Caeryl simply joining the debate for the first time. The druid looked at her and paused for a moment before responding.

'Of course I am afraid. Everybody in this place is afraid with the possible exception of you three.' His eyes narrowed in suspicion. 'Why is that?'

'I used a very weak potion from the blue flower' announced Ancastia simply. 'It was intended to allow the bad spirits that had entered Perris's body to be thrown out.'

'You . . . you used the blue flower?' said Morcant with increasing incredulity. 'You could have killed him, you must be aware of the propreties and strength of that plant. It is a killer.'

'But he does not die does he?' replied Caeryl. 'Ancastia is proficient in her work and Perris not only lives but the spirits are gone. Is that not so?'

'Perris remains enfeebled and weak' said Morcant, the colour having drained from his lined and bearded face. 'What are you trying to do?'

'What are you insinuating druid?' snapped Idon. 'That perhaps I want to kill my own son? The man I raised who has become a fearsome warrior Chief in the very image of his father?'

'I . . . I, apologise Lady' stammered Morcant, clearly perplexed by the attitude of the women. 'I have never ever dared use the blue flower to heal, it is a deadly plant.'

'And Ancastia is a skilled and proficient potion maker, would you not agree?' said Caeryl.

'She must be' agreed Morcant meekly, 'and my choice is clear. Having taken the step of administering what you have to Perris you must oversee his treatment and recovery, and' he added ominously 'bear the responsibility for his well-being. On your head must be the consequences of your actions.' He stood staring as if he had said something momentus.

'So be it' said Ancastia with a shrug of her shoulders. 'I shall need to speak with both his woman and his servant to advise them of what they need to do.'

Morcant, clearly offended by her matter-of-fact tone and what her perceived as a lack of respect to himself, snorted and turned on his heel, storming back into the daylight. The women smiled at each other.

'Now, if Morcant is leaving the care of Perris to us, we really do need to talk to Halen and whatever his servant is called' said Idon.

'Storril' said Ancastia. 'His name is Storril.'

The Same Day

Forrun, at Ancastia's bidding, had left the fortress, riding hard to fetch Marrad. Caeryl was angry with herself for the oversight of failing to consider the need to ensure a succession once Perris was dead, but had retreated into pragmatism and practicality as she now sat with Halen and Ancastia. Perris had been helped to his bed and lay groaning and drifting in and out of consciousness.

Idon was looking for Storril, the conversation would be similar to that with Halen; they were to be warned as to the seriousness of Perris's condition and the possibility of his death.

If Caeryl and Ancastia were expecting Halen to be a trembling and fearful woman, they were wrong. With her man incapacitated, Halen had taken on a mantle of competence and capability.

'I assume you want to discuss the fact that Perris may die?' A quick look passed between Caeryl and Halen, and it was not missed by Halen, who smiled wryly. 'I see' she said. 'I think we should talk openly. Can he hear us?'

'Not clearly' replied Ancastia. 'He wil be full of dreams and delusion and find it difficult to separate what is real and what is not.'

'In that case, speak your minds and speak truth. Will Perris die?'

'Yes' said Ancastia

'And you both think that this is for the best?'

'It is of course the will of the gods' replied Caeryl, not breaking eye contact with Halen.

'Or maybe the will of three women' said Halen, causing another brief glance between Caeryl and Ancastia.

'Perhaps four?' asked Ancastia.

'He is my man' said Halen 'and I have no argument with you lady.'

'Nor I with you' agreed Caeryl sincerely.

'Then you understand that I have a legacy to protect, should Perris no longer be with us.' Slowly she turned and looked at her children who were sitting eating and laughing. 'Perran is the son of a powerful Chief and his rightful place is as his successor, do you not think? And also his mother should live in a manner befitting her status?'

'These are matters of respect that would be due to you' agreed Caeryl. 'Should Perris not survive this illness, then his brother Marrad will rule over the lands formerly ruled over by his father Sisal. I think we can agree that Perran will rule this place and sufficient lands around, subject to the payment of a small tribute and allegiance to Marrad.'

'Perran will come of age and rule this place and its lands. No tribute need be paid and the bounds of family are stronger than any agreement. Marrad will teach him the ways of power until he comes of age. To maintain the appearance of respect, this place will always be called Caer Perris.'

Caeryl sat for a moment, her respect for Halen increasing with each passing thought, before, eventually she ended the growing tension in the hut by speaking slowly and clearly. 'It is agreed that should Perris die then what you say shall happen' said Caeryl. 'It is now in the hands of the gods' she added.

'I think not' said Halen, looking pointedly at Ancastia.

Idon's conversation with Storril was more direct and pointed. Used to dealing with servants and slaves she had bluntly told him that Perris's life was in mortal danger and had watched his shoulders visibly slump. Mistakenly she took this as a sign of sorrow on the part of the crippled man.

'I have been bound to Perris since he did this to me' said Storril. 'My own people spurned me for my injury and to survive I came to Perris as a matter of tribute.' He paused and Idon looked at him intently. 'I believe he is your son Lady, but that man has beaten and humiliated me at every opportunity. When he dies then I am released from my bond and I can make a life of my own.'

Idon, who was not used to being spoken to in such terms, looked at Storril as if he were dirt, but her words were kinder and more considerate. 'What will you do? You said your own people shunned you?'

'This is true, but over time I have developed skills and have traded through Corrilun. I have some silver and will clear some land and live there. Not here' he added quickly, 'but over the sea' in the land that Corrilun and Forrun live.' Idon stood quietly for a moment and then touched Storril on the shoulder

'May the gods smile on you Storril' she said.

'And on you Lady Idon' said Storril sincerely.

'I see someone watching you?' said Idon, and Storril turned slowly to see the eyes of the merchant's daughter turn away from him. 'You have hopes there?'

'Her father was butchered by Perris yesterday Lady. She is numb with shock and fear, but yes I have some hope. Whatever she decides she will be free to make her own choice in life. Her father was a merchant and she will have knowledge and skills that may be of use to Corrilun.' He shrugged his shoulders, a gesture that was as resigned to his fate as it was a show of strength of character.

'Storril, go now. Take the girl and get away from here before nightfall.' The man nodded agreement.

***

'Cwnsl is set for this night' said Halen. The three women had become four and all were now sat together in the guest accommodation, Halen's children were being looked after by one of the warriors' wives who had befriended Halen, she suspected to gain influence over Perris.

'Your point being that we should act now?' said Idon.

'It makes sense' agree Caeryl. 'Ancastia?'

'The potion is ready.'

'I administer it' said Halen. He deserves to go at my hand. There was a collective sigh and Idon explained that the argument had already been had. 'You need my silence'said Halen 'but I acknowledge your right' she said looking at Caeryl. 'And yours as his mother' she acknowledged to Idon.

'We can all be present' said Ancastia quietly. 'halen put it about that we, as women over whom he holds power, will make offerings to the gods to restore his health. No man will dare interfere. It gives us the right and the opportunity to be there, but get the children out and safe.'

'And cwnsl?' perisisted Halen.

'Marrad should be here by then' said Idon. 'We shall present him as the new Chief of the tribe, and protector of Caer Perris until Perran is of age. I can guide Marrad as to how to deal with the inevitable discontent.'

***

As the sun fell low in the sky, all was prepared. The children were taken out of the fortress by Storril, who had refused to leave. The merchant's daughter went with them. Ancastia had advised sufficient people that they were making offerings to the gods so that the word went round and a small group hung around the dwelling, a much smaller group than in Sisal's last days Idon noted with satisfaction. The four women were gathered around Perris's fetid body which still heaved and produced a fould smelling bile and liquid dung.

Ancastia reached into her robe and withdrew a small clay jar and stood over the man who was lying with his eyes open, the look of weakness and confusion upon his face.

'He knows' said Idon. 'you can see it in his eyes.'

'Good said Caeryl and spat in his face. Idon laid a hand on her arm and leaned over her son. She held her hand out for the potion and without ceremony tipped the contents into his mouth. Perris had no strength to resist but did not awallow and a quantity of the liquid leaked out and ran into his beard. Halen leaned over and pinched his nose tight so that the only way to take in air was to swallow.

Perris swallowed. He gulped air into his lungs and Idon was right, he knew what was happening. He tried to fight but was too weak, instead his head flopped around on the bed of furs as once again Idon leaned over him.

'You took what was not your Perris, you are now called to pay the price. Anything you did have or were given, you destroyed and now those things destroy you. I, as your mother, claim the right to end your life in as much pain as you caused to others. You will be denied a place with the gods and your body will be fed to the swine.' She turned on her heel and walked out into the fading light, shaking her head to the assembled people, to convey the message that Perris was beyong hope.

Perris had begun to change, his tongue lolled in his mouth which had become slack and help permanently open. His eyes remained wide open but his face turned a shade of red as his blood boiled inside his body. His limbs spasmed though he was too weak to control his movements and his body, already emptied of fluids heaved and retched.

Ancastia mopped the dying mans face with a cloth soaked in cold water, whilst Caeryl and Halen looked on dispassionately.

Perris did not take long to die, Ancastia put her hand on his chest and felt the drum beat within quicken and slow and then stop.

His dead eyes stared at nothing.

About the Author

A long time ago, I was born in Portsmouth, which is a great place to be hatched to be honest. I spent my childhood growing up just outside the city, in what was then a small village called Portchester, if you are interested in history, then take my word for it, Portchester has it all. In fact, don't take my word for it... go and see it for yourself ! And if you don't want to do that then stick around because the books are coming...

My education was mostly in the relaxed atmosphere of St John's College in Southsea; daily train journeys into the city, the constant threat of being stabbed because you wore a school uniform, and some very interesting characters as teachers to break the routine. From there, via Highbury College to re-sit my A levels (I was never very academic,) and then I embarked on the adventure of a lifetime to the north-east to study law. Ostensibly to make my fortune.

To any aspiring lawyer, I say this; don't do it.

I had fun, in the days when you could, and when being a solicitor actually paid a living wage; it was a job where creativity was paramount - after all you couldn't say the same thing to the same Magistrates about the same defendant week after week and expect to be successful. You needed to paint a picture with words, to enthral or captivate an audience of cynical shop owners, headmasters or accountants that mostly either wanted to exact retribution on my client or bugger off for a caffeine fix. And the story telling craft was learned - or was it inherent?

But then it all came crashing down and I was out of it, and looking for something new. I've tried things I've loved, and things I've hated but in every place and every job I've stored away the feelings, the people and the atmospheres and one day they will find their way into print.

For the moment I remain in the north east of England, hanging around Durham indulging in my other passion of photography whilst trying to avoid working too hard at the day job.

Dan.

Read more at www.dancanwell.com.